C000314887

the servants
of the storm

PRAISE FOR THE PILLARS OF REALITY SERIES

"Campbell has created an interesting world… [he] has created his characters in such a meticulous way, I could not help but develop my own feelings for both of them. I have already gotten the second book and will be listening with anticipation."

—Audio Book Reviewer

"I loved *The Hidden Masters of Marandur*…The intense battle and action scenes are one of the places where Campbell's writing really shines. There are a lot of urban and epic fantasy novels that make me cringe when I read their battles, but Campbell's years of military experience help him write realistic battles."

—All Things Urban Fantasy

"I highly recommend this to fantasy lovers, especially if you enjoy reading about young protagonists coming into their own and fighting against a stronger force than themselves. The world building has been strengthened even further giving the reader more history. Along with the characters flight from their pursuers and search for knowledge allowing us to see more of the continent the pace is constant and had me finding excuses to continue the book."

—Not Yet Read

"*The Dragons of Dorcastle*… is the perfect mix of steampunk and fantasy… it has set the bar to high."

—The Arched Doorway

"Quite a bit of fun and I really enjoyed it. . .An excellent sequel and well worth the read!"

—Game Industry

"The Pillars of Reality series continues in THE ASSASSINS OF ALTIS to be a great action filled adventure. . .So many exciting things happen that I can hardly wait for the next book to be released."

–Not Yet Read

"The Pillars of Reality is a series that gets better and better with each new book. . .THE ASSASSINS OF ALTIS is a great addition to a great series and one I recommend to fantasy fans, especially if you like your fantasy with a touch of sci-fi."

–Bookaholic Cat

"Seriously, get this book (and the first two). This one went straight to my favorites shelf."

–Reanne Reads

"[Jack Campbell] took my expectations and completely blew them out of the water, proving yet again that he can seamlessly combine steampunk and epic fantasy into a truly fantastic story. . .I am looking forward to seeing just where Campbell goes with the story next, I'm not sure how I'm going to manage the wait for the next book in the series."

–The Arched Doorway

PRAISE FOR THE LOST FLEET SERIES

"It's the thrilling saga of a nearly-crushed force battling its way home from deep within enemy territory, laced with deadpan satire about modern warfare and neoliberal economics. Like Xenophon's Anabasis – with spaceships."

—The Guardian (UK)

"Black Jack is an excellent character, and this series is the best military SF I've read in some time."

—Wired Magazine

"If you're a fan of character, action, and conflict in a Military SF setting, you would probably be more than pleased by Campbell's offering."

—Tor.com

". . . a fun, quick read, full of action, compelling characters, and deeper issues. Exactly the type of story which attracts readers to military SF in the first place."

—SF Signal

"Rousing military-SF action... it should please many fans of old-fashioned hard SF. And it may be a good starting point for media SF fans looking to expand their SF reading beyond tie-in novels."

—SciFi.com

"Fascinating stuff ... this is military SF where the military and SF parts are both done right."

—SFX Magazine

PRAISE FOR THE LOST FLEET: BEYOND THE FRONTIER SERIES

"Combines the best parts of military sf and grand space opera to launch a new adventure series ... sets the fleet up for plenty of exciting discoveries and escapades."

—Publishers Weekly

"Absorbing...neither series addicts nor newcomers will be disappointed."

—Kirkus Reviews

"Epic space battles, this time with aliens. Fans who enjoyed the earlier books in the Lost Fleet series will be pleased."

—Fantasy Literature

"I loved every minute of it. I've been with these characters through six novels and it felt like returning to an old group of friends."

—Walker of Worlds

"A fast-paced page turner ... the search for answers will keep readers entertained for years to come."

—SF Revu

"Another excellent addition to one of the best military science fiction series on the market. This delivers everything fans expect from Black Jack Geary and more."

—Monsters & Critics

ALSO BY JACK CAMPBELL

THE LOST FLEET
Dauntless
Fearless
Courageous
Valiant
Relentless
Victorious

BEYOND THE FRONTIER
Dreadnaught
Invincible
Guardian
Steadfast
Leviathan

THE LOST STARS
Tarnished Knight
Perilous Shield
Imperfect Sword
Shattered Spear

THE ETHAN STARK SERIES
Stark's War
Stark's Command
Stark's Crusade

THE PAUL SINCLAIR SERIES
A Just Determination
Burden of Proof
Rule of Evidence
Against All Enemies

PILLARS OF REALITY
*The Dragons of Dorcastle**
*The Hidden Masters of Marandur**
*The Assassins of Altis**
*The Pirates of Pacta Servanda**
Books 5-6 forthcoming

NOVELLAS
The Last Full Measure

SHORT STORY COLLECTIONS
*Ad Astra**
*Borrowed Time**
*Swords and Saddles**

*available as a JABberwocky eBook

The Servants of the Storm

Pillars of Reality
Book 5

JACK CAMPBELL

JABberwocky Literary Agency, Inc.

The Servants of the Storm

Copyright © 2016 by John G. Hemry

All rights reserved

First paperback edition in 2016 by JABberwocky Literary Agency, Inc.

Published as an ebook in 2016 by JABberwocky Literary Agency, Inc.

Originally published in 2016 as an audiobook by Audible Studios

Cover art by Dominick Saponaro

Map by Isaac Stewart

Interior design by Estelle Leora Malmed

ISBN 978-1-625671-39-4

To
my niece Candace

For S, as always

acknowledgments

I remain indebted to my agents, Joshua Bilmes and Eddie Schneider, for their long standing support, ever-inspired suggestions and assistance, as well as to Krystyna Lopez and Lisa Rodgers for their work on foreign sales and print editions. Thanks also to Catherine Asaro, Robert Chase, Carolyn Ives Gilman, J.G. (Huck) Huckenpohler, Simcha Kuritzky, Michael LaViolette, Aly Parsons, Bud Sparhawk and Constance A. Warner for their suggestions, comments and recommendations.

chapter one

The war-weary city of Minut shone under the rays of the rising sun as Master Mechanic Mari of Caer Lyn rode to the top of a ridge that looked down a long slope toward the once-busy port. She wore the dark jacket of a Mechanic, even though that Guild had long since banished her. Mari's horse shifted restlessly as a dozen cavalry troopers in blue uniforms with brightly shining cuirasses, sabers at their sides, and lances poised ready for use rode up next to her, one of them holding a staff from which flew the square banner of the new day, bright blue with a many-pointed golden star in the center.

A storm threatened the world of Dematr, a storm carrying winds of war, riot, and chaos, born of and fueled by the rage and frustrations of the people who had been forced to serve the wills of the Great Guilds for centuries. It was a storm which had begun in Tiae, breaking the kingdom into anarchy. Mari was determined to stop that storm, and she would counter it beginning here, in Tiae, where it had claimed its first victims.

She had scarcely quieted her mount when three more rode up, two of them cavalry in the dark green uniforms of Tiae, one of those carrying the banner of that kingdom, gold and green.

The third wore Mage robes. Despite the tension riding inside her, Mari smiled at the sight of him. "How does everything look? Are we ready to attack?"

Mage Alain of Ihris gave her a slight smile, which might have seemed a very restrained greeting in anyone but a Mage. From a Mage, trained to avoid any display of emotion, the gesture was almost flamboyant. "All is well. General Flyn is deploying your foot soldiers to the west, and Princess Sien is moving Tiae's forces into position to the east. We here are already blocking the northern side of the city."

Mari looked back down the slope at two hundred cavalry concealed behind the ridge and waiting for the order to advance. Waiting for *her* order. "We've come a very long way in six months, haven't we, my Mage? I never expected that we'd be retaking Minut this quickly."

A rattle of hooves announced the arrival of General Flyn and a small group of staff officers. "Your army is ready to advance, Lady," he announced, saluting her with a flourish.

Her army. That still felt unreal. In the half-year since forging an alliance with the sole surviving member of the royal family of Tiae, Princess Sien, and setting up a base at Pacta Servanda to the south, thousands of volunteers had made their way individually and in small groups to join the forces of the daughter of Jules, she who was foretold as the one who would overthrow the Great Guilds which had enslaved the world of Dematr for all of its history. Some of those volunteers had been taught to use Mechanic tools to construct more and better devices than the Mechanics Guild had ever permitted. The rest had been eager to fight to free their world. Without the help of professionals like General Flyn, Mari never would have been able to mold them into an army.

An army that was already equipped with rifles of a sort never before seen in this world. There were less than two hundred of those rifles as of yet, but they gave Mari's army a tremendous advantage in firepower in a world where the Mechanics Guild limited every other fighting force to only a few repeating rifles..

Mari raised her far-seers, grumbling under her breath as her horse shifted again, making it hard to focus on the waters just offshore of the city. This particular mare seemed to have an instinctive feel for when to move at just the wrong moments.

Her fleet was there, several large sailing ships also flying the banner of the New Day, blockading the port to keep any of the warlords trapped inside Minut from escaping by sea. Closer in, nearly twenty boats flying the flag of Tiae guarded against any escape attempt along the coast by the small-scale pirates who had infested the city in the decades since the Kingdom of Tiae had fallen into anarchy. "All we need to wait for now is whatever the Mages on their Rocs can tell us."

From here, even through the far-seers the towers and spires of Minut appeared to be in decent shape, only a few truncated by the loss of their upper portions. Mari wondered how intact they really were. Different sections of the city bore the scars of old fires, burned-out buildings still trailing tears of soot from windows broken ten or twenty years ago. Other areas of Minut appeared to be disconcertingly untouched, but that was probably because the far-seers couldn't spot the signs of neglect and decay from this distance.

The forbidden city of Marandur had died quickly and been left in total ruin. Minut had been dying slowly. But today would mark the beginning of its rebirth.

Hopefully the price of victory would not be high. Mari had suffered through another restless night the evening before, her nightmares haunted by the things she had already seen and had already survived. There had been too many deaths before this, but the knowledge that far, far more would die if she failed kept Mari striving to complete a task that she had not asked for but had to succeed at.

She lowered the far-seers as another small group rode up, led by a young woman who also wore green, but whose armor glowed golden in the sunlight. Instead of a helm she wore a gold circlet. Behind her rode a special guard carrying her banner, the flag of Tiae with the addition of a crown sewn from gold thread centered on it. "Good morning, Princess," Mari said. "We should have Minut back under your control before nightfall."

Sien smiled. "Tiae already owes you much, Lady Mari. I have heard from the agents who entered the city over the last week to prepare the way for us. They have been spreading word among those who still live in Minut that Tiae returns and that the days of the warlords are coming to an end."

"Princess," Flyn said respectfully, "did your agents confirm what we've heard of the warlords in the city?"

She nodded. "Yes, General. Three warlords, two of whom have used their fighting forces to hold large portions of Minut in thrall, and a third whose so-called army is little more than a large bandit gang. The remnants of *Colonel* Fer's fighters have joined with one of the warlords."

"I'm sorry we were unable to wipe out Fer's group yesterday," Flyn said. "But maybe the survivors who fled into Minut have stories to tell that will help unnerve the fighters there. And I can promise you that none of the warlords or their gangsters will escape from us this time."

"Escape is what they seek," Sien said. "We must offer it to them."

The sharp edge in Sien's tone hinted at the true nature of the "escape" that the warlords would see from the walls of Minut. Mari's infantry was visible to the west, and Tiae's reborn army, though still small, could be seen from the east. But here to the north the only forces visible from Minut would be Mari, her Mages, and the few cavalry with them at the top of the ridge. The warlords might wonder at such an elementary mistake, but with two real armies closing in on them they would head for the weak spot "inadvertently" left open for escape.

The country around Pacta Servanda had been pacified, but Tiae wouldn't be thought of as a kingdom again until a city like Minut once more belonged. And only such a victory would convince many of the people who had once belonged to the kingdom that it could be reborn after so many years of pain. Mari was still worried that the warlords and their supporters would dig in inside Minut, forcing a long and nasty fight that would further damage the already battered city and likely kill some of the surviving citizens. But both General Flyn and Princess Sien were confident that the warlords and their self-styled armies would not fight to the death as long as they saw a chance to run away. "They're criminals out for power and loot," Flyn had said contemptuously, "not soldiers fighting for a cause. They'll be afraid as we close in, and desperate to get away."

Mechanic Alli came riding up along with teams of horses pulling her two pride-and-joys, brand new artillery pieces bigger and better than anything the Mechanics Guild had ever allowed to be built. "Where do you want these, your daughterness?"

"Hi, Alli. Don't call me that. Over there."

"How about over *there*?" Alli suggested. "That will give me a better field of fire."

"Fine. Go over *there* but set them up behind the crest of the ridge," Mari ordered. "We don't want the warlords to realize we have big guns at this spot until they've already left the city."

A vast shadow swept overhead. Mari looked up to see a Mage Roc flying past, the huge bird moving with a grace that never failed to take her breath away. The engineer part of her knew that such a bird could not possibly fly, but the rest of her had decided not to worry about that. Mari could see Mage Alera and a man in a Mechanics jacket riding on the back of the Roc.

"Hey, Calu!" Alli yelled, waving.

"He's more likely to hear you if you use a far-talker," Mari said, bringing out her own. She paused to admire it, one of the products of the work shops that had been hastily built at Pacta Servanda in the last six months, using information from the banned technology texts and the labor of Mechanics who, like Mari, had left the Guild. Priority had been given of necessity to new rifles and Alli's new artillery, and the far-talkers required more complex electronic work. There were only about half a dozen of the new far-talkers completed so far, but they were smaller, lighter, and had better range than the Mechanics Guild models which had been deteriorating in quality for centuries. "I'm sorry we don't have enough yet to give you one. Do you want to use mine?"

"Later. Thanks," Alli said as she directed the positioning of the guns.

Alain pointed to the east and west, where two other Rocs glided high above Mari's infantry and the army of Tiae. "They will warn if they see any attacks coming from unexpected directions."

"Good, and Calu will tell us what's going on in the city." Mari keyed her far-talker. "Calu? You there?"

"I'm here," he replied, sounding breathless. "This flying still takes some getting used to."

"Just hold on tight. What can you see so far?"

"There is a bunch of people milling around on the docks, like they want to sail away but are afraid to with Tiae's coastal guard waiting just offshore," Calu said. "Most of the rest of the city looks deserted."

"The people of Tiae will be in their homes," Sien said. "Hiding from the battle they know is coming."

"But there are a lot of folks inside the north gate," Calu continued. "Looks like three separate groups of people with weapons. They're just standing there along the wide street that leads to the gate."

General Flyn nodded, smiling sardonically. "Their leaders are arguing over who gets to go second," he said.

"Second?" Mari asked.

"Yes, Lady. Whoever's soldiers lead the breakout attempt will take a lot of losses fighting through your forces. Whichever warlord comes last is likely to get caught by our pursuit. But the one who comes second will be able to use the sacrifices of those ahead and behind to protect themselves. I will confess to having been skeptical as to how much the Mage birds could help us, Lady, but this ability to see from above is remarkable when combined with your Mechanic far-talkers."

"That's what Alain and I kept finding out," Mari said. "Combining what Mages and Mechanics can do produces some real advantages. Unfortunately," she continued, "while seeing from above tells us what the enemy is doing, right now they're not doing anything. We don't want the warlords just standing around, giving them time to think and delaying our own assault."

"How do we get them moving, General?" Princess Sien asked.

"We're already offering them an apparently lightly held area here to the north," Flyn said. "If that doesn't lure them out, I don't know what else could get them moving. They could argue all day. If we attack, they are just as likely to fall back into the city in a panic as to try to escape from it."

"How about if we make it too hot where they are?" Alli asked. She gestured to her two new artillery pieces. "What if I drop some shells right behind them to encourage them to get their butts moving this way?"

"You can do that, Lady Mechanic?" Flyn asked. "Even though we can't see them?"

"And they can't see my guns, so they won't know where the shots are coming from," Alli replied. "Yeah. These guns are designed to allow long-range shots using a high arc. It's not complicated. I know the muzzle velocity of my shells and I can figure how far I want them to go. That gives me a trajectory and an angle of elevation. The shells go up over the ridge and come down behind those city walls." She held up a binder. "I had Apprentices back at Pacta Servanda work up range tables for these guns to simplify things. I'll just have to interpolate some numbers. Who's got the best map of Minut?"

Sien gestured to one of her escort, who brought a folded sheet of paper to Alli.

Alli and the soldier from Tiae spread out the map on the grass and crouched down to study it. "The north gate," the soldier said, gesturing toward the actual gate and then tapping a place on the old map.

"This is accurate?" Alli asked. "That's a nice wide street leading out to the gate."

"Yes. For the movement of trade goods, and sometimes for parades," the soldier added.

Mari thought that the soldier looked old enough to have taken part in some of those parades almost twenty years ago. She had noticed that the men and women flocking to the banner of Princess Sien to rebuild the army and the Kingdom of Tiae were often either older—veterans of the time before the Kingdom fell apart who wanted to recreate what had been lost—or younger than they should be, fired with idealism and the possibility that the long years of anarchy were finally ending. But the generation between the old and the young had been hit hard by the collapse of the Kingdom and the subsequent hardships, too often spending their own lives or health to give their children a chance.

"Can I have your far-talker now?" Alli asked Mari. She took it and knelt back by the map. "Hey, Calu darling, this is the reason for your happiness calling."

"Hi, Alli," Calu replied. "Is this a social call?"

"Business. Where exactly are those warlords' fighters? Their front is near the northern gate, right? Where's the rear?"

"Yes, the first group is just a little ways inside the gate. What's left of the gate, anyway. Then the next two groups…counting from the gate there are two cross streets intersecting the big street they're on. The rear is just past where the second cross street joins."

"Here," the Tiae soldier said, pointing.

Alli scowled at the map, then keyed the far-talker again. "I've got some concerns about the accuracy of the map outside the city, Calu. I don't think the distance from the gate to where I am is right, so I'm going to aim the first round to drop well behind where those terrorists are. I want to make sure it doesn't hit the front of the group and give them motivation to run the wrong way. There's nobody else on that big street, right?"

"Right. It's empty, except for trash and some piles of rubble."

"Stand by, but don't fly between where I am and my target, and let me know where the shot lands."

Alli made an adjustment to one of her guns, speaking to Mari as she did so. "We need better maps. For everywhere."

"I'll add it to the list," Mari said. The list of things they needed *right now* seemed to grow every day by at least one item.

"I'm going to fire the first shot," Alli told her gun crew. "Hold your horses!" she called out, then yanked the firing lanyard.

The crash of the shot startled even the cavalry horses, which had been trained to deal with loud noises, but the soldiers were holding their leads and none of them broke away.

The shell arced away into the sky, vanishing from sight.

After several moments, a muffled boom was heard from the direction of Minut.

"You nearly hit a building, Alli!" Calu called. "The shot hit on the east side of the street, just in front of a big building. And it was…two more intersecting streets back."

"Two?" Alli studied the map. "We are closer than the map says. All right. Let me tweak something…stand by for another shot."

The gun crew had already opened the breech, pulled out the shell casing, loaded another round, then closed the breech. Alli altered the angle of the gun a little, then yanked the firing lanyard again. Another crash, another pause, and another boom as the second shell hit.

"Pretty close to the middle of the street," Calu reported. "And only half a block behind the rearmost warlord group. Almost perfect. How do you do that?"

"I'm brilliant. We're going to fire two shots this time. Let me know where they fall." Alli adjusted both guns, crossed her fingers, then made a chopping motion. The gunners fired, one only a moment after the other.

"Got them!" Calu said. "One was right behind them and the other hit the rear ranks."

"I guess those goons are finding out how bad it feels to have someone bigger than they are beating on them," Alli said. "Mari?"

"Hit them again," Mari said, reluctance to give the order making her voice low.

"What?"

"*Hit them again!*"

Two more shots roared out, then two more.

"The group in the rear is pushing ahead!" Calu said. "You're doing some real damage and they're trying to get away!"

"Alli, let me see that far-talker." Mari gazed toward the city as she called Calu. "Are any of the bad guys scattering into the side streets?"

"Um…yeah. Some are trying to. Whatever passes for officers in the warlord ranks are trying to beat them back into place."

"Hold up, Alli! I don't want to hit them so hard that they spread out through the city."

Alli nodded, gesturing to her gun crews. "Hold fire, guys. Those scum have learned what we can do to them if they don't move."

"Mari?" Calu called. "I think...yeah, they're starting. Everyone at once. They're all coming out!"

The "armies" of the three warlords came charging out of the northern gate of Minut. Mari studied them through her far-seers despite the efforts of the mare to ruin her focus. The fighters in the first group wore an assortment of armor and carried a variety of spears, pikes, and pole-arms, but moved in a loose gaggle rather than a tight formation. Right behind them was a mixed group of mounted fighters and fighters on foot carrying swords and varied shields. The last group bore a wide assortment of arms and little in the way of armor, and unlike the first two was not even attempting to maintain any semblance of organization. "The last group is treading on the heels of the second, which is being slowed by the pace of the first group because of the heavy pikes some of them are carrying."

General Flyn nodded. "They're coming in our direction in hopes of breaking out. Just as we hoped. You know how to hold them, Lady. With your permission, I'll rejoin the foot soldiers and get them moving. Princess, your dragoons and other forces can move at any time."

"Tiae will advance," Sien said, waving a goodbye to Mari and Alain before she and her escort took off in a thunder of hooves.

Mari looked back at her own cavalry, still hidden from sight of the city on the back slope of the hill. "Rifles dismount and take up position on the crest!"

"Stay with the princess of Tiae," Alain directed some of his fellow Mages, who nodded once in acknowledgement and rode off after Sien. "Mage Asha, stay here for now."

Asha nodded, her long blond hair flowing in the wind off the sea. In the morning light, her beauty looked unearthly. "I sense Mages in the city. The traces of them are faint."

"Please let me know if they start moving," Mari said, fighting down a shiver as she remembered the last assassination attempt against her—by a Mage using a concealment spell. Less than a month ago. If not for Alain's ability to spot the Mage despite the spell, that attempt probably would have succeeded.

There were still far too few rifles to equip every soldier, but those of the cavalry who carried them dismounted, handing the reins of their mounts to other soldiers to hold, then scrambled up the slope to form a line along the top of the hill. By the standards of normal fighting, the line looked far too thin and too long to have any chance of holding against the oncoming warlords.

Alli and her gun crews had put their shoulders to the two artillery pieces and were rolling them the short distance remaining to the crest of the hill.

The line of rifles split, making room for Alli's artillery near the center of the line. Mari saw her setting up the guns and ordering the barrels to be lowered so that they aimed directly at the oncoming fighters.

"We wait," Alain murmured.

"I know," Mari muttered in reply. "You don't have to remind me. Let the warlords' forces get far enough from the city that our own forces can cut off their retreat." She heard signal trumpets to the west and started to raise her far-seers. Mari deliberately paused, smiled in triumph as the mare took the bait and prematurely moved a step, then got the far-seers to her eyes and looked across the battlefield. "General Flyn is moving his forces in against the left side of the warlords and has our dragoons galloping to the north gate." From the east the sound of Tiae's battle drums ordering the advance rolled like distant thunder. She swung her gaze to the right. "Here come the Tiae dragoons. Tiae's infantry is also moving up."

Mari put away the far–seers and picked up the far-talker again. "Calu, what can you see in the city? Are there any fighters left near the gate?"

"I can't see any near the gate," Calu said. "There are a few small groups along the wall. I can't tell who they are. That's it."

"Say hi for me!" Alli called from where she was helping reset the artillery.

"Alli says hi, Calu," Mari relayed. "Check out the rest of the city again."

"You got it."

Mari caught a glimpse of Mage Alera's Roc soaring high above the wall, then banking to glide back over the city so that Calu could see what else was happening in Minut.

"I think soon," Alain said.

Mari judged the distance to the increasingly disorganized mass of fighters headed for the apparent weak point in the forces surrounding them. Heading for where she was. The warlords could see the soldiers of Tiae closing in on one side and Mari's soldiers closing in on the other and were trying to outrace their attackers. "Alli? What do you think?"

"Are the dragoons in place?"

"Yeah. They've reached the gate and are dismounting now."

"Then I think it's time for some more payback against these guys!"

Mari knew what was about to happen, and no matter how necessary it was, it still left her unhappy and with a sick feeling in her stomach. "Go ahead, Alli. Rifles, hold your fire until they're closer!"

Alli sighted along each artillery piece, then pointed at the gunners. The big guns roared as one.

Mari could see the black dots of the shells flying toward the enemy and striking near the front of the group. Twin explosions tore apart earth and any fighters unfortunate enough to be close to where the shells struck.

The warlords pushed their fighters harder, the mass breaking into a run toward where Mari sat on her horse atop the hill. The thin line of soldiers near her must look far too weak to slow them down, let alone stop the surging forces.

Alli's big guns fired again, tearing two more holes in the attacking group.

"Open fire!" Mari yelled at her rifles, feeling an excitement and an urge to inflict justice on those who had preyed on those weaker than they for so long that warred with her earlier reluctance.

About thirty rifles opened fire from along the top of the hill. Even the old Mechanics Guild repeating rifles would have had an impact on such a concentrated mass of targets with that many firing, but Mari's forces were using A-1 semi-automatic model rifles newly made by Alli's workshops. Alli swore that the "A" stood for Advanced, but everyone else claimed the "A" stood for Alli. The A-1 rifles could fire much faster and more accurately than the Guild weapons.

The front rows of warlord fighters fell as if they had run into a wall, the rifles wreaking terrible havoc on them. Under the hail of fire and with their path blocked by the bodies of their fallen, the gangs of fighters stumbled to a halt.

Alli's guns fired again. Mari's rifles paused as all of her soldiers ejected spent clips and loaded new ones.

The rifles on the hill fired another volley. The renewed barrage broke what little discipline the warlords' fighters had. What was left of the first group fell back into the second group, while the third group pressed on into the packed mass of confusion and added to the chaos.

Mari heard the staccato rattle of rifle fire and saw General Flyn's infantry firing into the side of the enemy mass with more than a hundred weapons. The disorganized mob lurched away from the new threat, only to meet volleys of crossbow bolts and a few rifle shots from Princess Sien's soldiers.

Turning back, the remnants of the warlords' fighters saw their retreat to the city blocked by two lines of dismounted dragoons.

Flayed by fire from all sides, the fighters compressed so tightly they could no longer move as the outer layer of the mob tried to flee inward and the inner layers tried to flee outwards.

Mari stared, appalled, as the battle turned into a slaughter.

She yanked out her far-talker. "General! General Flyn! What are you doing?"

"Winning the fight, Lady," Flyn replied, his voice sounding grim.

"We're not giving them any chance to surrender!"

"They know what will happen to them if they surrender, Lady," Flyn said. "You've seen what they've done to their victims in the areas around Minut."

"I don't care what they did! We are not them! Give them a chance to surrender, General!"

A pause, then Flyn's voice came again. "I understand, Lady."

"Hold your fire!" Mari yelled to her rifles on the hill. "I said *hold your fire!*"

As the soldiers near her reluctantly ceased wiping out the enemy, Mari could hear the sound of shots from the infantry with Flyn also dwindling. Tiae's forces were still firing crossbows, but the damage they did was minor compared to that caused by Mari's army.

General Flyn's voice carried across the battlefield. "We will accept surrenders. Drop your weapons and walk slowly toward us with your empty hands held high!"

About twenty fighters hastened to comply, stumbling toward the ranks of Flyn's infantry.

Most of them were ridden down by their own comrades as the surviving mounted fighters charged out of the mob, heading straight for Flyn's soldiers in a desperate escape attempt.

Mari felt a mix of anger at the fighters and resignation over their fate as Flyn's troops opened fire again.

None of the mounted soldiers made it to Flyn's lines before dying, and now the army of Tiae had reached one side of the mob of warlord fighters and was coldly working vengeance on those who had helped terrorize the kingdom.

Some of the survivors bolted toward Mari's position, running in blind panic. She waved to her cavalry commander, resigned to the necessity of the next order. "Send your forces to finish them. Take prisoners if you can."

With whoops of exultation almost two hundred cavalry charged over the crest, through the ranks of the dismounted soldiers with rifles, and toward the remnants of the warlords' armies. The banner of the new day flew over the cavalry as they leveled their lances at what was left of their enemy.

"It is well they came out to fight," Alain said. "It will make it much easier to take the city."

Mari grimaced. "That was the idea. Minut has suffered enough. The people still living there don't deserve to have their city made into a battleground."

"You said you wanted to avoid anything like Marandur," Alain reminded her.

"I know. And we've achieved that. I'm sorry I can't be too comforted by knowing that. Let's—"

"Hold on!" Calu shouted loudly enough for Mari to understand him without raising the far-talker close to her ear. "A Roc just appeared down there! In the plaza in front of the abandoned Mage Guild Hall!"

"A Dark Mage?" Mari said. "I didn't know there were Dark Mages who created Rocs."

"I sense the spell," Mage Asha said, "but it does not have the taint of a Dark Mage."

"There's a Mage climbing on the Roc!" Calu continued. "There! It's in the air and…north! It's heading north!"

"Back toward safe territory," Mari said. "And toward us." She called out to the dismounted cavalry who were still with her. "There's another Roc heading this way! Not a friendly one! Wait to open fire until we identify which Roc is the bad bird!"

"I see it," Alain said, pointing toward a dark spot in the sky low over the city of Minut.

"It is climbing slowly," Asha said. "Is it overburdened?"

Mari brought up her far-talker. "Calu, was there only the one Mage on the Roc?"

"Yeah. Just the one. We're following it toward you. It's moving really fast."

Raising her far-seers, Mari tried to spot the oncoming Roc, only to have the perverse mare side-step a few times. "Somebody hold this horse!"

One of the cavalry grabbed the mare's reins so that Mari could dismount and look again.

There it was. The Roc was pumping its wings rapidly, growing visibly larger as it grew closer.

"Mari," Alli said, peering through her own far-seers, "that bird isn't just heading north. And it isn't trying to get much higher. It's heading straight for us."

All of the horses were shifting about nervously now, as if they could sense the approach of the giant raptor. The cavalry on the hill fought to control their mounts as Alain dismounted as well, and Alli and her gun crews went to help hold the horses in the teams that had brought their artillery pieces.

"Target the Roc in the lead!" Mari yelled to the cavalry with rifles who were still on the hill. "Make sure you do not fire on the Roc behind it, and if you can't tell which bird is hostile, do not shoot!"

She realized she had very little ability to judge the motion of something moving as fast as that Roc. No one had experience dealing with that kind of thing. Mari looked down long enough to free her pistol from its holster and let off the safety. "Alain, see if you can hit it with your fire spell."

When Mari looked up again, the enemy Roc had gotten much, much closer.

And it wasn't just heading for the group.

Mari could tell that it was diving straight at her.

chapter two

S he brought up her pistol, holding it in a two-handed grip, and fired several shots at the Roc. The bullets had no effect that Mari could see, and she suddenly realized that if she did somehow kill the giant bird its huge, dead carcass would still be heading straight for her at high speed. Alain must have realized the same thing as he turned to run toward her, skidding on the grass as he tried to place himself between her and danger.

Only one tactic made sense. "*Scatter!*" Mari yelled as loudly as she could.

The horses hadn't waited for Mari's command, either dragging at the soldiers trying to hold them or breaking free and running with snorts and squeals of fear. She lunged at a riderless stallion racing past and managed to grab on to the saddle, holding on one-handed for a few moments while the horse dragged her across the grass.

The Roc's claws, seeking Mari, hit the stallion's other flank, knocking the horse over. Mari lost her grip as the horse fell. One flailing hoof grazed her hip hard, but she rolled clear of the animal, still somehow holding onto her pistol. Mari looked upward to see if the Roc posed an immediate threat. Seeing it climbing and momentarily not able to attack, she jerked her gaze around in search of Alain.

He was on the ground only a short distance away and already getting to his feet. Alain came to stand by her, gazing upward at the Roc.

Some of the rifles were firing, but the rifle fire fell off as the enemy Roc rose higher from its attack, winging over to come around and strike again. Mari cast glances to each side, trying to decide which way to dodge.

Another Roc hit the enemy bird, coming in from above and to the side, screaming a raptor's battle cry.

Spinning away from the blow, the enemy Roc righted itself in mid-air and pumped its wings, shrieking defiance as it swung in to battle its attacker.

A second Roc appeared, slamming into the enemy bird.

As she knelt on the grass Mari caught glimpses of a fourth Roc approaching. She stared at the three giant raptors striking at each other about two hundred lances above her, their screeches deafening as the birds battled with wing, claw, and beak. In the flurry of strikes and flying feathers, Mari could no longer tell which two of the Rocs were controlled by her Mages and which one was the enemy.

A giant, dislodged feather plummeted to earth near her, sticking quill first in the dirt like a cast spear.

The fourth Roc dove into the fight, catching the attacker by surprise. Its massive claws closed about the enemy Mage and plucked the rider from his or her seat, hurling the Mage away in a low arc.

Mari stared at the falling body, expecting the Mage's arms and legs to flail helplessly. But the Mage stayed relaxed, accepting a fate that could not be altered.

Now unguided, the enemy Roc tried to climb away from its attackers, but Mari's three hit and tore at it repeatedly, landing blows that staggered the bird until it, too, fell to earth, crashing with enough force to make the ground jump slightly.

Alli ran over to Mari as she shakily got to her feet. "Far-talker!" The instant Mari handed it over, Alli called frantically. "Calu! Answer me! Are you all right?"

"Yeah, I'm all right," Calu said, though his voice sounded very wobbly. "I just held on as tightly as I could and hoped. Are you all right?"

"Yeah. We're all right," Alli said. "Are we all right? Yeah."

Asha had somehow kept her seat on her panicky horse and was riding toward where the enemy Mage had fallen, her long knife in one hand.

Mari winced as she stood with Alain's help.

"The Roc hurt you?" Alain said, for once having no trouble putting emotion into his words.

"No," Mari said, gritting her teeth as she tested her weight on both legs. "I got kicked by a horse."

"Welcome to the cavalry," a healer in uniform said, running up to her. "You've just endured the traditional initiation."

Mari grunted with pain as the healer pulled down one side of her trousers far enough to check the spot on her hip, probing carefully with his fingers. "Nothing is broken, Lady, but you'll have a very impressive bruise there and walking will be a bit painful for a while."

"Thanks," Mari said. "Go see if anyone was hurt worse than I was."

"I could not strike it with fire," Alain said as the healer went off to check others who might be injured. Alain's words, usually clear and precise, came out like a fumbling apology. "It moved too fast. My fire always fell behind it."

"We'll have to practice that," Mari said. "None of us expected that Roc to move that fast when it came at us."

"But I could not—"

"Alain, it's all right." Mari spread her hands slightly and tried to smile. "I'm all right. You can't do miracles."

"If you need a miracle, then I must," Alain said.

She could tell that he meant it with all of his heart, which both warmed and scared her at the thought of what risks he might run. "I need *you*. Don't forget that."

Alli gave Mari back the far-talker, then shook her head, wincing as she rubbed one arm. "Remind me not to wrap reins around my hand again. We've gotten these horses used to the sound of guns, but not to the presence of Rocs. We ought to fix that."

"I'll add it to the list."

Shouts sounded. "Lady Mari! Are you all right?"

Mari sighed heavily. "Somebody get me another horse. I'm going to have to mount up so everyone can see that I'm not hurt. Much."

She had just struggled back into the saddle with Alain's help, raising one arm to wave reassuringly to her soldiers, when Asha returned. "The Mage is dead," Asha said.

"Was he dead when you got there?" Mari asked, settling herself and wishing that riding wasn't so hard on her thighs and butt.

"Yes. He was not a Dark Mage, who would have revealed fear. His face showed nothing." Asha's impassive voice left no hint of whether she was praising the dead Mage or just reporting what she had seen.

"There are other Mages in the city," Alain said, looking toward Minut.

Mage Asha nodded. "I sense them, too. They wait. We will find them. Stay with Elder Mari, Mage Alain."

"I'm twenty years old," Mari grumbled as she watched Asha and the other Mages ride off. "I wish the Mages wouldn't call me Elder."

"It is a mark of their respect for you," Alain said.

"Then they can call me Master Mechanic!"

"Mages do not consider Mechanic titles to be marks of respect," Alain said.

"I'm looking for agreement, not explanations," Mari told him.

General Flyn called, sparing Alain the need to reply. "Lady? That was quite a show above the hill! You are all right?"

"Yes, General," Mari said. "You can assure our soldiers that I am fine. Almost fine, anyway."

"In that case, I recommend that we enter the city as soon as possible before anyone who might oppose us inside Minut has time to prepare."

"Let's do that," Mari said. "Princess Sien? Are the forces of Tiae ready to enter Minut?"

"We are," Sien replied. Six months ago, non-Mechanics were not supposed to even know that far-talkers existed, let alone how to use one. But Mari had made a point of providing Flyn and Sien with two of the few new far-talkers available at the moment. Some of the

Mechanics following her had been scandalized, but most had simply accepted it as part of the rebellion against the strict rules by which the Senior Mechanics had run both the Mechanics Guild and the world of Dematr. And it made coordinating actions on the battlefield a lot easier. "We shall enter the east gate as agreed upon," the princess added.

"My infantry will enter the west gate," Mari said, "and I'll lead my cavalry into the north gate. Princess, General, be advised that some of my Mages are already entering the city in search of enemy Mages Look for my armbands to know if the Mage is friendly."

Mari waved to the cavalry remaining with her. "Mount up!"

Alain had found another horse and climbed into the saddle, his lack of expression betraying how upset he was. Mari had noticed that when Alain was really unhappy he reverted to his Mage training to reveal no emotions. He brought his horse next to hers, clearly determined not to let any other danger threaten Mari.

Knowing that no words of hers would comfort him, she called to Alli. "We're heading into the city. Hold here with the big guns."

Her cavalry formed up around her, and Mari and Alain started down the slope in a rattle of harness and nervous snorts from the horses.

Directly before them lay the bodies of those who had helped three warlords terrorize the city of Minut. Mari looked away, but she couldn't avoid smelling the tang of blood that filled the air. She took deep breaths through her mouth, trying to block out the smell and the cries of the badly hurt and dying. Memories assailed her, of other fights and others hurt and killed, of moments when death had felt very close to her and Alain. Such things no longer frightened her, she told herself. The daughter of Jules could not afford to feel or show fear.

A small force of soldiers from Tiae was wading through the mounds of fallen, making sure that every one of them was dead. Mari was pleased to see that General Flyn had also sent out a force, this one finding wounded enemy fighters and taking them prisoner instead of finishing them off. As her force rode toward the north gate, the cavalry sent out earlier returned to swell the numbers of soldiers around her. How had she gone from being a Mechanic to this?

A Roc landed heavily between Mari's cavalry and the city, a man in a Mechanics jacket almost falling off on his way to the ground before the Mage left her mount with considerable more grace. Calu came jogging to meet Mari and Alain while Mage Alera held her Roc. "I don't know whether that was the scariest thing I've ever experienced or the most fun I've ever had," Calu gasped when they met. "But I don't want to do it again right away."

"Was Mage Alera's Roc hurt in the fight?" Mari asked.

"Not much. She said he used up a lot of power, though, and needs to sleep." He nodded back toward the Roc, catching his breath. "That's what Mage Alera calls it now when Swift goes away."

Mari saw the Roc disappear into a shower of dust that also vanished, leaving Mage Alera standing alone.

"Do you need me to go up on another one of the Rocs?" Calu asked, sounding willing but not particularly enthusiastic.

"Calu, if I sent you up again right away Alli would kill me," Mari said. "She's back there with the guns. Why don't you go join her so I can use your far-talker to let her know if we need her guns again while we're taking the city?" That had been an easy call to make since Mari could see the other two Rocs coming in to land as well. For the moment, her ability to see things from high above had run out of Mage power.

Calu continued through the ranks of advancing cavalry, heading for the hill where Alli's artillery sat silently menacing the city. Mari tried to use her far-seers again to catch sight of her infantry approaching the west gate and the soldiers of Tiae nearing the gate to the east, but the jolting of her mount's progress kept throwing off her attempts. And of course the mostly intact walls of the city kept her from seeing what new developments might await her army and the army of Tiae inside Minut. "Alain, I am really glad that you're beside me right now."

❧

Mage Alain of Ihris was very upset. He did his best to deny the emotion, to block it out, as he had been taught when an acolyte. Certainly no one watching him, except another Mage, would have guessed how unhappy he was. He knew that anger served only to distract and to weaken him, and would only aid his and Mari's enemies.

But he could not stop being angry with himself for having failed to protect Mari from the Roc's attack.

It was not until Mage Alera's Roc landed in front of them that Alain jerked himself out of his anger enough to realize how much it had distracted him. He had not even been aware that Alera was coming close.

And they were about to enter a city where threats to Mari might lie along every street and around ever corner, while he focused on a danger that no longer existed.

Some of the things the Mage elders had taught him had been false, but they had surely been right about the danger of selfish emotions like anger. He had no trouble recalling the brutal methods used to teach him to master and ultimately deny his anger, and now Alain used that experience to prepare himself for the task that lay ahead.

He breathed deeply as he banished his negative feelings to a place where he could no longer sense them. Alain glanced at Mari to see if she had noticed his self-absorption. Mari's feelings always lay so close to the surface, so easy to read, yet she retained depths he was still trying to grasp. At this moment, though, she was so distressed by the battle's casualties that it had driven many other concerns from her mind.

But as the column approached the north gate of Minut, Mari looked over at Alain, the question in her eyes easy to see.

"My foresight does not warn of danger," Alain said. "But that does not mean danger does not exist."

"We can hope," Mari said.

The north gate of Minut showed the scars of decades of war and neglect. One side of the great gate was wedged open. The other side had fallen to lie askew over piles of rubble where one of the former guard towers had been destroyed years before.

The commander of the cavalry called out orders, and forty soldiers urged their mounts forward.

Mari looked at them, surprised. "Why are they going in first? I should be leading this."

"This is still the front, Lady," Colonel Tecu assured her. "You will be leading the advance from the front. Just not as far in front."

"That is not right," Mari said. "I should not face any less risk than anyone else."

The colonel, who looked to Alain as if he would rather be leading a charge against a solid wall of pikes than trying to out-argue Lady Mari, hesitated in his reply.

Which gave Alain time to speak. "Colonel, where will you ride?"

"Next to the Lady," Colonel Tecu said.

"Behind those forty cavalry?"

"Yes, Sir Mage."

"Why are you not in the front rank?"

Tecu's face hardened. "If there is any question regarding my courage—"

"No," Alain said, realizing that this was one of the things commons and Mechanics could interpret as criticism. "There is no question of your courage. What I ask is, is there a reason why the commander rides a little farther back?"

The colonel relaxed and nodded. "I understand your question now. Forgive me, Sir Mage, for misinterpreting it. Yes, there is a reason. I need to be far enough forward to lead my soldiers, but far enough back that I can see what is happening and give the necessary orders to those both ahead and behind. If I am in the very front rank, I will be fully engaged with whatever is happening to those soldiers."

"It is your responsibility as commander of the force," Alain said.

Mari gave Alain a sour look. "All right, Sir Mage. I get it. We'll ride with the colonel."

"Your courage is unquestioned, Lady," Colonel Tecu hastened to assure her. "Everyone knows that you have personally faced and defeated dragons and trolls. And now a Roc as well."

"I've had some help," Mari said. "A lot of help. I don't want to expose those cavalry in the lead to risks that I am not sharing."

"You are here with us, Lady, and I think those cavalry would rather have you alive than in the front rank with them."

The first forty mounted soldiers having entered the gate, Mari, Alain, and Colonel Tecu rode after them, accompanied by the cavalry bearing both the standard of the new day and the banner of Tiae. They were followed by the remaining nearly one hundred and sixty cavalry.

Alain studied the pavement inside the gate, an act which he did without thinking. The paving stones of the street bore no resemblance to the fitted stone blocks on which his foresight months ago had shown Mari lying at some point in the future, her jacket wet with blood and herself apparently near death. That did not mean that Mari was safe here. It only meant that one particular future would not occur here. There were plenty of other future events which could take place at any time, any one of which might result in Mari's death before she reached whatever place contained those particular stone blocks.

The wide boulevard that stretched from the north gate of Minut was eerily deserted. Ahead, Alain could see a scattering of bodies and shattered paving where Mechanic Alli's shells had struck. Piles of trash, debris, and garbage lined the street, some obviously having been slowly decaying for more than a decade and others more recent. The heaps of junk narrowed the broad street, in places forcing the leading cavalry to ride only three soldiers abreast.

The buildings lining this once-grand thoroughfare had been majestic as well: multi-storied structures featuring the curves and arches favored in the southern cities, their facades of carved stone and hardwood doors now pocked with decay and damage. There did not appear to be a single intact window remaining, just shards of glass clinging precariously to the remnants of frames. In some cases the broken windows had been boarded up, but in many places the vacant windows gave free access to the dark interiors. Weeds and grass sprouted from between paving stones and anywhere else dirt had managed to accumulate, and small yards and gardens had degenerated into tiny, overgrown tangles of jungle.

Alain caught an occasional glimpse of a rat darting from cover to cover. He did not see any cats or dogs, and suspected that any such had long since become victims of Minut's lack of regular food supplies from the outside.

After the crash of Mechanic weaponry and the clash of metal on metal as soldiers fought hand-to-hand and sword-against-shield, the silence in the city felt oppressive. All Alain could hear was the jingling of harness, the clop of horseshoes on the pavement, and the blowing of the horses. The cavalry rode slowly, each soldier searching the buildings beside and ahead for any signs of trouble.

Alain heightened his sense of Mari riding next to him, hoping that would help trigger his foresight to warn of any danger to her.

A low call of warning came from the front rank of cavalry. Alain saw men and women coming out from the ground floors and down the entry stairs of some of the buildings ahead. No weapons were visible, and none of them wore any armor. Alain gained an impression of weathered dignity, as if the men and women were rocks which had been worn by hardship but still endured.

They stood at the edge of the street, amid the piles of rubbish, watching silently as the cavalry approached.

Alain swept his gaze over them, then across the buildings to either side, aware that most of the cavalry had fixed their attention on the people ahead.

He spotted a small movement in a second-story window.

A blotch of blackness appeared over that window, his foresight finally offering some warning of danger.

He knew the distance to that window would make for a long crossbow shot. But Mechanic weapons could hit an individual target at such a range. And his foresight said the danger existed now.

Alain lunged toward Mari and pulled her down with him as they both fell from their horses, the boom of a Mechanic weapon filling the street. Their startled mounts danced away as a soldier in the ranks behind them cried out and was knocked from his saddle as the bullet intended for Mari instead struck him.

Getting back on one knee, ignoring the horses plunging around him, Alain held out one hand and focused on creating the illusion of immense heat above it. He built it as strong as he could in a very short time, then imagined the heat not above his hand but in that window, where the end of the Mechanic weapon had once again appeared, pointing toward Mari.

Stone cracked and wood charred black in that window.

Alain heard a muffled cry and the weapon disappeared from view.

Colonel Tecu shouted orders, sending a dozen cavalry galloping ahead to dismount at the door to the building and charge inside, weapons at ready.

Alain, breathing heavily from the sudden exertion, helped Mari to her feet.

"Did you get him?" she asked, deadly calm in the way Mari could become in an emergency.

"I believe so."

Some of the nearby cavalry had caught Mari's horse. Now they held it while she swung back into the saddle of the nervous mare. Alain heard relieved calls as the rest of cavalry caught sight of Mari unharmed.

The soldiers sent into the building reappeared, one carrying a Mechanics Guild rifle and the others supporting a man with blackened clothing and hands who hung unresisting between them. "Is he dead?" Colonel Tecu called furiously.

"No, sir! Not yet, anyway! Passed out from pain or shock or both, we think!"

The cavalry column rode forward to meet the returning soldiers, who held their prisoner up for Mari to see. "A killer hired by the Mechanics Guild," Colonel Tecu commented.

Mari stared at the man's face. "No. He's not wearing the jacket, but he's a Mechanic. I saw him once, several years ago. He was part of a team who came to my Guild Hall and took away a Mechanic who had been too vocal a critic of the Guild leadership. He's one of the Mechanic assassins."

"We can finish him now, Lady!" one of the captors cried.

"No," Mari said. "We're not warlords. We don't murder the helpless. See if our healers can help him. Maybe he'll provide us with some worthwhile information."

She turned to Alain. "You saved my butt again, Alain. And you've been smart enough not to say 'I told you so' about me riding farther back."

"You have taught me much," Alain said. "He may not be the only assassin in this city."

"I know. Stay close."

Only then did Alain notice that the people who had come out into the street earlier had not moved. Even across the small distance between them Alain could see the fear in their faces, but they stood frozen in place.

Colonel Tecu had noticed as well. "Odd that they didn't run when the fighting started. Of course if they had, we would have thought they had known about the assassin going after the Lady."

Alain finally understood. "They have learned to stay still when confronted with danger. Running creates an impression of guilt, and for wolves or humans of wolfish mind a fleeing prey creates an incentive to chase and kill."

Tecu nodded slowly, his eyes on Alain. "I understand, Sir Mage. After so many years under the thumb of warlords and their arbitrary dealing of death and injury, these people have learned not to attract the wrong kind of attention. Like helpless animals, they simply freeze in place and hope the predators will pass them by."

"It is not right that people live in such fear," Alain said, his words coming out slowly as the idea crystallized in his mind.

"You figured that out for yourself?" Mari asked. "Good work, my Mage."

"I have had a good teacher in what is right," Alain said, feeling pleased that he had managed to work out the idea without asking Mari.

The cavalry column began moving again, except for those soldiers riding back toward the north gate as they took their wounded comrade and the Mechanic assassin back to the healers.

As the column came even with the people on the road, Mari called a halt. "We have come to bring Minut back into the Kingdom of Tiae," she told them. "Tiae's Princess Sien is leading the reborn army of Tiae into the west gate of Minut as we speak." The people gazed back at her wordlessly. "Don't you have anything to say?"

"Who are you?" one of the watching people finally asked.

Colonel Tecu replied, his voice carrying down the street. "This is Lady Mari, the daughter of Jules, come to free the world at last, and that is her banner that flies alongside the banner of Tiae!"

The cavalry cheered, and the faces of the men and women in the street took on expressions of disbelief and wonder. "Who will rule Minut now?" one cried.

"Princess Sien!" Mari called back. "*Your* princess rules Tiae, and today she once again extends her protection over the people and city of Minut!"

Alain could see that they did not believe Mari. But after Mari ordered the column back into motion, the people watched the rest of the cavalry pass and then followed, their numbers growing as more men, women, and children came out of hiding.

Up ahead, a large group of people pointed to a building. Colonel Tecu sent another detachment galloping ahead. "They say there are bandits in there!" the officer called back. "About a dozen!"

"Tell the bandits they can surrender or die! Make sure they know we have a Mage with us!"

The rest of the cavalry had nearly caught up when the reply came in the form of a prolonged burst of obscenity that Alain could easily hear.

"Let's go in," a lieutenant urged.

"Let's not waste lives," Mari said. "Alain, can you get them out?"

"I will have to leave you…."

"I won't go anywhere until you get back."

Alain nodded, dismounted and walked toward the building. He waited until he must have been clearly visible to the bandits inside before using his concealment spell. Normally, light in the world illusion showed someone's presence. But if light could instead be imagined to bend around a Mage, then the Mage would become invisible to shadows, as Mages called both commons and Mechanics. Alain could not sense any Dark Mages in the building who would have been able to see him despite the spell, so he created it, drawing on the power in the land around him.

He saw his success mainly in the reactions of the commons around him, whose eyes unsuccessfully searched the place where he had been visible.

Alain, husbanding his strength since the spell drew on his endurance to maintain, walked steadily up to the building. One of the empty windows provided easy access inside, where Alain saw two men standing to either side of the window with ready swords and fearful expressions.

Never fully having accepted his Mage training to regard all others as mere shadows of no consequence, Alain nonetheless found it far easier than Mari did to dispose of those shadows who sought to harm others. To his mind, these shadows had chosen to hurt, and therefore had no grounds to complain of being hurt in turn.

The first man never saw the Mage knife Alain used to stab him. He was still falling when Alain turned to the second and with brisk efficiency whipped his knife across that man's throat.

He left the room, walking softly, before the other bandits could react to the choking cries of their dying comrades.

Slipping nimbly between the three men who came running to check on the noise, Alain waited they were past, then stabbed the last.

He felt a powerful spell building behind him.

If Alain had been less experienced, he would have paused for a moment to think. That hesitation would have killed him.

In the same instant of realizing he had been lured into a trap, Alain swung behind him the body of the bandit he had just stabbed and then dove past the other two bandits toward the door of the room he had just left.

As he slid through the doorway at floor level, Alain felt the heat and crackle of lightning in the hallway. Bright light flared as the three bandits took the force of the spell, jerking under the impact, their clothes smoldering.

Before the bodies of the bandits could hit the floor, Alain was on his feet and sprinting for the window that he had entered. He dropped the concealment spell, knowing that it would be useless. His opponent was a lightning Mage, exceptionally good at hiding his or her presence and exceptionally powerful as well. Alain had no intention of trying to fight that foe on the attacker's chosen ground.

He lunged headfirst through the window without pausing, feeling a gust of sizzling heat behind him as another lightning strike filled the room.

Alain hit the worn pavement, grateful that his robes absorbed some of the impact. He rolled back to his feet to face the attacker, knowing that he had no chance of dodging a third strike.

He heard repeated thunder, but it was not the enemy Mage. The cavalry were still gaping in surprise and trying to control mounts which were splaying their front legs and rapidly swiveling their ears in fear at the lightning attacks, but Mari had her reins in an iron grip and her pistol out. She was firing rapidly into the room that Alain had just left, her face a mask of determination.

The cavalry was finally beginning to react when several bandits boiled out of the building. Alain could see their panic, but the cavalry shot or stabbed most before realizing that the bandits were also fleeing Alain's assailant.

Mari jumped down from her horse and stood over Alain as he straightened up, her weapon still aimed toward the building. "I don't know if I hit anything," she told him. "But I know nothing could have gotten to that window without taking at least one bullet."

Alain nodded, trying to regain his breath after the burst of activity and spell-casting. "You stopped him from making another strike at me that would have very likely hit."

"How did he get in there?" Mari asked.

"He was waiting inside, but I did not sense him until he attacked."

"Can you tell where he is now?"

Alain focused on the fleeting impressions he had gained of his attacker, trying to spot where that Mage was. He felt a sense of distance, of movement, then lost the trace. "He has left. That way."

"The back of the building," Mari said, then looked at the cavalry, hesitating.

It was not hard to understand why Mari had paused. The cavalry, brave when facing most opponents, were clearly unnerved at facing a powerful lightning Mage. Their horses were still stamping and moving about nervously. "I will pursue him," Alain began.

"Not alone you won't!"

"Mari—" Alain felt something else. "Another spell, in that direction. A powerful one. It does not feel like the work of any of our Mages."

A commotion in the street marked the arrival of Mage Asha and three other Mages, riding through the commons and soldiers who parted hastily to clear a path. "I know the feel of this Mage," Mage Dimitri said. "It is a Mage creating a Roc."

Mari's far-talker buzzed urgently. "Lady Mari! This is Princess Sien. We have spotted another Roc rising from the city, and the Mages with me say it is not one of ours."

"Where is it headed?" Mari asked.

"North. It has already gone out of sight and has probably left the city. We saw two Mages riding the Roc."

"The lightning Mage is making his escape," Alain said. "I know the feel of him. He is the same who attacked me in the Northern Ramparts."

"What about Palandur?" Mari asked. "Was that him there, too?"

"It may have been," Alain said. "He has become more capable since that time."

"If we meet him a fourth time we have to make sure he doesn't get away again. At least for now he can't—" Mari stopped speaking, her expression growing horrified. "Blazes! He casts lightning and he's heading north! Calu!" she yelled into her far talker. "Calu! Emergency!"

"…Mari? What's…?" Calu asked, his voice coming faintly from the far-talker. "Your signal…weak…buildings around…must…blocking…not getting…word."

"Listen! There's another Roc with two Mages on it headed for you! One of the Mages throws lightning! Get away from the guns! Everybody get away from the guns!"

"You…get away…guns? Why?"

"Lightning, Calu! He can hit the guns with lightning!"

"*Lightning?*" Through the far-talker, Alain could hear Calu yelling at the others near him. "…away from the…! …run!"

"What is the danger?" Alain asked Mari.

She stared to the north. "Lightning is a powerful electric charge. It can set off the ammunition for Alli's guns. If that Mage causes all of Allis's ammo to explode at once, it will wipe out everything on that hill."

Alain looked to the north as well, blaming himself for his failure to spot and stop the Mage. He did not doubt that the lightning Mage would try to kill him again. And next time must be the last time.

A titanic, prolonged crash of thunder rolled down from the north.

chapter three

"C alu!" Mari yelled into her far-talker as the echoes of the blast faded. "Calu! Answer! I need a better place to transmit from!" She looked around frantically, then spurred her horse to the other side of the street. "Calu!"

Alain followed, sick inside from seeing Mari's worry. If only he had—

"Mari?"

"Calu? Are you all right? What happened?"

"Mari," Calu said, sounding breathless but his words understandable. "I can't really hear you. Too much ringing in my ears from that explosion. Uh, I guess you need a status report. We're mostly all right. It looks like two...no, three folks got hit by fragments. I can't tell how bad yet. Alli had already hitched the horse teams back up to the two ammunition caissons, so when your warning came through she ordered the drivers to stampede in different directions while the rest of us ran like blazes. That left, uh, eight ready shells near the guns. I think they all blew when that lightning hit. It looks like one of the guns is a total wreck. The other one is damaged but I think repairable. Alli's all right, but she's standing near the guns cursing a blue streak, mostly about the terrible things she's going to do to that Mage who threw the lightning if she ever gets her hands on him."

Mari sagged with relief, rubbing her forehead with her free hand.

"Thank you, Calu," she shouted into the far-talker. "Tell us more when you can."

Another voice came over the far-talker. "Mari! This is Bev. What happened?"

Mari inhaled deeply before replying. "An enemy Mage caused Alli's ready ammo to blow. Nobody was killed. Why didn't General Flyn call?"

"He thought the far-talker was broken and asked me to look at it. I think he was just pushing the wrong buttons. Commons may be able to use these things but they sure aren't comfortable with them. So, we're all good? Attack continues?"

"Continue the attack," Mari confirmed. "Are you guys running into any trouble?"

"Just what General Flyn calls 'isolated pockets of resistance'," Bev replied. "He thinks it will get a lot worse when we push down to the waterfront."

"We're all converging that way. Princess Sien, did you hear?"

"I did," Sien replied. "The army of Tiae has met only minor difficulties and will meet you at the waterfront."

Mage Asha had ridden up to Alain as he returned to the saddle. She gestured to the hem of his robes, blackened from heat. "This one failed to find the Mage who attacked you."

"This Mage could not sense the one who attacked me even when close," Alain said.

"The Guild laid many traps in Minut," Asha observed. "Some Mage must have had foresight that we would come here. The one who casts lightning has tried to kill you before. Mage Siva is his name."

"You think that Mage Siva saw that I would come to Minut?"

"He has tried to kill you twice before, and was injured by Mari's weapon in Palandur. I heard after Palandur that Mage Siva was so greatly angered by your escape that the elders rebuked him for the emotion."

"He is angry again, then," Alain said, "for once again he has failed."

Their conversation was halted by Colonel Tecu calling out orders to advance. The Mages rode with the cavalry as it swept through the city, heading south.

The column reached the great central plaza, once a place of gardens and towering trees, now an emptiness marked by barren patches of dirt and piles of rubbish. After crossing the plaza, the cavalry spread out to enter several roads on the south side.

A trumpet sounded to the left. "Our flank has met up with the foot soldiers," Colonel Tecu told Mari.

A short time later, another trumpet gave the same call from the right. "We have established contact with the army of Tiae."

The crowds of people who had come out to watch their progress had fallen back, watching as the soldiers continued toward the waterfront.

Alain saw a stretch ahead where one side of the street was marked by piles of rubble that had once been buildings. From the old scorch marks on the ruins, fire had played a role in their collapse.

"This reminds me a little too much of Marandur," Mari murmured to Alain.

He nodded, looking around for signs of trouble. "Would your old Guild send only one assassin to Minut?"

"That depends on how much warning they had that I'd be here," Mari replied. "I thought we kept our plans pretty quiet. We certainly surprised the warlords."

"Mage Asha believes that I was attacked by Mage Siva, and that Mage Siva may have had foresight that I would be here," Alain said, keeping his eyes on the path ahead. "You remember what happened at Edinton, where the Mage Guild elders shared with the Mechanics Guild the foresight that you would come there. If the Mage Guild elders also shared with your former Guild foresight that you were expected in Minut, they may have had more warning than we hoped for."

A partial barrier had become visible up ahead, as if someone had begun building a barricade across the street using the rubble but abandoned the work after doing only a small section. Alain could hear a low rumble of sound coming from the waterfront and realized it was many voices crying, shouting, and yelling.

The leading cavalry reached the end of the street, where it let out onto the broad open area of Minut's waterfront. The soldiers paused, waiting for Alain, Mari, and Colonel Tecu to catch up.

Alain could see many people on the waterfront, almost all adults. The roar of conversation was falling off as the cavalry pushed their way into the crowd, which fell back without resisting. Men and women stared fearfully at the soldiers, their eyes coming to rest on Mari and the banners of the new day and Tiae which floated behind her. "Have mercy, Lady!" one person cried, and the others took up the plea, all raising their hands in surrender or supplication or both.

"Your orders, Lady?" Colonel Tecu asked over the uproar.

Mari shook her head. "What happens to them is up to the princess. But I do not want anyone hurt who is not fighting us. Alain, are they just trying to fool us?"

"I see fear," Alain said. "I do not see an intent to attack us."

"I see this, too," Mage Asha said.

"Extend our line toward the water," Tecu ordered the cavalry. "Maintain a solid defensive line and don't let any groups of soldiers get cut off from the rest."

A scattering of shots from Mechanic weapons erupted to the west.

"Mari? This is Captain Banda."

Mari yanked her far-talker up. "Here. What's happening?"

"A small craft left the outer breakwater, moving west and hugging the coast. A couple of Tiae's coastal guard ships moved to intercept and were met with rifle fire. I can't get any larger ships close in there but I can try to hit it with the *Pride*'s deck gun."

"Go ahead," Mari said. "Princess Sien? Can your army see the boat trying to escape?"

"I am sending dragoons to the coast," Sien answered. "They have two of your rifles with them."

"Send one of my Mechanics with them as well," Mari said. "If these are Mechanics, they will be more likely to surrender to another Mechanic."

The boom of the *Pride*'s deck gun, smaller than Alli's new artillery but much closer to the waterfront, drew the terrified attention of the people still crying mercy. When the shell explosion sounded a ways off along the coast, those on the waterfront relaxed a little, but their jumpiness worried Alain. "They might panic," he warned Mari. "If they panic, they will blindly attack."

Mari nodded, standing up in the saddle to yell over the noise. "We will not harm anyone who does not attack us!"

More shots came from the *Pride*, but Alain could see a measure of calm flow through the crowd as Mari's words spread like the ripples from a stone tossed into water.

"The small craft has run aground while trying to evade our shots," Captain Banda reported. "I can see mounted soldiers wearing the colors of Tiae approaching along the coast. There is one Mechanic among them. I would like to drop another shell near that boat, not aiming to hit but to encourage them to give up."

"Good idea."

Alain kept his attention on the crowd, noticing one figure who, unlike the others who milled about aimlessly, was instead drifting on a meandering route through the crowd that always brought him closer to Mari. Alain edged his horse between the man and Mari, watching and waiting.

Having reached the edge of the cavalry protecting them, the man suddenly darted between two horses and tried to race around Alain's mount, a knife in one hand. Alain urged his horse forward, the stallion's chest striking the man and knocking him down. Alain vaulted to the ground, catching the man as he tried to rise and holding him in an iron grip. "Demon!" the man shouted at Mari. "Demon and spawn of demons!"

Mari stared at the man, wide-eyed, as she calmed her jittery mare.

Two of the soldiers had dismounted as well. One of them brought the hilt of her sword against the back of the struggling man's head, knocking him out. The other searched inside the man's clothes, pulling out a sheet of paper well worn from frequent folding and unfolding. He passed it to Colonel Tecu.

Tecu scanned it with distaste. "The Demon Mechanic, spawn of demons and pawn of the Great Guilds," he read. "It calls you Mara, Lady."

"The Empire is still trying to discredit me," Mari said, her voice slightly shaky. "Its lies found a home in that man's mind."

"He must be ill in his mind, Lady," Tecu said. "To believe that and try to kill you for it."

"From his clothing," one of the soldiers offered, "he must have come south recently. His accent sounded like what I've heard around Marida on the northeastern coast of the Sea of Bakre."

"Working his way toward Pacta Servanda," Tecu agreed. "We met him before he could get there."

Mari turned a bleak look on Alain. He knew what she was thinking: that this man had left his home and braved the dangers of Tiae, all in hopes of finding Mari and killing her.

But before he could say anything, Captain Banda called again on the far-talker. "Those on the small craft must have seen how hopeless their position was, Mari. They are surrendering, wading and swimming ashore to where the Tiae dragoons are waiting. I saw two objects thrown out to sea from the boat. I am guessing they were rifles. We'll mark the spot as best we can in case someone wants to try retrieving them."

"Thank you, Captain," Mari said.

"Three more boats tried to put out, but the Tiae coastal guard nabbed them. Just run-of-the-mill pirates, probably."

"Hopefully no one I know," Mari said. "Almost everyone left here on the waterfront seems to be trying to surrender."

Alain saw another green and gold banner to the right and called Mari's attention to it. She rode to meet it, Alain staying with her as the crowd gave way and a large group of cavalry circling Mari protectively.

The cheering that began and grew told them that Sien was riding with that banner. Between the ongoing pleas for mercy, men and women chanted "Tiae! Tiae!" Their voices held a fervor which Alain could tell was real.

Mari and the princess of Tiae rode up to each other, both breaking into smiles. "I have the honor to present you with the city of Minut!" Mari cried.

"Tiae is honored by your assistance in regaining this city," Sien replied. "What can Tiae give you in return?"

Mari looked at the crowd, her smile fading. "Can you give them what they ask, Princess? Can you give them mercy?"

Sien studied the crowd, her own expression growing serious. Alain knew she was probably thinking of the hardships she had endured, and of whatever crimes those who had fled to the waterfront might have committed. "Tiae has had no luxury for mercy," Sien said, her voice ringing across the waterfront as the crowd quieted to listen. "Tiae's enemies have shown no mercy. Justice demands retribution for wrongs done. But justice also demands reasonable judgment and compassion. Tiae will this day once again open its heart to mercy. No one here shall be harmed without good cause and fair trial. No one here shall be harmed for reason of vengeance or in anger. This is my word as Sien, Princess of Tiae."

If the princess's words fell short of simple mercy, they were still far more than any of those listening had hoped for. The shouts of "Tiae!" redoubled as Sien leaned from her horse to embrace Mari.

Alain heard the cheers, but his eyes never stopped watching for danger.

The building had once been the home of a well-off trader and, though stripped of anything of much value, had still somehow survived the years of anarchy in Minut almost intact. For the moment, the crowds and the armies and the aides were outside and a measure of privacy and calm reigned inside the second-story room. Alain, restless, remained standing as Mari and Sien sat in mismatched chairs at a battered table, still wearing their weapons. Mari in her dark Mechanics jacket contrasted with Sien in gleaming vambraces and chest armor as they shared a drink from the princess's flask. "It's arak. The national drink of Tiae," Sien advised.

Mari choked, coughed, and managed to swallow. "That's…strong."

"We have to salute our victory." Sien sighed, leaning her head back and looking upward. "Seventeen years ago, Minut was the last city held by the central government before the final breaking of the Kingdom. Six months ago, I stood on the walls of Pacta Servanda and contemplated my death, since it seemed our defenses were about to fall to a warlord's band. And now I lead an army worthy of the name, and Minut is the first city to be reclaimed by the Kingdom. I cannot, ever, adequately thank you, Mari."

Mari shrugged. "Don't forget my Mage. Without him none of this would have happened."

"True. My apologies, Alain."

Alain gave her a small smile. "I am not the daughter. I only help her."

"You mean the demon?" Mari asked, sounding bitter.

"I heard of that," Sien murmured. "The daughter is at the heart of the hopes of many, Mari, but she is also the focus of the fears of others. I confess to not knowing much of Mara the Undying or how you and she became linked in the minds of some."

Mari waved toward the east. "It started when Alain and I escaped from Marandur. The Imperials have a lot of stories about Mara the Undying. She was supposedly the extremely beautiful consort of the first emperor, Maran, and wielded so much influence that she convinced Maran to make a deal with Mages to render her eternally young and beautiful. In order to stay that way, she needs to drink the blood of the young men she seduces, and according to superstition among the Imperials, Mara wants more than anything to regain the sort of power and influence she once had. Anyway, after we left Marandur we heard Imperials speculating about who had escaped from the city, because supposedly the Emperor Palan had sealed Mara into a tomb in Marandur. We heard all sorts of rumors that Mara the demon had escaped and was on the prowl again. That actually scared some of the

Imperials I heard! Can you believe it? At some point, the Imperial government apparently decided to fan those rumors about Mara in order to keep their citizens from looking to me, Mari, as the long-looked-for daughter of Jules. Supposedly I'm the Dark One, a danger to young men everywhere."

"I see," Sien said. "It cannot be easy to know that some think of you as being such a creature. I do understand the feelings inside you. Some of those who tried to kill me during the breaking of Tiae believed that the royal family was to blame and that wiping us out would finally bring peace to the land. One of them actually explained that it had nothing to do with me, it was not personal, but she had to kill me for the good of others."

"What happened?" Alain asked.

"While she was busy talking, I managed to get my hand on a rock large enough to end the conversation. I recommend that you use the same approach, Mari." Sien took another drink from her flask, then held it out to Alain. "Drink with us, honored Mage."

Alain rarely drank anything other than wine, but Mari had told him how to politely handle such requests, so he took the flask, touched his lips to it enough to drink a sip, then handed it back. The liquid burned a trail down his throat, but his Mage training suppressed any physical reaction.

Sien grinned as she took the flask. "If Mari ever tires of you, Alain, let me know. You and I could found a strong dynasty."

"It's a good thing I know you're joking," Mari said. "How long do you think you'll have to stay in Minut?"

"I'm not sure. We're looking for leaders of the city, those who have somehow survived from the past and those who have developed in the forge of the years of anarchy." Sien looked to the side, her mouth twisted in thought. "A couple of weeks, at least. I'll have to leave a strong detachment of Tiae's new army here to keep the city stable and at peace until things like a police force and city government can be recreated. I don't think there will be any resistance, though." She shook her head sadly. "The situation here is the same as in the smaller towns we have retaken. Everyone has suffered enough—has suffered too much. When they see we have the strength to stand, all grasp eagerly at the chance to see the kingdom reborn. Except for those who must be put down before they destroy again," Sien added.

"Thank you for offering mercy," Mari said.

Sien waved away her words. "Thank you asking it for them. I looked upon those and saw none who were well-fed and well-clothed. I wonder how many committed crimes in order to put food in the mouths of their families? We will take justice slowly in Minut, looking for those who preyed on others for profit. Some will have committed crimes that we cannot forgive. Others will be judged, I hope, appropriately. Speaking of others, I understand that there were Mechanics in that boat that tried to escape the city?"

"Yes," Mari said. She rubbed her eyes, grimacing. "They've refused to tell anyone anything about why they were in Minut. None of them seem to be Guild assassins; they're just run-of-the-mill Mechanics. From what the Mages could tell from their reactions to our questions, they were sent into Tiae to get more detailed information about what I was doing."

"They certainly found out where you were," Sien commented with a smile. "What do you intend doing with them?"

"I have half a mind to just let them go," Mari admitted.

"Why?"

"Because holding them prisoner would be a pain in the neck, and if I set them free it will help counteract the Mechanics Guild's propaganda that I'm a danger to all Mechanics and out to enslave everyone."

"Since these are Mechanics, the decision is yours," Princess Sien said. "But I think your 'half a mind' is correct. Consider this also: If you release these Mechanics, set them free to go back to the Guild, those who run the Mechanics Guild will wonder *why*. Why is Master Mechanic Mari freeing these Mechanics? Did they make a deal, perhaps? Can they be trusted any longer, can anything they report be believed, and should they be punished for the crime of being caught and released?"

Mari paused, thinking. Alain could see her reluctance, but eventually she nodded. "All right. I don't like sending people to be punished for acts they didn't do, but that sort of thing is what is needed to undermine the Senior Mechanics, and if the Senior Mechanics get undermined enough maybe the Guild will collapse from within. Sien, I asked how long you'd have to stay here for two reasons. The first is that General Flyn says the food and fodder my army brought will last us about another week. There are some ships bringing supplies on the way, but even with them Minut can't handle feeding all of us, so we'll have to either disperse through the countryside or head back to our warehouses in Pacta Servanda. The other reason is that the general thinks the campaign to retake Minut went well enough that we should seriously consider trying to gain control of Tiaesun as well before the rainy season hits. The strength of my army and your own are growing rapidly enough that Flyn thinks we would not be overextending to do that. But decisions about how and where to employ the army of Tiae remain with you."

Sien inhaled deeply, gazing into the distance. "I do not trust my own instincts on this, Mari. Tiaesun was not just the capital of Tiae, it was the jewel in the crown of the kingdom. My heart longs to see it again, though I am certain the Shining City must be much diminished. Over the years, different factions have fought for control of Tiaesun, each siege and each conquest doing more damage. To rule Tiaesun again, to begin rebuilding it…" She shook her head. "I will speak with my advisors. I want this too badly to make the decision on my own. What do you see in me, Alain? Am I lying to myself?"

Alain inclined his head respectfully toward her. "You are speaking truth to yourself. Like Mari, you do not take the easy path."

"Now you flatter me, Alain." Sien smiled at them both. "Our aides and advisors wait outside, doubtless frantic to ask our guidance on matters large and small. Are you ready to face them?"

"Our friends wait outside, too," Mari said.

"A princess cannot afford friends," Sien said. "I learned that the hard way. It is too dangerous for the princess and too dangerous for the friends. But, despite my resolve to have no more, I have two, and they are here with me now. Come, Lady Mari and Sir Mage Alain! Our people await!"

Alain felt himself smiling slightly as he walked with the two women out of the room and into a gaggle of eager men and women with dozens of questions that had to be answered. But the smile vanished as his foresight suddenly showed a vision of mobs rampaging through burning cities.

A small victory had been won, but the Storm still threatened the world.

Four days later, Mari led her horse to where Alli was supervising her guns being lashed onto large, flatbed wagons. Mari dismounted stiffly, her bruised thigh better but far from healed. "How are your girls, Alli?"

"They've been better." Alli hopped down off one of the wagons, dusting off her hands. "Number one may be a total loss, though I might be able to salvage the barrel. Number two can be fixed. When are you going to need them again?"

"Maybe in a month."

"A month?" Alli raised her eyes to the sky as if pleading. "It's a good thing you've got me working for you."

"I tell myself that every day," Mari said. "Alain and I are going to be heading out tomorrow for Pacta Servanda."

"With an escort? Because I'd like one for these wagons."

"Yeah. Four troops of cavalry. We're going to sweep the countryside for bandit gangs on our way east and south. You and Calu and the girls are more than welcome to come along."

Alli leaned back against the wagon, crossing her arms as she eyed Mari. The dozen cavalry troopers who were guarding her waited at a discreet distance, one holding the banner of the new day. "You're riding everywhere these days, your daughterness. And soldiers follow you around waving your flag. Very glamorous."

"Don't call me that," Mari said. "You know why I have to have the escort, with assassins from the Great Guilds and random killers of other kinds coming after me, you know how little I like it, and you're one of the people who insisted that I needed a banner. As for riding, I have to ride to get everywhere I need to go. I love horses, but I don't love what riding them does to my butt. And speaking of pains in the butt, Alli, I'm worried that the Great Guilds may be working together more frequently."

"Senior Mechanics and Mage elders talking to each other?" Alli asked. "If you're responsible for that, you've got another miracle to claim credit for."

"Gee, thanks." Mari yanked the reins to stop the mare's attempt to nibble on her hair. "Asha thinks the Mages had foresight warning that we'd come to Minut and that they tipped off the Senior Mechanics. That was how that assassin and the other Mechanics could get here."

"That's plausible," Alli agreed. "They already cooperated that way at Edinton. Speaking of those other Mechanics the Guild sent, I think I recognized one of them, and I'm pretty sure he recognized me. If he's who I think he is, I knew him from the weapon workshops in Danalee."

Mari jerked the reins again, wondering why this mare was so attracted to her hair. "Those Mechanics definitely weren't trained killers. It sounds like our guesses from questioning them were right. They were sent to see what we're building."

"The Guild must have heard rumors about you having access to banned technology. The Senior Mechanics would want to know if that was true. But we threw off their plans to carefully study the situation when we hit Minut and overran the city so fast. Still, those Mechanics would have seen some of the new rifles, and probably saw how we used them against the warlords."

"Yeah, but they didn't get to examine any of them closely, and there's very little chance they saw any of our new far-talkers. I wonder if they were able to pick up how we were using the Mages to support our attack?"

"I doubt it," Alli said. "I don't believe that stuff, even though I'm using giant imaginary birds to help spot for my artillery. Calu doesn't haven't any problems with it, because he goes off into la-la-theory-land and doesn't concern himself with whether or not anything makes sense. How did a greasy-handed Mechanic like me ever get involved with a theorist?"

"Are you asking me? The girl who married a Mage? We'll be meeting up tomorrow at the east gate just after dawn. See you there."

"Sure," Alli said. "Hey, you know I tease you to keep your head on straight, right?"

"I know it and I love you for it, when I'm not mad at you for it," Mari said.

"Aw, I love you, too. How are you sleeping these days?"

Mari paused, and sighed heavily. "About as usual."

"That bad? I wish I could do more to help with that," Alli said, all trace of levity vanished for the moment.

"I've got Alain," Mari said. "My dreams aren't so bad when his arms are around me."

"Then spend more time that way! Hey, try to look up Bev when you see Flyn. She's sort of gloomy."

"More than usual?" Mari said, trying to get the mare to stand still so she could get into the saddle. "Why do mares always give me so much trouble? Maybe I should try a stallion."

"Get a gelding. Once they're castrated, males behave a lot better." Alli grinned. "Male horses, that is. I'm not sure anything can make male humans behave better. Oh, hi, Alain!"

Mari turned a guilty look on him as Alain rode up. "I may have laughed, but I'm not endorsing what Alli said."

"And Alli didn't mean it," Alli added. "We love you guys as you are."

"And we love you women as you are," Alain said.

"Those Mage skills of yours give you a tremendous ability to keep a straight face when making a joke, don't they?" Mari said.

She and Alain rode together, her escort close behind, to the bustle of Flyn's headquarters, a large building still in decent repair that faced the central grand plaza of the city. Mari could see groups of people already working to remove the accumulated debris of nearly two decades of neglect from the streets, one of the first steps in the plan to get the city working again. A flagpole had been returned to the monument in the center of the plaza, from which the banner of Tiae once more flew.

Mechanic Bev was talking to some soldiers on the ground floor when Mari and Alain entered. Her face lit up when she saw them. "Long time no see."

"Sorry," Mari said. "Did you find anything in the vacant Mechanics Guild Hall?"

Bev shook her head. "Just squatters using it for living space. The Guild cleaned out the place when they abandoned it eighteen years ago, except for some workshops that are packed full of demolished equipment that has been rusting ever since. The Guild probably destroyed it as too heavy to move." She gave Mari a sardonic look. "The core of the Calculating and Analysis Device looks like it was yanked out at the same time. Nothing is left of that except some memory cabinets."

It took Mari a moment to remember what Bev was referencing: the orders the Senior Mechanics in Edinton had given Mari nearly two years ago to go to Minut and recover the CAD supposedly left there, orders that had convinced Mari her Guild had decided on her death. "I've been certain for a long time that the Senior Mechanics lied when they ordered me to recover that CAD. It's funny that I ended up here anyway."

"You came with an army. That was the only way to do it safely," Bev commented. "I recommended to Princess Sien's people that they clear out the squatters and offer the old Guild Hall to any of your Mechanics willing to work here. They can set up workshops again someday. I hope you don't mind."

"No. That's what we've been talking about doing," Mari assured her.

"Mechanic Ken has been wanting to set up a new Mechanic presence outside of Pacta Servanda, and this might be a great place to start."

"Ken could handle that," Bev agreed.

"Alain, what about the abandoned Mage Guild Hall? Would any of our Mages want to take that over?"

Mari, thinking like a Mechanic who had a store of both good and bad memories of her former Guild Halls, and who thought of such Halls as being the center of her craft, was surprised when Alain paused to consider the question. "I do not know. We are seeking a different wisdom, and being surrounded by the illusions of the old wisdom might make that more difficult. I will speak with others about it. Will Bev be coming back to Pacta Servanda with us?"

"If she wants." Mari looked a question at her. "You ready to head back to Pacta?"

Bev nodded quickly. "Truth to tell, I've been hoping to get back soon. I want to see how the kids are doing."

Mari smiled. Bev had taken over running the schools teaching Mechanic Apprentices as well as commons seeking to learn basic Mechanic skills. "I'm sorry we hauled you up here for this, but I wanted someone I knew with General Flyn. I'm sure the kids are fine. Everybody knows if they even look wrong at one of them they'll have to deal with you."

"Yeah," Bev agreed, glancing at Alain. "You never have told her, have you?"

"No," Alain said.

"Go ahead. Not now, but when you want. It's all right."

Mari knew that awful things had happened to Bev when she had been an Apprentice at the Mechanics Guild Hall in Emdin, but had never pried to learn more beyond that. "I already know everything I need to know about you, Bev."

Bev nodded to her. "I know you feel that way. That's why I told Alain it was all right. When and where are we leaving?"

"Tomorrow just after dawn. East gate. Make sure Flyn knows you're leaving so he can get any last-minute instruction on using his far-talker."

"Just between you and me," Bev whispered, leaning close, "I think the general considers that far-talker to be pretty much the same as a Mage spell, and he's no more comfortable using it than he would be trying to cast a spell."

Mari sighed and nodded. "The Mechanics Guild did too good a job of mystifying technology in the eyes of the commons. And even the Mages who accept technology can't grasp it. Try explaining far-talkers to a Mage some time."

Bev raised her eyebrows. "You've explained how far-talkers work to Alain?"

"Yes," Alain said. "The message delivers itself, using an invisible ocean."

"Waves," Mari said. "Invisible *waves*."

"Waves require an ocean," Alain said.

"He has a point," Bev said, smiling. "Are you going in to see the general now? Have Alain explain the far-talker to him. Flyn might actually feel more comfortable with it if he has that kind of explanation."

The long line waiting to see Flyn parted before Mari just as commons would have for a Mechanic. It was the sort of response that made her feel guilty, despite knowing that they would have similarly made way for Flyn if he were coming in to see her.

General Flyn looked very tired, but in the manner of someone who could see good results from their labors. "Leaving tomorrow, Lady? I won't be far behind you. I'm going to take most of the rest of our cavalry and sweep a bit north and east of the direct route back to Pacta. There's a minor warlord operating around there who avoided our advance and may be feeling smug enough at the moment to be caught by surprise."

"How much are we leaving in Minut to support Tiae's forces?" Mari asked.

"A regiment, Lady. Very much under strength, and older volunteers for the most part. They're good soldiers nonetheless, who can better serve your cause by keeping Minut safe and stable than by suffering on quick marches. The rest of our foot soldiers will march by various roads back to Pacta Servanda on a staggered schedule to avoid over-taxing the roads and the countryside."

"You're the expert," Mari said. "I'll see you in Pacta and we'll decide on our next steps." The thought brought another smile to her face. "It'll be nice to be in a place where I don't need soldiers serving as bodyguards."

"I'm glad that you brought that up, Lady. It spares me the need to do so. I know your escorts are a bit intrusive," Flyn continued, "but you know why we need them. Just yesterday your Mages caught a Dark Mage trying to enter the city, and there's little doubt why she was coming here." He reached back and plucked a sheet of paper from behind him. "The Dark Mage was carrying this, the latest public offer from the Mechanics Guild for your death."

Mari took a look, her eyes widening at the size of the newest bounty on her head. "That's…a lot. I guess I can't complain any more that the Senior Mechanics don't appreciate my value," she said, trying to make a joke of it.

"You should have escorts in Pacta as well," Flyn said, keeping his voice reasonable and measured.

"What?" Mari shook her head. "No."

"Lady, the danger is obvious, and as our experience in Minut has shown, that danger is spreading south. The Great Guilds may have been hoping that you would come north again into territories they control, or may have hoped that the Broken Kingdom would be the death of you, but they are clearly becoming more aggressive as your success continues."

"I can't live surrounded by guards!" Mari said. "Or locked up in a fortress! You know why I had to come to Minut along with the army. The…the daughter had to be here."

"I do not dispute that, Lady," General Flyn said. "I am trying to mold an army that can do your bidding without your personal pres-ence. We're still a ways from that. But if you die…" He let the words trail off, leaving unspoken dire results to echo in the silence.

"Alain is always with me," Mari said. "He was my guard from Ringhmon on, and he's my guard now."

Flyn nodded, looking at Alain. "I will not deny that Sir Mage Alain is worth at least a hundred ordinary guards in terms of his vigilance, his abilities, and his devotion to the task. But any man can slip, Lady, and even Mage Alain is a man in that respect. He's not perfect. Some other guards—"

"I'll consider it," Mari said.

She knew Alain could tell that she had made that concession just to end the discussion, and apparently Flyn could as well. The general gave Alain a look that combined understanding with pleading. "We will consider it," Alain said.

They left the building and Mari grumbled as she swung up into the saddle again. "Alain, aren't you as sick as I am of being followed around all of the time?"

"We do have our own room," he said.

"With guards standing right outside the door! Which is not soundproof! No healthy couple should have to worry constantly about whether they can be overheard when they're alone together." She shook her head at him. "I'm supposed to be freeing the world. Why am I in a prison formed of bodyguards?"

Alain paused before replying. "Is this one of the questions which is not supposed to be answered?"

"Rhetorical," Mari said. "Yes. I know you don't have an answer. I'm just venting. Do you mind if we ride to one of the foot soldier encampments? I should walk through and see how they're doing and...you know. Say hello."

"I know that such actions mean a great deal to those who follow you," Alain said.

They rode off slowly, past groups of people working on the street and lines of people going into and out of the buildings where the future of Minut was being forged. Mari's escort rode only a lance length behind, their weapons ready and their eyes alert. "If I can really make a difference," Mari said, looking around, "maybe I'm not being asked to pay that high a price. It's not like we'll have to live with this forever."

Her words must have triggered a memory in Alain. "Did you want to know what happened to Bev?" he asked.

Mari considered the question, then shook her head. "Not unless you think I need details. I've heard enough about how the Senior Mechanics at Emdin abused the Apprentices there, and how the Mechanics Guild just tried to hush it up without punishing the guilty or removing them from power. Did Bev ever tell you why she confided in you?"

"She worried that as a Mage I could see what she tried to hide," Alain explained. "Also, she thought that a Mage would understand feeling different. And I believe that she wanted someone she knew would not judge her as others might."

"Judge her?" Mari asked, incredulous. "She didn't do anything wrong!"

"She questioned her choices," Alain said, his voice growing impassive as it did when he became upset. "She questioned whether she had done things to bring it upon herself. I know those questions, which arise inside and seek to sustain the harm done to us. I felt them while I was a Mage acolyte. Those who do such things to others strive to shape the illusion we see around us, to alter the way we see the world and ourselves. A good teacher does something similar, and one who loves does it as well, but they shape the illusion in ways that make us stronger and better. Those who harmed Bev meant to create injury that would always cause her to doubt herself."

"What can we do?" Mari asked.

"What you have done. Bev has friends who value her and respect her. She has been given important tasks."

"If she needs more, I hope she'll tell us." Mari glanced at Alain. "You mentioned being a Mage Acolyte. There is something I've been wanting to ask. I know every scar on your body, every injury that was done to you in the name of making you a Mage, to teach you to deny or ignore every emotion and human connection and hardship and pain and pleasure. If that's the only way to make people into Mages—if mistreating children and young adults is required to do that—should there be any more Mages?"

He paused before replying. "This has been discussed. Mage Asha, Mage Dav, and I have talked of it. We do not know the answer."

"But you know what was done to you! How can the answer be hard?"

Alain looked at her, his face a mask. "What if it were Mechanics who were created so? What if your skills came at such a cost? And without that cost, no one could be a Mechanic? Would your decision be easy?"

Mari wanted to blurt out an immediate "yes," but hesitated as she thought. What if that was the situation? Being a Mechanic Apprentice hadn't been much fun. It hadn't been anything like the abuse suffered by Mage Acolytes, but there had been plenty of rough times and rough treatment in the name of teaching discipline and skills.

But she was proud of her Mechanic skills. Proud of what she could do. Just like Alain was proud of his Mage skills.

Suppose Mechanics were like Mages, and the decision was made that the cost to make Mechanics was too high? No new Apprentices, the existing Mechanics growing older and fewer as years went by, until the day the last one died and the last electric light shut off along with so much else. No more Mechanics, and everything that Mechanics could do gone, the hulks of their devices rusting away until Mechanics and what they could once do became the stuff of myth.

Mari shook her head, depressed by that vision. "I...I guess it wouldn't be that simple a decision, would it? Not if we thought about how we felt. But we have to think about the acolytes, Alain. Why can't there be another way to train them?"

"We are trying to imagine such other ways," Alain said. "I feel..." He paused again, looking downward. "If other ways cannot be found, this generation of Mages should be the last. I think...that would be the right thing. If the painful costs of becoming a Mage must be borne by those without the power or the knowledge to say no, then those costs are too high."

Mari reached across the space between them to grasp Alain's hand. "I'm sorry. Sometimes the good choices are the hardest ones."

"There may be other ways to teach," Alain said. "I will keep trying to find them."

"A few years ago, I would have thought a world without Mages would be great," Mari said. "Now I think it would be sad. As an engineer, I know how to make the world work in certain ways. But I've seen the importance of having a little magic in the world as well." Another depressing thought came to her. "All of these changes, Alain. Some of the things that we're doing are not just necessary but good. Like making the Mechanic arts available to all, and helping put Tiae back together. But we can't know where they'll all lead. Are they helping? Have you had any visions about the Storm being stopped or at least getting weaker?"

Alain shook his head. "No. My last vision still showed the Storm as a threat to the world, and to you."

"When was that? A while ago?" Mari asked hopefully.

"The evening after the city of Minut was retaken," Alain said.

She felt a gust of despair. "You mean nothing we've done yet has made any difference?"

"I did not say that," Alain said. "All I mean is that the foresight warnings have not changed."

Mari's anguish changed to irritation. "That does not help at all! Unless——" A thought occurred to her. "Maybe it's a tipping-point situation."

"A what?"

"There are situations where you add stuff and add stuff and nothing seems to be happening," Mari said. "Because it's not enough. But it's all adding up. Like trying to shift something by adding weight to one side. You add weight and you add weight and it just sits there. But then you hit the tipping point, which is when you add just a little more and the thing flips over all at once. Same thing with trying to boil water. You have to keep adding heat until the water boils. Maybe stopping the Storm is like that. We have to hit a point where the changes to this world have gotten big enough so that the Storm won't fade or get less worse, it'll just cease to be a possibility. Unfortunately, that means we'll have to achieve enough change to cause everything to tip. Anything less than that wouldn't save us from the Storm."

Alain was looking at her intently, a tiny furrow crossing his brow as he tried to absorb her words. "I think I understood that."

"There, you see?" Mari said, feeling better. "Maybe you've reached a tipping point in understanding Mechanic stuff!"

"Or a tipping point in understanding you," Alain said.

"That's— What do you mean by that?" Mari demanded.

He got that wary look which appeared when Alain was not sure what he had done wrong. "You see the world illusion very differently from how I do. The way you explain things is sometimes very different from how I see things."

"That's a pretty smooth explanation on your part," Mari commented. "Sometimes you go all Mage on me at very convenient times."

Alain frowned slightly again, then changed the subject in what he doubtless thought was a subtle way. "Speaking of Mages, if you wish to reach Pacta Servanda quickly and safely, you could ride on one of the Rocs. Mage Alera could bring you there in a day's time."

Mari laughed. "Oh, yeah. Me, flying to Pacta on the back of a Roc! Alli's already giving me a hard time for cavalry following me around when I ride. The last thing I need is to do grandstanding stuff like using a Roc for my chosen transport. I don't want my fellow Mechanics thinking I'm taking the daughter of Jules stuff seriously."

He revealed confusion this time. "But you take it very seriously. You have ever since I told you that you were…that one. It upset you very much."

"I don't mean it like that, Alain," Mari explained. "I take the responsibilities and the dangers that come with it very seriously. But I don't want people thinking that I believe I'm somehow special and deserve special treatment just because of the prophecy."

"You are special," Alain said.

"Thank you. I'm happy that my husband believes I am special," Mari said. "But other people shouldn't. Our world is facing the problems it is because some people decided they were more special than other people." They had reached a plaza where a few hundred of Mari's foot soldiers were camped, and within moments every soldier in the area gathered about to see her as Mari dismounted, made sure she smiled, and began talking to as many individuals as possible.

These men and women had left their homes and families to help her change the world. To help her overthrow the Great Guilds and free the world so that their own children could be free. Mari could see the looks in their eyes as they spoke to her, and their admiration and hope frightened her almost as much as assassins did. What if she herself ever started believing she was the person that these people idolized?

They left the east gate of Minut as the sun rose: four troops of cavalry, two large flatbed wagons carrying Alli's battered big guns, and a dozen other wagons which had come north loaded with food for soldiers and grain for their mounts but were now nearly empty. The column had not gone far before Major Consela sent one troop out wide to the right and another wide to the left with orders to find bandits camped near the road. The other two troops and the wagons stayed on the road, which recent dry weather had left hard but dusty.

As the day wore on, the dust the column raised on the road grew into a cloud that trailed them above and behind like some vast, nebulous monster. Like the others, Alain quickly fell into the rhythm of the journey. Everyone rode for a while, then all dismounted and walked their horses for about the same length of time. They took rest breaks, during which both humans and horses sometimes caught brief naps and the horses grazed along the road. At noon came a longer break, with some grain for the horses but only cold rations for the humans, then off again down the dusty road under the unrelenting heat of the sun.

Alain had read some of the heroic epics that had been composed in the centuries since humans had come to Dematr. Once he had begun to experience actual adventures—which Mechanic Professor S'san called "bad things happening to other people"—Alain had begun noticing the differences between those epics and genuine "adventure." Journeys such as this, in which a long day was spent just covering part of the distance from one place to another. Or horses, which in epics were untiring, even-tempered, and always perfectly obedient, but in actual use tended to wear out, bite, balk, and otherwise act like creatures with minds of their own.

Alain felt the same sense of relief as others when the column came to an unexpected halt, though of course he did not show it. That sense of respite vanished as he saw that one of the cavalry scouting ahead was riding back at high speed.

The scout rode up in a flurry of dust and saluted Major Consela. The two conferred briefly and then the major turned to Mari and Alain, who were riding nearby. "There is a large group of people ahead, just off the road. They are in defensive posture and appear ready for a fight. Your orders, Lady?"

chapter four

large group, just to the right of the road," the scout said, repeating his report to the Major. "Between one and two hundred of them. From their clothing, they're not from Tiae. They're in a semi-circle, facing this way. All on foot. No horses or wagons. We saw no armor and no pole arms or spears, but we did spot sunlight reflecting off blades. There were some Mechanic jackets among them."

"Mechanics?" Mari asked. "Did they have rifles?"

"No, Lady," the scout said, shaking his head. "No rifles were visible."

"They could be trying to lure you close, Lady," Major Consela commented, "before shooting with concealed rifles or crossbows. We'll prepare for a possible fight, but we need better information. I want you to ride close enough to them to exchange words," the major told the scout. "Ask them who they are and what they are doing on this road. See what else you can tell from that close."

"How about if I ride along to size up the Mechanics?" Bev asked.

Alain turned to see that Mechanic Bev had ridden up to them, her upper face a mask of dust and her nose and jaw incongruously clean where she had worn a kerchief. Bev gestured to Mari. "Loan me your far-seers and I'll get a good look."

Mari pulled out the far-seers, handing them over. "Bev, be careful."

"Not a problem."

As Mechanic Bev and the scout galloped up the road, Major Consela ordered the cavalry back into motion. "With your permission, Lady, I will not deploy my troops for battle until we are closer."

"It does not sound as if they are prepared to attack," Alain commented.

"No, Sir Mage," Consela said after a moment. She had joined Mari's forces only three months ago and was still getting used to speaking to Mages. "They are in a defensive formation, and all on foot. We would expect any bandits to either run or, if they could not run, to prepare to fight. But an ambush might present itself in such a non-threatening way before the trap was sprung."

The column crested a low hill, heading into the vale where the group could be seen ahead.

The scout and Bev came galloping back, their horses blowing from the exertion. "Lady," the scout said, "they claim to be travelers seeking refuge with the people of the daughter. They say they crossed the border from the Confederation about a week ago, coming south through the grasslands east of Minut. But this morning when they awoke, the guides they had paid to see them to the daughter's fortress had vanished. They were still debating what to do when they saw the dust from our approach and feared that bandits or the forces of a warlord were approaching."

"I didn't recognize any of the Mechanics," Bev said. "But they all appear to be unarmed. Most of the commons just have the sort of daggers and knives that everybody carries. I saw a few swords, and a lot of walking sticks, but that was it for weapons."

"Coming overland?" Mari said. "That wasn't smart. We'll have to ask them why they did that."

"We should proceed, Lady?" Major Consela asked.

Mari looked at Alain. "I see no warning of danger," Alain said.

"Then yes, let's get closer," Mari told the Major. As the Major called the order and the column surged back into motion, Mari gave Alain another glance. "Do I have a fortress?"

"Perhaps it is a surprise from Princess Sien," Alain said.

Mari grinned. "I'm sure that explains it. Why do you suppose they walked overland instead of coming by ship?"

"We have been told that the Great Guilds were trying to stop ships coming south," Alain said. "They may have been able to blockade the Strait of Gulls and the ports of the Confederation on the Jules Sea."

"That would complicate things for us," Mari said. "I hope you're wrong."

"Captain Banda has been seeking approval to strike at ships controlled by the Great Guilds," Alain reminded her. "With the port of Minut under control, your own ships can reopen passage at least from the Confederation."

"Remind me to talk to Banda and the others about that," Mari said. "I'll add it to the list. But I'm worried that striking directly at the Great Guilds outside of Tiae might provoke direct attacks here before we're ready to deal with them."

They had gotten close enough to the group for Major Consela's leading cavalry to confirm that the travelers were not a danger. Most of the cavalry stayed on the road while Mari, Alain, the major, and twenty soldiers rode up to the front of the defensive arc of travelers. "You're on your way to Pacta Servanda?" Mari asked, looking down from her seat in the saddle.

A man and a woman stepped out from the group. "Is that where the daughter is?" the man asked, then stared. "Is it you?"

Alain could see Mari's discomfort, but she smiled. "I am Master Mechanic Mari of Caer Lyn."

"Lady Mari!" The name was repeated again and again among the travelers, their postures finally relaxing and smiles breaking out.

A group of Mechanics came closer, the middle-aged man in the lead nodding to Mari. "It's nice to see you again."

Mari stared at him, then grinned. "Talis? From Dorcastle?"

"Not lately, but that's where we met." Talis gestured to indicate the other Mechanics. "We understand that you've got jobs available for Mechanics who want to work with forbidden technology."

"It's a little more complicated than that," Mari said with a laugh. "But I think you'll all be happy." She started to dismount, then looked again at Alain.

"He speaks the truth," Alain said.

"Good. I would have hated for Talis to have turned against me after he was so nice in Dorcastle." Mari swung down from her horse. "I'm glad you got away from the Guild," she told Talis.

Talis was looking at Alain, though. "Mari, I have to be honest. Having Mages around is going to take some getting used to."

"You've met this one before," Mari said. "Mage Alain of Ihris. He carried my tools for me when we inspected the damage to that trestle that almost wrecked our train on the way to Dorcastle."

"Him?" Talis stared. "You were with a Mage that early?"

"It's a long story," Mari said. "Since we have a ways to go to Pacta Servanda, I can fill you in on all of it. For now, let's just say that this Mage was the only reason I was still alive and on that train. The Mechanics Guild had already tried to get me killed before that, and the Mage Guild had already tried to cause his death."

"If you're really that daughter person, anyone with you would be marked," Talis said. "Up north we heard that Professor S'san was working with you. We know that she wouldn't have signed on if you weren't on the level."

"She's one of my senior people," Mari said. "And in case you're wondering, S'san hasn't lightened up one little bit."

"Still tough as nails, eh?" Talis grinned.

"Lady?" Major Consela asked. "There are some children here, and some of the adults are the worse for walking so far. We can load them in the wagons. I assume you wish us to escort these people to Pacta Servanda?"

"That's right," Mari said. "Alain, please have the Mages check over everyone to see if the Great Guilds have slipped any surprises in among them. Talis, I need to get this group ready to move so we can make the village we were planning to stop at tonight. I'll look you up later."

Mari led her horse over to the two commons who had first spoken to her. "Are you two the leaders of this group?"

"We have no leaders," the woman said. "We were following the guides."

"All right," Mari said. "You two are now leaders, because I need someone to pass word on to the rest of your group. We're heading for Pacta Servanda. It's still a long walk. Tell everyone to get ready to move."

"We're coming with you?" the man asked.

"Of course you are," Mari said. "My cavalry will protect you, and you'll be able to make better time by swapping people in and out of the wagons we have. There are going to be Mages moving through your group. Tell everyone not to worry. These are my Mages. They won't hurt anyone who doesn't try to hurt anyone else."

Alain heard a young girl's voice, audible over the other noises, which sounded oddly familiar. "Mari."

"Yes?" Mari frowned as she caught the voice, too. "Who is that girl?"

"You recognize the voice as well?"

The girl's next statement came clearly across the crowd. "I am *not* a child!"

Mari suddenly smiled in amazement. "It's Kath! Alain, that has to be Kath!" She pulled on her reins, leading her horse through the group of people to where some of Mari's soldiers confronted an angry girl.

Alain caught Mari's reins as she dropped them and ran up to the girl. "Kath! What are you doing here?"

"Mari! That's my sister!" Kath informed the soldiers before returning Mari's hug.

Alain looked beyond Kath and saw a woman he recognized, one who resembled an older version of Mari. Standing with her was a stern-looking man who was gazing at Mari as if unable to decide on which emotions to feel. Alain, used to easily reading the feelings of non-Mages, was surprised to see how many different emotions were warring within this common. "Greetings, Lady Kath," Alain said, then inclined his head respectfully toward Mari's mother. "Greetings, Eireen."

"Eireen?" Mari became aware of her mother and jumped up to embrace her as well. "Why didn't you send word that you were coming? I could have sent a ship. I could have sent a lot of soldiers or a Roc." She faltered as she caught sight of the man. "Father?"

He nodded stiffly. "Mari."

Mari hesitated, then hugged him as well. "It's been so many years."

He responded awkwardly, his face once again a tangle of emotions that Alain had trouble sorting out. "Your mother told me that you had grown," Mari's father said, sounding perplexed. "But it is very odd to see you now like this." His gaze, looking puzzled and sad to Alain's eyes, shifted to her Mechanics jacket and became unhappy enough that Alain thought anyone could see.

"It's been twelve years," Mari said. "And, well, a lot has happened. Oh. Father," Mari continued, her voice growing formal, "mother and Kath have met Alain, but you haven't. This is my promised husband, Mage Alain of Ihris." She said it proudly, with a smile that faded as her father only nodded stiffly, not looking at Alain. "Alain, this is Marc of Caer Lyn, my father."

Alain inclined his head toward Marc, trying to ensure that he put proper feeling into his voice. "It is an honor to meet you."

Mari's father said nothing.

Mari's mother intervened in the increasingly awkward scene. "We couldn't send word, Mari. We had to sneak out of the Sharr Isles. Imperial agents were coming by almost every day to question us, and someone in the Sharr government sympathetic to your cause warned us that they were preparing to arrest us and take us to Palandur."

"To use against me," Mari said, angry.

"Yes," Eireen agreed. "And Mechanics kept coming by as well, and even a few Mages. They kept asking questions even though we kept telling them we didn't know anything."

"Questions?" Alain asked, pretending he was not aware that Mari's father was still acting as if he didn't exist.

"Yes. Almost all of them about Marandur, of all places. I knew the Imperials had banned anyone from going there, but I didn't know they were so obsessed with it! The Mechanics, too! Why did Mari go there? What did Mari want? Did she bring anything out?" Mari's mother tossed up her hands in frustration.

Alain felt alarm stirring inside him. He was not yet certain what was creating that feeling, but something Eireen had said worried him.

"Lady?" One of the cavalry pointed to Kath. "Is this girl supposed to go to a wagon or not?"

"She can walk," Mari said. "Or ride with me when she gets tired."

"She said she is your sister?"

"Yes," Mari said. "This is my family," she added, waving to indicate her mother and father as well.

The soldiers all smiled. "They will be well protected, Lady," one assured Mari. "I will notify Major Consela."

"You're on your way to Pacta Servanda, aren't you?" Mari asked her parents.

"To wherever the daughter has her fortress," Eireen said. "Everyone tends to be mysterious about that."

"We don't want the Great Guilds knowing too much," Mari said apologetically. "Don't worry. You and the others will be escorted the rest of the way. Pacta Servanda is not exactly a fortress, by the way."

"It's fortunate that you happened to be traveling with this group of soldiers," her father said abruptly, sounding as if he was not certain whether or not he approved.

"I don't just happen to be with them," Mari said. "We're on our way back from Minut, sweeping the countryside as we go for bandit gangs."

"We?" her father pressed.

"This is part of my army," Mari explained.

Alain saw a flash of disbelief on her father's face, quickly replaced by impatience. Perhaps that was understandable in a parent who encountered part of his daughter's army, but it seemed odd to Alain.

"Minut?" her father asked. "That's a pirate den. We had to avoid it."

"Not any more," Mari announced proudly. "My army, and the army of Tiae, took Minut about a week ago. We destroyed the warlords who had been controlling the city and the area around it. The flag of Tiae flies over Minut once more."

Major Consela led her horse up to them. "Lady, we have talked to most of the people here. We haven't found anyone who was robbed, beaten, raped, or otherwise harmed. The guides they hired simply took off with the money they had been paid and left these people stranded. Do you want to send a detachment in pursuit of those guides?"

Mari shook her head. "Not if they didn't harm anyone. I don't want to risk a detachment alone out there given some of the larger bandit gangs that may still be operating between here and Minut."

"Yes, Lady. I understand this is your family?"

"That's right."

"I will assign an escort to them," Consela said. "We'll be ready to head out again soon. Do you want to bring in the troops on the flanks?"

"No," Mari said. "Have them keep sweeping for bandits. Whenever we're ready to start moving again, tell everyone to fall in and I'll rejoin you."

"Yes, Lady." The Major saluted before leaving.

"You're chasing bandits?" Kath asked.

"Gangs," Mari said. "Trying to clear them out."

"Shouldn't that be left to the authorities?" her father asked.

"I *am* the authorities," Mari told him. "I have full authority in Tiae, by order of Princess Sien."

"I want to join your army," Kath announced excitedly.

Mari's parents were both turning appalled looks on Kath when Mari spoke. "No, Kath. You're too young."

"I am not a child!"

"You're what, twelve years old now?"

"We would never approve," Mari's mother said.

"Why not?" Kath pointed a soldier standing nearby, holding the reins of her mount. "She can't be much older than me! Her parents must have been all right with it!"

Mari looked toward the soldier and recognized her. "Private Bete."

Bete nodded, then gave a impassive glance at Kath. "My parents died about five years ago at the hands of bandits, when I was a year younger than you. They were trying to get to Trefik in hopes of finding a healer for my two little brothers, who had the fever that went through that year. My brothers died of the fever not long after the bodies of my parents were found. I joined Lady Mari's army to put an end to the bandits, and the warlords, and to defeat the Great Guilds that out of greed and uncaring left Tiae to suffer."

"Oh," Kath said in a small voice. "I'm…sorry."

Private Bete relaxed enough to smile slightly at Kath. "The daughter has given me a new future, as she will give this world a new future."

"Mage Alain!" a woman's voice rang out coldly.

Alain looked that way immediately. Through gaps in the people between, he could see Mage Asha standing near a young man. The two cavalry soldiers accompanying Asha had already drawn their sabers as they confronted the man. "What is he?" Alain called, his own voice nearly as emotionless as Asha's.

"Not a thief," Asha replied. "A spy."

Alain began leading his horse toward the confrontation as the people nearest Asha and the accused spy drew away, leaving his path clear. But before Alain could ask any further questions, he heard Mari's father talking loudly. "That's absurd! We know this man! He's helped us out along the way!"

Alain waited for Mari to deal with her father. He walked up to the young man and studied him.

"Wait, Father, please," Mari said. A moment later, she was alongside Alain and eyeing the accused spy. "Who are you working for? The Empire?"

The man, looking alarmed in a very innocent way, shook his head.

"Not the Empire," Asha confirmed. "But something was left unsaid."

"The Mechanics Guild?" Mari asked.

Another shake of the head.

"He lies. It is the Mechanics Guild," Asha said.

"I see this as well," Alain agreed.

"I—I'm not—" the young man began.

Mari shook her head at him. "You can't fool Mages. Bind his hands," she directed one of the soldiers. "So, you've helped my family on the way down here, huh? Have you been tailing them ever since they left Caer Lyn? Ingratiating yourself with them? Does he have any weapons?" she asked another soldier who was searching the man.

"Just a knife, Lady. Nothing odd about that."

"What are you doing, Mari?" her father demanded, coming up behind her. "What is that woman doing? Stop that! Stop it now!"

The soldier who was binding the spy's hands behind him raised one eyebrow toward Mari's father but did not pause in his task.

Mari looked at her father. "Please do not countermand my orders to my soldiers, or attempt to give them orders yourself. Major," she added as Consela arrived, pointing to the spy, "ensure that this man stays with us when we resume our march. We'll have a long talk with him tonight and find out what his orders were."

"Yes, Lady. We'll tether him to one of the wagons."

"Thank you, Mage Asha," Mari added.

Asha nodded once in reply, her bland expression unchanged. "This Mage will continue her task." She turned and walked slowly toward a small group of commons who eyed her fearfully.

Alain looked toward the nearest officer, a captain. "Assign more escorts to Mage Asha so they can assure the people here that she is no threat to the innocent."

"It will be done, Sir Mage."

Mari's father had finally found his voice again. "You are arresting a man on the word of a *Mage*?"

"On the word of one of *my* Mages," Mari said, her voice sharpening in that way which Alain knew meant someone was getting perilously close to making her really angry.

Whatever her father might have replied was cut short by Mari's mother, who said one word. *"Marc."* She leaned close to him and spoke in a low voice. No one else could hear what was said, but Alain could read the emotions in her and Mari's father.

Apparently, one did not have to be a Mage to see those emotions. Alain saw every other person turning away or pretending not to be aware of the drama.

"Fall in!" The shouted command set everyone in motion back toward the road.

Mari, her mouth set in a thin, hard line, beckoned to Alain. "Let's go."

"Kath," he murmured, keeping his voice so low that only Mari could hear it.

She flinched, nodded thanks to him for the reminder, and turned back to look at her little sister. "Did you want to walk and ride with me?"

Kath cast a measuring glance at their mother and father, then shook her head. "I'd better keep an eye on them, Mari," she said in what Kath probably thought was a whisper but carried to those nearby.

Mari smiled. "You're a good daughter." Something about those words, though, erased Mari's smile almost instantly. She nodded to Alain again and they walked to rejoin the cavalry on the road, everyone else moving along with them.

The afternoon was far advanced when the soldiers and refugees reached the village where they intended to stop for the night. A couple of wells and a stream cutting through the village—spanned by a miraculously surviving bridge—offered water for the thirsty horses as well as the soldiers, but everyone knew the only food available would be what they had brought.

In the golden light of the late-afternoon sun, the village glowed with a false vision of health and prosperity when the cavalry column first caught sight of it. As they came down the road, which wound between abandoned farm fields overgrown with saplings and weeds, it became increasingly obvious that the village had barely survived the years of anarchy. Past the outer, forsaken farms, those closer in showed the marks of repeated raids. Closer yet it became easy to see that many of the village's buildings were abandoned, some having been burned or vandalized. The remaining inhabitants, who had gazed with amazement at Mari's army as it marched to Minut, welcomed the news of Minut's recovery with disbelief at first, then a cautious and small celebration.

Mari had any rations that could be spared distributed to the villagers. The old town hall had been looted long ago but remained structurally sound, so she and Alain took over one room in order to deal with any decisions that needed to be made before Mari could relax, a constant stream of officers and people of the town or from the refugees going in and out of the improvised office.

Well after full night had fallen, the moment finally came when the last official visitor had come and gone. Mari stretched and yawned, her shadow on the wall wavering in time to the flickers of the oil lamp providing light. "Is there any wine left, Alain?"

He shook the flask, then shook his head. "I can look for more."

"Maybe you should." Mari slumped over the small table that the town had provided for her use. She felt worn out from the long day of riding and walking, capped by all of the work needed to keep this part of her army working right. But nagging guilt told her that she shouldn't yet rest. "I need to talk to my father. You should be here when I do. Or maybe you shouldn't. I don't know."

Alain took a few moments to respond, carefully considering the matter before replying. "Your father showed many emotions when meeting you. He was…confused in his feelings."

"Confused? You mean he was unhappy?"

"No. I mean he did not know how he felt. That is the best I can describe it." Alain paused again. "I believe it would be best if you spoke to him without me present. He would be more likely to settle on his feelings about you if he did not have feelings about me to distract him."

Mari felt anger stirring and tried to tamp it down. "He has no right to have negative feelings about you."

"I am a Mage. I have been seen as inhuman and abhorrent, so this is not an unknown thing for me. The experience was always difficult, though, even when I pretended I did not care. But that was in the past. Now the only feelings about me that matter are yours," Alain said.

Despite everything, his last statement made her happy. "Are you sure you'll be all right if I speak to my father alone? You won't feel left out or excluded?"

Alain gave her a trace of a smile. "I will spend the night beside you, will I not? How could I feel left out?"

"You are too good for me, my Mage." Mari smiled back. "Please ask one of the guards to invite my father here for a talk. Where will you be?"

"Not far. I will be watching, close by if any more assassins appear."

Mari tried to relax after Alain had left. That was not easy. The room bore the marks of having been ransacked, and now contained only some chairs and the single small table borrowed from various homes. The remnants of their evening meal—hardtack bread, pork jerky, and the last of the cheese—had been set aside. Outside the one small window the darkness of night was relieved only by a few small lights showing from the still-inhabited homes of the village.

One of the guards sounded a brief knock on the door and looked in. "Marc of Caer Lyn, Lady."

"Send him in."

Her father walked into the room, his gaze wandering about. He came to a stop a lance length away from where Mari sat and looked around as if the bare walls held great interest, then finally gazed directly at her. "Do you have to wear that, Mari?"

As conversation starters went, it wasn't good. Mari looked herself over, knowing that her clothes bore the marks of a long day of travel.

"Good evening, Father. Please sit down. Do I have to wear what?"

"That…jacket," her father said, making no move toward any of the chairs.

"My Mechanics jacket?" Mari composed herself, remembering the many grounds her father had for being angry with the Mechanics Guild. "Yes. It's not a sign of my former Guild, Father. It's a mark of what I know. Of what I can do. I'm working to make the jacket a sign of knowledge, not a sign of oppression." She opened it wide to emphasize her point. "Taking it off wouldn't prove anything, and would make it harder for other Mechanics to believe that I'm on their side against the Guild."

Her father stared at her. "Is that a weapon?"

"This?" Mari realized that opening her jacket had exposed the pistol in the shoulder holster under her arm. "Yes. It has saved my life quite a few times."

"You always carry a Mechanic weapon?"

"Always," Mari said, refusing to accept any feeling of guilt over that. "I'm a target, Father. There were three attempts to kill me in Minut, and two other assassins in that city who were stopped before they got close enough to make a try. Alain, my husband," she emphasized, "personally stopped two of the attempts."

Her father looked away. "Why have you made yourself a target?"

"Why does it sound like you're blaming me for being a target?" Mari rested her elbows on the table. "The Mechanics Guild decided to kill me because they were worried I might some day challenge the leadership of the Senior Mechanics. Are you saying I shouldn't have tried my best to be a good leader and look out for everyone else? I didn't choose for the Mages to see me as the woman of the prophecy. I sure as blazes didn't want it. But they did, and the moment the Mage Guild learned of it, their elders wanted me dead. I've been doing the best I can to stay alive and try to fix a broken world. I think I've been doing some good things. Why am I only hearing criticism from the father I haven't seen in so many years?"

Her father grimaced, running one hand through his hair. "It is… difficult. You were stolen from us when you were so young."

"I never forgot you, or the things you had already taught me," Mari said.

"You never contacted us."

Guilt tied a knot in her stomach. "Mother must have explained that to you. I was lied to, and when I realized it I came to see you."

He nodded sharply. "Those who took you lied to you. You didn't have good, honest, firm guidance, a father's guidance, growing up."

"I think I turned out pretty well regardless," Mari said. "I know it must be hard to see me all grown up now, but I am. I have some very serious responsibilities. I could use your help and support."

"How can you claim to be fighting the Great Guilds when you have Mechanics and Mages lording it over the common folk just as in the rest of the world?" her father demanded.

Mari rubbed one hand on her face in exasperation. "Walk around, listen, see how we do things. These Mages and Mechanics do not act like those you're used to. I insist on that."

"Mages are inhuman and cannot change—"

"My husband, your son-in-law, is a Mage, and he is an exceptionally fine man!" Mari insisted. "I am not the only one who believes so! He is *honored* by our soldiers for his actions."

"Mages can confuse people. I can't believe that you would do some of the things—"

"Things? What things?"

"I can't avoid hearing the stories going around," her father said.

"Stories?" Mari asked. "You mean the rumors about what happened in Dorcastle and the Northern Ramparts, and at Altis?"

"Wishful gossip about a mythical hero arriving to save the day," her father said disdainfully.

"It's too bad you see them that way," Mari said, leaning back in her chair to try to force herself to relax. "They happen to be substantially true."

Her father paused before speaking again. "I'm talking about the stories specifically linked to you."

"The stuff from Dorcastle and the Northern Ramparts is specifically linked to me," Mari said. "Unfortunately, so is what happened at Altis. What other stories?"

"About your behavior! About what you're doing!" her father burst out.

"What are you…?" Mari's voice trailed off as she realized what he must mean. "Are you talking about the trash being bandied about by the Mechanics Guild? About me being crazy and incompetent and sleeping around with anybody who's willing? You believe that?" She didn't feel the outrage she would have expected, but rather a deep sense of disappointment. "You believe that I'm like that?"

"That's not the point," her father said brusquely. "Many other people have heard them, and your…known actions lend them credence."

"Credence?" Mari breathed in and out deeply to regain her calm before saying more. "What about the stories the Empire is spreading about me, Father? The ones about me being Mara the Undying? Do you think those stories have credence, too? Do you want to check my teeth to see how sharp they are, so you can be sure I'm not the Dark One?" Mari smiled in an exaggerated way, pulling back her lips to show her teeth clearly.

"This isn't funny, young lady!"

"I am well aware of that, Father! And I am not nearly as young as you appear to continue to believe! Give me something specific, and I will refute it."

"You want something specific? How could you let that little girl join?" her father demanded. "The one who talked to Kath?"

"Private Bete?" Mari shook her head. "Didn't you hear her? I let her join, I granted her a waiver, because I thought it would offer her the best chance of both surviving and finding something else to live for besides revenge. She had raised herself since her parents were killed, and had been planning to go out to hunt bandits, Father. How long do you think she would have lasted? And what would she have been like when she reached twenty? If she lived that long?"

"But she's only sixteen!"

"Not inside, Father. I have hundreds of orphans like her, some in the army if they're old enough, but many in the workshops back at Pacta Servanda. They're learning trades and skills, but most importantly they're learning that society works by rules and that laws do matter." Mari sighed in distress. "The first time I saw Bete…she was feral. Thin as a stick and ready to lash out at anyone. It was all she knew. There are too many like her."

"But making them soldiers at that age, Mari!"

"I'm using the tools I have, Father! Being a soldier is risky but not nearly as dangerous as the lives those boys and girls barely survived before we started restoring order to this land. I am saving their lives by giving them steady jobs and teaching them skills. If I was wrong, if I was harming them, then Princess Sien would be the first to call a halt to it. But this is the least bad option I have, and hopefully it will help turn the victims of anarchy into a generation with the strength to help rebuild Tiae."

Her father stared at the floor, once more running a hand through his hair. He didn't say anything for a while, then finally spoke in a halting voice. "I love my daughter. My Mari. But…this *Lady* Mari. This *Mechanic* Mari. This…*daughter* of someone else. I don't know who they are."

"They're all *me*," Mari said. "Your daughter. First and foremost. Always."

"Then leave *him*."

"Him?" Mari felt fury bubbling up inside her as she bolted to her feet. "Alain? You're telling me to leave my husband? The man who has saved my life countless times already and who I love and who loves me with a devotion that outshines the sun? Who would I be if I left Alain?"

"My daughter!"

"*No*," Mari said with all of the force she could put into one word. "Your daughter would not do that."

He fell silent again for a while, then shook his head, still not looking at her. "This was a mistake. I was certain it would be and I have been proven right."

"I'm sorry that you feel that way," Mari said, wishing that her father had a Mage's skill to see how much she meant it. "There are plenty of places in Pacta Servanda where you will not have to—"

"We'll go back north in the morning. Your mother, Kath, and I. We'll find a better place for a new home."

Mari felt her jaw drop. "Father, you can't do that! The countryside still isn't safe. This road still isn't safe! If you head north without a strong escort you'll run into bandits before the day is out!"

"Don't tell me what I can't do!"

"In this case I have to! You will not be permitted to leave this column until we reach Pacta Servanda. Once there we can arrange safe transport north for you on one of my ships. But you will come to Pacta Servanda with us."

Her father, his body tense, turned and walked out of the room.

Mari dropped back into her chair and lowered her face into her hands, wondering whether there was any possible way the conversation could have gone worse than it had.

She wasn't sure how much time passed before one of the guards knocked again and looked inside. "Eireen of Caer Lyn, Lady. She says you wanted to see her?"

"Yes," Mari said, taking deep breaths and trying to compose herself.

Her mother came in, sat down across from Mari, and gave her a sympathetic look. "How are you?"

"Rotten," Mari said. "Thanks for knowing I needed to see you without me even asking. Has he always been like that?"

"No. Not that bad. But tension brings out the worst in us all, doesn't it?"

"I tried to explain things to him, but he wouldn't listen! Why is he so stubborn?"

Her mother shook her head. "It runs in the family."

Mari tried to keep her glower going, but eventually let it become a rueful smile. "Guilty as charged. You always did act as a referee between me and Father, didn't you?"

"You remember?"

"A bit." Mari looked down, biting her lip and twisting her fingers about each other. "I can't recall everything that I should. I spent so many years trying not to think about you two. Trying to pretend that I no longer cared about you."

"Your father and I went through the same thing, you know, trying not to think about the daughter we had lost." Eireen sighed. "But we never pretended not to care. Instead, we pretended that you'd come back some day."

"Mother—" Mari felt tears starting and rubbed them away. "I did. It took too long. I don't deny that. But I did come back. And I never would have if not for Alain, the man who my father refuses to look at or say the name of. He asked me to leave Alain! Why would he do that?"

Her mother looked to the side as if watching old memories, staying silent for a long moment before finally speaking. "Your father has always viewed the world in terms of certainties. Among those are that all Mechanics are arrogant and evil, and all Mages depraved and evil. It's like the numbers he deals with for a living. A number is. Five will always be five, and will always mean five. That is how your father thinks. Then you were taken by the Mechanics to become one of them. Your father struggled with that. Were you the little girl he loved, or the arrogant and evil Mechanic he detested? He made a fuss about you wearing the jacket, didn't he? I knew he would. It confuses his certainties. Are you Mari, or the Mechanic? He loves Mari, but she won't fit into his neat categories anymore, and he is reacting to that by lashing out. If he drives you away, then he'll no longer have to try to understand who you are. He'll no longer have to try to understand all of the things you now are."

Mari leaned forward, staring miserably at her mother. "He can't handle change. My own father hates the Great Guilds, but also hates change as much as they do. Mother, what can I do?"

"I don't know." Eireen covered her eyes with one hand. "Giving him orders is probably not a good idea, though."

"Mother, he said he was going to take you and Kath north in the morning! Just the three of you!" Mari waved a hand to indicate the outdoors. "My army and Tiae's army have taken down the warlords in this area, but this country is still crawling with bandits and the remnants of the warlords' fighters. I can't let Father take you and Kath to ugly deaths just because he has a stubborn on!"

"He was probably just venting," her mother said, lowering her hand and gazing at Mari. "Your father is very worried about Kath. When you came back to us, your little sister went from loathing the sound of your name to worshipping her big sister. Ever since then your father has feared she might be lured into the grasp of the Mechanics Guild."

"If Kath wants to learn Mechanic skills she can do that now without going to the Guild," Mari said. "I have schools already functioning that are teaching people those skills."

"It's the same difference to your father," Eireen said. "And then Kath saw your soldiers and said she wanted to join the army!"

"That is *not* going to happen," Mari said.

"Your father and I are worried that Kath won't take no for an answer, that she'll sneak off and try to join anyway."

"If she does that," Mari said, "I will have her assigned to a classroom in Pacta Servanda. My friend Bev runs the schools, and Kath wouldn't get away with anything if Bev was watching her."

Eireen smiled with relief. "You could make that happen? For certain?"

"Mother, it's *my* army."

"Your father doesn't believe that, you know. He thinks you're being used as a figurehead by the Mechanics and the Mages, and are too young and naïve to know better."

Mari tossed up her hands in frustration. "Mother, I wouldn't have gotten this far if I was that naïve. And as long as Sien is advising me I know I won't fall for any tricks."

"Sien?"

"I'm sorry. Princess Sien. Ruler of Tiae."

"You're on an informal-name basis with a princess?" Eireen laughed. "Wait until Kath hears that! And your father, well…" She sobered, gazing at Mari. "And you, my little girl, who lived only in my memories for so long, and who I have to be careful not to forget to worry about now that she's so much bigger. Even though you're a person out of legend, leading her own army. Slaying dragons. Changing the world. A hero."

"Mother—!" Mari began.

"But there is a shadow on you." Eireen leaned closer. "A shadow *in* you. That young soldier whom Kath admired isn't the only one with some scars inside her, is she?"

Mari paused, tempted to deny it or laugh it off, before finally making a weary gesture with one hand. "There have been…things…that are…difficult to remember. And…well, I told Father there had been three attempts to kill me in Minut. And two other tries. One of them involving a man who was convinced that I was a demon. There have been a lot of other tries to end my life. The Great Guilds are going to do all that they can to kill me, and if I fail the Storm will cause so many, many deaths. Even if I succeed…it's a bit scary to think about what the future holds. Or how short it might be for me."

Her mother closed her eyes and inhaled deeply, her distress clear to see, then opened her eyes to study Mari once more. "Why don't I see fear? I know how frightened I am for you. I see worry in you, but not fear. Why not?"

Mari hesitated again, trying to put into words what she had rarely tried to explain. "Mother…my fears…the more I thought about them the worse they got. I couldn't get rid of them. I couldn't pretend they didn't exist, even with Alain's help to show me how Mages do it. Princess Sien gave me some advice, though. She helped me figure out how to do what a good Mechanic should do. I rebuilt the fears.

"I have an anvil. That anvil is what I know is right. It is all the lives that depend on me doing the best I can. And I have a hammer. The hammer is my determination to do the job, and to do it right, and not to give up, and not to fail anyone. I took my fears and I put them on that anvil, and I hammered them into a new shape, into a weapon and a shield. They don't threaten to paralyze me anymore. Instead, they drive me on. When I should be the most scared, I become more unwavering in doing what I have to do. Because the only thing I am scared of now is failing."

Her mother watched Mari for a long moment, then sighed heavily and shook her head. "Mari, there is going to be a cost some day for those suppressed emotions. You've found a way to redirect them, but they aren't gone."

"I know." Mari shrugged, pretending nonchalance. "I'll fight that war when I've won this one. Alain gives me strength when I need it. Mages draw on something they call power, and I've realized that I sort of do that, too. Only what I draw on when I really need it is the love of those who care for me. Alain, and you and Kath and—" She couldn't finish.

"Your father. Please remember this," her mother said, looking straight into Mari's eyes. "Your father does love you. But that love is being chained by his stubbornness and his prejudices. If he can overcome those, he will show you that love again, *if* you have not helped burn all of the bridges between you two before then."

Mari nodded. "I will remember that. I'll do my best. Tell Father I'm sorry our conversation went so poorly. Don't tell him that I think it was mostly his fault."

Her mother smiled sadly. "We had almost that exact same conversation when you were six."

"Really?"

"Yes. What was it you said? *I'm sorry that Father is wrong. But just tell him I'm sorry.* That's what you said."

"I was probably right then, too," Mari said. She sighed. "I'll do my best. I don't know if Father will ask about that man we arrested in front of him today, but if he does, tell him that we asked a lot more questions and got a lot more answers he did not mean to reveal. You were allowed to escape Caer Lyn because the Senior Mechanics hoped you would lead them to me. That man was befriending you to find out exactly where I was staying and as much as possible about the security around me. And when the Mechanics Guild had learned enough and decided to strike, he would have acted as an insider to help their killers reach me." She paused. "And Kath."

Eireen stared at Mari, stricken. "They want to kill your little sister? Why?"

"She could also be a daughter. She could be like me. The Great Guilds want to eliminate that chance. But only after they would have used Kath to help get to me."

"Your father will have to know," Mari's mother said in a low voice. "He'll blame you, Mari."

"Everything else bad in the world seems to be my fault, so why not?" Mari saw her mother's worry and instantly regretted her words. "I'm sorry. You three will still have a special cavalry escort tomorrow and every day until we reach Pacta Servanda. I'm also going to ask Mage Asha to watch over you during the march. She will spot any threats that the cavalry doesn't. You've already seen Asha. She's the one who caught the spy earlier today."

Her mother stared at Mari. "That beautiful blonde? She's really a Mage?"

"Yes," Mari said. "She's a very good Mage. And a very good friend. If Kath wants to speak with her, Mage Asha will be happy to talk. She won't look happy or sound happy, and she's still learning small talk, but Asha will enjoy it."

"Oh, that would thrill your father!" Eireen smiled half-heartedly. "Then he would start worrying about Kath wanting to become a Mage."

Mari managed a smile in return. "Why can't Kath follow whatever path her heart leads her to?"

"Because life is rarely that simple, Mari," her mother said. "Sometimes life demands we take other paths. Like the path you're on right now."

"Alain calls that fate. He says fate gives us choices. We're free to decide which of those choices to make, but our decisions drive the next set of choices."

Eireen nodded. "I hope your father comes to see how fine a man your Alain is. Oh, I wanted to ask if you had a spare knife I could borrow. We had to leave so precipitously that I forgot mine, and it has been no fun being on the road without a good knife."

Mari pulled the knife from her belt and offered it. "You can borrow this one until we can find you another."

"Thank you." Her mother looked it over. "Is this a sailor's knife? Why are you carrying a sailor's knife?"

"It was given to me by sailors," Mari said. Her mother looked a question at her, and Mari bowed to the inevitable. "After I…became a pirate."

"A pirate?" Eireen examined the knife again, then shrugged. "You'll have to tell me about that sometime."

"Mother, I'm getting this awful feeling that nothing I do would surprise you."

"Nothing that you *would* do would surprise me," her mother corrected gently. "Because I know that my Mari would not do anything I would not be proud of once I learned the hows and whys. But for the time being, I'll avoid mentioning to your father why you have this knife. I'll see you in the morning, Mari."

"Thank you, Mother." Mari sat for a while, feeling better, but still thinking about the choices she had made this day and wishing she could revisit a few. And wishing she didn't have to deal with this when everything else was going on and…

Alain came in and she got up and held him, breathing deeply. "Can you forgive me?"

"For what?" Alain asked.

"I was sitting there feeling sorry for myself because I was having trouble with my family, or just my father really. And I finally remembered how much you would give to have family troubles, how much it would mean to you to have your parents alive. I shouldn't be so self-centered."

"Self-centered?" Alain gazed back at her. "No one thinks more about others than you do. Who else would have saved the life of a Mage she had never met?"

"You're going to keep throwing that in my face, aren't you?" Mari said, smiling despite her upset. "I'm still sorry. I'm sorry I couldn't convince my father that I am doing all right, and that you are…the best man in the world."

He managed a smile for her. "Words will not convince him. We will show him, he will see who you are, and your father will learn just how wise his daughter is."

"His son-in-law is pretty wise, too," Mari said, kissing him.

Alain's words stayed with her. She slept calmly that night with her arms about him.

As they walked their horses down the road the next morning, the dust not yet too bad, Alain listened as Mari and Mechanic Talis talked to each other, Mari telling Talis about what was happening in Tiae, and Talis telling Mari about events within the Mechanics Guild.

"We've all heard rumors that you're using banned technology," Talis said. "The Senior Mechanics absolutely deny it, say it's impossible, so most of us figure there must be some truth to it. One thing I knew before I bolted for Tiae was that the Senior Mechanics wanted to find out where you could have gotten access to it, because even while they said you couldn't possibly have it they kept asking us to report any rumors or specific information about the tech, especially any copies of plans."

"I'll bet they want to see copies," Mari said. "They want to know who is getting them to me."

Alain could easily see that Mari was unhappy with deceiving Talis to protect the true source of the manuals, but the other Mechanic couldn't tell. "Yeah, but since the only available source is in the vaults at Guild Headquarters," Talis said, "it's strange that the Senior Mechanics keep asking *where* you got them."

Something had been bothering Alain since yesterday, but he had been unable to sort out what it was. As Mari and Talis talked, though, he gradually realized the reason for his concern. And as that realization hit, Alain had trouble managing his Mage composure.

The Imperials and the leaders of the Mechanics Guild were on the trail of Mari's greatest secret—and might have already discovered the answers they were seeking.

chapter five

Talis finally left to rejoin the other Mechanics. Alain made sure his voice was composed. "Mari, we must speak of something."

She clenched her jaw. "I hear you using your Mage voice, which means you're upset. I hope this isn't about my father. I really don't want to talk about that today. I've been spending the whole morning trying not to think about it."

"It is about what your family said when we met them. It connects to what you and Mechanic Talis just discussed."

Mari gave him a puzzled glance.

Alain checked to ensure no one else was too close and that the background noise of the people and horses on the road would cover their conversation, but still lowered his voice. "It is about Marandur."

Mari's tension grew as she frowned at him. "What about Marandur?"

"Your family spoke of the Imperial agents who had questioned them."

"Yes." Mari nodded, looking ahead as she concentrated on the memory. "The agents asked about Marandur. I thought that was probably part of the Imperial attempt to discredit me by linking me to Mara, or trying to learn how we got in and later escaped."

"Your mother said the agents asked *why* you went to Marandur,"

Alain said. "They asked if you had found anything there. And if you had brought anything out."

"That's because the Imperial Ban doesn't allow—" Mari inhaled deeply. "We did bring out something. The banned technology texts. Do you think the Imperials are starting to put two and two together?"

Alain let himself frown slightly to show his own puzzlement. "Put two together? Two what? With what?"

She shook her head at him. "I mean, do you think they're starting to figure out that we got those texts from Marandur?"

"I fear so. And not just the Imperials. Mechanic Talis said that the leaders of the Mechanics Guild have been trying to learn as much as they can about what you have. They want to see copies."

Mari nodded. "We've been leaking information to the Guild that someone in Guild headquarters at Palandur has been providing us with copies. You heard Talis tell me that the Guild is still conducting witch hunts to try to find whoever is supposedly helping us. Why do you think they would change their minds and focus on Marandur?"

"According to your mother and Mechanic Talis, the Imperials and those from the Mechanics Guild want to know where you got the texts, even though they know there should be only one answer. That implies they believe there may be a second answer."

"A second answer." Mari breathed deeply as she considered his words. "But if that is what they are on the trail of, why seek copies of what I have? What could they learn from the copies we got out of Marandur that the librarians in Altis didn't notice?" She stopped speaking, growing dismay on every feature. "Libraries. The copies. Alain, the texts we got from Marandur have markings and letter/number combinations on them. We don't know what they mean. They could be identifiers, like those used on library books to tell which library owns them and what shelf they belong on. What if those markings on the texts from Marandur are different from those on the texts in the Guild vaults? Or maybe the letter/number combinations could identify whether our copies came from the original headquarters in Marandur. That's why the Senior Mechanics would want to see my copies of the tech manuals! Alain, if they discover the markings are different, that would point my former Guild straight at the source of the texts."

"I remembered your regret at having to leave so much behind in Marandur."

"Regret? It was heartbreaking! We could carry only a small part of what was there! We had to leave so much behind. This is awful! If the Senior Mechanics or the Imperials figure out the truth—that those texts in Marandur were not destroyed during the siege—stars above…it could all be lost." She reached out and grasped his hand. "Thank you so much for keeping an eye on the big picture while I was drowning in details."

"We thought out the problem together. We are a team," Alain said.

She smiled at him despite the worry evident in her eyes. "The best team ever. Those texts are incredibly valuable, but not half as valuable as you are to me. As soon as we all get back to Pacta Servanda we'll hold a meeting and try to figure out what to do. That item just went to the top of the list."

Unfortunately for their plans, days later when they finally arrived at the outskirts of Pacta Servanda they were met by Mage Alera and her Roc in a field off the road. Alain dismounted from his horse, which had become skittish in the presence of the giant bird, and walked to speak with Alera as Mari ordered the column to halt. The Roc sat quietly, as if half-dozing, radiating what felt to Alain like a sense of contentment, while Mage Alera sat on the ground next to its colossal head. "You have returned to this place," Alain observed.

"The general of Elder Mari asked that we look ahead of his march for what he called trouble," Alera replied. "We saw none."

"How far off is General Flyn?" Mari asked as she walked up.

"Elder, he said he would be at this place in two days, perhaps three."

"Three days?" Mari looked at Alain. "Do we need General Flyn at the meeting?"

Was the general needed for a meeting to discuss what to do about the texts remaining in Marandur? Alain paused, recalling the first battle he had been in with Flyn. "I have great…respect. Is that the right word? Respect for the opinions of General Flyn. So do many others, including many of the commons. What he has to say may be of great importance."

He could tell she wanted to hold the meeting anyway, but finally yielded to necessity. "You're right. General Flyn has to be here when we decide things."

Mari paused, looking west toward the Umbari Ocean. "We should wait for Captain Banda's input, too. He's sailing the *Pride* back from Minut, but depending on the winds he might not get here until after the general does." She sighed. "Another item on the list. We need to get the *Pride* retrofitted with a steam propulsion system to aid the ship's sails. Don't look like that, Alain."

He let surprise show. "I was revealing some feeling?"

"Yes. Every time I mention steam or boilers you get this worried look in your eyes."

"I saw no emotion in Mage Alain," Mage Alera said.

"It is the rings we wear," Alain told Alera. "They allow Mari to see into my mind."

"She's going to think you're serious!" Mari said. "How are you and Swift, Mage Alera?"

Alain could see Alera's pleasure in being asked about her Roc, though it probably would have been impossible to spot for anyone not trained as a Mage. "We are well, Elder."

Mari paused again. "You're not going anywhere soon, are you? I think you should be at a meeting we have to hold. No, make that two meetings. I will need your knowledge and opinions."

This time, Alain thought that even a common could have seen the surprised pleasure on Alera's face. The elders of the Mage Guild looked down on Mages who created Rocs, disdaining their emotional ties to their birds. Alera was still unused to being respected. "I will be here, Elder." Alera struggled to say more. "Tha◻ Than—"

"Lady Mari understands," Alain told her.

"I must learn to say it."

"You did say it," Mari replied. "You're welcome."

Alain and Mari walked back to the road, where the horses were pricking up their ears as they sensed the herds and stables not far distant and the soldiers were straightening their uniforms and grinning as they thought of both the people and the taverns awaiting them. "I never should have taught you how to tell jokes," Mari commented. "Alain, in case you're not reading my mind, I am still considering immediately getting together the people we do have here and seeing what they think we should do about those copies left in Marandur. Any delay feels too long."

Alain had remembered something else. "Mechanic Dav is with General Flyn."

"Dav?" She nodded reluctantly. "You're right. No matter what, Dav deserves to be with us when we tell others the truth. We'll wait."

Reaching his mount, Alain swung back into the saddle. He had grown to enjoy riding, and had been trained to endure and ignore all physical hardship, but after so many days on a horse even he welcomed the fact that their journey was almost over.

Mari pulled herself back onto her own horse, the mare shying to one side so that Mari came down hard on the saddle in a way that made her wince. "I like horses. Why do all horses hate me?" Mari grumbled as she ordered the column back into motion.

"I overheard some of the soldiers saying they thought that mare liked you," Alain offered.

"She's got a strange way of showing it." But Mari's expression brightened as she looked ahead. "Pacta has really grown, hasn't it?"

Six months before, Pacta Servanda had been a town under siege, its walls barely holding, its dwindling number of defenders worn to the last extreme, and the refugees inside the town despairing of what the next days would bring.

Now, Mari and Alain rode down the recently widened and paved main highway leading from the neglected Royal Road which ran east of Pacta Servanda and linked Minut to the north with Tiaesun to the south. The growing number of inhabitants, as well as new industry, had spilled outside the walls, onto equally new streets marked out in neat grids to control and channel the growth. Tent encampments, new buildings and Mechanic workshops, and a string of outer fortifications flying the banners of the new day alongside that of Tiae sprawled over more than twice the area of the old town, even covering the place where warlord Raul's besieging army had camped before being wiped out half a year ago. The town's waterfront, then nearly barren and abandoned, was home once more to the nets and boats of local fishers as well as warehouses and merchant offices. The small harbor was crowded with ships bringing in raw materials, workers, volunteers for Mari's army, food, and trade goods to meet the demands of the rapidly growing metropolis.

Alain looked over at Mari. "You have wondered if our efforts are making a difference. You can see how much change they have caused here."

"Yeah," Mari said with a small laugh. "I guess I hadn't noticed all of the changes while they were happening. But after having been away, this is amazing to see."

"In six months," Alain assured her, "Minut will be the same."

"Did you see that?" Mari asked, turning serious. "Did your foresight show you that?"

"No. What has happened here shows me that."

People were running toward the sides of the road, gathering to cheer the army's return. She saw mostly common folk, but with plenty of the dark jackets of Mari's Mechanics among them, as well as here and there a Mage's robe. All mingled together in a shared cause. *A daughter of your blood will someday overthrow the Mage Guild and the Guild of the Mechanics,* the ancient hero Jules had been told by a Mage who looked upon her and saw that future through his foresight. *She will unite Mages, Mechanics, and the common people to save this world and free the common people from their service to the Guilds.*

Alain saw Mari look down with embarrassment as the cheers grew, then nerve herself and raise her gaze to smile back at the onlookers. As the chants of "Lady Mari!" grew louder, Mari raised her free hand, clenched into a fist, and began yelling "Tiae!" and "the New Day!"

The crowd picked up that chant, too, as Mari pumped her fist skyward.

Alain had been trained to see the world as an illusion, something which could be changed temporarily by the right use of power, skill, and training. But that ability dealt only with the world itself, not with the people in it. The Mage elders taught that those people were shadows: another illusion, but one that Mages could not directly change because even Mages could not completely accept that what appeared to be other people were in fact nothing.

But at times such as this Alain saw Mari changing the people around her by using a different kind of power, one that grew out of their belief in her and out of her own instinctive actions. Mari herself discounted that, insisting that she only tried to do what was right. Alain looked at the people, felt the power of their belief and their enthusiasm, and knew that whatever power she wielded, it was as real as Alain's own Mage skills.

He looked back, catching glimpses of Mari's family where they walked surrounded by their escort. Kath was almost glowing with pride in her sister, Mari's mother was trying hard not to look the same, and her father…her father looked confused. Which, from what Mari had told him, was a good thing. Perhaps her father was questioning the certainties he had held firm to.

They reached the gates of Pacta Servanda, where the smiling town leaders and Princess Sien's representatives were waiting along with Mari's senior representatives.

Professor S'san, Mari's old instructor, clapped lightly, then gave her a dry look and called out over the chants. "Welcome back, Master Mechanic Mari. There is a lot of work to do once you've finished your little victory procession "

"Save me, Alain!" Mari cried in mock horror. "I'll take the column through to the city plaza and then wrap it up, Professor."

"Make sure she doesn't try to run away, Mage Alain," S'san said.

Alain nodded to her, feeling a natural smile appear on his lips. To be accepted by someone like S'san was something he had never expected.

For this moment, life was good.

Mari walked into the conference room with a sour expression, massaging her hand as she sat down at the table. "Who would they get to sign all that stuff if I hadn't come back from Minut?" she grumbled.

"Life is hard," Mechanic Calu agreed with exaggerated sympathy.

Alain, judging that Mari was too tired to appreciate further attempts at humor, gestured to the others who had already seated themselves. "Those you have asked for are present," he said. "Mechanics Bev and Calu, and Mages Dav, Asha, Hiro, and Alera."

"Thank you," Mari said. She paused a moment, looking around the table. "I'll try to keep this short since it's already getting late. Mage Alain and I discussed this in Minut. There's a much more critical short-term matter we need to meet on when General Flyn and the others get back to Pacta, but while we're waiting I wanted to talk about a long-term issue. Mage training."

Mechanic Bev made a face. "I can wait outside."

"No. I want you here, Bev. You're our conscience on this stuff. You all know the problem," Mari said. "The training for Mage acolytes is brutal. This is done to children as they grow and become young adults. I would like your thoughts on whether we can figure out a different way to train Mages, or if we should plan for a gradual loss of Mage skills rather than continue to mistreat acolytes in a fashion we find impossible to justify."

"You can't do that," Bev interjected. "That second thing. You can't just stop training Mages."

Mari stared at Bev. "You are the very last person I would have expected to say that."

"You have to understand what I'm saying," Bev insisted. "Suppose everyone who thinks like we do stops training Mages in the bad, old way. What about all of the Mages and their elders who still follow that old way of thinking?"

"The old wisdom," Mage Hiro said. "Yes, they would continue training acolytes in the old way."

"Which would mean that after a while there wouldn't be any Mages like Alain or you others left, but there would still be Mages who acted like the Mages everyone hates," Bev said. "You haven't made a better world. You've unilaterally surrendered that world to the people you disagree with."

"Why did we Mages not think of this?" Asha asked.

Alain shook his head, as surprised as Asha that it not occurred to him. "Perhaps because we have been taught not to consider such things. Deny the world and deny all others. We do not consider how our actions might change that world. Or not change it."

Mage Hiro inclined his head in agreement. "That is the flawed wisdom we were taught. Perhaps the elders did not want us to think through such things." He paused in thought. "I was only recently an elder, but I remember those older than I discussing the need to avoid causing acolytes and Mages even to think about change. Their reasoning was that if change was not thought of, it could not occur."

"Let me get this straight, Bev," Mari said. "You're right, but are you actually arguing that if we can't find any alternatives that work for training Mages, we should still use the old, abusive ways?"

"*No!*" Bev breathed slowly, calming herself. "No," she repeated. "What I am arguing is that we can't accept failure. We *have* to find another means of training Mages, a means that doesn't involve such brutal treatment of kids."

"What if there is no other means?" Alain asked.

"Alain," Bev said, "you have told us that to Mages this world is an illusion! Something we make up with our minds. Why isn't there room in that illusion for more than one way to train a Mage?"

"No one has ever trained a Mage in any other way," Asha pointed out.

"Has anyone tried?" Calu asked. "Has anyone been allowed to try? We have experience with that in the Mechanics Guild. We'd suggest some different way of doing something, and the Senior Mechanics would say no, it won't work. They wouldn't test it or allow us to try it. They'd just pronounce that it wouldn't work, and then they'd ban it. Have the elders of the Mage Guild worked the same way?"

Mage Hiro revealed a tiny measure of approval as he looked at Calu and Bev. "They have. This Mage left the Guild because he decided that the Mage Guild elders erred by dictating only a narrow path to wisdom. Now these Mechanics, their minds not set on the same rigid paths, have grasped what those elders do not. If we view the illusion in only one way, if we allow ourselves to see only one path, then we ourselves create the illusion that the only alternative is failure."

"Yes!" Calu said, pointing at Hiro. "It's like, um, a frame of reference. If we create that frame in a certain way, it's going to affect how we see everything."

"Are there other means of seeing Mage training?" Mage Dav asked.

Hiro nodded. "Every heresy suppressed by the Mage Guild elders is a possible alternative. I studied many of these heresies, using the excuse that I wished to be able to quickly identify anyone trying to revive them. My actual reason was to search for answers the elders' wisdom did not provide. Thus this one remembers many of the ideas in the heresies. We must speak of them. We must look at the heresies not as something known to be error, but as something that might show the way to a different wisdom."

"I feel a different wisdom when aloft," Mage Alera said. "I feel… closer to something. Something…vast. It is hard to say in words."

"The elders have never listened to those Mages who create Rocs," Mage Dav observed. "Perhaps there is a road to wisdom there."

"Perhaps there are many roads," Alera said.

Alain could see that Alera instantly regretted her impulsive words, though no one not a Mage could have detected it.

But Mage Hiro simply nodded in agreement. "We shall look down every road. As the Mechanic Bev said, we cannot surrender the world illusion to those whose wisdom is flawed."

~~✦~~

Two days later, Alain and Mari sat in another room in the old section of Pacta Servanda, part of the original town. Alain had been told that in the past traders had used this room to make agreements with each other. Solid walls and a heavy wooden door ensured no one could overhear what was said inside.

The emotions of those arriving for Mari's meeting were, as usual, easy for a Mage to see: mostly curiosity, but worry, too. Only Mage Dav, Mage Asha, and Mage Alera offered a serious challenge. Though greatly muted, their thoughts appeared similar to those of the Mechanics and commons present.

Mari's feelings were mixed. She revealed anxiety, anticipation, but also annoyance. "Changing the world requires too many blasted meetings," she grumbled. "I never realized how many meetings Jules must have had to sit through."

"You're the one who called this meeting," Mechanic Alli pointed out. "Maybe you're starting to like them."

"That's really not funny, Alli. Some days I think I'd rather take a bullet than sit through another meeting."

"Do not joke about such things," Alain murmured, knowing his voice must carry far more emotion than usual. Was it only his fears that caused the foresight vision of a badly injured Mari to reappear for an instant?

She gave him a startled look that quickly became apologetic. "Sorry, love. I know how you worry."

Once more he felt guilt that Mari did not know of that vision, that he had shared it with only one other person. Across the table, Mage Asha met Alain's gaze with her own, wordlessly conveying her understanding.

Mechanic sailor Captain Banda entered, the guards outside closing the door behind him. "I'm last? Apologies, all. We ran into some contrary winds entering port."

"This Mage must work on his wind spells," Mage Dav said impassively.

The statement drew blank looks from almost everyone present, who knew that Mage Dav had not been on Banda's ship and that Mages had said they could not control winds.

"That Mage makes a joke," Alain explained to the Mechanics and commons. "He pretends to berate himself for not having skills no Mage can employ."

"Good one!" Mechanic Calu said with a little too much enthusiasm, but Alain could see that Mage Dav was pleased by the words.

Mari's old instructor, Professor S'san, gave her a sharp look. "All right, Mari. We're all here. You said this was an extremely important matter. About something you found in Minut?"

"Not directly." Mari looked around the table. "It's about something from Marandur."

General Flyn looked surprised. "The stories that you went there to find something left by Jules are true?"

"No. We went there to find something, but the supposed link with Jules is just to cover what we really found. One of you knows the truth about this already. I'm going to tell the rest of you now. The banned technology texts that Alain and I acquired came from Marandur— from the old Guild Headquarters there."

Mechanic Dav reacted first. "But those texts were destroyed."

"No," Mari said. "When the siege ended, the Guild didn't know whether the texts had survived the destruction of the old Guild Headquarters. The ruins of Marandur were about to be sealed by order of Emperor Palan, so a Mechanic was ordered to determine whether the texts had been destroyed, and if not to finish the job. But he didn't. He saved them, because he knew how important those texts were. He was your ancestor, Dav. Mechanic Dav of Midan. Do you remember how surprised I was when you told me your name the first time?"

"Yeah." Dav rubbed his chin, his eyes full of wonderment. "That's what he did? He didn't just die in the siege?"

"No. He defied the orders of the Guild, but sent out word that the texts had been destroyed. Then he stayed in Marandur to ensure the texts were kept safely and to make sure the Guild wouldn't find out. That's where he died, on the grounds of the old Imperial University, and that's where the texts were hidden until Alain and I found refuge there."

"Refuge?" Captain Banda asked. "In the ruins of the university?"

"The university isn't ruined," Mari said. Alain could see her relief at finally being able to share the story with more people. "It wasn't destroyed in the fighting—it had a wall around it—and so the descendants of the teachers and students who were trapped there have been able to survive. They're barely hanging on, but they are hanging on."

"Astounding," S'san murmured. "And that explains why you have not produced any other texts? It's not because your source in Palandur has stopped providing them?"

"Yes," Mari said. "The Guild had copies that it moved into the vaults in Palandur when the new headquarters were built, so we've fed the impression that someone there was leaking copies of those copies to us. It was critically important to keep the Senior Mechanics from learning the true source of those texts, because Alain and I could carry out only a small portion of what was saved. I had to focus on those texts that would be most useful in overthrowing the Great Guilds. But there is so much more, and all of those texts that we couldn't carry are still in Marandur."

"Why tell us now?" General Flyn asked.

"Because the Mechanics Guild and the Imperials are trying very hard to learn where the texts came from," Mari said. "Alain and I think that both the Imperials and the Guild may be close to realizing that we got the texts from Marandur."

Master Mechanic Lukas sat back, looking very unhappy. "Based on the texts we already have, whatever you left must be of incalculable value. The Senior Mechanics would defy the Emperor's ban if they knew those texts were there. And if the Imperials realized it, they would lift the ban long enough to get their own hands on the texts."

S'san nodded, her own expression bleak. "If the Senior Mechanics get their hands on those texts they'll be lost to this world. If the Empire gets them, they'll keep them and everything in them for themselves, sharing nothing.. How much is there, Mari?"

"A lot more," she said. "And what it is…I can't begin to describe it. Mechanic Dav of Midan, the one who saved them, called those texts the future of our world, and he was right."

"They're even more advanced than the texts you brought out?" Calu asked.

"Some of it is lower-level knowledge in areas that weren't as critical to defeating the Great Guilds," Mari explained. "The highest-level technology in the texts is…well, magic," Mari said, turning an apologetic look at the Mages. "Not your magic. Just technology that's way beyond what we have, like systems that use equipment based on far-talker technology to monitor weather and predict dangerous storms."

"That doesn't make any sense," Master Mechanic Lukas said. "The things in the texts you have are better than what we've got, but I can see where they came from. How could there be technology that far beyond what we have? How did the Guild ever develop that, and then keep it all secret?"

"The Mechanics Guild did not develop it," Mari said.

"Are you finally going to tell them about the ship?" Mechanic Alli asked.

"What ship?" Calu looked at her. "You know this stuff?"

"Mari had to have one other Mechanic she could talk to about it," Alli explained. "Tell them, Mari!"

"The technology came on a ship from the western continent?" Captain Banda asked.

Mari pointed upwards, her expression solemn. "No. It came on a ship from a world that is warmed by another star. The stars, most of them, are suns like our own. It was a special kind of ship designed to travel through the empty space between worlds. It was the same ship that brought people and animals and many plants to this world. The voyage took many, many years."

Professor S'san, for the first time that Alain had ever seen, appeared totally astounded. "How could you know this?"

"There are people who saved artifacts," Mari said. "Librarians. You cannot…it is impossible to describe the equipment they have preserved. Unfortunately, most of it either doesn't work anymore or they don't know how to make it work. You remember that ancient far-talker you showed me once, Professor? The oldest one in existence? The librarians have some, and they are among the most minor of their technological treasures. Those who founded the Mechanics Guild stole the knowledge brought from that other world, allowing only enough of it to make sure they could control Dematr. And they hid from everyone else knowledge of the ship that brought our ancestors here. I haven't been able to tell you about the ship or the librarians because the Guild only permitted the librarians to continue in case the Guild ever needed what they had. But the Guild apparently kept them so secret that the Guild itself has probably forgotten about them. We cannot afford to let the Guild be reminded of the librarians and what they have."

She pointed to one the forbidden technology texts she had brought to the meeting. "You've all asked what that means. Demeter Projekt. That was the name of the ship. Demeter. It gave its name to this world, though over time we must have altered that to the name we know, Dematr. The texts like this were designed to allow civilization to rebuild if ever there was need. They provide step-by-step instructions for recreating the sort of things that allowed a ship to cross from one star to another."

"That is why history is so short?" General Flyn said, his own expression reflecting wonder. "Only centuries, and with no mention of any time before the first cities like Landfall. I had thought the Great Guilds had destroyed any accounts of earlier times."

"In a way they did," Mari said.

"The Mechanics did," Alain corrected. "The Mages did not come into existence until later."

"Right. That's one crime the Mage Guild was not guilty of."

"Which star did the ship come from?" S'san asked.

"The librarians don't remember. They may have records that show it, but they can't access them anymore. The planet was named Urth, though. That's where the ancestors of all of us came from. The Mechanics aren't the only ones who came from the stars. Everyone did."

"I didn't know that any Mechanics still believed that," Lukas said. "Strange that it turned out to be true. Can we visit these librarians and see what they have?"

"I wish you could! But not yet. We have to keep their location secret until the Mechanics Guild is defeated. And one thing they don't have, because the founders of the Mechanics Guild did not want to risk the librarians sharing the knowledge, is copies of the banned technology texts." Mari paused. "So you see the reason for this meeting. If we are to ensure those texts remaining in Marandur are safe, we have to figure out a way to get there and safely depart with them. And we need to do it as fast as possible."

Every eye turned toward Mage Alera. She looked at the map of Dematr on one wall, then at Mari. "Elder, the journey by Roc would be long, over difficult areas and ground held by our enemies, and the Rocs would be seen as they arrived and departed."

Alain saw the concern underlying Alera's impassivity. "You are uneasy about using Rocs for this task?"

"It would be very difficult."

"Would it matter if they're seen?" Calu asked. "As long as no one can attack them when they're flying?"

"There are Mages capable of creating Rocs who could attack," Mage Alera said. "You saw this at the city to the north. And on such a long journey the Rocs would have to land and rest many times. Anyone could strike at them then. How much must be carried?"

Alain picked up a box that Mari had prepared. "Like this. Only twenty."

"Twenty?" Alera hefted the box, shaking her head. "We do not have enough Rocs. They could not carry so much."

"Is there a different means of…operating your Rocs that could make it feasible?" S'san asked.

Alera gave her a look that was vacant even for a Mage. "I have told you what a Roc can do."

"She does not speak out of fear for the task," Alain told all of the non-Mages in the room. "That is not a concern for her. It is the ability to do the task."

"You can't make a machine exceed its capabilities," Captain Banda commented.

"Or overload horses and expect them to just keep going over long distances," General Flyn agreed.

"Having had first-hand experience with being attacked by another Roc," Calu added, "I can see where we can't afford to risk that."

"You're our expert on Rocs, Mage Alera," Mari said. "I was really hoping we could get this done easily using them, but if you say it can't be done, then we need to look at other options."

Calu looked at the map as well. "I assume that walking or using horses is out of the question."

Alain nodded. "It was very difficult for Mari and me to enter Marandur on foot, just the two of us. Departing was also very hazardous. Since our visit to Marandur became known, the Imperials have surely further tightened the security around the city. Only an army could fight its way in and back out."

"Against the Imperial legions on their own ground?" Flyn said with a snort of disbelief. "There isn't any army nearly that big. And how would we even get them there? Overland through the southern mountains and the great waste, which have stopped every Imperial attempt to traverse them? Impossible. By sea? Lady Mari's fleet is too small and too weak to face the Imperials and whatever the Great Guilds would throw at it. No offense intended, Sir Mechanic," he added to Banda.

"None taken," Banda replied. "I agree with you. It would be suicide."

"Are we deciding this is impossible?" S'san demanded. "There must be a way."

"If we decide that the air and the land are closed to us, there is one more way," Banda said. He pointed to the map. "The Ospren River runs through Marandur, and then the new capital at Palandur, and thence down to Landfall where it joins the sea."

Alain saw the look of dread on Mari's face and knew that she was remembering their perilous crossing of the Ospren inside Marandur. "It is a wide and swift river," Alain said.

"And cold," Mari said. "Really, really cold."

"And deep," Banda added. "Before gaining command of the *Pride*, I was second in command on a steam ship the Guild runs on the Ospren. I know that river from years of sailing on it. I could take a steam-powered ship nearly the size of the *Pride* all the way to Marandur."

"Why would the Imperials keep the river dredged and clear all the way up to the old capital?" Master Mechanic Lukas asked. "Wouldn't they only worry about keeping the river navigable as far as Palandur?"

Banda smiled. "These are Imperials, governed by Imperial bureaucracy. Yes, it was nigh on two centuries ago that Emperor Palan ordered no one be allowed to enter the ruins of Marandur, and built the new capital some ways down river. But the instructions given to the Imperial offices charged with keeping the river clear never changed. They still do their work all the way up to the edge of the forbidden zone around the city. We used to joke about that when we took Senior Mechanics on pleasure cruises up the river, stopping short of Marandur of course."

"Well enough," General Flyn commented, "but I don't think the legions would just stand and watch as you went up the river."

"No," Banda said. "That's the big problem. Deception, using a smaller ship that we could try to pass as an Imperial vessel, could get us as far as Marandur. But once we were seen entering the city we would be dead in the eyes of Imperial law. And we *would* be seen. The legions would be ready for us when we came out. I cannot imagine any way to survive the journey back down the river to the sea."

"Could one of the Mage concealment spells…" Mechanic Alli began, then trailed off as every Mage shook their heads in negation.

The long period of silence that followed was eventually broken by Professor S'san. "I will admit to have begun expecting Mages to do anything needed whether it was physically possible or not. But it seems that here we have run into a problem that neither the Mechanic arts nor the Mage arts can defeat, and the cost to this world may be immeasurable."

"Hold on," Calu suddenly said. "Concealment. Alli brought that up. I…where is that?" He started looking through the technical texts on the table. "There is something in one of these— Here! How about a ship that goes under the water so the Imperials couldn't see it going to Marandur and leaving again? —Why is everybody looking at me like that?"

"For signs of insanity," Lukas said. "A ship that goes under the water?"

"It's called a submersible. Look!" Calu held up the text so everyone else could see.

To Alain, the picture resembled some sort of odd sea creature, as if Mechanics had built a fish just as they built their other devices.

Lukas took the text and studied it intently. "The ship can be sealed tightly, and uses tanks that can be filled with air or water to change its buoyancy."

"Like taking on or removing ballast?" Banda asked, leaning to look as well.

"Sort of, but more so." Lukas nodded, his lips pursed as he thought. "Mechanic Calu is right that this is the design for a ship that can sail either on the surface of the water or below it. But there are some practical problems." He pointed at the text. "Some of the potential power sources cited are unknown to me and certainly beyond our current abilities, but I've seen diagrams of these internal combustion engines. We could make one—we have the metallurgy and machining capabilities—but it would be an experimental model. Would we want to use something like that for a mission this important? And those engines are very loud, according to the descriptions."

"Why are they loud, Sir Master Mechanic?" General Flyn asked.

"Because they work by setting off a continuous series of little explosions inside, as if four or more rifles were being fired again and again and again without pause. Maybe not that loud, but still loud."

"The legions wouldn't miss something like that," Mari agreed, looking disappointed.

"But those engines need air," Calu pointed out, "just like steam boilers do, so they're only used on the surface. Underwater, they use batteries."

Lukas shook his head. "I see that. Again, some of these batteries are beyond us at this time, and the basic ones the text speaks of are described as potentially dangerous because of the chemicals used. This is a great idea in terms of concealment, Mechanic Calu, but it is not practical given what we can build."

"It's too bad we can't use a boiler," Mari said. "That's one power source we know well."

"Hey," Alli said, also leaning in to look. "Why *can't* we use a boiler in this design? No batteries and no explosion engine?"

"How would that work when it was submerged?" Lukas asked. "Where would the boiler get fresh air, and how would the exhaust gases be vented?"

"How about if we built something like this in which almost all of the boat or ship or whatever was under the water, but a small part always stayed above?" Alli said. "That way there would be a constant source of air for the people and for the boiler, and somebody could see to steer the thing."

"Even a small portion above water would be seen," General Flyn pointed out, then paused. "But it could be concealed. Not using Mage spells, but in the way commons do, with branches and sticks and leaves. We call it camouflage."

"Like a raft of driftwood?" Captain Banda said. "Such drifts are found on the river."

"Big ones?" S'san asked. "Large enough to conceal the sort of thing we're talking about and not appear strange to the Imperials watching the river?"

"Certainly," Banda said. "Sometimes entire large trees drift down the river before the river patrols snag them. If we only travel at night while going against the current, we should be able to remain unnoticed."

Lukas studied the diagram again. "Steam propulsion, most of the hull underwater, using ballast tanks to adjust how deep the craft lies… we can build that," he finally said.

Alain had understood very little of what the Mechanics were discussing, but he saw every other Mechanic relax and smile at Lukas' words. To them, if Master Mechanic Lukas said it could be done, it could be.

"I still see one problem," Banda said. "You would want a short stack for the boiler, as short as possible to keep it from being seen on the river. But the thing we're talking about would have to enter the river from the sea, and the swells on the surface of the sea would swamp that short stack. The water would put out the boiler and sink the ship."

"We could put an extension on it," Mari said. "Like the one on that Dark Mechanic barge that pretended to be a dragon in Dorcastle. Remember that, Alain?"

"No," Alain said. "I remember you using many words as you spoke of the Dark Mechanic device, but I understood none of them." He wondered why the Mechanics present smiled as if he had told a joke.

Mari shook her head. "Anyway, they had a collapsible funnel that they could raise and lower to hide the presence of the boiler at times. We could do that. Use a longer stack at sea that can be lowered when the, uh, thing enters the river."

Banda nodded, rubbing his mouth with one hand as he looked at the diagrams. "That should work. It would still have to travel as much as possible by night to avoid anyone noticing a raft of driftwood moving upstream against the current, and to minimize the chance of anyone seeing exhaust smoke if we don't maintain the fuel-air mixture just right, but…it should work."

"We've got some gifted Mechanics and commons when it comes

to ship design and construction," Lukas said. "We can get this done."

Everyone looked triumphant. Except for the Mages, of course, and except for Mari, who looked steadily at Alain.

Alain nodded to her. He knew he had to be the one who said what came next. "There is the matter of who must go on this journey."

"We'll pick the best," Professor S'san vowed.

"There are two who must go," Alain repeated. "I must be one of them, because Master Mechanic Mari is the other."

chapter six

I f Mari had said it, the room would have erupted with protests. But since Alain had spoken, everyone just stared at him in wordless disbelief.

"Sir Mage," General Flyn said, having recovered the ability speak first, "Lady Mari cannot—"

"Let me explain," Alain said. He had discovered that his ability to speak without emotion gave his words more weight with Mechanics. He was not sure why that was, but he made use of it at times like this. "Those who survive at the university in Marandur were tasked to ensure they provided the texts only to the right person. They had abided by that promise, and denied to Mari knowing anything of the texts when she asked after them. It was only after she proved that she was the Mechanic they had waited for that the masters of the university told her where the texts were."

"How did she prove it?" Mechanic Dav asked.

"I repaired their steam heat system and taught them how to run it themselves," Mari said. "I didn't ask for anything in exchange or in payment."

Professor S'san nodded in understanding. "You said you had proven that commons could operate a steam boiler. I had wondered where you could have done that without the Guild knowing. That was very good thinking."

"It was Alain's idea," Mari hastened to add.

"If any other Mechanic goes to the university," Alain continued, "the masters will once again deny any knowledge, in case those Mechanics have been sent by their Guild to destroy the texts."

"But Mari knows where they are now, right?" Alli asked.

"I was told they were going to move them," Mari said. "Hide them again in case Alain or I got captured and were forced to tell someone where the texts were."

"But Mari, the risks of you going back there through the heart of the empire—"

"Do you think I want to go back to that awful place, Alli?"

"Lady Mari is irreplaceable," General Flyn said in a low voice.

"So are those texts," said Master Mechanic Lukas, as reluctantly as if the words had been dragged out of him.

"Do we risk the irreplaceable to save the priceless?" S'san asked. "How can we in good conscience do that, and yet how can we not?"

Alain spoke again, keeping his words unemotional. "I know of these texts only what I have been told, and I have understood little of that. What I have understood is that Mari does not often cry, but she cried when seeing what those who came here on the great ship could once create. I have also understood that the founders of the Mechanics Guild stole this wisdom from everyone, not just the Mechanics who came after them. One other thing I know. The Great Guilds and the Empire fear what Mari is doing and what she will do next, but none of them will expect her to revisit Marandur by going up that river in a ship which sails under the water."

"Alain," Alli said, "you're arguing in favor of sending Mari into an incredibly risky situation."

"I know this." Alain paused, remembering Dorcastle. "You know I would not argue so by choice. Nothing is more precious to me than she is. But one of the first things Mari taught me was the need to do the right thing. As much as it worries me, this is the right thing."

"If it were for anything less…" Professor S'san muttered.

"I hate this," Lukas said. "No one here can replace you, Mari. You know that. We've got depth when it comes to things like technical knowledge. We've got the general and his officers to command the military forces. And we've got a surprising number of Mages who render invaluable services to us. There's only one person the commons see as the daughter, though, and only one Mechanic that the Mages will accept as a leader. And I'll be the first to admit that you have been a very effective leader, showing an ability to inspire and to combine our strengths that I would not have believed before joining you. On top of that is the deal with Tiae, which the Princess insisted on making with you personally. I'm not telling you anything that you don't know. But I also know that the Senior Mechanics would burn every piece of knowledge, no matter how precious, to try to keep themselves in control for another day. And the Empire would be no better. We have to do this. I can get the ship built. I hope you aren't planning on just you and Mage Alain sailing it up the river to Marandur."

"You need a good sailor who knows the waters," Captain Banda said. "I must go as well."

"And me!" Mechanic Dav insisted before anyone else could speak. "My ancestor started this. He saved those texts. It's my job to finish the work he began."

Mari nodded to him. "I can't argue with that."

"If Mechanic Dav goes," Mage Asha said dispassionately, "I will go." Despite the lack of feeling in her words, Alain noticed that even the Mechanics and commons had caught the determination behind them.

"That has to be it," Lukas said. "This mostly-under-the-water boat thing has to be as small as we can get away with. We already have to worry about the boiler and fuel for it. Three Mechanics should suffice to oversee the boiler while you're moving on the river, and two Mages can provide what could be critical backup if you have to fight at any point. But five people and food for them will take up enough space as it is, and we need to leave room for those texts."

"Do you see a need for a common among the crew?" S'san asked Flyn.

"No, Lady Mechanic," Flyn said, shaking his head. "Lady Mari represents us all."

"General," Mari said, "if I knew any other way to safeguard those texts, I wouldn't do this."

"I do understand, Lady. At this moment, there are at least two injured men in a hospital who would be dead if not for some of the medical devices in the texts you *did* bring back." Flyn grimaced slightly, looking down. "I once told Mage Alain that I had a son who died of illness when very young. What still lies in Marandur could perhaps have saved him, and could save many other sons and daughters in the future. It does not surprise me that you see the importance of that, and are willing to risk yourself for it."

"Thank you," Mari said in a small voice, looking down herself in embarrassment.

"We need to keep anyone from knowing that Lady Mari is gone," General Flyn added, looking resigned. "We can do that for a few weeks by pretending she is visiting other places. But any longer than that and uncomfortable questions will be asked. Is she supposed to sail that thing up through the Umbari Ocean and the Jules Sea, then across the Sea of Bakre and up the Ospren River, and then back? That round trip could be months."

Captain Banda grimaced as he thought. "The thing can be towed by a larger ship like the *Pride*. But that would still mean Mari being gone for all that time on the ship."

"Rocs could take her and Mage Alain to the ship," Mage Alera said, surprising the others. "Carry them up and across the sea, stopping to rest in the grasslands and the Southern Mountains. It would be much easier and faster than trying to cross the waste and southern Empire as well. The journey should only take three days, four at the most, if the Rocs are pushed."

"That would be much better," General Flyn said.

"How do Mari and Alain get from the bird to the ship?" Calu asked. "Can Rocs land on water?"

"Rocs cannot land on water," Alera said. "No. Elder Mari and Mage Alain would jump into the sea."

"We would what?" Mari demanded.

"The Rocs carrying you and Mage Alain would glide slowly as low as they could, and you would jump into the sea near the ship," Mage Alera explained.

"This would work," Alain agreed.

"Excuse me!" Mari said. "You want me to jump off a giant bird into the sea? What happened to all of this concern that I might get hurt?"

"We would put a boat into the water when we saw the Roc approaching," Captain Banda said. "There should be little risk."

"Little risk to you, maybe!"

"Mari," Alain said, knowing that she probably would not thank him for bringing this up, "I have jumped from a Mechanic ship into the water."

"We didn't exactly have a choice, Alain."

"And I have jumped from Mechanic trains at your request."

"Only once!"

"Twice," Alain corrected her. "The first time was supposed to be into water, but it was mostly rocks. The second time was only rocks."

Mari set her mouth and glared at him. "The second time was dirt with rocks mixed in. Fine. I didn't think I could hate anything more than I did the idea of going on this trip to Marandur, but now I do."

"Speaking of things no one wants to do, who tells Princess Sien of this when she returns?" General Flyn asked.

"I will," Mari said. "She won't accept it from anyone else."

"Good luck dealing with the royal wrath, Lady. Princess Sien knows you carry the future of Tiae with you."

"Needless to say, but I will say it anyway," Professor S'san added in her harshest tones, "no one is to breathe a word of Mari's upcoming trip to anyone who wasn't in this room. And don't talk about it among yourselves anywhere where anyone can overhear. Better yet, don't talk about it at all. Mari's survival will hinge on whether we can keep secret the fact that she is returning to Marandur. You can talk about the experimental watercraft among yourselves. We'll do our best to keep it secret as well, but the need to construct it will require letting a lot more people in on that. But not what it is intended for. We need a name for the craft, Lukas."

"The texts call it a submersible," Calu pointed out again. "But that's for something that completely submerges."

"We want a name that is misleading," General Flyn suggested.

"Misleading?" Lukas asked. "It's essentially a boiler that can be floated somewhere."

"It is very dangerous, then," Alain said.

"No. Not if properly operated. Why do you think a boiler is very dangerous?" Lukas asked.

"Because—" Alain suddenly realized that what he was about to say might not be welcomed by Mari. "They can explode. And create fires."

"How did a Mage—?" S'san began, then looked at Mari. "What did you do?"

"I made a boiler explode," she said, with an aggravated look at Alain. "And set a fire in the boiler room on the *Queen of the Seas*."

"That's right!" Calu said. "You blew up a boiler in Dorcastle, right?"

"You blew up a boiler." Lukas stared at Mari as if seeing her for the first time.

"It wasn't an accident!" Mari protested. "I did it on purpose!"

"You did it on purpose." Lukas looked at S'san as if hoping she would have a rational explanation for such behavior.

"There was a dragon," Alain said.

"And Mari used the boiler explosion to kill the dragon," Alli explained. "She told me all about it. Hey, that's what we could make people think the thing is. A way to sneak a powerful bomb next to a ship at sea. The *Queen*! That might sink her. And Mari already tried once."

"I didn't try to sink the *Queen*," Mari corrected. "I just wanted to disable the ship. But the Senior Mechanics probably think I did want to sink her."

"And fanatical, crazy Mari would be obsessed with finishing the job, wouldn't she?" Alli said.

"Could you put that some other way?" Mari asked.

S'san nodded, smiling thinly. "Yes. That is exactly what the Senior Mechanics would think. And that thing could be a sort of mobile bomb potentially useful against a steel ship like the *Queen of the Seas*. Or at least it could be in the eyes of a dangerous, unpredictable opponent."

"We don't want the Mechanics Guild to be too worried about this thing if they hear about it," Captain Banda said. "That would attract too much interest."

"Not if they think it's a piece of junk," S'san said, smiling again. "We can plant plenty of rumors that the thing is not working, that the design is the flawed product of a flawed mind. The Senior Mechanics would be eager to believe that Mari's obsessions were driving her to such irrational schemes."

"Excuse me," Mari said. "Still sitting here listening, and not enjoying this. Aren't we supposed to be deciding on a name?"

"The *Terror*," Calu suggested. "That's the sort of name an obsessive, insane leader would pick, right, Mari?"

"Why are you asking *me* that?" she replied coldly.

"Um...and the nickname would be the *Terrible*," Calu finished, trying to pretend that he hadn't heard Mari's response.

"I like that," Lukas said. He gave Mari another look. "You do understand we don't want this one to blow up?"

"Yes, I do understand that," Mari replied, her tone of voice flat now. "I have a very strong desire to get back from this alive."

S'san nodded. "Remember, everyone, an incautious word could doom Mari. Banish the name of Marandur from your minds from this moment on, and don't even hint that Mari will leave Tiae at any point in the future."

Alli stood up and walked up to Mari. "Since we can't talk about this once we leave here, I'm telling you right now, your daughterness, that you had better come back safely. You and Alain both. If anything happens to you, if you die, I swear that I will find your grave, dig you up, and yell at you until my voice gives out!" She blinked back tears, then embraced Mari.

"She means it," Calu said to Mari. "Alain, you'll get Mari back to us, right?"

"I will," Alain said.

After everyone else had left, Mari shut the door again and sat down next to Alain, burying her face in her hands. "Thank you for convincing the others that I had to go," she mumbled.

"I am sorry," Alain said.

She looked over at him, smiling crookedly. "I wasn't being sarcastic. If I had told them I had to go, each and every one of them would have accused me of being irresponsible and misguided and impulsive and...lots of other things. But they knew you wouldn't have proposed it unless it really was necessary. When it comes to me, they trust you more than they trust me."

"When it comes to most other things, they trust you a great deal. But they know you place a very high concern on what you see as your duty, and a very low concern for the dangers that duty may place you in." Alain put his arm about her, worry and guilt filling him now that he had helped convince the others that Mari must go into danger again. "I hope what I said about no one expecting this is so. We might be able to get into Marandur and escape again without anyone in the Empire knowing."

"My darling Mage, I am certain you are right about no one expecting me to do this." Mari closed her eyes tightly. "Jumping off a Roc into the sea. You've wanted to get back at me ever since I made you leap off that second train, haven't you?"

Concerned that Mari was serious, Alain began to deny it, then looked closely at her. "This was a joke?"

"Not much of one, but yeah." She looked at him again. "I'm starting to be as bad at telling jokes as Mages are. You're rubbing off on me. Did you have to bring up the boiler explosion in front of Master Mechanic Lukas?"

"Yes?"

She tried to keep a straight face, then laughed. "If I stay sane, my Mage, it will be because of you."

∽

A week later, Alain stood by Mari's side as she explained to Princess Sien about the mission. Sien, who had sat down with a happy expression at being reunited with Mari, grew increasingly stone-faced as Mari talked.

When Mari had finished, Sien said nothing for a while. Finally she stood up, drew her dagger, and slammed it point first into the table with enough force to partially bury the blade. "How can you do this to Tiae?" Sien demanded. "How can you do this to me?"

"I am doing it *for* Tiae," Mari insisted. "This is part of fighting the Storm."

"You are rushing to your death when your life means hope for everyone!"

"Sien," Mari said, "these texts are the most valuable things in this world."

"That will mean nothing if Tiae remains a broken kingdom!" Sien clenched her fists and glared at Alain. "You permit her to do this?"

Alain, surprised at the way the question was phrased, shook his head. "I do not control Mari."

"No one does, it seems! And no one can guarantee that she will return to Tiae! If I had ever doubted that she bears the wild spirit of Jules within her, I would know that for certain now!"

"Sien," Mari said, "the contents of those texts, what they could mean to everyone in this world, is impossible to describe. You know Mechanic lights? One of those texts tells how to make panels that can turn sunlight into the electricity needed to power those lights and a lot of other devices. Every building could have them. There's another that shows how to make devices that let Healers see inside the bodies of people. Instead of having to cut into people to see what was wrong, Healers could just look through their skin and muscles! And devices for farms that would let them grow a lot more food with less labor, along with means to preserve food for longer periods. No more famines!"

Sien shook her head angrily. "Mari, I understand how these things could benefit everyone, but you yourself have said the Storm approaches. If you die, the Storm triumphs, and there will be no future to build those devices."

"And if I win there has to be a foundation for a better future! I can't just aim to win and have no plan for afterwards!"

The two women looked at each other, both upset, neither yielding. Something occurred to Alain that might break the impasse. "Princess Sien, when Mari returns to Tiae, she will have the texts with her."

"What does that matter to Tiae?" Sien grumbled.

"The most valuable things in the world will be in Tiae," Alain said.

Sien paused, shooting a sidelong glance at Alain. "But they will belong to the Mechanics."

"They will belong to everyone," Alain said. "Is that right, Mari? You have said these texts belong to everyone."

"Yes," Mari said. She gave a knowing nod and half-smile to Alain. "But they will need a safe place to be located. Tiae could be that place."

Sien stood straight and crossed her arms, eyeing Mari. "Tiae would not control these texts. But Tiae would be their home."

"Everyone would have to come to Tiae to see them," Mari agreed.

"You are clever, Mage Alain," Sien said. "You offer me something that would help make this kingdom respected once it is reunited. But still, Mari, it must be reunited. I am…disappointed to hear that you will risk yourself in this way."

"Have you ever risked yourself for Tiae, Princess Sien?" Alain asked.

"Too clever," Sien said. "And you know I am only Sien to you in private. Yes, I have risked myself for Tiae. Mari, does your heart tell you that you must risk this?"

"Yes," Mari said. "For the world. Believe me, if my brain could think of a good alternative, I would be doing something else."

"Then I cannot stop you, because the one person in this world more stubborn than I is Lady Mari. I can only give you my blessing and hope with every bit of my being that you will succeed and come back whole to me." Sien looked down at the table, grasped her dagger, and pulled unsuccessfully. "Alain, can you aid me in getting my dagger out of this?"

Alain focused on the wood next to the blade. The illusion of a table was there, but he could overlay on that for a little while the illusion that some of the wood was missing.

A small section of wood next to the dagger blade vanished, Sien catching the weapon before it could fall. "My thanks, Mage Alain." She studied the dagger blade as she spoke to Mari. "I know of Mage Asha, and have been impressed by your Mechanic Captain Banda, but have had little experience with this Mechanic Dav."

"He's a good man, reliable," Mari offered. "He has a family obligation to fulfill."

"I understand better than most the burdens of family obligations," Sien said. "More important than those are your judgments of him. Mari, you have spoken of your troubled nights. Do you not fear that returning to Marandur will worsen the nightmares that plague you?"

"I'm learning to handle them," Mari said.

Alain gave her a look, knowing that she would understand his meaning without words being spoken.

She did. "Alain's opinion may differ."

"It does," Alain said. "Part of Mari has never left Marandur."

Mari gave him a cross look. "I didn't need to hear that."

"But," he continued as the thought came to him, "it is possible that when we return, she will find that part, and be able to finally leave Marandur behind."

Sien raised her eyebrows at Alain. "You may have spoken wisdom indeed. I have tried to help Mari in my own ways."

"Your advice has helped a lot," Mari said.

"I'm glad to hear that. Let me know what Tiae can do to assist you both. Will this require our hoped-for campaign to establish control over Tiaesun to be postponed?"

"No," Mari said. "I don't think so, anyway. There's some uncertainty as to how long it will take the ship thing to be built, but even though it will take time to prepare for the campaign, and to get the newest volunteers integrated into my army, we need to capture Tiaesun before the rainy season hits."

"And it does *hit*," Sien said. "Any army trying to move during the rains will drown in the mud."

"I'm not looking forward to that. Anyway the, uh, *Terror* isn't going to be ready that soon."

"Tiae needs more time to grow its own army," Sien admitted. "Though that army grows much faster than anyone could have expected. It is a comfort to me to know that you will be present when we retake Tiaesun. Our armies have grown, but so have you. You are much more comfortable with giving orders, Mari."

Mari looked surprised. "I don't feel much more comfortable doing it."

"That does not show. You do not hesitate to lead even though those you lead have grown greatly in number. You do not like making some of the decisions, but you make them." Sien paused. "Speaking of decisions, on the matter of rifles…"

Mari made a face. "How many do you need?"

"How many are to spare?"

"You know there aren't any to spare. I'll talk to Alli. Would you be willing to accept ten out of every hundred new ones for Tiae's army?"

Sien smiled at Mari. "Surely my dearest friend and companion could find a way to offer twenty out of every hundred?"

"You wish for more than that," Alain said.

"Of course I do! I would take fifty out of every hundred if I could get it, but I know that Mari's army is the one that will face the Great Guilds." She gave Alain and Mari a searching look. "However, the open comments of those such as Colonel Yuri do not help."

"Colonel Yuri?" Mari looked to Alain for help with the name.

"He came with three hundred troops of the Western Alliance," Alain said. "That force arrived but two days ago, and Colonel Yuri has begged off seeing you since, saying that he must tend to his soldiers. General Flyn told me that he was unhappy that the three hundred are all a single unit rather than a group of volunteers. He suspects it is an attempt by the Western Alliance to subvert your control."

"And what has this Yuri been saying?" Mari asked Sien.

"In public, that Tiae will only ever receive token numbers of the new weapons, which will instead go to 'reliable' soldiers such as his."

Mari's expression hardened. "Alain, if you speak to Flyn before I do, tell him I want this Colonel Yuri to be politely told to go home. I don't want to offend the Western Alliance, but I don't want them playing those kinds of games here. Sien, you must have known that I would never do what Yuri suggested."

"I know this," Sien said. "But others do not. Tiae has always been a proud land. It is hard to accept our need for foreign assistance, even while feeling bitter that more help was not coming from other lands. I was informed of the problem with Yuri as soon as I arrived, which tells you how much it concerned my advisers. If I may suggest…"

"Always," Mari said.

"Send the errant colonel home, but keep the soldiers and break them up among your other forces so that they can no longer act as a single force under Western Alliance control."

"This is wise," Alain said.

"And," Sien added, "it will make clear to those who planned this that the daughter is not so easily undermined. Make those soldiers your own, so that they become an instrument to use against the Western Alliance if necessary."

Mari jerked in surprise. "Against the Western Alliance? Why would I ever need to do that?"

"Better that I say, against some of the *leaders* of the Western Alliance," Sien said, reaching out to touch Mari's shoulder. "The people are yours. That is not something that many leaders will be happy about. But if enough of the people are yours, it might give pause to leaders planning to do something stupid."

"Alain," Mari said. "Please go talk to this Colonel Yuri yourself. See what he reveals when a Mage is there to read him. I want to know exactly what he and his bosses were planning. And tell General Flyn that I want Yuri gone and the soldiers he brought scattered among the rest of my army."

Sien smiled. "You might tell General Flyn to inform Yuri that these measures are necessary because the daughter fears that otherwise the Western Alliance might become the direct target of the wrath of the Great Guilds. No one could object to the daughter's concern for their own welfare."

"One of our Mages who rides a Roc could also deliver such a message directly to the Western Alliance," Alain pointed out.

"They could! I will be happy to assist in drafting the message."

Not long afterward, Alain walked with General Flyn through one of the large encampments of new volunteers for Mari's army. "Colonel Yuri finally checked in with me yesterday," Flyn said. "But if I judged him right, he took my orders as suggestions. I'm looking forward to having him face both of us this time."

"Perhaps we should have brought Mari as well," Alain said.

Flyn smiled. "I think perhaps Lady Mari's temper might be too sorely tested by the likes of Yuri." His smile vanished as they approached Yuri's command tent. "It's still up."

Alain gazed at the flag of the Western Alliance flying in front of Yuri's tent and understood Flyn's unhappiness. "You told him to take it down?"

"In no uncertain terms, Sir Mage." Flyn, a stern look on his face, marched up to the sentry at the entrance to the tent. "We're here to see Colonel Yuri."

"Yes, sir!" the soldier replied, saluting smartly. "I will see if the Colonel—""There's no 'if' about it, soldier," Flyn interrupted. "Tell him that we're coming in."

Alain and Flyn walked into the tent right after the sentry had announced them. Colonel Yuri, a handsome enough man in a uniform adorned with ribbons and medals, looked up from his field desk with barely concealed annoyance. "Yes, General?"

Flyn's frown increased slightly. He gestured toward Alain. "I am not your only guest, Colonel."

Yuri glanced at Alain, who had let his face settle into a Mage's menacing lack of emotion. Unnerved by that, Yuri stood up quickly. "Sir Mage."

"Do I irritate you?" Alain asked in his most unfeeling voice.

That question rattled Yuri a bit more. "No, Sir Mage."

"Why is the Western Alliance flag still up?" Flyn demanded.

Yuri looked only mildly apologetic. "My soldiers are proud of their unit and its history serving the Western Alliance—"

"They're either here to serve the daughter, or they're going home," Flyn said, his voice taking on a sharper edge. "Flying that flag on the soil of Tiae without invitation is an insult to the army of Tiae."

"The army of Tiae?" Yuri asked, smiling slightly. "Do you mean the children, or the gray-haired elders?"

Alain saw General Flyn's expression tighten even more.

"I am not impressed by your disrespect for capable, motivated, and reliable troops," Flyn said. "You may count yourself fortunate if your soldiers never have to fight them."

"If?" Yuri stood straighter, looking affronted. "You issue threats? The Western Alliance has sent soldiers to fight for Lady Mari—"

"Despite the fact," Alain said, his emotionless Mage voice slicing through Colonel Yuri's words, "that Lady Mari has instructed governments not to send entire units of soldiers, since that could cause the Great Guilds to retaliate against them before the daughter is prepared for such a confrontation."

Yuri paused, then a smile flickered on and off. "We of course deeply respect Lady Mari—"

"You do not," Alain said, having seen the lie clearly.

"How can you—"

"You're trying to lie to a Mage," Flyn said, now sounding exasperated rather than angry.

"But he's Lady Mari's…" Colonel Yuri's eyes went from Flyn to Alain.

"I am a Mage," Alain said. "Do not mistake my ability to feel emotion as a sign of weakness. Should you make me angry, you will see how strong my skills are, and your words and the meanings hidden behind them are indeed making me upset."

"Um…Sir Mage," Yuri began nervously.

"Come with me, Colonel," Flyn said. "Right now. We have to talk, commander to commander."

"But I—" Yuri glanced at Alain, obviously was worried by what he saw, and nodded. "Sentry!" Colonel Yuri gestured peremptorily when the soldier stuck his head in the tent. "Get Captain Patila in here."

An aide rushed out, returning quickly with a woman Alain recognized. "Yes, sir?"

"I need to speak with the general. You're in command until I return."

Alain waited until Flyn and Colonel Yuri left, Yuri not realizing that he had not joined them, then spoke to Patila. "Captain," Alain said. "It has been long since Lady Mari and I saw you at Altis."

She nodded. "Yes, Sir Mage."

"Do you still aid the daughter?" Alain asked.

"I do." Patila hesitated, revealing worries and conflicting emotions easy for a Mage to see.

"You will not see Colonel Yuri again. He will be taken under escort to a ship that is sailing for the Western Alliance and given a message to deliver to his leaders." Alain did not mention that the same message was also being sent north by Roc and would arrive by that means long before the ship did.

Patila gazed warily at Alain. "What are your intentions, Sir Mage?"

"None of the soldiers in your unit will be harmed or mistreated, but the unit will be broken up, the soldiers scattered among the rest of the daughter's army."

Patila grimaced. "I warned our leaders this was a bad idea—that you would see through it. They made me second in command anyway because of the time I aided both you and Lady Mari on the docks of Altis, which they thought might incline you well toward me."

"What was the plan?" Alain asked. "I saw contempt for Mari in your colonel, but not hostility."

"No, no, it wasn't about hurting her, it was about trying to gain an advantage for the Western Alliance," Patila explained. "We were supposed to stay with you long enough to be issued as many of the new rifles and as much ammunition as possible, and then arrange for a transport from the Western Alliance to show up. We'd march aboard before anyone knew what we were doing and head home with the new weapons."

"And the Great Guilds would have learned that the Western Alliance had those weapons, and would have moved to crush you," Alain said.

"Yes," Patila agreed. "But try talking sense to some people who can view situations only in terms of how they might personally profit. Colonel Yuri is highly ambitious, and has close connections in the highest levels of the Western Alliance. He was in many ways a bad choice because he is…not the most diplomatic of men. But he knew the right people to get the job. I don't know whether this whole game was his idea, but he is not the highest-placed player in it."

Alain nodded, eyeing Patila. "And your loyalty was torn between your oath to the Western Alliance and your sympathy for the daughter's work. Will you serve Mari well, Captain?"

"If I am allowed to," Patila said. "Her victory would be the greatest victory for the people of the Western Alliance as well, and my orders did send me here."

"There is no lie in you," Alain said. "Tell your soldiers that the unit will be broken up to ensure that the Great Guilds do not attack the Western Alliance for providing direct military aid to the daughter. Any who do not wish to serve wherever they are needed in the daughter's army may return to their own lands. There is something you wish to say."

Captain Patila hesitated. "I was thinking that another commander who suspected Colonel Yuri would have used this unit as cannon fodder in the next engagement, allowing it to be cut to ribbons in combat and only then dispersing the survivors among the rest of the army."

"Lady Mari does not think that way, and does not act that way."

"Then I did not misjudge her." Patila paused again. "There are rising concerns in some quarters. The daughter's power is growing. The Broken Kingdom is being mended. The world is not used to such changes in such a short span of time."

"What do you suggest?" Alain asked.

Patila looked startled at being asked for her opinion. "If you truly wish to know, I would advise sending messages to every city explaining Lady Mari's intentions. I know this has been done with some cities, but tell everyone. Let them know that the daughter's only enemies are the Great Guilds."

"And those commons who ally with the Great Guilds."

"Yes. The Great Guilds are moving slowly, Sir Mage, but do not doubt that they move. They play on the fears of some of the leaders of the commons and on the greed for power or wealth of other leaders."

Alain nodded. "I will advise Mari to do as you say."

"You...have come far, Sir Mage," Patila said. "Have you heard that the Mage Guild says you have lost your powers because of your feelings for Lady Mari? They are telling everyone that you are a...fraud."

"Are they?" Alain found himself amused instead of upset. "That may work to my advantage."

Only a few days later, Alain found Mari poring over some strange drawings in the small upstairs safe room. The house they had been given in Pacta Servanda had once belonged to a merchant who had constructed on the second floor a room with one door, no windows, and solid walls to allow for private negotiations and deals. Decades later, that room offered a secure place for talking about much more grave matters. "Take a look at these," she said.

He studied the drawings, seeing many different aspects and views of what looked like two large boats that had been joined deck to deck to form a single flattened fish-like shape. "What is this?"

"It's the blueprints for the *Terror*," Mari explained. "Master

Mechanic Lukas has already approved them, but he wanted me to see them before work starts on the thing. See, the hull will be watertight except for these places, where water can enter or leave the tanks that adjust the buoyancy of the ship." She pointed. "This is where the waterline should be, so almost all of the ship will be underwater except for a low deck around this oval compartment that the captain will steer from. The low deck extends back to where the stack for the boiler sticks up, giving us some room to work. It will all be covered in carefully crafted camouflage so that the upper portions are hidden behind what looks like a big pile of driftwood."

Alain frowned as he tried to make sense of the drawings. "This is the deck inside?"

"Yes. There's only one deck inside."

"If I stand on it, I will be under the water?"

"Yes," Mari said. "Wow. You got that!"

"This is the boiler creature?" Alain asked, pointing.

"Right again!"

"It is…very close."

"Umm…yeah," Mari admitted. "There is very little free room inside this ship. These things near the boiler are for the whole steam cycle, circulating the feed water, condensing the steam when it's done its work, and all the rest. These things convert the steam pressure into work like driving the ship's propulsion. This is the fuel tank. These tanks on the outside are for ballast, which is water. We had to put in a big enough boiler to drive the ship's propulsion and the pumps to adjust the ballast and drain the bilges and…I lost you, didn't I?"

"Yes," Alain said. "Soon after you said there was little room inside." He looked from the drawing to her. "This is what we need?"

"I think so," Mari said. "Lukas did an amazing job coming up with these plans so quickly. I don't see any flaws in them."

"Then I know all that I must know."

Mari smiled at him for a moment, then lowered her head and exhaled slowly. "Seeing these plans drives home for me that this is going to happen. I don't want to do it," she whispered. "If you weren't coming along I don't think I could muster the courage. The last time we went there we were hardly known. We could hide among the populace. Now...the entire world knows that Master Mechanic Mari of Caer Lyn has been proclaimed the daughter by Mages. If anyone figures out I am there, if they get their hands on me..."

Alain watched her helplessly for a moment, trying to think of what to say that would not reveal his own fears for her. "Whenever I have expressed concerns, Mari would tell me to make use of our plan that has never failed."

She raised her head enough to frown at him. "What plan of ours has never—" Her expression cleared and she laughed. "You mean our plan to make up a plan as we go along? To improvise? Alain, sometimes we have survived by the skin of our teeth!"

"But we have survived," he said.

"This time we need to not just survive, but to get the stuff we had to leave behind last time."

"If that is our job," Alain said, deliberately using the Mechanic term, "then we will do it."

She smiled again. "Thanks, my Mage. Let's get these back to Lukas so I can go back to worrying about how to conquer another city." Mari began rolling up the plans into tubes.

Alain, following his usual habit during quiet moments, ran his gaze around the room, checking the ceiling, floor, and walls for anything unusual and giving his foresight a chance to give warning, if it happened to work at all. He rarely saw anything, but since encountering the Mechanics Guild assassins in Altis and being kidnapped in Julesport he had made a habit out of constantly watching for trouble, even in places where none was expected.

Which was why he saw a wavering patch of darkness appear on one wall as his unreliable foresight chose to give warning this time.

On the other side of the wall was a bedroom, and beyond that the wall to the next building, which was supposed to be guarded.

Alain whipped out his long knife, walking toward the wall.

Mari's eyes locked on him. She said nothing, but kept rolling the papers with one hand, while her other reached into her coat for the weapon she always carried there.

Feeling a sudden sense of urgency, Alain activated a spell to create the illusion of an opening in the illusion of a wall. Fortunately, there was a good supply of power here, so the effort was not very tiring.

A doorway-sized opening appeared in the wall. Two men were there, one already moving toward the bedroom door, the other still facing the wall as he held a Mechanic device.

chapter seven

The first man bolted out the bedroom door and away. The second dropped his device and pulled out a pistol that looked like Mari's. Before he could bring the weapon to bear, Alain brought his knife around and slashed it into the man's upper wrist. With a howl of pain the man dropped the weapon, fixed enraged eyes on Alain, and with his other hand yanked out a dagger that he swung at Alain's face.

Alain twisted his long knife and shoved it point first into his attacker, who staggered back and fell.

Mari leaped past Alain and the man he had taken out, racing in pursuit of the other spy.

Alain kicked the fallen man's pistol and dagger into the safe room, then relaxed his spell so that the wall was whole again and the weapons out of reach. He ran after Mari, wondering where her guards were.

He heard the front door slam open, startled cries, and the sound of the door slamming open again as Mari went through. By the time Alain reached the doorway the shocked sentries were beginning to chase after Mari in a belated attempt to protect her. "Two of you go inside for the man I wounded," Alain ordered.

The center of the street was fairly clear, the second spy bolting along it as people on either side began to realize that something was wrong.

"Everybody down!" Mari shouted, her voice carrying such a strong force of command that nearly everyone within earshot dropped to the dirt without hesitating. Everyone except the spy, who kept running.

Mari aimed carefully, holding her weapon with both hands. She fired.

The running man jerked from the impact of the bullet but kept moving.

A few soldiers had realized what was going on and were scrambling to their feet to intercept the fleeing spy.

The spy pulled out a weapon that looked similar to Mari's and swung it about, apparently uncertain whether to aim at Mari or the soldiers closer to him.

In that brief moment of indecision, Mari fired again. This time the spy staggered and fell.

The two soldiers who reached him first pinned him to the ground and wrested the weapon from him.

Mari lowered her pistol as Alain reached her. She wore the expression he had become used to seeing on similar occasions, a remorseless resolve that hid inner regret and unhappiness. Hid from most of those around her, at least; Alain could see through it clearly. "What about the other one?" she asked as she carefully did things to her weapon before returning it to the holster under her shoulder. Her voice stayed steady, but Alain saw the way Mari's hand shook now that the danger was past.

Alain glanced back to the building, seeing some soldiers carry the other spy out and lay him on the street. A healer bent over him and began to work. "He still lives."

Mari's eyes went to the blood on Alain's knife. She grimaced and nodded, then began walking to the group that had formed around the spy she had shot.

Mechanic Calu was part of that group. As he noticed Mari approaching, Calu moved between her and the fallen Mechanic spy. "You don't need to worry about this, Mari. I've got it."

"I shot the guy," Mari said. "The least I can do is to look him in the face." She went around Calu, looked down at the wounded man, and stopped, her expression going blank.

"What is it?" Alain asked Calu.

"We know him," Calu said. "Roge was an Apprentice with us when we were younger and used to hang around with our group. Long story short, the Senior Mechanics told all of us, repeatedly, that hanging with Mari wouldn't do our future Guild careers any good. Most of us didn't listen. Roge did. We didn't see much of him after that."

Mari finally spoke, her voice thin. "Hi, Roge."

"*Mechanic* Roge," the wounded man got out between teeth clenched against pain as two healers worked to save his life.

"I'm sorry we had to meet again like this," Mari said. "Maybe after the fight is all over, we can work together again."

Roge's attempt to smile mockingly was distorted by agony. "When this is over…you'll be dead…traitor."

Her expression hardening, Mari shook her head. "I've never betrayed my friends. And I'm not going to lose this fight." She looked at General Flyn, who had just arrived, breathing hard from running. "Make sure this one is kept separate from the other prisoners. No communication with any of them."

"What about the other one?" Flyn asked. "Your Mage stuck a knife in him, but he'll likely live."

"Put them in the same cell. Away from everybody else."

"Yes, Lady. Did they hear anything?"

"They heard something," Mari said. "I'm pretty sure one of them, the one Alain stabbed, had a far-listener. We can check when we get back to the building. But they didn't hear any locations. I'm certain of that." She paused, closing her eyes and breathing slowly, then looked at Flyn again. "How did they get in?"

"We're checking on that, Lady," Flyn said, with an expression that boded ill for anyone who had failed in their duties.

A lieutenant ran up, saluting. "They came in through the basement, after entering the building next door through the basement of the building behind it."

"Why wasn't the digging detected?"

"We're looking into that, General. If anyone—"

"There is no *if* about it," Flyn interrupted. "That basement should have been checked on every guard shift. Find out why it wasn't."

"Yes, sir. I deeply regret—"

"Don't apologize to me! When those two had finished listening in, they probably would have tried to kill the Lady."

The lieutenant came to rigid attention and saluted again. "I understand, sir. I will find out what went wrong."

"See that you do," Flyn said in dismissal. He shook his head at Mari. "You should be berating me now, Lady."

"What good would that do?" Mari said, looking down the street to where the man Alain had stabbed lay under the hands of the healers. "Is there anything I could say that would make you feel worse about this or more determined to make sure it doesn't happen again?"

"No, Lady, there isn't." Flyn shook his head. "In one more week we head south for Tiaesun. Which at least will make you a moving target once more."

"Many people know we are preparing to move the army again," Alain said. His anger at the danger to Mari had been balanced by relief at having been able to identify the threat in time and take the right steps.

"Yes, Sir Mage," General Flyn agreed. "But they will discount reports of how soon we're going to move. It's far earlier than anyone will expect, and if not for the way your army is growing and the weapons you are providing it would also be far too risky."

Calu came up again, carrying the weapon the spy had dropped. "It's not a standard model Guild revolver, Mari. It's a semi-auto pistol like yours. I'll have Alli take a look at it, but from what I can tell it's almost brand new. Hardly ever fired."

"Tell Alli she can have it," Mari said, gazing at the weapon. "So the Mechanics Guild is making more pistols."

"We figured they were," Calu said. "But this one has maker's marks on all the parts. The Guild is still crafting each weapon, one at a time. They can't have made very many."

"There's another the first spy dropped when Alain chopped his wrist. You can keep that one."

Calu stared at her, smiling awkwardly. "Are you sure, Mari? These things are worth their weight in gold. Actually, they're worth a lot more than that."

She smiled slightly in return. "I'd rather my friends had them than the people who are trying to kill me."

General Flyn listened as another officer ran up with a report. "Both spies had daggers, and both daggers apparently have some sort of poison on them," Flyn said, offering one carefully for their inspection.

Calu took a close look. "Cyanide, from the looks of it. A small quantity can kill pretty quickly. Make sure nobody touches it, General."

"Why would Mechanics have such a thing?" Alain asked.

"Cyanide is an industrial reactant. We use it to make stuff. But it's also a really nasty poison."

"Mari would have walked past the door to their hiding place on her way out of our meeting," Alain said.

Mari stared at the dagger blade, then looked away.

Alain turned to Calu. "Could you help General Flyn dispose of those daggers so they do not harm anyone?"

"Sure." Calu's expression darkened as switched his gaze from Mari to the poisoned weapons. "Yeah. I'll get rid of them. You take care of Mari."

"We should get the plans," Alain suggested to Mari, who nodded wordlessly in agreement. She led the way back to the safe room.

They collected the plans and were most of the way to Master Mechanic Lukas's offices before Mari finally spoke again. "One of them tried to stab you, didn't he?"

"Yes." He had been thinking about the danger to her, and was not surprised that she had been thinking about him.

"We can't let them win, Alain. Not people who would use weapons like that. I won't let them win. We're going to beat the Storm and every idiot working for it and we're going to save this world."

"Yes," Alain said once more.

〜〇〜

A week later Alli bade them farewell as most of Mari's army marched away from Pacta Servanda. "I have to stay here to supervise some of the work on the *Pride*. I found some cool recoil mechanisms that should allow us to mount a pretty big gun on her. Along with the steam propulsion system we're retrofitting, the *Pride* soon ought to be ready for…anything."

Mari nodded. "Keep an eye on that special construction project for me, will you, Alli?"

"Sure. But Lukas is there almost constantly. I doubt that I'd spot any problems he didn't." Alli's smile slipped as she looked at Calu. "Keep an eye on my husband for me, Mari. I'd kind of like to have a family when this is all over, so don't let him lose any important parts."

"I love you, too!" Calu called.

"I've been thinking I should tell him to stay," Mari admitted.

"No," Alli said, shaking her head and offering Mari a squeeze of her hand. "If you and I are going to go off and do stuff, then we have to let them do the same. Calu would let me go, so I'll let him go. Have a fun adventure, and bring the big goof back to me in one piece."

"I will, sister."

Alain saw Mage Asha and Mechanic Dav watching from a distance and raised one hand toward them. Asha raised her hand in answer while Dav waved. It felt absurd to have a sense of heading out alone when he and Mari were accompanying her army, but Alain found he had become very used to having those other Mechanics and Mages around. "You are certain that you do not wish to say farewell to your family?" Alain asked Mari.

She shook her head, sadness in her eyes. "They're safer if I stay away from them. What if those last two had taken Kath hostage?"

"I can drop by and let them know you couldn't," Mechanic Bev offered. "Since I can't do anything else," she added pointedly.

Mari smiled. "Bev, you know that we'd love to have you along, but your work with the schools here is far more important than nursemaiding me and Alain. It's a full-time job now, and you're good at it."

"Yeah, yeah," Bev said dismissively, though Alain could see her pleasure at Mari's words. "I'll keep an eye on things here. But you two be careful. No matter where you end up."

Orders were called and repeated down the road, and the column of soldiers and wagons lurched into motion like an immense and deadly creature. Mari and Alain mounted their horses, waved farewells again, and joined the movement.

Feeling both depressed at leaving some of the friends he had never expected to have and elated at the excitement of being part of the campaign, Alain looked along the road, seeing hundreds of cavalry and many more foot soldiers moving south. Out in the harbor, ships loaded with more soldiers were getting under weigh, including the *Dolphin*, which had been built to land soldiers anywhere they were needed. Somewhere in all that activity was Captain Patila.

They stopped for the first long rest about noon, men and women tending to their horses and getting some rest as they themselves ate. "General Flyn wants to try to maintain a pace of forty thousand lances a day for the cavalry," Mari explained to Alain. "That's tough, but should be manageable, and should get us to Tiaesun in a week. The supply train and the infantry will be trying to maintain about twenty thousand lances a day, so they'll fall behind as we march. The infantry and supplies on the ships should easily keep pace with our cavalry and be there before us for the attack on Tiaesun."

"General Flyn knows the art of his profession just as you know that of the Mechanics and I of the Mages," Alain commented. He saw the banner of Tiae approaching among a small group of riders. The figure of Princess Sien was easy to spot in the lead.

"Greetings, friends and allies of Tiae!" Sien called as she rode up and dismounted.

"You're in a good mood," Mari observed, smiling for the first time that morning.

"We've had a good omen," Sien said, gesturing to an officer who had also dismounted nearby. "Hasna of Trefik has rejoined Tiae's army. She was but a captain when the kingdom broke, but she held together the remnants of the army long enough for many citizens to escape the ruin of Tiaesun. I have made her a colonel in the new army of Tiae."

Alain's gaze on Sien sharpened as a gray shadow passed across it. Why would his foresight warn of this hero of Tiae? The feeling of the warning was odd. Not of immediate danger, which always showed as a black shadow, but of something else.

Hasna stepped forward with an agility at odds with the signs of age she showed. Or perhaps, Alain thought as he looked closer, she had been marked less by age than by many years of stress.. She was not young, but not as old as she appeared.

"These are true friends of Tiae," Sien told Hasna, waving toward Alain and Mari. "Lady Mari and her Mage."

Hasna saluted, her expression showing formal politeness, but Alain caught a flash of resentment in Hasna's eyes that anyone not a Mage would surely have missed. "You have returned to serve the princess?" he asked, deliberately seeking an answer that would reveal Hasna's loyalty.

"Yes, Sir Mage," Hasna said, not pausing before replying or showing any other sign of deception in her words or manner. "I serve Tiae again. I serve only Tiae."

He felt it again, a vague sense of warning. But what in Hasna's words foretold danger?

"I'm happy to meet you," Mari said. "We're doing all we can to help the new army of Tiae become strong enough to defend your kingdom, and we welcome your assistance in that."

Alain once more saw Hasna's unhappiness, though she hid it well. "Tiae's defenders have long fought alone," said Hasna, a truth which Alain thought might explain her resentment that aid had been so long in coming.

"Hasna will be with us when we retake Tiaesun," Sien said proudly. "The final defender of Tiaesun will be among those who reclaim the capital city of Tiae."

After Sien and her escort had left, Mari eyed Alain. "What? The way you looked at Hasna seemed a bit intense."

He tried to think how to best answer her. "I felt vague warnings from my foresight. It was not a warning that she was a direct danger to us, but something related to her perhaps."

"Tiaesun?" Mari asked. "Could it be that retaking the city might expose us to some particular danger?"

"It may be, but I could sense nothing further," Alain said. "I do not know what the warning meant."

"When you get a chance, ask some of the other Mages," Mari said. "Without mentioning Hasna's name."

"I will do so, but because the Mage Guild elders have discouraged any study of foresight, I doubt that the other Mages with us will know more than I do."

General Flyn kept the army moving at a punishing pace through the day, halting for the night only so that humans and beasts could sleep where they stopped.

The next day, as the army neared the borders of the areas already pacified, Flyn and Sien sent out most of the cavalry to range widely along both sides of the road. Throughout the day Alain and Mari heard the rattle of distant gunfire as the cavalry overran startled bandit camps and freed towns and villages from any petty despots who had been ruling them in the absence of central authority and protection.

The column of infantry following the cavalry shrank a bit as they marched, detachments of troops being left behind in the larger towns as garrisons. The citizens of Tiae were amazed to see armed men and women who wore uniforms and acted as defenders and protectors rather than predators. Alain noticed that Mari always perked up upon seeing the gratitude of the people finally liberated from the anarchy that had plagued the Broken Kingdom for so long.

Forty thousand lances a day pushed the men, women and horses to the limits they could sustain. By the time the column stopped for the night not far from Tiaesun, even Alain was feeling worn out.

"The warlords occupying Tiaesun may well have heard we're coming,"

Flyn told Mari as they sat in the darkened camp chewing on cold rations to avoid kindling fires that would warn of their presence. Alain, having endured worse conditions, listened half to Flyn briefing Mari and half to the grumbles of tired soldiers bedding down near their mounts. "But they won't expect us so quickly, so they won't be prepared when we show up at dawn."

"Are you sure they'll run rather than hole up in buildings and fight?" Mari asked.

"We'll be coming in from the north, with the routes heading south from Tiaesun apparently clear," Flyn said. "The thugs who make up the armies of these warlords don't want to die. They'll run."

Everyone was roused in the darkness well before dawn. By the time the sun began to rise, the army, arrayed for battle, had reached the Royal River. On its far bank lay the battered old capital of the former Kingdom of Tiae.

The branch of the great southern river that flowed past Tiaesun was both wide and deep. It formed a formidable obstacle to travel, as the bridges that once spanned it had been destroyed during the wars that broke the kingdom. But among the ships that had sailed south from Pacta Servanda were several towing barges with segments of bridges atop them. The night before the army appeared, the barges had been lashed together to form a floating passageway across which the cavalry stormed. Mixed in were Mages ready to provide their own form of special weaponry and means of getting through obstacles if needed, while Mechanics followed ready to employ their own weapons or fix those of the others.

Alain felt a thrill of excitement as the horses thundered across the wooden planks making up the surface of the floating bridge. He held his horse back a bit, knowing that Mari would not ride ahead on her own, so despite her frustrated glances at him Alain kept them near the center of the cavalry column as it split to head for the two nearest gates, both of which had been damaged too badly in earlier battles to serve as barriers now.

Each gate had been guarded by a few gangsters who collected

"taxes" from anyone using them to enter or leave the city. Faced with a flood of cavalry, the brutes took to their heels. None of them made it very far as citizens of the city, waking to see soldiers flying the banner of Tiae riding into the city, hurled objects at the warlords' followers to hinder them until they could be ridden down.

The cavalry had to slow down once inside the city walls, their horses needing a break after the charge and the roads hazardous from the same sort of uncollected debris and garbage which had plagued the streets of Minut. Alain heard deafening cheers erupt near the other gate and knew that Princess Sien had ridden into the city.

A small group carrying swords and clubs stumbled out of a building, roused by the noise. They took one look at the oncoming cavalry and ran.

Mari pulled out her far-talker. "Calu. What are you seeing?"

Alain looked up to where the vast wings of a Roc swung lazily over the city.

"It's like looking at shockwaves spreading out from the two gates," Calu called back from his perch on the giant bird. "Citizens spilling out of buildings, and the various bad guys taking to their heels. The news of the attack is moving faster than you guys are."

"That's all right," Mari said. "We knew that would happen. Is anyone forming defensive lines or gathering into units?"

"Nope," Calu said. "Most of the people I can see from up here are just gathering in the streets and looking to the north where the cheering is coming from. The rest are running south individually or in small groups. Looks like…yeah, I think the ones running by themselves won't get too far. The crowd seems to be jumping them when they realize what's happening. Oh, your ships are in position and blocking the mouth of the harbor. I saw some people running toward boats but when they saw your ships they changed direction and started heading south, too."

"Is there anyone on horseback or in carriages or wagons?" Mari asked.

"A few, yeah. I'll ask Mage Alera to circle over them."

"All right. We'll watch for that, but don't get too low. If anyone in this city has firearms, it would be one of the bosses. And their guards might have crossbows."

"Got it. See us? There are six or seven riders below us, and two wagons."

"Make sure they keep heading south when they leave the city," Mari ordered. "We might have to chase them down if they head too far east instead."

Alain urged his horse forward, staying with Mari as the cavalry was slowed further by the surviving population of Tiaesun crowding into the streets, faces lit by joy and enthusiasm. The intensity of the emotions surrounding him dazzled Alain and he tried to maintain his focus. But no danger threatened this time as the cavalry forced their way through to the great plaza of Tiaesun, which was so large that the diminished population of the city could no longer fill it.

Another column of cavalry entered the plaza farther down, the banner of Tiae and the royal banner flying side by side. Mari headed that way, Alain and several cavalry serving as her guards following as closely as they could.

He had never seen Princess Sien so happy, as she greeted her people and accepted their cries of allegiance.

Mari rode up to Sien, saluting the princess with a broad grin. "Princess Sien, I know your birthday isn't for a few weeks yet, but I wish to present you with the city of Tiaesun as an early present!"

"You are too kind!" Sien shouted back over the noise of the crowds. "Tiae is forever in your debt, my friend Lady Mari, daughter of Jules in truth!"

Colonel Hasna brought her horse close to them. "The scum are escaping to the south. I will take our cavalry in pursuit."

"No need!" Mari called. "Hear that?" Far to the south, the rattle of rifle fire could be heard. "Last night the *Dolphin* and some of our other ships landed an infantry blocking force far enough south of the city to be out of sight. All of the warlords and their followers fleeing that way are going to run right into that force."

"Half of our cavalry are bypassing the city," Alain added, "and will head south to pin those fleeing against the blocking force. Few should escape."

"Tiae had little to do with saving Tiaesun, it seems," Hasna said.

Mari did not need Alain's help to see the unhappiness in that statement. "That's not so. We couldn't have done it without Tiae, and if my army had entered this city without the army of Tiae alongside it, the citizens would not be celebrating. This is your victory as much as ours."

Sien bent a sharp look on Hasna. "I am told that before the kingdom broke, Tiae made much of its own pride and desires and cared little for the feelings of those outside our borders. As a result, when our own strength failed, Tiae had few friends willing to join their strength with ours, and we have paid a terrible price for that. I long ago vowed that should true friends appear, I would not disdain or turn them aside out of a desire to stand alone. No man or woman stands alone. Nor does any country."

"I understand, Princess," Colonel Hasna said.

Alain detected no falsehood in the words, but he wondered just what it was that Hasna understood.

Those concerns were forgotten over the rest of the day, however, as Alain and Mari had to focus on gaining full control of the city, preventing the civilians' celebrations from getting out of hand, restoring order, and sweeping the nearby countryside for criminals who had escaped Tiaesun. Many people kept pressing close to see and to touch the daughter, and Alain had to watch every one of them, constantly on guard for danger. This time, though, Mari had apparently blindsided her enemies with the speed and direction of her attack. No assassins materialized.

The next day, Alain grew increasingly exhausted from watching every person who came within sight of Mari as the crowds around her grew. Word had gone around the city that the army of the daughter had made the liberation of Tiaesun possible, and everyone seemed to want to thank her personally. The only break of sorts came during a ceremony that Princess Sien held at midday, where she declared the Broken Kingdom formally reborn and pledged to protect the people of Tiae.

After that, Mari and General Flyn toured the encampments of some of Mari's soldiers. Now it was Mari who seemed intent on personally thanking every one of the men and women in her army.

"How much longer until we take on the Great Guilds?" one asked, to murmurs of assent from those within earshot.

"Many of you came with little or no experience as soldiers. All of you are still learning to fight as an army," Flyn said. "An army with more Mechanic weapons than anyone has ever carried, with Mechanics and Mages providing direct assistance during the fights. You're making remarkable progress, but campaigns like this one are teaching us all how to best use these forces so that when we confront the Great Guilds directly we can beat them."

"We're showing the world that a place without the Great Guilds controlling everything can exist," Mari added. "I know you're all impatient. It's been so long that the Great Guilds have ruled this world. We almost have Tiae pacified, so that our bases and the families of those of you who brought your relatives here will be safe. And what the general said is very true, especially about the Mages and Mechanics who work alongside you. You know how remarkable that is."

"The rainy season will strike any day now," Flyn added. "You'll all get to rest a bit except for dealing with flash floods."

"Will it be another year?" a second soldier asked, looking disappointed.

"Less," Mari said confidently. "When we hit the Great Guilds, they won't stand a chance. Our Mages will protect you from the Mage Guild's attacks, and our Mechanics are already making better devices than the Mechanics Guild."

"What about after, Lady? My family came with me. My children are learning Mechanic arts in your schools. Will Tiae be open to us?"

Mari smiled. "Princess Sien has told me that anyone from my army who wishes to stay in Tiae may do so."

As they walked away from that meeting, Flyn cast a questioning eye on Mari and Alain. " 'What about after' is an apt question, Lady. I admit that when I first met you I was filled with hope but also worry. How could even the daughter prevail in a fight against the Great Guilds and their common allies? But now I lead for you an army the likes of which this world has never seen, one whose strength grows by the day as new volunteers arrive and new weapons are delivered. What will become of that army and those weapons should you succeed?"

Mari turned a troubled look on Alain. "I can't just tell everyone to go home, not with their weapons."

"It's something we have to think about, Lady," Flyn said. "You're dealing with the Mechanics and the Mages, who are finding new ways to live. But the commons in your army will be an immensely powerful force. It can't simply be dissolved on the day the Great Guilds yield."

"Will it not depend," Alain asked, "on how victory is achieved? What the state of the world is at that time? Once the Storm is defeated, we will face a world such has never existed on Dematr. Perhaps we must wait to see the form this world takes before making such decisions."

Flyn nodded, but he also looked troubled now. "Lady, I know you well, and Sir Mage, we have become close. Were you anyone else, I would be greatly worried about what someone with so much power might attempt."

"General," Mari said, her voice sharp, "I have made it clear from the first that I have no desire for power."

"I believe you, Lady. I know that you would act only in pursuit of what you consider to be the greatest good. But you have learned that power is necessary to accomplish one great deed. Can you be certain that you would never yield to the desire to accomplish another if you had the means?"

Mari paused, her expression somber. "I have my friends to keep me honest. I have my Mage." She looked at Alain. "My Mage knows that he can always speak the truth to me. About anything. If I ever push him aside, General, then you should worry. But that will never happen."

Alain nodded to Mari, keeping his expression solemn. He should have perhaps smiled at her confidence in him, but her words stung in ways that Mari could not guess. *My Mage knows he can always speak the truth to me.* Except about his vision of her perhaps mortally wounded, the vision Alain was determined to keep from coming to pass. Asha had convinced him to keep that secret from Mari, but the deception often troubled Alain.

Two days later the rains began, the legendary rains of southern Tiae, which gossip in northern lands claimed were so heavy that the fish became confused where water ended and sky began, swimming past people who could reach out and grab them.

Mari had wanted to head back north to Pacta Servanda, but Alain and General Flyn had convinced her to stay at longer at Tiaesun, where she was close to Princess Sien and far from assassins sent by the Great Guilds. Alain had said finally won the argument by pointing out one of Mari's own greatest worries. "I know you wish to be where you feel you are needed, but if you are always needed, then you will always *be* needed."

It was not as if Mari lacked for work, as couriers struggling along the flooded, muddy roads and ships daring the storms along the coast arrived with requests for decision or direction. The Mechanics still looked to her whenever a dispute arose with either commons or Mages, and the Mages sought both her instruction and her counsel, which continued to baffle Mari.

Eventually, killers made their way south. Mari's guards stopped two. Alain stopped a third who had come almost within reach of her.

Alain got very little rest.

The rains were beginning to slacken when Alain received two visitors he had awaited, and had not looked forward to seeing. He left them to eat and rest, going himself into the next room where Mari was struggling with something she called "allocating limited resources."

But she immediately noticed that Alain was tense. "What's happening?"

"Mage Alera and Mage Saburo arrived today, riding on the Rocs of other Mages," Alain said. "They are well rested. Before dawn, they will create their Rocs to carry us north on the mission we planned before leaving Pacta Servanda."

Mari covered her face with both hands. "I've been dreading this day. Let's find Sien and Flyn and let them know."

Flyn was easy enough to find. "I will escort you outside the city myself. Lady, you know how little I want you to go on this mission, but if you feel so strongly that it must be done, perhaps the spirit of Jules is speaking to you."

Sien was much harder to locate. Alain and Mari, encircled by the guards whose presence had become all too familiar, trudged through the intermittent rain of late afternoon, finally finding the queen's escort standing outside the gates to one of the ruined palaces. They left their own guards there and went into the palace.

Inside, they found Sien standing alone in an upstairs room, looking out a long-shattered window onto a tangled mass of tall weeds. Once-bright paint on the walls had faded and peeled, the cartoonish images of happy children and animals on them distorted by time and damage. "Are you all right?" Mari asked.

"As well as may be," Sien replied, looking at the floor. "I somehow always expected that when I came back the toys and dolls would still be here. But of course those were carried off long ago." She gestured out the window. "That was the garden where we played. The royal children, blessed by the land of Tiae." Her voice carried bitterness but also sorrow for the lost past.

"Why did you come here?" Mari asked.

"Sometimes ghosts must be faced down," Sien said. She looked slowly about the stained walls of the room. "So much to rebuild. No matter how much longer I live, I will never lack for a long list of tasks to complete." She focused on Mari. "You're leaving, aren't you? It is time for that?"

"Yes. That job that has to be done. I'll be back," Mari said.

"You've never broken a promise to me, Mari. Don't let this be the first. Alain, I would grieve to lose you as well. Bring her back."

"I will," Alain said. "What is it you have not told us?"

Sien shook her head at him. "Fool that I am, trying to deceive a Mage with silence. My dreams have been haunted of late. Perhaps it is only because of being in Tiaesun again and seeing how little is left of what a very young girl once knew. Have you seen anything of my future, Alain?"

Alain shook his head regretfully. "Nothing. I have been preoccupied with concerns for Mari, but even of her I have seen no visions recently. It is…odd."

"Odd?" Mari asked.

"It is hard to explain," Alain said. "I have a sense that too many images seek to crowd upon me and block each other. As if—" An idea finally came to him. "As if the future near us is so unsteady that no one image of a possible event can prevail. Too many possible futures hang in the balance."

"That isn't reassuring," Sien said. "Remember your importance to this world, Mari."

Mari sighed and shook her head. "If I am important, it's because of who I am, Sien. And…that means I'm going to do certain things if they need to be done."

"Then go with my best wishes." Sien hugged her, eyed Alain, then kissed his cheek. "You too, Sir Mage. Make real the future that we all want."

"Nothing is real," Alain said. "Mari knows as well as I do how many dangers we will face beginning tomorrow. But I will do all I can to make this illusion the right one."

He hoped that all he could do would be enough.

chapter eight

mari felt a strange sense of fate hovering over her the next morning when they were awakened well before dawn by General Flyn. It was not in any way reassuring. She had struggled with nightmares again, fighting off visions of dungeons, torture, and death, nonetheless grateful that unlike Mages, whose visions might be of actual future events, hers were fantasies born of the fears she denied during her waking hours.

She stayed close to Alain as they walked through dark, nearly silent streets, along little-used ways that Flyn had scouted out. They left the city through a recently repaired sally port and moved silently through the open area outside the walls. A thin drizzle of rain fell through near-total darkness as Mari and Alain followed the barely visible glow of Flyn's heavily shielded lantern. She grasped her coat tightly to her, wishing it was her Mechanics jacket. But that garment, too easily tied to Lady Mari, had been left behind in Calu's keeping, and the coat Mari wore would be much warmer.

Large shapes loomed out of the murk. General Flyn came to a halt, exchanging a few words with Mage Alera and Mage Saburo. "They are ready for you," he told Mari, his expression shadowed by the night. "Lady, come back to us. Please."

Mari, already tense, tried to sound confident. "I will. You take care of things here. Alain and I will be back. With the texts." She blinked rain from her eyes, everything blurring for a moment. Fear rose again inside her, but she fought it down ruthlessly, focusing on the job that needed to be done. The job that only she could do.

Alain and the general exchanged a few murmured words, then Alain put both arms around her. "You will be safe on Swift," he said, holding her.

"You promised me that we'd ride on a Roc *together* some day," Mari said, trying to joke to hide her nervousness. She had avoided flying up until this day, and wasn't looking forward to her first flight on an imaginary bird.

"We will," said Alain. "But it will be another day."

"A Mage's promise," Mari pretended to scoff. She kissed him. "You'll get another kiss when we rest for the night."

Mage Saburo and Alain walked off into the gloom.

Mage Alera led Mari to what appeared to be a wall of giant feathers. Swift lowered enough for Alera to assist Mari up to a position on his back. To her immense relief, a harness tied to a line around the Roc's body waited there so that Mari could fasten herself securely, lying face down.

Alera took position ahead of Mari, riding just behind Swift's neck. "Are you ready, Elder?"

Mari exhaled a shaky breath. *I will never be ready for this*, she thought. "Yes."

Swift's huge wings spread to either side, then Mari felt like she did when a locomotive surged into motion. But no locomotive accelerated like this. Her stomach felt as though it had remained behind, while the thin rain and a suddenly much stronger wind lashed at her. She wanted to look for the dim glow of General Flyn's lantern, but feared to raise her head.

The play of impossibly strong muscles beneath her was both exhilarating and frightening. The darkness was so complete that she could not see the movement of Swift's wings to either side, but could feel the rhythmic pumping as each sweep drove them up and forward, with jogs and pitches to either side at unpredictable intervals as wind gusts caught the Roc.

Face pressed against the feathers of Swift's back, Mari wondered if this was how Alain had felt the first time he had ridden on a Mechanic train.

The darkness grew somehow deeper, and the rain changed to what felt like dense fog. Swift jerked abruptly up, down, and to side as the Roc kept climbing.

Suddenly, the air cleared and became bright enough to see. Mari stared to one side as a moonlit ledge of fog went past. How could there be fog this high?

She felt a thrill of terror as she realized the truth.

It had been a fragment of cloud. She was higher than the rain clouds, riding above them, nothing between her and the ground but the body of this giant bird that her Mechanic training told her could not actually exist.

How high were rain clouds, anyway?

High enough for it to be cold. High enough that Mari felt herself breathing more deeply, as if she were once more among the highest peaks of the Northern Ramparts where the air was thin. She closed her eyes, grateful for the warmth of the heavy coat, and wondered how she would survive an entire day of this.

The air was definitely thinner. There must be a way to use that to determine how high she was. Didn't air density change at a steady rate as you got higher? Mari found herself trying to figure out how to build a device to measure the effect, and surrendered gratefully to the distraction.

It wasn't until bright light struck her closed eyelids that Mari remembered it had been only an hour before dawn when the Rocs began flying. She cautiously opened her eyes, squinting against the sun rising over what looked like a rumpled field of fog—the top of the rain clouds. Mari felt a sense of wonder overawing her fear as she realized that rain was probably still falling down below, but up here she was seeing a sunny day. She turned her head, catching a glimpse of the moon near setting, the Twins that followed the moon blazing like bright sparks in the light of the rising sun.

The air was thin, sharp with cold, but also clean and amazingly clear.

Mari felt herself smiling, almost laughing, at the thrill of it. "Thank you," she whispered, breathing the words not to anyone, but to that *something* that Alera had spoken of, a something that somehow felt nearer up here.

She hadn't slept well before leaving, and now felt both physically and emotionally exhausted. Mari did not even realize that she had fallen asleep until she woke abruptly as her stomach protested a sudden lurch downward.

Mari looked around cautiously. The sun was much higher, uncomfortably warm on her heavy coat even though her face was tingling with cold. She raised her head enough to see past the edge of Swift's body. The layer of cloud was gone, replaced by a few wisps that barely obscured the ground. She stared, fascinated, at the view, wondering if the river visible below was the one which originated in the Southern Mountains and flowed south and then west until reaching the sea at Edinton.

A bird rose into view, flying near Swift. Mari saw Mage Saburo riding on his own Roc and behind him the shape of Alain lying prone just as she was. Worried about moving, Mari slowly raised one arm high enough to wave at the other bird.

Alain's hand rose and he waved back.

This was so cool.

By the time the sun sank toward the western horizon, most of the novelty and wonder had worn off, replaced by the ache of muscles that couldn't be stretched, very dry lips and throat, hunger, and a headache from breathing the thin, cold air.

Thankfully, Swift was now sinking through the sky, gliding ever lower. The peaks of the Southern Mountains could be seen ahead, but still far off. Below she could see what must be the rolling plains of the southern Bakre Confederation, occasional towns and villages looking like children's toys from this high and clumps of dots marking the presence of horse and cattle herds. Around the villages, farms could be identified by the long rectangles of their fields, the crops or bare, harvested fields standing out against the wild grasses of the rangeland.

Despite Mari's growing discomfort, both Swift and the Roc carrying Alain flew onward as the sun set with what felt like excruciating slowness. Only after twilight was well advanced did the two birds head for an isolated area well away from the nearest town, finally coming to earth with a jolt.

Free at last to move, Mari just lay still, afraid of how her muscles would protest. "Stretch," Mage Alera said, looking back at her. "A little at first, then more, then I will…help…you off of Swift."

Feeling grateful that she had made a point of teaching all of her Mages what "help" meant, Mari followed Alera's instructions, wincing as her stiff muscles protested. Once on the ground, still feeling wobbly, Mari realized that after a day confined to the back of a Roc she had a far more urgent need than food, water, or exercise. Fortunately, there was a stand of trees not far away, and what the trees did not conceal the growing darkness took care of.

Once that vital task had been completed, Mari rejoined the others. Her muscles ached, but the last thing she wanted to do was sit down, so she paced restlessly while digging into her pack. Alain came to walk beside her. "Are you all right?" he asked.

"It was fun for a while," Mari said. "Breathtaking. It's funny how breathtaking can turn into tedious and tedious can turn into torment, though. I suppose you three Mages are taking this all in stride?"

"It is physically difficult," Alain said. "You will feel better after eating."

"I hope so." Mari pulled out her dinner, a portion of jerky and a slab of hard journey bread. Before tackling either of those, she fished out the canteen and drank long and slowly. "Do you have beeswax for your lips?"

"No."

"I didn't think you would. Mages just endure such things. I don't want it hurting you when I kiss you though, so you can share mine." As Mari replaced her canteen, she felt something else in the pack. "The jar of honey. I may survive this after all."

Even jerky tasted great after a day without food. After wolfing it down, Mari sat next to Alain and used a nearby rock to break off a piece of the journey bread, then placed it in her mouth to soften before trying to chew it. "How do you navigate, Mage Alera?" she asked around the bread.

"Navigate?"

"How do you know which way to go to get where you want to go?"

"I tell my Roc."

Mari waited for more. "That's it? You tell Swift where you want to go and Swift goes there?"

"Yes."

"Do you have any idea how that works?" Mari prodded gently, having grown used to coaxing Mages to elaborate on replies that tended to be as brief as possible.

Alera took a moment to respond. "The Rocs are birds. Birds know how to reach the places they want to go."

"So even though you don't know exactly how it works, you're creating something that works like a bird?"

"Yes."

Like many Mage things, it actually made a kind of sense.

"This one has questions," Mage Saburo said.

It took Mari a little while to realize that had been directed at her. "Uh…sure. What?"

"Why does Elder Mari ask how the Rocs find their way? The Rocs do find their way. Why does the how matter?"

That took her some thought to answer. "It's because that's how I do things," Mari said. "How I work my version of Mage spells. I learn how things work, so I can figure out how to change them or fix them or…well, to be honest, just because I like knowing how things work."

Mage Saburo, his face impassive in the moonlight, pondered Mari's words. "This is acceptable wisdom? To want to know not for any purpose, but just because one wishes to know?"

"Absolutely!" Mari said. "Who is wise enough to know what might be important to know? Something that seems insignificant might lead to something great. Or maybe just knowing that thing might make you happier. There's nothing wrong with pursuing knowledge for its own sake."

"Mechanics believe this?" Mage Alera asked.

"Not all Mechanics, no," Mari admitted. "Some, especially among the Senior Mechanics who run the Mechanics Guild, want people to learn just what they are told to learn and nothing else. They don't want people thinking about new things, or what they consider the wrong things. So they try to put strict limits on what people are supposed to learn. But I think just about all the Mechanics who have joined with us are the sort who want to learn new things."

Alain nodded. "This is so of the Mages as well."

"Yes," Saburo agreed. "We all seek something different. The elders in the Mage Guild would rebuke me for asking too many questions. I will think on your wisdom, Elder," he told Mari.

"As will I," Alera added.

Alain intervened to ease Mari's embarrassment. "I first followed Mari because she asked me questions and did not believe she knew all the answers. I wanted to see what I could learn from her."

"You followed me out of curiosity?" Mari asked. "I'm sure you weren't the first or last to do that."

Despite not looking forward to another day in the air, as Mari and the others settled to sleep she found it strangely idyllic to be far away from other humans. Only the huge shapes of the two Rocs nestled nearby as the birds, too, slept.

She was roused as dawn was just beginning to lighten the sky to the east, eating a hasty breakfast but being sure not to drink too much water before what would be another full day of flight.

This time, it was light enough to see when Swift leapt into the air. Mari stared as objects below grew rapidly smaller, and her range of vision grew larger the higher the Roc flew. The sun appeared to jump into view with startling speed. Mari comforted herself by trying to work out the math for the difference in her view of the dawn from high up in the air compared to that of someone on the ground.

Soon enough the grasslands began to blur into monotony. There were fewer villages or other signs of human presence this far inland.. Mari wondered how much this land had changed from before the great ship came. Had there been grass on the ground or birds in the sky? How much of what she saw had been here when the ship came, and how much had grown and multiplied since then?

How high had that ship been when it performed what the librarians called "orbital surveys"? Much, much higher than this. The thought made Mari momentarily dizzy.

It was afternoon before they reached the outskirts of the Southern Mountains. Mari was at first interested in seeing how the foothills and lesser mounts looked from such a vantage, but as the Rocs flew deeper into the mountains strong air currents began to buffet them. Mari clung to her harness as Swift's flight experienced sudden drops and abrupt rises, the steep sides and jagged rocks of the mountain peaks all around. As the wild motion created painful nausea, she found herself increasingly grateful for the fact that her stomach was nearly empty. At least that discomfort distracted her somewhat from the terror of being flung around the sky amid the jagged peaks, her body jerking against the harness that now seemed entirely too lightweight to hold her safely against such stresses.

By the time the Rocs spiraled down toward a small, high valley resting like a bowl between three towering peaks, Mari felt like a piece of laundry that had been pummeled all day in cold water by unusually strong and enthusiastic washers wielding clubs.

They landed on a thin layer of soil in which a few shrubs and clumps of weeds had taken root. A small stream trickled down from one of the peaks, fed by snowpack slowly melting. The valley was high enough that the air was still noticeably thin and chill. There was nothing even remotely idyllic or comfortable about this resting place. "At least I don't have to worry about rolling off a ledge in my sleep," Mari mumbled, looking at the rock walls rising on all sides.

She slept that night huddled against Alain, the other two Mages fighting the cold by lying next to their Rocs.

Awake before dawn for the third and hopefully last day of flight, Mari gazed blearily at the undimmed stars overhead before nerving herself to climb back onto Swift.

The first part of the day was a brutal repetition of the day before, with the Rocs and their passengers jolted by vicious air currents that roamed the mountains like invisible giants who enjoyed slapping around anything within reach. But finally the mountains fell behind them, though the range still stood tall off to the west. Below the Rocs a great expanse of dirt, sand, and rock stretched to the north and east with little sign that humans had ever traversed it.

With a shock, Mari realized that they were skirting the edge of the desert waste around Ringhmon. Having privately vowed never to come near Ringhmon again, her relief at leaving the mountains was tempered by fear that the Rocs might have to land in the waste because of a storm or other emergency.

Late in the day, she caught sight far to the east of a low-lying bank of dark cloud that probably marked the smog hovering over Ringhmon.

Mari thought she was catching occasional glimpses of sunlight reflected from the waters of the Sea of Bakre when the Rocs once more descended to land. Disappointed, Mari watched the details of the wasteland below grow larger as the birds flew lower. Was that—? "We can't land near the train tracks," she yelled to Mage Alera. "I don't know what schedule they're running now. One might come by and see us."

"The smoke snakes never do anything when they see us," Alera yelled back. "Swift tells me this is the only place there is water."

Swift landed with a thump not far from a natural spring-fed pond. Mari unstrapped herself and fell off, barely feeling the sand and gravel under her. She struggled to her feet and gazed to the south, seeing the train tracks they had flown over tinted gold by the rays of the setting sun. They were only a few hundred lances away, and just beyond them were a small station house and a water tank for servicing locomotives running this route. Of course the Mechanics Guild had constructed a station house here, where there was water to be found. Normally there would only be a single Mechanic and an Apprentice occupying that station house. How many were there now with rebellion seething all around the Sea of Bakre?

She was not surprised to see a Mechanic appear in the door to the station house, checking on the noise the Rocs had made when landing. The last thing she expected was for that Mechanic to then start walking steadily toward them.

Alain, standing beside her, looked at Mari. "What is the Mechanic doing?"

"I don't know," Mari said. "Mechanics Guild policy is that spell creatures can't even exist, so any sightings of Rocs, dragons, or trolls are supposed to be ignored. But that guy is walking toward us in a way that means he is admitting the Rocs are here."

"If he desires to speak with Mages," Alain said, "then it is best that he see only Mages."

"Good idea. That Mechanic can't have made us out in any detail. You, Alera, and Saburo remove your armbands so you look like Mages still loyal to the Mage Guild." The sun had slid behind the peaks of the western mountains as Mari faded back behind Swift, wondering how much the Mechanic had seen of her in the growing dusk.

She drew her pistol, made sure it was ready for use, then waited, tense, worrying that she might have to shoot—might have to kill—a Mechanic whose only crime known to her was to be too inquisitive.

The scrunching of the Mechanic's boots on the gravel drew closer, halting so close that he must be facing Alain, who was now flanked by both Mage Alera and Mage Saburo. "Is there a message?" the Mechanic asked in tones which were so grudging and resentful that the words were a little hard to understand.

Alain replied, his own voice impassive and devoid of feeling. "No. Is there a message?" he asked in turn.

"My Senior Mechanics want to know what Mari is doing! Didn't you come from the south?"

"We do not concern ourselves with what Mechanics want," Alain said, the blandness of his tones only adding to the insult of the words. It was a perfect imitation of the old Mage tactics for infuriating Mechanics.

"Watch it, Mage," the Mechanic growled. "Didn't I see four people here?"

"There is a common," Alain said. "She offers us…entertainment."

Mari winced at that, knowing exactly what Alain meant, what any Mage would have meant not so long ago, when all Mages regarded other people as playthings at best. It hurt all the more because some Mechanics had been equally willing to mistreat the commons for their own amusement.

This Mechanic apparently wasn't one of those who cared little for commons. His voice quivered with rage. "If I didn't have orders from the Senior Mechanics, I'd—" His words choked off.

"Neither your Senior Mechanics nor the Mage Guild elders care what you think," Alain said, his words cold and emotionless and thus striking harder.

Mari worried that Alain had gone too far and prepared herself to leap out and fire if the Mechanic lost control of himself. But after a long pause she heard the sound of boots stomping away through the gravel and the growing darkness.

She was putting away her pistol when Alain came walking around Swift's back to join her. "Our former Guilds are working together in ways they never have before," Alain said.

"Yeah," Mari agreed. "I was afraid you might have pushed that Mechanic too hard."

"I wanted to cause anger within him at both his allies in the Mage Guild and his own leaders," Alain said.

"And you succeeded admirably," Mari said.

"Is this what you call ironic?"

She paused. "Is what ironic?"

"The prophecy said that the daughter of Jules would unite Mages, Mechanics, and commons to free the world, but you have also united Mages and Mechanics to keep the world enslaved."

Mari laughed softly. "Yes. That is sure as blazes ironic. Are the birds all right?" she asked Alain. "I see Alera and Saburo fussing over their Rocs."

"The Rocs were created with much power," Alain explained, "but they have used much on this journey. They will not last much longer. Perhaps two days."

"Oh." Mari felt guilty, as if she were actually killing the huge birds with her demands upon them. But then another thought occurred that drove away all guilt and replaced it with worry. "Can they just disappear in midair? While we're riding them?"

"In theory," Mage Alera said, having heard the question. "But we can sense when our birds grow weak, and would land before then."

Already worn out, Mari spent a nervous night, waking up often to look toward the lights of the station house and listen for the approach of a train. But the Mechanic and the Apprentice who should also be in the station made no more appearances, the Mechanic apparently having had his fill of trying to communicate with Mages, and no trains passed by.

They took off again before the sun rose, the Rocs winging northeast toward the sea. Mari felt tremendous relief as the desolate plains gave way to coastal salt marshes.

The Rocs soared over the Sea of Bakre, the sun casting their shadows on the waves rolling in to strike the coast. Once well out to sea, with land still visible to the south, the birds turned and began flying parallel to the coast.

The mountains dwindled as the coastline curved northeast toward the Imperial city and port of Landfall. Mari looked to the southeast as the Rocs followed the coast, thinking that inland a ways sat Longfalls, site of the Mechanics Guild prison. But she could do nothing for the prisoners there, nothing except try to win so that the Mechanics Guild, its power broken, would no longer be able to maintain such a prison.

The birds kept going as the sun sank lower again, until sunset once more loomed near. Where could they land this time?

Swift dipped suddenly, diving toward the sea. Mari, her heart seeming to have jumped into her mouth, tried to see around Alera. "What is it?"

"The *Pride*," Alera said.

Mari looked to the side as Swift raced past the masts and sails of the *Pride*, the large ship gliding along the surface at a pace that Mari would once have characterized as fast. She caught glimpses of the flag the ship was flying, not Mari's banner of the new day but that of an Imperial merchant ship, and of Mechanic Captain Banda waving from the quarterdeck. Up forward crouched the shrouded shape of the new heavy cannon. Mari knew that Alli had personally overseen the reinforcement of the *Pride*'s hull to withstand the shock of that gun firing, but still worried about it. Amidships, the stack for the new steam boiler had been lowered to lie flat on the deck so that the *Pride* appeared to be a regular sailing ship to anyone spying her. A heavy tow line led to the *Terror*, most of the strange vessel lurking below water but dimly visible from above.

Swift came around again in a long, slow turn as the *Pride* put one of her boats into the water. The sun was sinking below the western horizon, throwing a glare into Mari's eyes as she looked toward the *Pride*. But as the Roc finished its turn, the sun set and the darkness to the east began spreading overhead.

Swift skimmed along just above the surface, heading back toward the *Pride*. It still looked too high to jump as far as Mari was concerned, and the water beneath was going past entirely too fast for her peace of mind. "Release your harness," Alera called back. "I will tip up Swift so you can slide off his back."

That didn't sound like something she really wanted to happen, but Mari loosened the straps of her harness. She also unbuttoned the heavy coat, and reached back to open the laces on her shoes.

"Are you ready?" Alera asked.

No! "Yes!"

Swift's wings flared, braking the bird and flinging his head and body up as the tail dropped. For a moment, Swift hung suspended above the waves before his wings beat again, propelling the Roc upward. It took all of Mari's control not to grab at the harness as she slipped down the feathers and off the Roc, nothing between her and the water below.

She hit the water feet first. Stunned by the impact, Mari shrugged out of the coat and kicked off her shoes, struggling toward the surface, hoping she would make it and that the boat from the *Pride* was nearby.

Alain stayed on Mage Saburo's Roc, watching Mari drop into the water with a mighty splash. "Take us to where she fell," he yelled at Saburo. "I want to drop as close to that spot as possible."

The Roc winged over, gliding lower.

"Now!" Saburo called. The Roc tilted upwards and Alain fell.

He saw Mari surface not far away just before he hit the water and sank deep.

Alain had shed his robes already, and now slipped off his shoes as well, stroking inexpertly but without panic toward the surface. It seemed to be much farther away than he had expected, and as the darkness in the sky grew it was harder to tell which way was up. Holding his breath was getting painful.

One hand broke the surface and he realized that he had been swimming just beneath the surface rather than up toward it. Alain jerked himself upwards and got his head clear of the water, inhaling deeply. Looking around, he saw the *Pride's* boat not far away, a lantern on the bow casting light forward. "Here!" Alain called, waving one arm. "Where is Mari?"

"We already have her." Within moments the boat had pulled up to him, the rowers on Alain's side taking care not to brain him with their oars before he was helped into the boat. "Welcome back to the *Pride*, Sir Mage," Mechanic Deni greeted him.

Alain sat down in the stern next to a wet, bedraggled Mari, who instead of expressing relief glared at him. "Why did you try to kill me?"

"I did not," Alain protested.

"I finally get back to the surface, I finally start breathing, and a certain Mage comes plummeting down into the water, his feet landing practically on my head!"

"I was not that close," Alain said.

"It felt really close."

"I wanted to be able to help you."

She grinned. "I'm kidding, Alain. I'm so glad that is over." Mari looked upwards. "I can't see the Rocs. Did either of them say where they were going?"

"To the mountains of the Sharr Isles," Alain said. "Their Rocs are tired and will cease there, but once Mage Alera and Mage Saburo have rested they will be able to renew their Rocs and fly back to the coast near here."

"Good." Mari shivered, leaning against him in a way that made Alain happy. "I'm cold and tired and this adventure has just started."

The boat came alongside the *Pride*. Alain let Mari go up the ladder first, then followed, finding that Mechanic Dav and Mage Asha were waiting on deck along with Captain Banda. "How was it?" Dav asked.

"It was great!" Mari said. "See how I can barely stand? I need dry clothes, a soft place to sit, and warm food."

Not long afterwards they were seated in the cabin next to Captain Banda's, Mari and Alain huddled together in a blanket as they ate. "How was your trip?" Mari asked Dav and Asha.

"Long and uneventful," Dav said. "Ash and I spent most of our time trying to find out as much as we could about the part of the Empire we'll be going through."

"Ash?" Alain said.

Asha gave him a bland look. "It is a friend name that Mechanic Dav uses. Between ourselves," she added, her tones staying largely emotionless but still causing Dav to wince apologetically.

"We'll stick with Asha then," Mari said, amused by something that Alain did not understand. "How far from Landfall are we?" she asked.

Banda gestured to the north. "Another day's travel. Dav and I will transfer to the *Terror* in the morning to get her boiler going. Mage Asha will come with us to help get everything ready. We'll maintain a pace to arrive near Landfall as darkness falls, go in as close as we dare, then cut loose the *Terror*."

"Alain and I can help with that," Mari said.

"Yes," Alain agreed.

"Take the day to recover," Banda advised. "Tomorrow night will be a very long night."

By the time Alain awoke much of the next day had already passed. Mari was still asleep, so he quietly put on the new Mage robes the *Pride* had brought along for him and went out on deck.

All that could be seen of Imperial territory was a thin gray line on the horizon to the east, but Alain could see the masts of numerous ships which were close enough to be spotted. "We're getting close to Landfall," Mechanic Deni told him as Alain walked onto the quarter-deck. "There's always a lot of traffic around that port. As long as it's still light, we're trying to stay far enough from any other shipping to keep anyone from wondering about that mess of driftwood following us around."

Alain looked over the stern. Two heavy lines formed low arcs that ran from the back of the *Pride* to the front of the *Terror*. As Deni had said, the parts of the strange craft above water had been well concealed by what looked like a tangled mess of branches and logs that had locked together. One log rose incongruously nearly straight up, though. "Why is that one positioned so oddly?" Alain asked.

"That's the stack for the boiler," Deni said. "Made to look like a weathered log. Once you get into the harbor at Landfall the swells will be gentle enough that the stack will be lowered onto its side and look more natural. There are a few other branches that are hollowed out the same to serve as air intakes and exhausts. It's a funny-looking ship, but the design has all sorts of clever touches like that. The Captain, Mechanic Dav, and Mage Asha are all aboard, getting the ship ready."

Deni turned to judge the position of the sun. "You can let Master Mechanic Mari rest a while longer. We'll start our run in toward the port soon, but it will be well after dark before we're close enough for the two of you to transfer to the *Terror*."

As it turned out, Mari didn't rouse until nearly sunset. That was just as well, since once she had dressed and they had both eaten there was nothing to do but wait.

As they stood at the rail of the *Pride*, looking at the lights of other ships visible in the night, Mari shrugged her shoulders uncomfortably. "They had a Mechanics jacket for me," she explained to Alain, "but it's new and stiff. I miss my old one. I've been through a lot in that jacket."

"You feel an attachment to an article of clothing?" Alain asked.

"Yes." She gave him a look. "Don't you? You've never mentioned that sort of thing, have you?"

"No," Alain said. "I have not imagined having any feeling for clothing. If others feel as you do, it must be because of my Mage training."

"Very likely," Mari said. "You're taught not to care about people, so it's no surprise you don't care about clothes. And maybe you're better off not worrying about something that really isn't all that important. That's the breakwater, isn't it? We must be entering the harbor."

"The motion of the ship on the waves has lessened," Alain said. Off to one side he could see one of the harbor fortifications, a light shining atop it, oblivious to the danger posed by the *Pride*. Ahead, the waterfront of Landfall blazed with lights flickering through an increasingly dense forest of masts from ships and boats.

"Time to go," Mechanic Deni said, coming up to them and speaking softly. "Take good care of Captain Banda for us, will you? Once we set the *Terror* loose, we'll head back out to sea and stay well away for the next week to avoid running into Imperials. After that we'll come in as close as we can to the harbor each night until we hear from you. If for some reason we miss a rendezvous near the harbor, Captain Banda has a position to head to at sea where we'll be looking for you during the day."

"He thinks we can do this in a week?" Mari asked. "It's a long way up the river to Palandur and then Marandur beyond that."

"It'll be slow going on the way there," Deni agreed. "You'll be fighting the current and not able to move in daylight. But the way back down should be a lot faster."

Deni led them to the smallest of the *Pride*'s boats, which was carefully lowered once Alain, Mari, another Mechanic from the *Pride*'s crew, and two rowers were seated. Once on the water, it only took a few strokes of the oars to reach the *Terror*. Asha stood amid the tangle of wood, helping first Mari and then Alain onto the strange craft. The sailors in the boat maneuvered to the tow lines and began unshackling them from the *Terror*.

The other Mechanic from the *Pride* and Mari went to the fake tree trunk standing straight up and began doing mysterious Mechanic things to its base. "Careful," the Mechanic cautioned as the trunk opened as if cut through. A piece on one side allowed it to pivot down. Alain felt a gust of hot air from the foreshortened stack as Mari helped fasten down the trunk, then assisted in getting the tow lines loose. "Fair winds and following seas!" the Mechanic from the *Pride* whispered, then jumped back across to the boat. Alain had only a moment to watch as the boat returned to the ship, breaking their last contact with the others.

Asha showed Alain the hatch that led into the ship. He went down the ladder, finding himself in a room of metal that conjured up unpleasant memories of his and Mari's captivity onboard a Mechanic Guild ship. Light came not from lanterns, but from some of the Mechanic "bulbs" whose glow never changed. Asha came down the ladder behind him. "The bunks where we sleep are there. Behind that wall," she said, pointing to a metal bulkhead, "is the room where Mechanic Dav and Mari will tend the creature they call a boiler. Dav has been in there all day. In the other direction there is another ladder leading up to where Mechanic Captain Banda sees to steer the ship, and beyond that an area holding food, a table, and the space where Dav says most of the texts will be placed when we have them."

Mari came down the ladder, pausing at the top to swing shut the hatch and dog it securely. "Not a lot of room, is there? Sorry."

"Why?" Asha asked.

"Because we had to cram in the boiler and the steering mechanism and a small generator and the intake and exhaust fans and the generator and food and—" Mari stopped speaking, then laughed. "Oh, you wanted to know why I apologized, didn't you?"

"Yes."

"I don't know. They did the best job they could in the time we had," Mari said. "One thing about dealing with Mages that's nice is you guys never complain about the food or the accommodations. Alain, I'm going to go back and help Dav with the boiler."

"What tasks must Asha and I do?" Alain asked, worrying that he would only be a passenger while Mari did all the work.

Mari pointed to the second ladder. "There's just enough room up in the steering area for two. On this trip, Dav and I will be tending the boiler, and Banda will be either steering us through the night or sleeping during the day. That leaves you and Asha to look out for trouble from the Imperials or any other source. You're our sentries. We'll need you mainly during the day, but depending on how heavy the river traffic is at night we might need one of you up there all the time."

"I have been in the steering area," Asha offered. "Mage Alain should see it as well."

Perhaps because it was mostly underwater, the *Terror* felt to Alain as stable as a much larger ship. He nonetheless moved carefully around the tubes and pipes and other Mechanic devices, remembering the many times that Mari had cautioned him about what might happen if something was damaged or shoved in the wrong way. Asha came with him, and as he reached the forward ladder she gestured around. "Does this feel odd, Mage Alain?"

"It does," Alain admitted. "We are surrounded by the illusions the Mechanics have made. There is nothing familiar to us."

"There is Dav," Asha said.

"And Mari," Alain agreed.

"We will speak later," Asha said, stepping back.

Alain went up the ladder a short distance, finding himself in a small, low space ringed with circular windows each about the size of his outspread hand. Captain Banda sat in a seat fastened to the deck, looking forward in the direction of the *Terror*'s motion, before him a small ship's wheel and various Mechanic devices. The views out of the windows were partially obscured by the driftwood camouflage. Directly overhead was another hatch.

Captain Banda glanced back to see his visitor. "Welcome, Sir Mage. There is another seat there and you are welcome to it. Would you do me a favor first, though? There is a curtain suspended down below that can be drawn around the ladder to ensure no light from inside the ship shines through these windows. It could be fatal if we betrayed our presence that way. Please draw the curtain and then rejoin me."

Alain went down, but his task was interrupted by Mari dashing past and up the ladder to talk in a low voice with Banda. She came back down within a very short time. "Sorry, love. I needed to make sure I knew what we were planning on doing tonight. I'd love to sit up there and hog the view, but you need to familiarize yourself with the situation and be ready to react if you have to." She leaned to kiss him. "Here we go!"

"It is exciting," Alain said.

"You sound calm, not excited," she said. "But I agree. Exciting. And scary. Let's get this done and go back to the relative safety of Tiae, where all we have to worry about is armies of assassins."

Alain returned to the seat behind Banda. It was a bit cramped, but he could see in all directions. The surface of the harbor lay close to the lowest edge of the windows so that the water seemed uncomfortably near. Occasionally it lapped across the very bottom of the windows at the front.

He looked at the lights of the harbor. Some were moving, probably small boats in motion, others stationary, marking anchored ships or buildings on shore. Watching those lights, Alain realized that the *Terror* was moving as well, heading steadily toward the place where the Ospren River flowed through Landfall and into the harbor.

A dark shape looming to one side gained detail as they drew closer. They were passing just astern of an anchored Imperial war galley, only a single light burning on the prow to mark its position. As the *Terror* glided by, Alain could see above him a solitary sentry leaning on the galley's rail and staring out across the harbor, oblivious to the strange craft almost right beneath his nose.

"It's good we have that driftwood around us," Banda muttered, his voice tense with concentration as he peered into the night. "Any boats that see us are steering clear so they don't risk damage from colliding with a bunch of heavy, sharp-edged scrapwood. But it also means I have to keep our speed down. I can't make it obvious that this wood is moving faster than anything drifting in the harbor should be. Tell me for my future knowledge, Sir Mage, if it is needed can you use one of your spells against something you see through one of the portholes, or would you need to view it directly?"

"If I can see something, I can place a spell on it," Alain said. "There is little power available on the water," he added. "My abilities are limited."

"Will that be true on the river as well?" Banda asked.

"I will learn that when we reach the river."

The river's mouth was guarded by a large watch tower on each bank and by another war galley that was moored nearby. Banda cursed under his breath as he struggled against the current to get the *Terror* into the river and past the Imperial defenses without being noticed. Under the push of the water, the *Terror* swung close to one side, where the sentries on the nearest watch tower could have easily looked down and perhaps spotted the dark shape beneath the driftwood. Alain felt the ship drag on the right as it brushed against a subsurface sandbar. Banda tried to wrestle the *Terror* back toward the main channel, leaning forward toward another tube. "I need more power!"

Alain heard Mechanic Dav's response come out of the same tube. "Understood." The *Terror* shook a little more, but Alain could feel the drag on the right side of the ship increasing. The ship slowed further. He leaned to look up through the nearest windows. They had almost drawn even with the Imperial guard tower on this side of the river. He could barely see the top of the tower, which must provide an ominously good view of the struggling ship below.

"Reversing," Banda called into the tube, his voice clipped with anxiety.

The *Terror* slid backwards slightly, twisting a little, but then halted again.

"Going forward." This time the *Terror* barely moved at all.

Two more attempts to go forward and back produced no result.

Mari stuck her head up the ladder. It was too cramped in the steering room for her to join them, so she stayed there, her expression not easy to make out in the dim light filtering in through the windows. "We're not moving. Are we stuck?"

"Yes, we're stuck," Banda said angrily. "All of this effort, all of this work, and we have come this far to run hard aground on a submerged sandbar under the noses of Imperial fortifications with the journey barely begun. It is entirely my fault, Master Mechanic Mari."

CHAPTER NINE

What can we do?" Mari asked, her voice low, calm, and yet insistent. "How do you free ships when they run aground?"

"When we're hard aground like this? Wait for the tide to lift them," Banda said, bitterness filling every word. "But look out there at the water marks on the rocks. You can't see any. We're at high tide already. When the tide goes out, we'll not only be stuck, but we'll be sticking out of the water enough that any fool will see us."

"Alain?" Mari asked.

"I cannot think of any spell that Mage Asha or I could do that would free this craft," Alain said. "We could make some of the sand or mud holding us disappear, but only if we could tell where it was by seeing or by touch, and that might be only a small portion of what holds this ship."

"Captain," Mari said, "I did not endure riding a Roc for four days so I could abandon this job when it was barely begun. What other options do we have?"

"Unless you know a way to get under the ship and pick it off the bar, there are no options," Banda said.

Mari frowned at him in a way that Alain recognized. She was thinking. An idea was close. "We have to raise the ship?"

"Yes," Banda said.

"I talked to Calu about this ship, and about the ships it was based on, the ones that could ride fully on the surface or fully underwater. I know we can adjust the buoyancy of the *Terror*. That was planned in so that when we used fuel and food we could lower the ship to keep it concealed, and when we took the texts on board we could—"

"Increase the buoyancy," Banda broke in, slapping his forehead. "Blazes! I'm an idiot! I'm in a totally new kind of ship, but I'm still thinking as if it were like all other ships! We can pump out some of the water in the ballast tanks and make the ship ride higher, which means the bottom of the ship will rise, hopefully enough for us to clear that sandbar!"

He paused. "We'll have to fire the boiler at full pressure to have enough power to run the pumps and keep enough propulsion to make sure we don't get pushed the wrong way when the ship gets free. That will make some noise, and we're right next to one of the Imperial watch towers. The pumps will also make some noise, and the water we shove out may create some noticeable turbulence on the surface. So will the screw while we're stuck and it's thrashing away. And the higher we rise the more of the actual ship will be exposed above the surface of the water for anyone to see."

"We don't have any choice," Mari said. "Alain, you and Asha watch for trouble. Captain Banda, Dav, and I are going to be fully occupied trying to get this ship free. If the Imperials start reacting to us, you and Asha do whatever you think is best, but keep in mind that we want to raise as little fuss as possible."

Alain waited, hearing Mari and Dav rushing around and calling out to each other. Asha appeared at the foot of the ladder and nodded to Alain to indicate her readiness.

There was only a moderate amount of power here. Not much at all. If he and Asha had to use spells they would quickly deplete it.

"If we use spells, the elders and other Mages in Landfall will know we are here," Asha said. "We should only use spells if there is no other choice."

"You are right," Alain said. He felt frustratingly helpless. The

Mechanics had built this ship. In a way, they had created this world and this situation, and only they could fix the trouble it was in. He wondered if Mari had felt like this when riding on the back of a Roc, able to do little but watch and wait.

"Ready at the pumps!" Mari called, her voice echoing oddly off the metal sides of the ship. "Dav is bringing the boiler up to the highest safe pressure!"

Alain could hear a soft roaring sound, like that of a blazing fire muffled by distance. The boiler. He had never forgotten the noise they made, and how it could rise to a bellow before they destroyed everything around them.

Captain Banda called back to Mari. "Start the pumps. Be ready to stop the moment I call. I'm advancing the throttle now and will hold it at full."

A low rumbling was added to the other noises, along with a deeper hum of Mechanic devices laboring. The vibrations shaking the *Terror* increased.

Alain looked upward as far as the window permitted. He was just able to see the edge of the top of the tower. As the noise and shaking increased, Alain saw the silhouette of a sentry lean out, gazing down. The night was dark, and darker in the river away from the lights on the shore, and darker yet under the water. What could be seen from up there?

Apparently, not enough. Another sentry joined the first, their bodies canted out and down as they stared toward the commotion in the river. Alain waited for one or the other to jerk back in alarm, for indications that warnings were being shouted from the tower, but as the moments passed the sentries kept studying the scene beneath them.

"We're not rising!" Mari called. "The gauges say water is being pumped out of the ballast tanks but I can't feel us rising!"

"There's suction holding our hull to the sandbar! It's mostly mud," Banda called back. "We'll need enough buoyancy to break the suction. Be ready to reverse the pumps and take on more water, because we might jump as much as a lance length higher in the water when we finally break free. How is the boiler doing?"

"Dav says it's holding pressure. Do you need more?"

"We'll see!"

In the midst of the Mechanics' furious activity and the noises and vibrations, Asha maintained total, impassive calm where she stood at the foot of the ladder. Alain realized that he was doing the same, reverting to Mage training in the face of the emergency to be ready for the worst.

One of the sentries high overhead raised a torch, holding it out from the tower in an attempt to get a better view of the activity below.

The *Terror* suddenly lurched upward just as if it were a Roc caught by a strong updraft. Alain and Asha grabbed for support as the ship surged forward and up while Captain Banda, a sheen of sweat visible on his face, steered toward deeper water near the center of the river. "Stop the pumps!" Banda yelled. "Stars above, we're about a half-lance higher in the water! Start taking on ballast again!"

"Are we clear of the sandbar?" Mari yelled back.

"Yes! Definitely! We're past the buoys that mark the edges of the main channel down the river that the Imperials keep dredged. We're all right. I'm throttling back now. But we need to get the *Terror* lower in the water again before somebody spots the bulk of the ship beneath the camouflage."

The shaking of the ship had fallen off a great deal. Alain could hear the hum of the Mechanic devices again.

"Dav!" Banda called into the tube. "You can reduce pressure to standard steaming. We're clear."

Alain spotted something odd on the river alongside the ship, bubbles bursting to the surface. "There is something next to the ship." He checked the other side. "And there as well."

"That's air being vented from the ballast tanks as we take on water," Banda said. "Can't be helped. Did the Imperials notice that show we just put on?"

"The sentries were watching, but did not show clear signs of alarm, just curiosity. I saw no signs of reaction to a possible threat."

"Let's hope you're right. Mari! Slow the pumps. We're almost low enough in the water again."

A short time later, Banda ordered the pumps stopped as the *Terror* drove up the river. "This will do until we get enough light tomorrow to readjust our depth," he said. "I assume you want to continue with our job?"

Mari joined Asha at the bottom of the ladder. "Yes. We'll keep on going upriver and see if the Imperials react. They may not have had any idea what was going on."

"Let's hope so," Banda said. "We can't do much in the way of inspecting the hull for damage, but it would be wise to pull up the deck plates and see if any leaks can be seen in the bilges."

"I'll do it," Mari said. "We forgot to bring an Apprentice along to handle jobs like that."

Banda laughed, and Alain realized that Mari had shared a Mechanic joke with him.

Alain turned and looked back through the branches of the camouflage. The lights around the watch towers were receding as the ship labored up the river. But he could see new movement at the base of the one they had just left. "There are lights leaving the Imperial watch tower and going down to the river near where we were."

"I wonder what they'll make of the gouge we left in that sandbar? They shouldn't be able to send a diver down to look at it until daylight," Banda said.

Mari came back, breathing heavily. "I checked under the deck plates. Those things are heavy. No sign of a leak. Are the Imperials chasing us?"

"No," Alain said.

"We'll see what day brings." Banda exhaled heavily as he finally relaxed a little. "There shouldn't be much traffic on the river at night, so I'll stay right in the center of the channel. I'm getting a better feel for handling this thing. We need to get far enough past Landfall to be able to find a spot on or near the river bank to hide during the day. But not too far, or the river banks might be crowded with barges and other small craft that have laid up for the night."

The lights on either side of the river that marked the fraying edges of the city were dwindling, replaced by darker areas of open country. From what Alain could see of the river banks, the land was losing its civilized, contained, controlled, and built-up appearance, instead slipping into the anarchy and lack of discipline that nature gloried in. Even the Empire had not been able to impose order on every piece of the land it claimed as its own.

"You've only been to Landfall the one time?" Banda asked, his voice hushed to match the quiet outside.

"Yes," Alain said. "When Mari and I were heading for the Sharr Isles."

"Landfall is what they call the first place a ship reaches shore," Banda said. "Is this where the ship from another star first set people on this world? How many people have lived here since, not having any idea of what the name truly meant? It will be a great day when they can be told. When everyone can be told. Do you think we'll go back to calling the world Demeter instead of Dematr?"

"I do not know. People can be…stubborn," Alain said.

"Truth from a Mage," Banda replied, using the old saying for something wildly improbable, but now giving it another meaning. He fell silent after that, as did Alain, until the growing light to the east warned of dawn approaching.

As Banda had predicted, there were a number of boats and barges tied up or anchored near the riverbanks. But they had chosen spots easy to reach, avoiding areas where vegetation, indents in the river, or rocks complicated getting in and out.

Captain Banda cautiously brought the *Terror* close in to the river bank where several trees leaned out over a rock ledge. The current had scooped out a deeper spot next to the bank, giving plenty of room for the bulk of the *Terror*'s hull underwater, and the natural obstructions of nearby rocks made the pile of driftwood atop the *Terror* look perfectly natural in this spot. "Those trees should keep us shaded much of the day," Banda said to Alain. "Which will make it much harder for anyone to spot anything under our camouflage. Dav!" he called down. "Come out the aft hatch and see if you can find a way to tie us up that no can spot. Otherwise we'll anchor."

Mechanic Dav popped up through the deck behind the steering room, waved at them, then clambered over the wood hiding the *Terror* until he found a boulder in the water that he could loop a line around.

Banda opened the forward hatch above himself and Alain, allowing fresh air to enter along with the smells and sounds of the outside. "We should keep the hatches open during the day as much as possible to air out the ship." Banda yawned. "It's been a long day. I need to get as much sleep as I can. When is Mage Asha relieving you?"

"Very soon. She will take half the day, and I will take the other, just as Mari and Dav will share time on the boiler creature."

"It's...not really a creature, you know."

Alain shook his head. "I know Mechanics do not consider it so, but it breathes, it does work, it gives off heat, it must be fed."

Banda paused. "Yes. But it's not alive."

"Neither are a Mage's spell creatures such as dragons," Alain said.

"Oh." Banda thought, then shrugged. "I suppose by a Mage's definition it is sort of a creature, then. How does Mari take it that you call boilers creatures?"

"She says it is something required of her in life." Alain took a moment to recall. "Those are not the exact words. What she says is that it is something...she has to live with. But that means the same thing."

"Not exactly," Banda said, smiling as if Alain had just told a joke.

In some ways he would never understand Mechanics.

About noon, after Asha had spent the morning on watch, Alain came back up to the steering room to take his turn at sentry duty. Asha was sitting where Banda would to drive the ship, so Alain took the seat behind it that he had occupied the night before. "There has been nothing of concern," Asha said. "I have seen nothing but boats passing us." She bent a sharp look on Alain. "Have you seen anything?"

"My foresight?" Alain asked. "No. It has given no warning."

"We have not spoken for some time, because Mechanic Dav and I were on the *Pride* while you were flying by Roc. Have you seen anything else of Mari?"

He knew what she meant. The vision of Mari at some future time, lying on a surface made of fitted stone blocks, her jacket wet with blood, apparently near death. "No."

"If you cannot stay with her at all times, you can always call on me," Asha said, gazing out one of the portholes. "We will keep that vision from happening. You and Mari must stay with each other. — Mechanic Dav has asked me if I would promise myself to him," she added in a sudden burst of words.

"What did you tell him?" Alain asked.

"I said I must think." Asha stayed silent for a while. "A Mage does not marry. A Mage has no family."

"This is not so. Mari has shown us a different wisdom."

"But is it the same for me as for you? Some things are different for women."

"Does Mechanic Dav think it is different?" Alain said.

Asha's lip twitched in a tiny Mage smile. "He does not. He said we could be as…happy…as you and Mari."

"But you do not think so?"

"I do not know. I am a Mage." She closed her eyes and Alain saw a shadow of pain flit across her features. "Mechanic Dav has a family. They are Mechanics. What happens if he brings a Mage to them?"

"They should be happy if he is happy," Alain said.

"You know what Mages are," Asha said. "What we have lived with. What others see when they look at us. Like Mari's family."

"Mari's mother and sister accept me as a Mage. Does Mechanic Dav see ill in you being a Mage?" Alain asked.

"He…" She looked down. "He says I am a gift to all who know me. How could anyone believe that?"

"When I say such things to Mari, she laughs."

"Why would she laugh?"

"I do not know. But it is a happy sound." Alain gave Asha the most encouraging look he had learned to make. "You fear that a Mage would not be accepted by the family of Mechanic Dav, and you fear that a Mage is not someone Mechanic Dav should exchange promises with. I will tell you what Mari would say: that anyone would be fortunate to have your promise. Would Mari count you as a friend if being a Mage was so ill a thing? And for the family, there is a place in Marandur you should see. It will tell you much of importance about the family of Mechanic Dav."

"In Marandur?" Asha nodded slowly. "You are much wiser in such things than I, Mage Alain."

"I often do not feel wise," Alain admitted.

"Doubt about your wisdom can be the clearest sign of wisdom," Asha said. "I will decide after I see this place in Marandur that you speak of." She paused, but Alain could sense that she was going to say more and so stayed quiet. "Mage Alain? Had things been different, could you and I have been such a pair?"

He had deliberately avoided thinking about that for some time. "I do not know. But it was something that could not happen, not unless I met Mari and relearned how to feel."

"I do not know, either," Asha said. "We met only because the Mage Guild took us as acolytes, but because we were acolytes and then Mages we could not even be friends. I do know that I am happy I was free to be with Dav. You once said that Mari defined the world illusion for you. It shocked me. But now I understand, for that is how I feel about Dav. I will—" She stopped speaking, looking toward the trees screening them from the river bank.

Alain felt it, too. "A Mage approaches along the road. She is making no attempt to conceal her presence."

Asha raised herself enough to peek through the hatch. She held the position, then slowly lowered herself and whispered to Alain. "I hear the sounds of orders being called. I know voices of this kind from my contracts with the legions. Legionaries approach along the road from the direction of Landfall."

He wondered whether to call Mari and the other Mechanics, but the decision was taken from him as a head wearing the helmet of the Imperial legions stuck through the far side of the trees.

"Yeah, it's a bunch of wood, Centurion!"

The reply came faintly but clearly to Alain. "Is it wreckage? Recent wreckage?"

The legionary had already looked away from the raft of driftwood hiding the upper portion of the *Terror* and was gazing across the river. "Nah. Not wreckage at all. Just a bunch of branches and stuff that drifted down river and got stuck here."

"Any sign of a kraken?"

Another voice sounded from a legionary who must be near the first. "Centurion, aside from wreckage, what else are we looking for?"

"Tentacles, you idiot! Tentacles attached to a body large enough to break a ship! The watch towers reported what must have been a kraken that got stuck in the shallows near one of them last night. It might have headed up river once it got free. Didn't you get a briefing from your section leader before you were put on scout?"

"Uh, no?"

"Unless there's something else worth checking out over there, get your butts moving!" the centurion ordered, his voice now carrying clearly to Alain as the legionaries marched by. "I want us to hit the boundary marker so we can report the river all clear and get back to Landfall before dark!"

"Soon as we check out the underbrush for any signs of the kraken, Centurion!" Alain heard the nearby legionary continue speaking to his comrade, though in a much lower voice. "A kraken. Gah. No wonder we got that Lady Mage with us."

"Maybe we ought to take our time checking out this spot," his companion suggested. "Get some rest from all the marching, you know."

"Not for me! For once, I'm all for doing what the Centurion says. I don't want to be out here after dark."

"Why? You afraid of Mara?"

"Blazes, yeah! Aren't you?"

"Nah. I'm too old for her tastes. She'd snap you up, though. Mara likes young blood."

"Shut it! That's not funny! Come on!"

Alain heard the two legionaries leaving. He and Asha waited until they could see the Imperial search group come into sight well down the road, still heading upriver.

"I understand now why the Mage was not hiding her presence," Asha said. "If there was a kraken and it sensed a Mage, it would be drawn to her."

"I did not know that of krakens. Will you stay a little longer here so that I can tell Mari what we have heard?" Receiving her assent, Alain left Asha on watch. He went down the ladder quietly, around the curtain that was now blocking light and sound from getting into the parts of the ship where Mechanics Banda and Dav were sleeping, then back to where growing heat marked the presence of the Mechanic boiler that Mari tended. The roaring sound from the boiler was much softer. Alain had always thought that meant the creature was sleeping, even though Mari insisted it did not sleep.

Mari listened to Alain's report, then shook her head. "A kraken?"

"If I did not know of this ship," Alain said, "and heard the noises last night, and saw the marks left by a large body in the sandbar this morning, I would think it was a kraken that had done it."

"The only logical explanation they know of," Mari said. "We're lucky that krakens are real— Oh, no, I said it. Go ahead."

"What?" Alain asked.

"Say it!"

"Nothing is real," Alain said.

"Right. Wouldn't the Mages in Landfall know whether or not a kraken had been created?"

"Not if the kraken was not created there. It could have been created elsewhere and slipped away from the control of the Mage who made it. If no other sign of the spell creature is found today or in coming days, they will assume it ceased and vanished."

"Good. Did you hear anything else from the legionaries?" Mari asked, wiping sweat from her forehead. While the front of the ship was cold from the river water surrounding it, this back area was very warm because of the heat from the Mechanic boiler creature.

"They wanted to get back into the city before nightfall, because they were worried about Mara."

"Mara?" Mari made a face. "Not seriously."

"One spoke in fear when her name was mentioned. He sounded like a young man," Alain added.

"It's the Empire's own fault. They keep spreading rumors that I'm that undead blood-sucker, and their own people are believing it."

"We might be able to use that," Alain suggested. "If we encounter legionaries—"

"No."

"Mari, their fear of Mara might give us a very important advantage."

"No."

"But—"

"I'm not posing as Mara the Undying!" Mari insisted. "It's a ridiculous idea, anyway. Anybody who sees me isn't going to be fooled into thinking I'm the Dark One. Even if Mara wasn't a myth, she's supposed to be extremely beautiful. Irresistible to men! Why are you looking at me like that?"

Alain tried to find the right words. Mari looked tired from the long night and too little sleep on top of her work so far this day, sweat marked her skin and spotted her shirt, but somehow that all made her even more attractive in his eyes. "Because you are the most beautiful woman I have ever seen."

She stared at him, then laughed. "You're complimenting me by saying I could pass for the Dark One, who I will remind you is rumored to drink the blood of young men to keep herself looking young and gorgeous. Am I supposed to thank you? Alain, everyone else in the world doesn't view me through love filters."

"Love filters?"

"It means…Alain, when someone is in love and they look at that person they love, they see everything they want to believe is in them, all the good and all the rightness and everything else, and that comes out as beautiful. Maybe that wears off after a while. I don't know. I hope not. That's why you think I'm better looking than Asha. No other man on Dematr would agree with you, but I'm good with that. As long as you believe it, I'm good."

Alain thought about her words. "You see something like that when you view me?"

"Yes." She laughed softly. "That's when I first realized that I was in trouble. The first time I looked at you and saw this amazing guy instead of just Mage Alain. To get back to the point, I really don't think that anyone besides you who sees me would think I was attractive enough to be Mara."

"But under the right conditions, the illusion could be important," Alain said.

She sighed. "I suppose. You know what? I'm sitting *under* the Ospren River, and heading back to Marandur, so I can definitely say that stranger things have happened. I'll keep it in mind. If playing at being Mara might get us out of a tight situation, my dignity isn't worth even one life that might be saved."

Alain went back to his watch, and Asha went down to the bunks to sleep for a while before taking over from him again. He sat in the steering room with the small, round windows circling it, listening to the sounds coming in through the open hatch as barges and boats and the occasional larger vessel went past. None of the people on them spared a second glance for the pile of branches and trunks snagged under the shade of the trees.

He felt oddly moody. Though his eyes strayed from the river to the river bank and his senses remained alert for any other Mages who might draw near, Alain's thoughts kept coming back to two visions. One was of Mari as he had just seen her, rumpled and sweaty and tired, but happy because she was working on one of her devices. Was she right that no other man could see her beauty even at such times? It was still a matter of amazement for Alain that such a woman had chosen to promise herself to him.

The other vision was the one he had had almost a year ago. A vision of some future time. Of Mari, to all appearances near death. When would that happen? Could he stop it? As Asha said, there must be a way.

Even if that meant taking Mari's place as the one to suffer a terrible injury.

The crew of the *Terror* met briefly for a shared meal as the sun neared the horizon. Mari assured Alain that the boiler creature would be fine if left unsupervised for a short time while it was at rest, so all of the Mechanics were present. Only Asha was not at the small table forward of the ladder, being back on watch for danger, but she was within earshot of those eating.

"River traffic has already fallen off," Banda commented. "That's normal. Any boat that can't make its destination by sunset is finding a good spot to stop for the night. Not many risk the river in the dark."

"Why not?" Dav asked, looking morosely at the cold, salted meat and cold, hard bread in front of him.

"Because of junk like what we're pretending to be," Banda said, jerking a thumb in the general direction of the driftwood camouflage. "It makes a good disguise for us because that sort of debris is common enough on a river like this. Even in daylight a mostly submerged tree trunk could put a hole in a barge if there was a collision. At night, it's far too hard to see trouble like that in time to avoid it."

"Especially if it's a kraken," Mari said, drawing smiles from the other Mechanics.

"There's another problem this time of year," Banda added. "Especially as we go farther up the river, we're likely to run into mist or fog in the early evening. It will usually dissipate by midnight, but before then the mist could be so light we barely notice it, or heavy enough to make it hard to see. The stretch between Palandur and Marandur is notorious for it. I heard once that Emperor Palan chose the location for Palandur in part because it was far enough down river to avoid the worst of the river fog that had created problems for shipping near Marandur."

"How are we doing on getting to Marandur?" Mari asked. "Did we get as far last night as you'd hoped we would?"

"I think so," Banda replied. "I'll know better how we're doing when I get a look at some of the towns along the way. If we can maintain speed as I hope, it will be about six days to Marandur, running only during night. You and Dav will have to keep a close eye on our fuel level. We had to estimate how much it would take to fuel the boiler for the whole trip. Extra fuel oil isn't very easy to obtain along the banks of the Ospren." He paused, looking thoughtful. "There is a place we could get some if we needed it. But it would be a bit risky."

Alain saw the tension that Banda hid from the others. "More than a bit risky, is it not?"

"Very risky," Banda admitted. "I wouldn't even consider it if we didn't have you Mages along. We'll know when we reach Palandur if we should make a try. Mari, once it gets dark enough and the river traffic has let up, I'm going out to check on the screw for damage. I think it's all right, but I'd like to be sure."

"This one has questions," Asha called down softly from above. "What is a...screw?"

"It is something that Mechanics use to hold their illusions in one piece," Alain said.

"No," Mari said. "That's a different screw, an inclined plane wrapped around a shaft to hold things. Whereas the screw propelling this ship is a rotary device using inclined blades extending from a central hub to move things. Same principle, I guess, but very different. You know, Alain, it is absolutely amazing how blank your expression can get when I'm explaining Mechanic things to you."

"This one has questions," Asha repeated. "I have seen that Mechanics place great importance on using the right word when speaking of things, as Mari just did when…explaining to Alain."

"That's right," Mari said. "Using exactly the right technical term is very important."

"Then why is the same word used for two things you say are very different?" Asha continued.

Alain saw Mari and Dav exchange glances, then both looked at Banda, who shrugged and shook his head.

"We have no idea," Mari said.

"You know," Dav commented, "I've heard a lot of stories about you, Mari."

"Most of them aren't true."

"That's not what Alli says. The point being, you kept asking questions like that one from Asha when you were an Apprentice. That's one of the reasons the Senior Mechanics never liked you."

"It was one of the reasons," Mari agreed. "Are you trying to say I should have been a Mage?"

"You would not have made a good Mage," Alain said.

"That's comforting."

"Yeah," Dav said. "What I meant, though, is that maybe part of you thinks like part of them. And maybe that's why you were able to get to know Alain the first time you two were together. Your minds weren't totally different, just mostly different."

"Huh," Mari commented. "What do you think, Alain?"

Alain brought up his memories of their first meeting. "I remember thinking that I could not understand anything you were doing."

"Has that changed?" Banda asked, grinning as Mari threw a glare his way.

"Yes," Alain said, "mostly. But there came a time when I realized she was saying things I did understand. That we…shared something. It was disturbing for a Mage to feel like that. Trying to understand Mari caused me to do things and believe things that a Mage should not. After that I could not go back to being what the elders had made me."

"You broke him?" Banda asked Mari.

"Yeah," she said. "I broke a Mage. But it turned out he still worked, and better than ever. Getting back to business," Mari said to Banda, "do you think we'll encounter any more kraken search parties?"

"Doubtful," Banda said. "If none of the searches today bore fruit and none of the boats in the river reported seeing anything, the Imperials will probably conclude the beast swam out to sea rather than upstream. I don't see why they'd stumble around in the dark of the night looking for a kraken they couldn't find in the daylight."

"Asha said they were worried about staying out at night," Dav said. "That doesn't sound like what I've heard about Imperial legionaries."

Mari sighed. "They're scared of Mara the Undying. The Imperial government has been feeding rumors that the Dark One has returned so they can try to discredit me, but it's been having a negative effect on their own people."

Dav looked puzzled. "No offense, Mari, but from the stories I heard, Asha would fit the description of Mara better than you would."

"And it's right that you think so," Mari said, "but Asha's hair is the wrong color, she didn't come out of Marandur—at least not yet—and she's not the daughter of Jules who has the Emperor worried."

"Oh, yeah," Dav agreed. "And I guess the name Asha isn't anything like Mara, but Mari is pretty close."

"Thank you."

Alain did not understand why Mari had said "thank you" in such a way that it sounded as if she was not thanking Dav. It was one more thing he would have to ask her about someday.

"Can we use that?" Banda asked. "The Mara thing? If the legionaries are scared of her..."

"Alain and I have already discussed it. If the right opportunity arises, I'm willing to, even though the idea of being linked to Mara has an even worse effect on my appetite than this salt pork." She held up the meat from her plate. "I mean, seriously, this looks like some of the wood that's camouflaging our ship."

"The wood probably tastes better," Banda said, "and is easier to chew. Normally we'd boil that stuff, but we can't risk having cooking smells reveal our presence."

The next few days settled into a pattern of making as much progress up the river at night as possible, followed by spending the daylight hugging one of the riverbanks as the ships and boats that used the Ospren River as a highway steered well clear of what looked like a dangerous mass of driftwood. On the third day, as Alain sat the watch, he saw an official Imperial craft of some kind cruise by, the men and women aboard making particular note of the camouflaged *Terror*. But Banda expressed no worries when told of it. "That was one of the Imperial river watch boats. They look for hazards and for any boats that need help, so they were tagging our location for someone to come out and get rid of the problem before the mass of driftwood we look like breaks free and hurts someone. By the time the clean-up crew arrives, we'll be long gone."

But Alain did note that Captain Banda's worries kept growing over another matter. Every afternoon as they prepared to get underway again, Banda would measure the fuel, growing progressively more gloomy as each day passed.

Finally, on the afternoon before the *Terror* would run the gauntlet of the river as it passed through the Imperial capital of Palandur, Banda dropped a piece of paper on the table as they ate. "Mari, Dav, feel free to check my numbers."

Mari picked up the paper, studying it. "Fuel consumption, fuel remaining…I knew it wasn't looking good. I don't see any errors in your math. It's this bad?"

"You already know the answer," Banda said, frowning unhappily. "We're burning too much fuel because of having to fight the current. All we had to go on before we started was estimates of how much drag having so much of the ship underwater would create and how much fuel it would take to maintain the speed we need. If we could have tested this ship in a river like the Ospren, we might have discovered how badly off our estimates were, but it was too important to keep the ship and its purpose secret."

"We'll make Marandur," Mari said.

"Yes, and then we'll have to conserve fuel as much as possible on the way back down river, mostly by coasting with the current. It will prolong our trip by a week, at least, and we'll be running on fumes when we reach Landfall. The *Pride* will still be waiting, but getting worried and running a risk every extra day they stay near Landfall, and we won't have any means to sail out to sea to meet them. Anything unexpected would doom us."

"They told me they were providing enough fuel to give us a margin of error," Mari said, angrily rapping a fist against the side of the ship.

"The error has proven to be bigger than the margin," Banda said.

"You said there was another place to get fuel," Dav pointed out.

"Yes. The only other place on the Ospren short of Landfall. It's the Mechanics Guild pier at Palandur," Banda said.

"The Guild's pier?" Mari asked, incredulous. "No wonder you said it was risky. Isn't that inside the Imperial military dockyard?"

"Yes. When I was last there," Banda added, "security consisted of alarms on the pier and two Mechanics or Apprentices on watch. The Senior Mechanics worried about the Imperials trying to learn our secrets. And since the pier is inside the Imperial dockyard area, there is also Imperial security to worry about. Boat patrols in the water, roving foot patrols, sentries at the entrance to the dockyard, whatever various Imperial warships and their crews that might be in the dockyard, and a cohort of legionaries on call."

"How about the fog?" Dav asked. "Asha says we've started seeing it on the river and the river banks in the early evening. Could that provide enough concealment?"

"No. It's still fairly light. We might run into a little fog in Palandur, but we can't count on it to be there at all, let alone to be heavy enough to hide us."

"And that's the only place we can get more fuel?" Mari asked.

"That's the only place."

chapter ten

There are two fuel oil tanks there for any Guild ship that needs filled up right away," Banda explained. "Located near the end of the Guild pier. Not huge tanks, but each would have more than enough fuel to top us off. It's not that far beyond Palandur to Marandur along the river, so that would leave us a lot of fuel for the trip back."

"But how do we get to the oil tanks?" Dav asked. "It sounds impossible."

"Are there any Mages helping to guard the area?" Alain asked.

All of the Mechanics looked at him with dawning hope. "Not that I ever saw," Banda said. "This isn't something that Mari, Dav, or I could manage. Do you think that you and Mage Asha could provide the edge we need?"

"What must we do?" Alain said.

Banda sketched a rough map in the air. "Sneak in past the Imperial guard towers at the entry, sneak past the picket boats, get past the alarms on the Mechanics Guild pier, either avoid or neutralize the Mechanic guards on the dock, tap into one of the fuel oil tanks, top off our tanks, then get back out without being spotted. Oh, I forgot to mention that the Mechanics Guild pier is brightly lit at night."

Mari's and Mechanic Dav's expressions had grown steadily more appalled as Banda listed once again all the security measures they would face.

Alain took his time answering, thinking through what must be done. "Any spells used by Mage Asha or myself would advertise our presence to the other Mages in Palandur, and there will be many."

"Even if we could use them, what spells could be used to conceal so large a thing?" Asha asked.

"I do not know," Alain said. "I do not know how we can prevent ourselves and you Mechanics and this ship from being noticed."

Dav nodded ruefully. "Especially in the case of Asha. She tends to draw a lot of attention."

Alain paused, an idea coming to him. "Perhaps that is the answer."

"Use Mage Asha to distract people?" Mari asked skeptically.

"Use Mage Asha and myself." Alain felt his plan forming. "Mages will go wherever they want to go. They do not acknowledge the rules of others, and the commons fear to stop them. Suppose that two Mages openly enter this place, ignoring the protests of the Imperial sentries who will not dare halt the Mages? Suppose those Mages go to such parts of the place where they will distract anyone from looking at where this ship and its Mechanics are?"

"Instead of hide our presence," Banda said, "we'd use you two Mages to make everyone aware *you* were there? And then slip past while their attention was on you? That just might work."

"Who tries to sneak into a place by making a ruckus?" Dav said. "It wouldn't be something that they'd expect. But even though it might work, wouldn't it place Asha and Alain in some serious danger?"

"Commons will not attack Mages," Asha said.

"There have been some attacks in the last few years," Mari said. "Random, crazy stuff that's a forewarning of the Storm."

"These will be Imperials under discipline," Alain said. "They will act as ordered."

"All right," Dav said. "Fine. But they'll be watching you and following you through the dockyard, right? How do you Mages break contact when it's time for us all to leave?"

"Mage Alain and I could leave by another way, along the land beside the river," Asha said. "Then rejoin you outside the area where the Imperials watch."

"They won't follow you on land?"

Alain saw Asha's amusement at the question. "No one follows a Mage, Dav. Not closely enough to be a problem for us. What if the Mage took offense? What if the Mage simply desired to play with a nearby human toy before discarding it?" Her inner humor faded. "I never did such things, but I know those who did. You are shadows, remember? Illusions on an illusion. That is what Mages are taught. Doing harm to you is of less importance to a Mage than swatting a fly would be to a common."

Dav stared at her, distraught. "But you don't believe that."

"For years I tried very hard to convince myself that I did believe it, Dav."

"So did I," Alain said. "Dav, you have become more at ease among Mages because of the changes that Mari has wrought, but Mages who have not accepted a different wisdom are dangerous to those around them. To the world beyond Mari's control, Mages are still objects of fear and loathing."

Mari looked away, unhappy. "I'm sorry. I hate hearing you say that."

"It is so."

"I know. That's why I hate hearing it, because once I would have looked on you and Asha that way." She gazed at the others. "Alain's plan to conceal by distraction seems like it might work, and it will pose a lot less danger than trying to hide from that much security by...is sneakiness a word?"

"How would we know?" Banda asked. "We're engineers, not scribes."

"You might have had to look it up once," Mari said. "Are you all right with this plan, Asha? Good. Unless someone else comes up with a better idea, let's run with this one. Captain Banda, if you remember enough about the layout of the dock area, you can plan out with the Mages where they should go to keep attention centered on them while we steal the fuel we need."

"What about their transport?" Dav asked. "Asha and Alain need a way to reach the shore before we sneak in after them."

"We will find other transport," Asha said. She gestured lightly toward the river banks outside. "Many boats will be available in Palandur."

"What are we going to do to the crew of the boat you pick?"

"We will do nothing. They will help us," Asha said.

"Yes," Alain agreed. "The crew will do what two Mages demand."

The night was distressingly clear, but dark nonetheless since the moon had set early. The boats and barges tied up at the landings bobbed gently in the current, for the most part silent or with only a single small light showing.

"That one should do for you," Captain Banda said as he brought the *Terror* close enough to a landing for Alain and Asha to step onto it. "That barge. You saw the Imperial docks when we cruised past them. Have that barge head down river, and we'll follow in your wake."

The crew of the small barge had settled for the night, but one of them poked his head up when Alain and Asha boarded with loud footsteps on the deck. Looking about with angry suspicion, the sailor's eyes fell on the two Mages and froze in fear. After a long moment, the sailor ducked below again. Alain heard him frantically waking the rest of the crew.

But no one else came up on deck. The sailors had apparently decided to hide below in hopes the Mages would leave. Alain walked to the low deck house and, drawing his long knife, slammed the hilt once against the wood planks.

The silence below was replaced by fearful, muttered conversation as the sailors debated who would go on deck.

Asha walked up beside Alain. "I grow impatient," she said, her voice something only a Mage could achieve, so lacking in feeling and human attributes that commons always referred to the sound as "dead."

A moment later, another sailor came on deck and bowed to Alain and Asha, visibly trembling. "Wh— Wh— What do you de- desire, h- h- honored Mages?"

Inwardly, Alain flinched at creating such terror in another person. Even before he met Mari he had not liked seeing people react to him like this. But he betrayed none of that, keeping his own face as dead as Asha's. Alain pointed down river. "Take us."

The sailor looked in the direction indicated, hesitated, then bolted back below. In a very short time, three men and two women came on deck. Alain and Asha ignored them, acting as if they were alone in the world, as the sailors cautiously moved about to release lines and begin poling the barge down river.

Mages did such things, commandeering transport when they wanted to, and commons did what they were told for fear of what the Mages might do if they were disobeyed. Everyone knew that. Too many commons had experienced it, or knew someone who had, or had simply heard horror stories about what could happen.

The entry to the Imperial dock area appeared ahead, illuminated by lanterns burning on the small guard towers on either side.

Alain pointed again, clearly indicating that entry.

The fear emanating from the barge crew grew in intensity. Four of them looked to the fifth, who must be in charge, but he just shook his head helplessly and gestured for them to do as Alain directed.

Alain and Asha walked to the bow, standing silently as the barge veered and slowly headed for the entry.

Somewhere behind them the *Terror* should be creeping in the barge's wake, but Alain could not turn to look without possibly causing someone else to do the same.

A legionary appeared at the top of one of the towers, waving off the barge. "You're not allowed here!"

The trembling sailors looked at Alain, who pointed into the entry again.

"You got dirt in your ears? No entry! Veer off!" The legionary emphasized his commands with another strong wave-off. Other legionaries appeared on the towers, drawn from their watch duties by the unusual activity.

The sailors, their heads averted from not only the Mages but also from the sentries, as if that would render them invisible, stole glances at Alain and Asha and kept poling.

The sound of a small ballista being loaded came clearly across the short distance remaining to the guard towers. The legionary leaned down and yelled. "The only reason you're not already dead is because I don't want to have to fill out the blasted paperwork after we kill you! This is your last…"

The legionary had finally spotted the two Mages on the bow of the barge as it grew closer to the lights on the guard towers. Alain and Asha raised one arm each to point between the guard towers to the dockyard beyond.

"Sir," one of the sailors said to the legionary, pleading in a voice hoarse with fear, "we don't have any choice. Please!"

The legionaries on sentry were rushing out of the guard towers to stare at Alain and Asha, arguing among themselves as the barge began to enter the dockyard. One who seemed to be in charge yelled over the debate. "Get the commander! Wake the supervisor! On the double!"

Two legionaries took off at a run.

"What do we do?" another legionary demanded of their leader.

"Uh…follow them! Keep them in sight! Alert the boat patrols! Move it! No! Not all of you! We can't leave the entrance unguarded, you mindless clods! Odd numbers follow that barge. Even numbers stay in the towers!"

Alain pointed again, slightly to the right. As the barge shifted course, he also moved a little to give himself a sidelong view of the guard towers that were now behind the barge. Even though half of the legionaries had remained to guard the entrance, everyone in the towers was staring at the barge rather than watching the entry. The other legionaries were running down the quay forming the outer wall of the dockyard, keeping pace with the barge but trying to stay slightly back so they weren't in the direct line of sight of either Mage.

He could not see the *Terror*. He could only hope that the ship was taking advantage of the diversion.

The barge moved slowly under the push of the crew's poling, giving plenty of time for the Imperials to react to the slow-motion intrusion. Alain pointed again, toward the Mechanics pier but not directly at it, keeping everyone else guessing as to where the Mages intended to go.

Two boats driven by oars and carrying extra guards were rowing up, taking position on either side of the barge. The barge passed an Imperial war galley tied up to the quay, the crew coming up on deck and lining the rail to stare at the spectacle. More legionaries could be seen streaming toward the area of the dockyard closest to the barge. From their numbers, Alain estimated that the rest of the on-call cohort had been called out. Leading them was a woman still buckling on armor and her sword, but already wearing a helmet with the plume of a cohort commander waving above it.

A smaller group was running toward the scene from another part of the dockyard. From their dress, most of them seemed to be workers. However, the man leading that group wore the suit of an Imperial official of moderately high rank.

Alain pointed once more, directly at the Mechanic pier, which as Banda had said was impossible to mistake. The pier was large, extending out a substantial distance and wider than the main thoroughfares in Imperial cities. A fence and gate blocked access to the pier from shore, but the sides and end were open. Mechanic lights, what Mari called eel-ectric, shone brightly over the pier. Alain could see the squat, round shapes that he had been told would be the fuel tanks located near the end of the pier where Banda had said they would be. The barge was coming in on the opposite side of the pier from the tanks, and a little ways closer to shore. In addition to the fuel tanks, a few small buildings were scattered along the far side of the pier, and near the fence a guard house.

A woman, unmistakable in her Mechanics jacket, was standing on the pier and staring at the circuses headed her way by land and sea. A male Mechanic was hastening to join her.

The Mechanics began yelling at the Imperials, making wave-off motions, but the legionaries in the boats looked at Asha and Alain and pretended not to notice the Mechanics. Alain had expected that. When the Great Guilds came into conflict, commons always tried to get out of the way rather than get involved.

The barge came alongside the pier, bumping against it as Alain grabbed a ladder and climbed.

Alain went up the short distance to the pier first, Asha following. The two Mechanics, both holding the sort of rifles that Mari called lever action repeaters, were facing Alain as he came up. The woman was younger, perhaps just recently having been promoted from Apprentice. Both Mechanics were trying to project toughness and authority, but Alain could easily read the uncertainty in them. Before he left the *Terror*, Mari had once again told him how Mechanics thought. "They're used to being treated to their faces as the biggest dogs on the block. They're used to deference and respect and a bit of worry about what a Mechanic might decide to do. If you don't react like that, if you do the Mage thing of not even admitting they are there, they won't know how to handle it. And if they don't know how to handle it, they'll first try to bluff you, and then when that doesn't work they'll call for instructions from the Senior Mechanics."

Reassured that his old Mage training and guidance from Mage elders on how to ignore and annoy Mechanics was in this case still the best course of action, Alain pretended that the two Mechanics were not even present, let alone speaking.

"You! Hey! You don't belong here," the female Mechanic said. "You— what?" She turned to look at the guard house as a bell began ringing continuously.

The male Mechanic scowled. "They set off the alarms coming up that ladder! Go shut the alarms off. You…Mages…is there a message?"

Alain and Asha ignored the question.

"If there isn't a message," the Mechanic said, "then get back on that barge."

The woman ran to shut off the alarm system, which as planned would allow Mari, Dav, and Banda to reach the fuel tanks on the other side of the pier without alerting anyone. Alain eyed the male Mechanic with total disinterest, then looked down the pier away from the fuel tanks. Asha stood beside him. They exchanged a look. She nodded once to him as if they had also soundlessly exchanged words. Mages were not supposed to play games, weren't supposed to enjoy them, but every acolyte heard of ways to frighten and confuse shadows by pretending to powers that even Mages did not have.

The bell had ceased ringing. Asha was facing Alain, able to see the fuel tanks beyond him. She caught his eye and this time did pass on a wordless message. Something was happening near the tanks.

She turned and began walking slowly toward the shore end of the pier. Alain walked with her as the male Mechanic followed in angry impotence, soon rejoined by the woman Mechanic. "What do we do?" she whispered. "Stars above, they're disgusting."

"If they keep going, we just walk them off the pier," the other Mechanic replied. "If they don't... I don't know. I'm going to call—" His voice lowered dramatically as he realized he had been about to spill a Guild secret within earshot of Mages. "I'll let the Guild Hall know. You stay with them."

"Me?" The female Mechanic sounded very unhappy at the prospect. "What are they doing here? What if they do something else?"

"Just watch! Maybe this is what Mages do on dates." The male Mechanic laughed scornfully as he sprinted ahead to the guard house.

Alain turned a dead look on the female Mechanic, who backed a step, raising her rifle.

"Don't get any ideas, Mage!"

The revulsion on her face took any fun out of the performance for Alain. But his movement had let him surreptitiously scan his surroundings while still appearing uncaring. He thought he had caught a glimpse of some sort of large tube running over the far side of the pier to the fuel tanks. The barge he and Asha had arrived on was being ushered away by one of the Imperial guard boats, the sailors on the barge working their poles with the enthusiasm of people who believed they had just escaped a dire fate.

He was trying to figure out how to draw out the encounter so that the others would have enough time to get the fuel they needed. Banda had spoken of a certain number of minutes required, but Alain still had only a vague idea of what "minute" actually meant.

The male Mechanic had reached the guard house and was standing partly concealed by the door. From his posture, Alain could tell that he was using a far-talker but ensuring that neither Mages nor Imperials could see it. The female Mechanic had her eyes fixed on Alain. The Imperials were watching on boats and land from varying distances, this part of the dockyard now lit by dozens of lanterns and torches as well as the bright, unwavering lights of the Mechanics.

But how could he maintain their focus on him without being obvious? He and Asha had to keep moving or people would begin to look away. But if they left the pier too quickly the Mechanics and the Imperial harbor boats might go back to watching for other intruders.

Alain looked over at Asha, a question in his eyes. She judged the distance to the end of the pier, nodding in understanding.

Asha stopped, forcing Alain to stop as well. She turned to face him, her expressionless demeanor giving no clue to her intention. Before Alain realized what Asha was doing, she had pulled him close and brought her face to his, their faces only partly concealed by the cowls of their robes.

If it had just been a common man and woman, the watchers would have probably looked away. But these were Mages. Alain kept his eyes open, catching glimpses of Imperials watching them with revolted fascination. Very likely none of them had ever seen Mages do such a thing, and very likely none of them had ever wanted to see it, but now they could not look away.

Even though Asha was not actively kissing him, just pressing her lips against his and moving her head slightly as if doing more, Alain found himself torn between a small measure of enjoyment and a large amount of guilt.

Asha finally drew back, still revealing no trace of feeling. Alain maintained the same cold lack of expression as she did, imagining that the watchers would be further appalled by the inhuman nature of the Mages' physical relations. And unable to resist keeping their eyes on the Mages in case some other disgusting thing happened.

They began walking slowly toward the shore end of the pier again. Both Mechanics were close once more. "What did they say?" the female Mechanic hissed to her companion.

"Just keep watching them. There's a Senior Mechanic and reinforcements on the way," the male Mechanic muttered in reply.

Had it been long enough yet? Had the *Terror* been able to get the fuel it needed? Alain and Asha reached the barrier at the end of the pier, standing impassively before it. The male Mechanic edged forward and flipped the gate open, then stepped back.

After a long pause to keep everyone watching for whatever the Mages would do, Alain began walking again. He and Asha went through the gate without showing any awareness of the male Mechanic standing beside it, who once again betrayed frustrated anger at the Mages.

The gate slammed shut behind them. Alain heard the lock clicking and almost betrayed himself with a smile over how the Mechanics thought such a thing could keep Mages out. He was tempted for a moment to demonstrate how easily he and Asha could get back on the pier. But a spell to regain access to the dock would be sensed by other Mages, and some of them might recognize Alain or Asha as the one who had cast the spell.

However, Alain did pause, turning slightly as if deciding whether to go back, knowing that this would keep the Mechanics' attention centered on him. The legionaries had formed up nearby, almost like an honor guard, the shipyard official and the cohort commander together in front, both watching the Mages. After waiting as long as he dared, Alain started walking again, Asha alongside.

As they passed the legionaries, giving no sign of admitting to the presence of the Imperial soldiers, the official and the cohort commander cautiously fell in behind the Mages.

Alain, apparently disregarding everything around him, concentrated on hearing the hushed conversation between the cohort's commander and the dockyard supervisor. "I can't do anything else. Didn't you get the orders?" the commander asked as if continuing a discussion. "No incidents with Mages. No provocations, no challenges, no confrontations."

"It's not like anyone starts any of that with Mages anyway if they can help it," the supervisor grumbled. "What's going on?"

"Word is, the Emperor is trying to make some sort of deal with the Mage Guild and doesn't want anything happening that might cause trouble with getting things settled. Most people think it has something to do with that daughter business out west."

"Huh," the supervisor commented. "If she's who rumor says she is, even the Emperor could use the Mages' help in taking her down."

"I wish they'd let me at her! I'd get together a special strike force of the best female legionaries, and while you men were falling at her feet we'd take her head off. Let her try to cast spells after that."

"But what are these Mages doing? Does it have anything to do with the Emperor's negotiations?"

"Who knows? Do you want to be the one to ask them?"

Alain glanced at Asha, who was maintaining a perfect Mage attitude. A legionary looking their way caught Asha's eye and nearly fainted from the force of her indifference and cold dismissal of his very existence.

Alain and Asha walked along the dockyard's waterfront as long as they could, keeping the security forces in boats as well as those on land occupied in watching them. Surely by now the *Terror* would have gotten far from the pier and headed out through the entry?

"I sense other Mages," Asha murmured. "They approach."

"Then we must leave." The Mages might be coming this way by chance, or they might have been sent by the Mage Guild elders in Palandur who had heard of Mages acting oddly in the dockyards. Alain and Asha turned, walking toward one of the large gates controlling access to the dockyard. They were in the right area to depart, upstream of the entry.

The gate they walked toward was closed, but the cohort commander still following them gestured commands and the sentries opened one side before stepping away and clearing a path. Alain and Asha, still acting totally unaware of the existence of anyone else, walked out onto the broad street running alongside the wall protecting the military dockyards.

Far down the street behind them, Alain could hear the rapid clop of hoof beats that spoke of a carriage pulled by more than one horse moving fast. That was probably the Senior Mechanic and other reinforcements. He could also sense the Mages that Asha had detected earlier, their presence drawing closer at what felt like a walking pace. Well past midnight and still not close to dawn, there was very little other traffic on the street, and those commons out right now were making every effort not to approach Alain and Asha.

Alain and Asha walked at a faster pace along the street, a small detachment of legionaries still following at a distance. The Imperial soldiers displayed little enthusiasm for their assignment, but in keeping with the reputation of the legions they kept diligently following the two Mages as they had been ordered.

"There." Asha had spotted the darker bulk of the trees where Captain Banda had said to watch for them. It was a park running down to the water, where small landings offered moorage for pleasure boats and water taxis as well as footing for those fishing in the river.

They veered into the park, moving silently into the deeper darkness among the trees, secure in the knowledge that Imperial gardeners would not leave any obstacles marring a lawn. Alain could hear the sounds of the legionaries behind them, proceeding more cautiously to avoid running into the Mages by accident.

Banda had told them to look for a small landing at the far side of the park. Alain could see it now, overshadowed by trees whose branches grew down toward the water. He paused to look out at the river and almost immediately saw a large pile of driftwood not far from the landing, and not drifting with the current but holding position.

He and Asha looked back to ensure no legionaries were close

enough to see them, then waved. Captain Banda appeared out of the forward hatch, spinning a line that he tossed their way.

Asha caught it, passing the end to Alain while hanging onto it as well. Both Mages stepped into the water as quietly as possible while Captain Banda and Mechanic Dav, hard to see in their dark jackets, hauled the line in. Alain saw that the *Terror* was moving, drawing away from the landing and bringing them with it. The gentle roaring of the boiler creature could barely be heard over the sound of the river.

Alain felt his robes soaking up water, gaining weight, the chill of the water eating into him. Only the rapid pull of the line kept him and Asha afloat.

"Do you see them?" a legionary cautiously called in the park behind them.

"No, they're not here, either. It's like they disappeared."

"They're Mages."

"Yeah. I guess they did disappear."

"We did our job. Let's get back."

Asha had reached the *Terror* and was being helped up by Dav. Alain arrived a moment later, pulling himself up against the weight of his water-soaked robes and grateful when Dav was able to assist him as well.

Banda dropped back into the driving seat. Alain felt the *Terror* surge ahead, fighting the current to push farther up the Ospren toward Marandur.

Dav helped Asha to the aft ladder, then Alain, before following and sealing the aft hatch. "We should have thought about what to do with the robes," he said as Asha and Alain stood in the midst of puddles that drained down through the deck plates into the bilges.

"I have a shirt and trouser to wear until the robes dry," Alain said.

"I have nothing," Asha said.

Dav grinned. "Maybe I can loan you a shirt. Excuse us, Alain."

He watched the two go forward past the curtain, realizing that his shirt and trousers were in the same place they were going. He had a feeling that Asha and Dav would want some private time. Resigning himself to a long, wet night, Alain went back to the boiler place to speak to Mari.

She was sitting in the control seat watching the dials, but switched most of her attention to him. "Good job, my Mage. At the entrance to the dock area I saw a guy look at the *Terror*, but then he got distracted by you two and didn't give us a second glance. Everybody else watched you and Asha while we got a hose on the fuel tank and filled up."

"You got what we needed?" Alain asked, grateful that the heat from the boiler creature was drying his robes.

"As much as we could," Mari said. "When we were about to leave, Banda got the idea of leaving the valve on the tank open far enough to drip, so if anyone sees any fuel we spilled and measures the tank, they'll think there was a long-term slow leak that the security watches failed to notice. What about you?"

"We heard the Imperials talking about orders not to have any confrontations with Mages. They believe the Emperor is trying to negotiate a deal with the Mage Guild, and they think it involves you."

Mari nodded sourly. "That's to be expected. I wish I knew the details of whatever the Emperor was trying to arrange, but gossiping Imperials aren't likely to know that."

"There were more Mechanics coming, and Asha and I also felt Mages approaching, but we left before either arrived. I do not think the other Mages sensed our presence."

"Great," Mari said. "Is that it? Did anything unexpected happen?"

"No."

"No?" Mari gave him an inquisitive look. "How was it?"

"How was what?" Alain asked, feeling a surge of irrational guilt.

"You and Asha, locking lips for looooong time."

Alain felt a momentary sense of panic. "You saw that?"

"We couldn't miss it, Alain. There was all this noise, and then it suddenly got almost quiet, so we looked, and there you and Asha were, engaging in a deeply meaningful game of tongue-wrestling."

"It was not actually a kiss," Alain protested.

"No?" Mari asked. "Your lips didn't make contact?"

"Yes. They did. But it was not a kiss. There was no sense of it being a kiss." He felt terrible, and wondered how angry Mari might get, but instead she laughed.

"I believe you," Mari said. "First, because I trust you, and second, because I know you're too smart to cheat on me where I can see you, and third, because I also trust Asha. Oh, and fourth, because if it had been a hot and heavy kiss, you wouldn't have sounded a little bit disappointed when telling me it wasn't a kiss."

"I did not sound disappointed," Alain said.

"Yes, you did. You finally got to kiss Asha, and it was no big deal. That's good, Alain." She laughed again. "I admit I'm very relieved we got away with stealing fuel out from under the noses of the Mechanics Guild and the Empire, but even if I wasn't I wouldn't be angry with you."

Something else had just occurred to Alain. "Mechanic Dav also saw it."

"Yes, he did."

"I should—"

"Not even mention it. If he holds it against Asha, he doesn't deserve her. But I have good reason to think he thought it was funny that two Mages were freaking out everyone by kissing each other." Mari rose up enough to kiss him. "There. That's better, right?"

"Much better," Alain said. "I would like to stay so my robes would dry more, but I must go stand my watch with Captain Banda."

"Yeah. It'll be a while before we clear Palandur, and it won't be long now before we get close to Marandur." Her humor fled, Mari waved him away. "Keep us safe, my Mage."

After the adventure in Palandur, Alain expected the rest of his watch to be boring. But instead he was kept alert by sensing the frequent presence of Mages along the river. Alain concentrated on keeping his own presence concealed from them as the lights of Palandur fell behind and gave way to open country outside the city walls. It was not until the *Terror* had left the city well behind that the sense of other Mages searching finally faded.

"We have to stop soon," Banda told Alain. "We spent a lot of time getting the fuel. There are not enough hours of darkness left to get to Marandur tonight, so we'll lay up when I find a good spot and get to the Forbidden City tomorrow."

"I see few boats along the river." Alain said.

"That's all you will see, boats going to and from a few small towns upriver, and most of that traffic can make the journey in a day so they don't tie up along here. We'll be past those soon, and then we'll have the river to ourselves except for barges resupplying the legionaries that enforce the quarantine of Marandur."

By the time Asha came to take over the watch, Banda was bringing the *Terror* to shelter under an overhanging bank of the river.

Only a single boat came down the river the next day as Alain watched while Asha and most of the Mechanics slept. The barge had legionaries sprawled on the deck, relaxing and enjoying the ride. Alain guessed that they were either leaving duty around Marandur or getting a brief break from the isolated assignment.

He watched the legionaries talking and joking. Their uniforms and armor were different, but otherwise they looked much like other soldiers Alain had seen. Change the uniforms and they would have fit in among those who followed Mari.

But that, he knew, was partly illusion. These legionaries shared some things with the soldiers who fought for Mari. But in other ways, they were very different. Just as he and Asha had looked like typical Mages to the Imperials at Palandur, but inside were not the same at all.

The right thing. Mari had taught him that, or perhaps only reminded Alain of things his parents had tried to teach him when he was very young. The legionaries fought for their Emperor, doing what they were told. It did not matter whether the Emperor told them to do right or wrong, because whatever the Emperor said was right. Just as the elders of the Mage Guild insisted on total obedience, and just as Mari said the Senior Mechanics who ran the Mechanics Guild did as well. That was the difference. Mari's soldiers had decided for themselves what to fight for, and Mari did not want to force others to obey her own desires. She wanted to give them the choices, the freedom, that the elders and Senior Mechanics and common rulers of Dematr like the Emperor had kept to themselves.

Alain looked at the relaxed, happy legionaries and understood Mari's distress at the thought of war. These men and women would face death along with her own soldiers. But he could not think of any alternative that would save this world, not as long as some were willing to fight to enslave others. Little wonder that Mari saw the responsibilities of the daughter as a burden, not a blessing.

That night, Captain Banda waited until well after sunset before starting out. "The closer we get to Marandur, the more we'll be the only thing moving on the river, and the more sentries on the shore will be watching for anything unusual. We need the night's protection. But we can't approach the limits of Marandur too early. It has to be close to sunrise, because the river within the city has not been cleared or dredged since the siege that destroyed Marandur. We have to be able to look for obstacles ahead."

The increased tension as the *Terror* steamed up the last stretch of river contrasted oddly with their seemingly peaceful surroundings. There were few signs of human presence on the river banks, and no boats or barges to be seen.

The evening fog had come on fairly dense when the *Terror* started out. Banda kept quiet, concentrating on steering the ship.

The mist slowly dissolved as they traveled, until Alain could see ahead and behind a short distance as well as both river banks at once.

"See that?" Banda suddenly asked, keeping his voice low even though the hatch was closed.

Alain spotted something on the river bank that from this distance resembled a huge, dark snake coming out of the water and extending up the river bank before vanishing into the mist. "What is it?"

"The chain. That's a very heavy chain that can be raised to block the river. It was built when Marandur was the capital, to keep an enemy from sailing up the river and attacking the city. You can't see it, but there's a building a little farther up that bank of the river that contains a winch maintained by the Mechanics Guild. In an emergency, a lot of Imperials would put their backs to the poles on that winch and raise the chain."

"The city is a complete ruin," Alain said. "Why is the chain still here?"

"Because it's well outside the walls of the city," Banda said, sounding amused. "Which means it wasn't affected by the Emperor's ban, which means no one ever told the Imperial offices responsible for maintaining that chain that they should stop. So they didn't. Just like the Imperial work crews that keep the river dredged even though the only boats that come up this far are resupply runs for the Imperial troops maintaining the quarantine of the city." He pointed to the other bank of the river. "Over there the chain also comes out of the water a ways, but there isn't any building or winch on that side. The chain is just anchored securely enough to hold it against just about any imaginable load."

"That chain could stop this ship?"

"It could," Banda said. "Especially with so much of this ship under the surface. I can't imagine why the Imperials would raise the chain without good cause, but that's one more reason to be very careful we aren't spotted going into the city. If they knew we had gone in, they would raise the chain to prevent us from getting out again." He peered forward. "I've never been this far. The Mechanics Guild ships I brought up always stopped short of the chain. Did you and Mari see anything of the defenses along the river when you were here?"

"No," Alain said. "We entered on the north side of the city, crossed the river near the center, and then left from the south side. We never saw the city where the river entered or left." He paused to remember the frightening river crossing he and Mari had made on an improvised raft with barbarians in pursuit. "I do not clearly recall if I looked down to where the river left the city, but I have no memory of seeing anything standing in the river but the remnants of the bridges."

Banda nodded. "Even the Empire might have trouble building a guard tower in the middle of the Ospren. Let's hope they only watch the river from each side."

When they had approached Landfall and Palandur, or even just towns along the river, Alain had seen the glow of lights as the ship drew closer to civilization. But the only light he saw as the *Terror* drew closer to Marandur came from the Imperial watch towers spaced around the city and the fires between them. Directly ahead, all was dark.

Alain sensed another Mage. It felt as if he or she was asleep, and not close to the river.

"Here we go," Banda muttered as the *Terror* drew closer to the towers built on either bank of the Ospren. Strong lanterns cast light across the river, leaving no area of complete darkness between them. "We'll have to creep along so it isn't obvious we're moving against the current." As the *Terror* slid little by little between the watch towers, Alain looked to either side, watching for signs of alarm from the sentries whose shapes were silhouetted against the night sky by the lanterns on the towers. But his first warning of trouble came when the light on one side of the *Terror* brightened.

Alain shaded his eyes against the light coming in through the small windows, vaguely making out two legionaries who had swiveled a mirror to focus the light of a powerful lantern on the *Terror*. The light played slowly over the driftwood camouflage, searching for anything that looked wrong.

"If anything on this ship reflects the light of that search lantern, we'll be spotted," Banda whispered. He eased off the throttle to let the *Terror* appear to move with the current.

Alain tried to see past the light to the legionaries. One of his hands went down to grip the hilt of his long knife. It would not be of much use if the alarm was sounded, but it was the best weapon he had.

The legionaries were talking. One of them pointed, and the light swung back slowly over the *Terror*.

chapter eleven

What are they doing?" Banda murmured, as if the legionaries could have been able to hear him.

"I cannot tell," Alain said, squinting against the light of the lantern.

The *Terror* began drifting backward with the current. The light illuminated different parts of the ship as the *Terror* moved.

A loud *thwak* broke the silence as a crossbow bolt struck the top of some of the driftwood disguising the Terror and ricocheted off.

"That's it," Banda growled. "They saw something. Get ready—"

"Wait," Alain said. Despite the shock of hearing the bolt hit, he held himself from jumping into action. Why?

Because something was missing. As Alain listened, he realized what it was. "There have been no other shots."

Banda frowned at Alain. "No. Just the one. If we were being attacked there should have been a dozen more bolts hitting us right after that one."

"Why would the Imperials only fire once?" Alain asked.

"Maybe trying to provoke a response? Maybe…" Banda shifted as much as he could to look toward the river bank.

Alain did as well. He could just see the shapes of two legionaries on one of the watch towers. One, with a larger helmet crest, was leaning in toward the second. Neither of them faced the river. "What are they doing?" Alain asked, mystified.

Banda began laughing very softly. "Oh, I know what they're doing. I've seen those exchanges before! That one legionary decided to enliven a dull night by taking a shot at some passing driftwood, and judging from the helmet crest on the other, his centurion is letting him know in very clear terms that it was a bad idea."

The concentrated light had left the *Terror* as the ship slowly drifted and was now focused on an empty part of the river. "Can you see the legionaries on the opposite watch tower?" Banda asked.

"Yes. Though not well. They are...looking across at the tower on the other side."

"Watching their friend get chewed out by the centurion," Banda said. "A bored sentry distracted his own comrades. We got lucky." He cautiously advanced the throttle again, steering away from the direct focus of the light as the ship moved forward once more. Alain kept an eye on the towers, but the centurion was apparently long-winded, inadvertently keeping the attention of the nearby sentries fixed on him while he berated the legionary for failing to keep a good watch. No one gave any sign that they were still paying attention to the driftwood, or had noticed that it had begun drifting the wrong way, toward Marandur.

The sky was beginning to pale in the east by the time the *Terror* got far enough upriver to reach the walls of the city and pass between the remains of the two fortified towers that had once guarded the river entry. Nothing except their location identified the piles of decaying rubble as once having been part of the city's formidable defenses.

"How are we doing?" Mari asked.

Alain looked down to see her standing at the foot of the ladder. "We have just entered the city."

"Can you still see the watch towers outside the city?"

He looked back, seeing that the towers on either river bank were still visible. "Yes."

"Let me know when the towers are hidden behind the city walls. I'll go out on deck then and help spot obstacles in the water."

"Good idea," Banda said, his voice tight with tension. "I'd feel stupid if after making it this far we ran hard aground in Marandur or punched a hole in the hull by running into a wreck."

By the time the watch towers outside the city were out of sight, Asha had appeared at the ladder to take over the watch. Alain went down, then aft where Mari waited impatiently. "It is safe to go up now."

She raced up the ladder, popped the hatch, and went out on deck. Alain followed, climbing over the driftwood to make his way forward on top of the *Terror* as well. Mari paused to open the forward hatch so Banda could easily hear them, then settled to watch the water ahead.

As he made his way past the steering room, Alain realized that he had forgotten how the city smelled, like a vast mausoleum, dust and old death mingled. His gaze traveled along the north side of the river, and Alain stared as he recognized the stub of a quay protruding into the water. "It is the dockyard."

"What?" Mari looked that way and inhaled sharply. "Stars above. It is."

If Alain had held any doubts that Palandur had been copied from Marandur, that sight dispelled them. A short time ago, he and Asha had traversed the living image of the crumbling, dead dockyard Alain now saw in Marandur. Even for a Mage it was emotionally jarring.

He looked away, but not before catching sight of the decayed ruins of other structures he recognized from seeing their intact counterparts less than two days before. Those recent memories populated the ancient wreckage like modern ghosts against the remnants of the past. Alain remembered when he and Mari had first come to Marandur and how Mari had reacted when seeing places she had recognized from Palandur. He had not understood until now how hard that must have been for her.

In the growing light, the *Terror* moved cautiously up the river, threading a path between sunken boats and ships that might or might not retain the stumps of masts protruding above the surface. Alain could see the hull of the *Terror* underwater until it curved down and out of sight at the bow. Beyond that, he could not tell how deep he could see. "The water is not clear," he said to Mari.

"River water," Mari replied. "Sediment, plant life, fish, bugs, and I don't know what else. Do the best you can. Maybe your foresight will kick in." She gazed ahead. "We shouldn't have to go past the first big bridge!" Mari called to Banda.

"Good!" Banda called back, not trying to hide his relief at the news. Even from a short distance it was easy to see how the tumbled wreckage from the bridge and its supporting piers had laced the river with obstacles. "I wish the Imperials had cleared that before they sealed the city!"

"If it hadn't been for that junk, Alain and I never would have made it across the river last time!"

Alain spotted something between the ruins of taller buildings on the south side of the river. "That tower is part of the university."

"You see it?" Mari craned to look. "You're right. We're probably as close as we can get to it on the river. Captain, see those landings up ahead? Pick one."

"Should I try to come alongside one of them? There might be enough depth."

"No!" Mari warned. "You can't tie up. If the barbarians can get to you, they'll attack. You're going to have to stay anchored a little offshore."

"I think I see a good spot," Banda said. He steered the *Terror* that way, easing the ship into place. "Let's drop anchor here."

Mari darted back inside to release the anchor. Alain stayed on deck, watching the ruins. He heard the clank of the anchor's release, followed by the low rumble of the chain running out.

Banda let off the throttle to allow the current to push the *Terror* backwards, until the anchor reached its limit and jerked the ship to a halt.

"Are you sure this is a safe spot?" Mari asked, coming back on deck and looking over the side. "That's a pretty strong current running through here."

"You were the one who warned about the barbarians," Banda said, climbing up onto deck himself and stretching. "Anyone who tries swimming out to this ship will find themselves getting swept downstream. But the same current will help carry our boat down to that landing." He pointed. "It seems relatively intact compared to the rest of Marandur."

"We have a boat?" Alain asked.

"A hidden boat," Captain Banda said. He leaned into the hatch. "Hey, Dav. Put the boiler into standby status so you can come up here and do some work!"

Dav appeared in a short time, accompanied by Asha. He looked around, a smile of anticipation fading into dismay as he took in the ruined city. "I didn't think it would be this bad."

Captain Banda handed Mari his shoes, then pulled off his shirt and pants. "I need to get into the water to release the boat. Help me out, Dav."

"I could have helped," Mari said.

"You don't know the setup," Banda explained. "Dav and I had the chance to go over it a few times and practice. Here, Dav. We've got a decent current going past, so tie yourself off with this line. I'm sure Lady Asha would be happy to hold onto the other end to keep you from being swept away to your death."

Alain, feeling useless, was grateful when Banda handed him the other end of his own safety line. "Just hang on and pull us in if there's trouble. Mari, get yourself down low enough to see what we're doing."

Banda and Dav jumped into the water, both gasping from the shock of the cold. Alain almost immediately felt the line he held grow taut as the current tried to take Banda downriver. The two Mechanics worked their way to a point on the starboard side, each reaching under the water with his free hand as he clung to the ship with the other. "See, Mari? The boat is fastened on bottom out, its own bow in the same direction as the *Terror*'s. Here's what holds it. Loosen these… flip this up…and the boat comes free."

Mari, lying on the driftwood to look out into the water, nodded. "That is cool. Who designed it?"

"Master Mechanic Lukas," said Dav, helping Banda slide the boat upward and drain it of water so the small craft could flop bottom-first back into the water and float. "It took him longer to tell us the story of where he was, and how he learned this and that, and why Mechanics have to think about finesse, than it did for him to design the thing."

"It takes two people?"

"One can do it in a pinch now that we've loosened the fittings," Banda said as he climbed up enough to sit in the small boat, remove the line from his waist and tie it to the boat. He and Dav came back aboard the *Terror*, shaking off water.

While Dav and Banda dried off, Mari went into the ship again, surfacing with two Mechanic weapons and four backpacks. "A couple of Alli's finest A-1's, fresh out of the workshop. That leaves two onboard for the captain. Alain and Asha, you've got your knives? Good. We'll each carry a pack stuffed with sacks to hold the texts once we get to them. As soon as Dav gets dressed again we'll row ashore." She looked up at the sun. "There should be plenty enough time left to reach the university before nightfall. We should have done this the first time, Alain."

Alain looked at her. "We did not have this ship. We did not know Captain Banda. We—"

"I know. I meant it would have been nice if we could have done this the first time." She gave Banda a worried look. "We're going to have to spend at least one night at the university, leaving you alone out here. Make sure you keep the hatches closed except for short periods, especially at night. Alain and I didn't see the barbarians using boats or swimming, but if they figure out you're here they might do whatever it takes to try to reach you, even if it seems suicidal to us."

Banda nodded, looking at the shore. "They're that impossible to reason with?"

"We didn't have any success." Mari grimaced. "They lives they've led…they can't imagine anything better, and death probably doesn't seem all that bad."

"Death would be preferable to being captured by them," Alain said, remembering the way the barbarians had looked at Mari.

"Yeah," Mari agreed sadly. "They're...lost souls."

"And they are condemned to those lives because their ancestors failed to make it out of Marandur before the Emperor's ban took effect?" Banda asked.

"Yes," Mari said. "Some of those ancestors undoubtedly stayed because they were rebel survivors hiding in the ruins, but a lot of others were probably just people who didn't want to leave what was left of their homes."

Banda nodded once. "That's Imperial justice for you. For all the rules and the laws, it comes down to whatever the Emperor and the aristocracy dictate. Mari, I know you aren't going to try to overthrow the Empire, but do you think there's any chance that the changes you bring about could help the poor devils in what was once Marandur?"

"I hope so. I've already promised to do what I can for the inhabitants of the university, who managed to retain civilization, but maybe I can find a way to help the others as well."

Dav finished getting his clothes on, took one of the rifles from Mari, and helped Asha into the boat. Alain eyed it warily. The boat was small and made entirely of metal.

"Hold on," Banda said. "Let me test." He brought out another line, coiled most of it, spun the end about quickly, then let it fly. The end of the line flew in a high arc, finally thumping down on the landing before Banda pulled it back to him. "I wanted to be sure I could reach it with a cast."

"How do you throw a rope like that?" Mari asked as she and Alain helped each other into the boat.

"It's this weight," Banda said, holding up a ball-sized knot on the end of the rope. "It's called a Mankey fist."

"Like a Mankey wrench?" Mari said. "What does that weight have to do with a wrench? Why would they have the same name?"

"You see?" Dav said. "She does ask the same sort of questions that Asha does."

"And gets the same sort of answer," Banda said. "I have no idea what a Mankey is, or why this and a big wrench are named for him, her, or it."

Alain, sitting cautiously next to Asha, touched the metal side of the boat. "This is very thin," he said.

Mari nodded as if every boat was built that way. "See those tubes running along the top and the sides? Those reinforce the thin metal so the boat holds its shape."

"It does not seem safe," Alain said, since Mari did not seem to get the hint that he was worried.

She stared at him. "I spent three days— No, *four* days high in the air on an imaginary bird, and you're worried about this boat?"

"Yes. What do the Rocs have to do with it?" Alain asked, realizing that some tension might have entered his voice. His memories of his last raft trip on this river were all too vivid, with the crumbling wood breaking up beneath them as Mari walked them across the submerged wreckage of a bridge despite nearly succumbing to the cold.

Mari paused, then leaned close. "I'm sorry," she whispered. Sitting back again, she rapped the side of the boat. "This is safe, Alain. It's not heavy duty, but it can carry us ashore and back again."

Alain nodded. "It is just—"

"You don't have to explain. I just flashed on the same memories you probably did. I'm amazed you got in the boat without protesting. You good?"

"I am good," Alain said.

Dav and Mari shoved off from the *Terror*. Each began rowing toward the landing as the current helped carry the boat that way. But the boat nearly overshot and Alain had to make a long reach and grab a stone standing up from the side of the landing.

Alain had wondered why the Mechanics had kept the line tied to the boat, but now he understood. Captain Banda hauled the boat back to the *Terror* and tied it securely to the driftwood. Banda waved farewell, as did Dav and Mari, then the small party faced inland. The

sun had reached its highest, shining down through a clear sky to minimize shadows and show every detail of the ruined city.

The ancient landing was mostly intact, but littered with debris.
Looking ahead at the tortured ruins of Marandur and remembering
his and Mari's last trip through the city, Alain knew that crossing the
landing would be easiest part of their walk.

Dav checked his weapon. "All right. I heard what you told Banda
about the barbarians, so I know what to do if we encounter any. Do I
need to know anything about the people in the university?"

Mari shrugged as she also looked over her rifle. "It's run by the
masters, who are the most senior professors, and other professors
make up the rest of the leadership. Almost everyone else there is
called a student. It doesn't matter how old they are. Except for babies
and little children, they're students. They spend most of their time
on things other than studying, like growing food and guarding the
wall."

"The professors, the masters, are suspicious of strangers," Alain
added. "The students were more accepting and more…"

"Curious," Mari said. "Maybe even innocent. They've lived all their
lives in the small world defined by the walls of the university. But
they're also tough enough to have survived under these conditions."

"A mess of contradictions," Dav summed up. "Like most people."

"You got it," Mari said. She faced toward the ruins, pointing. "I
can't see the tower any more, but the university should be in that
direction. Let's go."

Alain had thought his memories of Marandur had remained sharp,
but as the group moved through the ruins he realized that conditions
were worse than he recalled. Not only was it difficult to move through
the tumbled debris among the tottering wrecks of buildings, but a
pervasive feeling of death and menace lurked all about. The brooding
silence still lay over the city, but this time Alain knew that silence
masked many dangers.

"How long were you in Marandur last time?" Dav asked when they
stopped for a brief rest. He scanned the remains of the city, fingering

his rifle nervously and jerking when a skinny cat darted across some wreckage behind them.

"It took us a couple of long days to reach the university," Mari said, "then one long day on the way out. When you're inside the walls of the university, it's a lot easier to handle this place."

Dav looked down at the skull fragments and other bones mixed in the wreckage. "What must it have been like when my ancestor was here? All the bodies still lying where they fell, all the wreckage fresh… and yet he stayed. How did he manage it? I'm going to have nightmares about this, guys."

"It is gone," Asha said. "Do not give the dead power over yourself."

"This doesn't bother you?"

"It is the record of horror in the past, not the horror itself," Asha said. "It creates the illusion within us that we are viewing the actual awful events instead of the aftermath of what happened long ago."

Dav nodded, then glanced at Asha. "Does it make you feel anything?"

"I look upon this and think of the waste, and think that this is what Mari is trying to save all the world from becoming, and this makes me want to help her all the more. Is that feeling?"

"Yes, it is. The right feeling, I think. It's sure motivating me," Dav said.

They had scarcely begun picking their way through the ruins again when Alain saw a black haze float across his sight. "Stop," he said, his voice soft but carrying enough force that everyone halted immediately. "There is something wrong ahead."

Mari knelt, rifle ready, studying the decaying buildings to either side and the rubble-choked street before them. "Where?"

"On the street itself," Alain said. He pointed. "There."

Dav moved ahead with extreme caution, checking before taking each step. "There's some sort of…there's a pit here. But it's got something covering it." He examined it carefully. "This isn't any random bit of junk. Somebody tried to cover this pit with enough stuff to hide it, but not enough to support anyone who walked on it. It's a trap."

"For animals?" Mari wondered. "Or for people? Can you tell where the edge of the pit is, Dav?"

"Yeah. Here and here. See? Come along this side of the street."

"All right. But stay alert."

Alain looked around, but saw no other warning of danger. "Mechanic Dav, the trap might have been intended to cause people to take the path you are now following. Be careful."

"Believe me, I—" Dav paused, looking down. "Tripwire. Mari, it looks like something pulled out of Mechanic electrical cables."

"The old generators and power lines at the destroyed Guild Hall had a lot of wires sticking out," Mari said. "Can you tell what the tripwire is connected to?"

"It runs to…a big stick. A stick that seems to be holding up the front of this building."

They moved ahead, each stepping carefully over the wire.

Not long afterwards, Asha gestured for everyone to halt. As they waited, a herd of tiny deer bounded out of a crumbling building a little ways ahead, leaping along the debris as several small, wolfish dogs raced in silent pursuit.

"Not completely dead," Dav muttered. "How will we know if there are any of the barbarians around?"

"You will know," Alain said. Nothing else happened as they struggled through the wreckage except for a few near-falls that could have resulted in twisted ankles or broken legs. The journey had not seemed that it would take so long, but he realized that despite their experience he and Mari had underestimated Marandur.

"Do you think we'll make it?" Mari asked him a low voice as she studied the position of the sun.

"We should be able to," Alain said, voicing more confidence than he felt.

Climbing over a solid wall of debris higher than their heads, they found on the other side the edge of what had once been a park. "There is the wall," Alain said.

"At last," Mari sighed, before abruptly coughing from inhaling dust, the sound carrying across the field. She stiffened as a low whistle sounded somewhere in the ruins off to their right. "I don't believe I did that. We've been seen…or heard. Let's get to the gate."

The small group headed out into the field. Once grassy and dotted with trees, now only charred remnants of tough wild grasses and weeds remained where the citizens of Marandur had once relaxed and played.

Another whistle sounded, off to their left this time, then a third from behind them. Mari picked up the pace, she and Alain moving at a trot and Dav and Asha right behind. It was still light, but the trip through the ruins had taken so much time that the sun was down in the west, casting long shadows from the wreckage and the buildings that still stood inside the university. "Should I discourage them?" Dav asked, hefting his rifle.

"No!" Mari called back. "They don't discourage that way, and we don't want to shoot unless we have to. If the legionaries outside the city hear the shots they'll know something is happening that shouldn't be happening in the city."

"How much farther is it?"

"Right up there! We're almost to the gate." She came to a halt just before the sealed gate, breathing hard, looking up and around. "Alain? Do you see the sentries?"

Alain shook his head. "I thought I saw some movement in the guard posts above the gate while we were running here, but I cannot be certain."

"Inside the university!" Mari called. "This is Master Mechanic Mari and Mage Alain. We've come back to see the masters of the university. Please open the gate."

As they waited for a reply, all they could hear were more whistles in the ruins that told of barbarians gathering.

"Alain, why would they leave the main gate unguarded?" Mari asked.

"They would not," Alain said. "Perhaps the barbarians found another way in and no one survived the attack."

"If that had happened, why would the barbarians have left this gate closed?" Mari stared above one part of the wall. "See that? Dav, that's exhaust from a boiler, right?"

Dav craned to look. "Yeah. Are they burning wood?"

"That's all they've got. But if they can still run the boiler, why aren't they guarding this gate?" The sun had fallen enough to put the former park into dusk. More whistles sounded, some of them nearer. "Alain?"

"We should enter," Alain said. "Asha can open an entry for us, you and Dav with your weapons ready and me with my heat spell, and we will go inside and see what awaits. Whatever is inside, we cannot stay out here."

"Good plan. Nobody shoot until I do."

"No noise. Right," Dav said.

"That and we don't want to hurt the wrong people." Mari hefted her weapon in both hands, as did Dav. Alain mentally prepared himself to imagine heat, and also drew his long knife from beneath his robes. Asha already had her knife out as she gazed fixedly at the wall next to the gate.

An opening appeared in the wall, one large enough for two persons to go through at once. Mari and Alain dashed forward, Dav and Asha on their heels.

Mari went only a few steps inside, then stopped, her weapon pointed toward a group standing directly behind the gate. Several crossbows were pointed back at her.

Alain relaxed his developing spell but kept his knife out as Mari lowered her rifle.

"Hi," she said in a voice that sounded exaggeratedly relaxed to Alain. "I know you guys. You, anyway. And you and you. You're all students. We worked together. Why wouldn't you let us in? Why didn't you answer us?"

"You must leave!" one of the guards cried, gesturing with a short sword. "Now!"

Alain indicated the wall. Asha had relaxed her own spell, and the wall was solid once more. "We cannot leave."

"We'll open the gate—"

"After dark?" another student objected. "The rules say we never—"

"I am in command here and I say—" the one in charge, wearing the same frayed robes as the other students, began to insist.

"Oh, stuff it!" A student with a crossbow lowered it and gestured apologetically. "We're sorry, Lady. We have orders to not let you into the university."

"Why?" Mari asked.

"Don't answer her!" the officious commander of the gate guards cried. "We have orders."

Alain, feeling an un-Magelike level of annoyance with the guard leader, knew that Mari would want to avoid any kind of confrontation nonetheless. He could also see the tension in several of the students. They were trying to present the illusion of steadiness, but their jumpiness was betrayed in the shifting of feet and eyes, the set of their mouths, the way they stood, and the nervousness with which they held their weapons.

He did not see enough hostility or resolve in them to worry him, but their fear could too easily cause them to over-react. Especially the officious commander of the guard, whose bluster did nothing to hide his insecurity. That commander needed to be given something else to think about. "You had orders that we should not enter?" Alain asked that student.

"Yes!"

"But we are inside. What are you orders if we are inside?"

The commander paused, looking suddenly panicky.

"Maybe we should be taken to the masters," Alain suggested. "So that they may provide new instructions."

"But we weren't supposed to let any of you inside! You need to get back outside!"

The student who had apologized spoke in a horrified voice. "We can't make them go outside! You heard the barbarians out there!"

A low murmur of assent came from most of the guards.

"We're not your enemies," Mari said, her weapon pointing straight up. "Asha, Alain, put away your knives. It's just a misunderstanding that I'm sure the masters can clear up. I'm sure that none of us want to do anything that would be contrary to the wishes of the masters."

The commander of the guard relaxed a bit as the long knives were put away and Dav raised his rifle to point up. He was bright enough to recognize the out that had been suggested and to embrace it eagerly. "The masters are in charge. I will bring you to them so that they can decide your…what to do."

Several of the guards stayed behind at the gate while one ran to carry word to the masters. The others walked with Mari, Alain, Asha, and Dav as the commander of the guard led the way. Alain looked around as they walked, seeing few changes from the last time he and Mari had been here. Some dead trees which had been left standing had been cut down, doubtless to feed the Mechanic boiler. An abandoned building was also gone, perhaps sacrificed as well to feed the appetite of the Mechanic creature.

"Have you had any problems with the boiler or the steam-heating system?" Mari asked one of the student guards.

"No, Lady," the guard said, grinning. "All has gone well, thanks to your instruction and guidance."

"All I did was teach you the basics," Mari said. "I'll take a look at things before I go to make sure no problems are developing anywhere."

In a short time, they were in the same large, vaulted room where Mari and Alain had met the masters on their last visit, and once again the masters faced their visitors from behind a long table. But Alain immediately noticed that Professor Wren, who had been the head master during their last visit with a seat at the center of the table, was now seated off to one side. In her place, the center seat was occupied by a very lean, tall man whose expression was far from welcoming.

"Why have you returned?" he said, sounding as if Mari and Alain had violated some agreement by doing so.

Alain noticed Mari's temper flaring at the man's attitude, but she controlled it and simply raised an eyebrow at him. "Maybe we should all know who we're talking to. You all know me and Mage Alain. This is Lady Mage Asha of Ihris. I'll let our other companion introduce himself."

Dav faced the masters. "I'm Mechanic Dav of Midan."

Alain saw the reaction that rippled through the masters when they heard Dav's name. Surprise and guilt appeared to be equally mixed, but there was also some skepticism.

"An ancestor of mine began a job here," Dav continued. "I'm here to help finish that job."

"We…will see about that. I am Professor Don, headmaster of the University of Marandur in Marandur by charter of the Emperor," the lean man declared.

"The charter was revoked when the Emperor Palan declared all within the borders of Marandur dead," Professor Wren said heavily, her attitude that of someone restating an old and unresolved argument.

"Our oaths stand!" Professor Don insisted.

"Our predecessors also swore an oath to this Mechanic's ancestor!" Wren said, pointing at Dav. "I take such oaths seriously."

"The oath to the Emperor takes precedence over all others," Don said. "Do you deny that?"

Mari broke into the argument. "All we want is to collect what I had to leave behind. We'll depart tomorrow if we can get everything out by then."

"There is nothing for you here," Professor Don said.

"You know that is not true," Alain said. He gestured to Asha. "Few dare to speak falsehoods before even one Mage. Do you seek to mislead two?" He had let his voice become emotionless again, and it rang with strange menace in the room.

"If I may," another of the masters interjected into the resulting silence, "we remain very grateful for the assistance you once granted us, Master Mechanic Mari. But in the wake of your departure, there was extensive debate over whether or not giving aid to you, in any form, was in violation of our oaths of loyalty to the Emperor. After much discussion, votes were held, and those who felt our loyalty to the Emperor must be paramount won the day and now run the university."

Mari shook her head. "We went over this last time. I'm trying to help the Emperor by overcoming the forces that, if left unchecked, will turn every city in the Empire into a howling wilderness like Marandur. How is that contrary to your oaths?"

Alain was grateful that the masters did not also have a Mage to tell whether or not Mari was telling the truth. She was speaking truth as far as her words went, but left unsaid had been the fact that the Emperor would want these masters to turn the texts over to him rather than Mari.

"Have you warned the Emperor of this looming disaster?" asked a soft-spoken woman professor.

"Yes," Mari said. "I've sent messages to him."

"And what has he replied?"

"He has not replied," Mari said.

"If this matter is so serious," said Professor Don, "why haven't you gone to the Emperor in person?"

"Are *you* serious?" Professor Wren demanded. "She has been to Marandur. We all know what that means. The Imperial court would kill her immediately for violating the ban."

"And yet," another master observed, "she has once again not only made her way to Marandur, but passed safely through the legion enforcing the ban."

"Getting what was left here was important enough to justify the risks of coming back," Mari said. "And I tell you again that those texts are important to the future of the Empire as well as every other country and city and person on Dematr."

Dav had been listening with growing impatience. "Mari told me that my ancestor stayed here not only to protect those texts but also to help your ancestors. I don't understand why you'd dishonor his sacrifice by disregarding the promises you gave him to keep the texts safe and provide them to the right Mechanic when she or he came."

The silence that followed Dav's statement was finally broken by Professor Don. "We have other responsibilities, other vows, that we must observe."

"But is there a conflict here?" Professor Wren said. "We could not ask Master Mechanic Mari again after she left, but there she is before us now. Lady Mechanic, do you swear that what you mean to do will benefit the Emperor?"

"Yes," Mari said without hesitation.

"Would the Emperor agree with what you're doing?" a male professor asked.

"I don't know," Mari said. "Would he agree with what you're doing? All either of us can do is what we think is best for the long-term interests of the Emperor and all of his subjects. I do know that anyone who works against what we are trying to do isn't serving the Emperor. They're serving the Storm that will sweep away the Empire and the Emperor if it is not stopped."

"We?" Professor Don asked. "What *we* do you speak of?"

Mari waved to indicate her companions. "Myself, other Mechanics, these Mages and others, and many common folk."

"We have the word of Master Mechanic Mari," Professor Wren said. "We have the descendent of the Mechanic Dav to whom our predecessors gave their word. And you all know we have what they came for, which is not and never has been ours except to hold in trust."

"It has stayed here for generations and can stay longer," Professor Don insisted.

"Not unless we break faith without cause! I call for a vote of the masters."

Professor Don did not try to hide his unhappiness, but he nodded. "You have the right to call for a vote. Before the vote is held, I remind everyone that their oath of loyalty to the Emperor takes precedence over any other oath."

"And I remind everyone," Wren said, "that Master Mechanic Mari has said she is not working against the Emperor. Do you wish to repeat that, Lady Mechanic?"

"I am working in the best interests of the Emperor," Mari said.

Alain, trying to judge the attitudes of the masters, could not be certain how they all felt. But it was clear that fear ruled many of them. "Has any ill befallen the university since we left?" Alain asked.

"Why do you ask that?" a master inquired.

"I see in you a worry that was not there when Master Mechanic Mari and I were here last," Alain said.

The soft-spoken woman answered. "When the Master Mechanic started the heating system again and taught our students to operate it, our first response was gratitude and nothing more. But we know the old rules by which the Mechanics Guild operated, and we know her action must have been in violation of those rules. And we know of old that the Emperor demands his people accept no gifts from those outside the Empire. More, we knew that the Mages of old did not traffic with other people, but stayed within themselves."

"You fear that you have violated all of those rules?" Alain asked. "But you knew when we were here—you heard Master Mechanic Mari say—that her intent was to overthrow the Great Guilds."

"Intent," Professor Don said, "is not action, and is not success."

Mechanic Dav laughed. "You think Mari is all talk and would leave you to the tender mercies of the Great Guilds? She's made big changes in Tiae. Changes that have helped people there a lot."

"We have only your word on that."

"You know we have to change things!" Mari said. "You want the Emperor to consider your petition to revoke the ban so that you can be free of this city. That's a big change! Do you think your loyalty to the Emperor requires you all to die because Emperor Palan declared your ancestors to be dead?"

"It is not so simple," a male master said. "We have vowed obedience. We have nothing else, Master Mechanic. As long as we hold to that, we have a purpose. But if we lose our sense of mission, then we are the slowly dwindling and doomed remnants of those who made a tragic error."

"I'm sorry," Mari said. "I can't change what happened when Marandur was destroyed. All I can do is try to change the future to ensure that Palandur and every other city doesn't share the same fate. What about your children? If I don't change things, what happens to them?"

"We must have faith in what we have served all of our lives, just as our parents did, and just as their parents did," Professor Don insisted. "You wanted a vote, Professor Wren. Let it be done. Who believes that we should allow this Master Mechanic to remove more items from this university?"

The vote went down the table, each master giving a yes or a no. Alain spent the time trying to work out the best means of getting the texts that Mari needed if the vote went against her. He had heard her speak too many times of their importance. He had seen her looking through all of them, moved sometimes to tears and often by wonder.

It was easy to spot the tension in Mari as the vote took place, and he could see her dismay at the number of votes against her.

The last master to vote, the soft-spoken woman, looked at Mari before saying anything.

"The vote is tied," Professor Don said. "Give us your vote, Professor Jan."

"I vote that we give to Master Mechanic Mari that which was promised her," Jan said.

Alain relaxed, but tensed again as Professor Don spoke. "The masters have voted, by a bare majority, to give the Mechanic—"

"Master Mechanic," Mari interrupted, her eyes fixed on the professor.

"To give the Master Mechanic the materials held in trust by this university. This discharges our obligation to her and to the Mechanic Dav of Midan from the days of the siege. There will be no other assistance provided to the Master Mechanic or her companions by the masters of this university," Professor Don finished.

No one said anything. Alain, fighting down an urge to set fire to the air around Professor Don, could see Mari struggling for control, so he spoke in a steady voice that only his Mage training made possible. "Will someone show us where the materials are, or would that be considered assistance?"

The flat, emotionless words made even Professor Don twitch as if he had been threatened.

Professor Wren stood. "I will show you. I was walking that way anyway, so no one should be able to consider this to be undue assistance to the men and women who have risked so much and done so much for us," she added in a voice dripping with sarcasm.

Mari, her jaw tight, followed Wren, along with Alain, Asha, and Dav. Nothing else was said until Wren had led them down a hallway and two flights of stairs, then into another building. "I am sorry," Professor Wren said. "Please do not hate them."

"I don't hate them," Mari replied, her voice reflecting her inner turmoil. "I am frustrated with them and angry with them, but I don't hate them."

"What are they frightened of?" Alain asked. "The answer I was given was not a full one. I saw that, just as I saw fear in many of the masters, but not in you."

Wren stopped walking and leaned against one wall, her face distressed. "You probably think they're afraid of the Emperor, because of all that talk about the oath. But that's just something they're using to hide the real thing they fear." The professor looked at the nearest window, which showed little but the night's darkness now that the sun had fully set. "You look at our lives here and see hardship. And there is plenty of that. You see us locked within this dead city, prohibited from leaving, besieged within the walls of the university. And that is indeed what we live with."

She paused, her expression changing. "One thing we have not had to face is change. Within the walls, we remain as we were. Individuals are born, age, and die, but the university goes on as it has since the days of the siege. Our days are hard, but predictable. Tomorrow will be like yesterday. There is a comfort in that, especially for those who have never known anything else."

Dav shook his head. "Even in the outside world controlled by the Great Guilds people can change their routines or where they live. I can't imagine never having had any changes in anything."

"But they cannot imagine such change," Wren said. "They cannot deal with it. That is what they fear."

"Then why don't they shut off the boiler that provides you with heat?" Mari said angrily. "That was a change."

"Master Mechanic Mari, there have been arguments that we should do exactly that." Wren waited for Mari's shock to lessen slightly. "Yes, you gave us heat, and that saved lives last winter. Yet even as those lives were saved there were complaints. Students' schedules had to be adjusted, with new responsibilities added. Schedules had not been adjusted for more than a century. Some people thought they never should be, that our routines should be more unchanging and enduring than the stones of our buildings."

Alain suspected that Professor Don was among that number.

"We have to acquire more wood to burn," Wren continued, "and students are learning new skills. New skills! The horror! But those who fear that are absolutely sincere. They imagine more changes, more alterations in a pattern that has seen no variation in the memory of any living here. They imagine being able to leave the confines of the university someday if the ban is lifted, and it scares them."

Mari's shoulders slumped and she lowered her head, cradling her face in one hand. "Can't they realize that without change they're doomed? You showed us last time that the population here has been dropping slowly for decades. Your small herd of domestic animals is dwindling, the water in more and more of your wells is being contaminated by leakage from the ruins outside, and…oh, what's the point. I'm sure you've talked about all that."

"I have," Wren said. "I have to remind myself that they do not intend harm by refusing to take action."

"But they do harm," Alain said. "I was trained as a Mage, as was Mage Asha, and we were taught that our actions toward commons meant nothing. There was no harm in what we did to them because they did not matter. But that wisdom is flawed. Harm is done. Those who stand aside and refuse to help are choosing to aid the forces that harm others. That is an action. Mari showed me this: that it is not enough to see danger threatening, not enough to see that others will face the danger. It is necessary to help. If the Storm triumphs, it will sweep away the legionaries guarding Marandur, and then you can leave. But the world outside will then be like this one, and they will have worked to cause that to come to pass."

Wren shook her head, looking miserable. "I have made those arguments. They cannot overcome the fears."

"People can't make decisions based on fear," Mari said, raising her head to look at Wren. "Leaders, especially. I can't afford to let my fears dictate my actions. If I did, I sure as blazes wouldn't have come back to Marandur! I've got a responsibility to face those fears and get things done."

"I wish you the best of luck," Wren said, leading them down another stairway into a basement area. "I wish I could do more." She indicated a nondescript door and offered Mari a key. "In there."

Mari opened the door and stepped inside. "It looks like they maintained everything the way I shelved it when they moved it here," Mari said, studying the rows of texts. She dropped her backpack on the floor and sighed heavily. "What do you think, Dav? With just us four carrying these, how many trips will it take?"

Dav looked around. "I'm guessing they'll fill roughly twenty containers. We've got twenty-four—five sacks in each backpack and the packs themselves—so we'll be all right there. But that would mean at least five trips to the river and back. We couldn't carry more than one each and clamber through those ruins and defend ourselves."

"That would be hard enough if we didn't have to worry about the barbarians. After one trip back they'll be watching for us. Laying traps. Ambushes." Mari gave a despairing look at Professor Wren. "We'll never make it."

Wren stared at the floor. "I can do nothing else," she whispered.

chapter twelve

Perhaps an idea will come to us in the morning," Wren said. Alain was sure even the Mechanics could tell that Wren did not believe her own words. "Come and rest. Surely rooms for the night will not be considered assistance."

"I'm going to sleep here," Mari said. "I want to keep on eye on these."

"I will stay with you," Alain said. He glanced at the stone floor, seeing tiles that did not match the fitted stone surface in his awful vision of Mari. That did not mean she did not face other dangers, though, or that she could not die before reaching that place.

"We'll take a room," Dav said. "It's too tight in here for all four of us to lie down. But before we go there, I'd like to see two other things. Mari told me my ancestor's grave is here. And there's a room where he lived."

"Of course," Wren said, her expression firming with determination. "I don't care whether they consider me showing you that a form of assistance or not. You deserve to see those, and I will wait as long as you wish to linger at them."

"This one can come as well?" Asha asked Dav.

"Yes," Dav said, smiling for the first time since they had entered Marandur. "Uh, this one would like you to be there with me."

"I'm going to see your boiler," Mari told Wren. "I promised some of the students that I'd check it for any problems that might be developing."

"I will come with you," Alain said.

"You don't have to, but thank you," Mari said. "Professor, we'll go with you as far as the grave, because I want to see it, too. Alain and I can find our own way from there and then back here."

Wren nodded, distressed again. "Master Mechanic, if there was anything—"

"I know. I don't blame you. Nobody ever said being the daughter of Jules would be easy."

Alain followed the others, his mind going over possible other ways to get the texts to the river but coming up blank each time. When they reached the place of memory for the university, Wren led them to an unobtrusive corner.

The plain stone bore only a name whose chiseled letters had been slightly blurred by time. Dav of Midan. Dav knelt next to it, reaching out to touch the stone, saying nothing. Alain saw Asha hesitate, her hand reaching out and retreating as she fought her Mage training, until she was able to place her hand on Dav's shoulder.

"Let's leave them to their own thoughts," Mari whispered to Alain. "Come on."

They walked quickly across the darkened grounds, the route familiar from their earlier visit. Alain hesitated for just a moment as Mari opened the door to the place where the boiler creature lived, but followed her without anyone noticing. He was not sure whether to be pleased with growing more comfortable with the strange creations of Mechanics, or worried about it.

Inside, the room was lit by a single lantern turned low. The university did not have the luxury of wasting resources. Two students, both young adults, had been watching over the boiler and talking, but they sprang to their feet when Mari and Alain entered.

Alain had spent the walk worrying about the response Mari would receive here. A rejection by those she had trained would have hit doubly hard after the rest of the day. But he knew he need not have been concerned when both students broke into broad smiles as they recognized Mari.

"Welcome, Lady," the woman said. "We were told you might come by, but didn't really expect it."

"We have been very careful to follow your instructions and training," her male companion added.

"I remember both of your faces," Mari said, cheering up a little at the reception, "but I'm sorry I can't recall your names."

"Student Ndele," the young woman said eagerly.

"Student Leo," the young man said, smiling.

"I'm going to look for anything that might need repairing," Mari said, her return smile slightly strained because of the tension inside her. "From here, though, everything looks great. You guys are doing a good job of keeping this equipment clean and maintained."

As Mari worked her way over the equipment, Student Ndele turned to Alain. "Sir, is something wrong? The Lady seems upset about something."

Alain wondered whether to speak of Mari's mood to others, especially the secrecy surrounding the texts.

"If we're doing something wrong here, we want her to tell us," Leo said.

"She has not told me of any problems with your work," Alain said. There seemed no good reason to deny the obvious. "She is unhappy because while the masters of the university have given us what we came for, something which was left here long ago by another Mechanic, the masters have refused any assistance."

Leo made a face. "What does she need?"

"We have…texts, which must be carried to the river. There are many. It will require five trips or more."

"Five round trips?" Ndele gasped. "Through the ruins? The barbarians will see the pattern in no time and ambush you."

"They won't help at all?" Leo asked. "After she did this for us?" He waved around the boiler room.

"No," Alain said.

"What exactly did they say, sir?" Ndele asked.

"They said the masters would provide no more assistance to us of any kind."

"The masters would provide no more assistance?" She looked at Leo as Mari rejoined them. Leo smiled in understanding, leaving Alain wondering what they were thinking.

"It looks good," Mari told them, "but you're using more grease than you have to on those valves. Put on just enough to keep them turning. You're some of the best Apprentices, I mean students, I've ever worked with."

"Thank you, Lady," Leo and Ndele chorused.

"Sir Alain has told us of your problem. How much is it that must be taken to the river?" Leo asked.

"About twenty sacks," Mari said. "Heavy enough that a person could only carry one at a time. We'll figure something out. Um… we should go get some sleep. We'll be starting out just before dawn tomorrow."

"We are sorry that the masters will not provide help," Ndele said.

As they left the home of the Mechanic boiler, Alain leaned close to Mari. "Students Leo and Ndele reached some decision after I told them of the problem."

"What decision?" she murmured back.

"I do not know. I sensed…something that felt like mischief. There is no ill will in them. I am certain of that."

"Maybe it's not even something to do with us," Mari said. "Those two look like they're into each other, and they do make a nice couple, don't you think?"

"What…makes a nice couple?" Alain asked, thrown off by the unfamiliar term.

. Mari smiled briefly at him despite her obviously lingering upset. "Like you and me. Let's get some sleep. Tomorrow will be another long day. I should have asked Wren for blankets, but that would probably be assistance."

Once back in the small room lined with shelves filled with texts, Mari did not sleep. Alain watched with growing weariness as she insisted on packing the texts carefully into the backpacks and then the sacks. Mari alternated between trying to be quiet so he might sleep, and keeping him awake by trying to carry on conversations with him about the contents of the texts as she saw various titles. Since Alain did not understand most of the words she was using, all he could do was make occasional noises that implied interest or comment.

She finally put out the lantern and lay down with him. He felt her shaking and held her. "Is it because of Marandur?" .

"Yes," she murmured. "No. Why do we have to fight so many people, Alain? Why does the Storm have so many allies while we have to struggle to change things for the better?"

"I do not know. Fear is part of it, as the professor said."

"I'm afraid! But I do what's right anyway! People are counting on me!"

He could not think of a reply to that, so Alain held her until she finally fell asleep. He followed her into dreams of which he remembered nothing.

The next morning, Alain awoke to a tapping on the door. At least, he assumed it was morning; it was pitch dark inside the room. On his way to the door he tripped over the bags that Mari had packed, while she struggled awake.

"Mari said to be here a little before dawn," Dav said. He and Asha looked inside the room using Dav's Mechanic hand light. "You guys already got the stuff bagged? Great. These, uh, students said you'd asked them to be here, too."

"Students?" Mari got to her feet, running her hands through her hair as she tried to put it in some sort of order.

"Good morning, Lady," Student Ndele said. Beyond her, Alain

could see Leo and others. "We have brought friends to help you carry your burdens to the river today."

Mari blinked in surprise. "But the masters said they wouldn't provide any more assistance to me."

"Yes, Lady." Student Leo grinned. "The masters said *they* would provide no more assistance to you. But they did not prohibit the students from helping you on our own initiative, and nobody has told us not to."

"Did you ask?" Mari pressed.

"No."

"It's the same rule everywhere, isn't it?" Dav said, smiling as well. "Don't ask the question if you don't want to know the answer."

"And," Mari added, "it's easier to beg forgiveness than to ask permission. This is…thank you." She looked down, rubbing at her eyes. "Every time I start believing that this whole daughter job is just too big for my friends and me, I find out I have more friends than I realized. Um…here are the bags. Dav and Asha, take your packs and go up with the first students, then everybody wait until we're all up there."

As Alain led Mari out after the last of the student volunteers, more students approached out of the darkness, bearing weapons. Alain scarcely had time to be alarmed before the new arrivals were greeted by the others. "They'll help guard us while we're out in the ruins," Leo told Alain.

It was still dark, the sky just beginning to lighten in the east, when the now large group was ready. "Can I have one moment?" Dav begged.

"As long as it is very short, sir," Ndele said. "We need to get out of the university before any of the wrong people realize what is happening."

"Very short," Dav repeated, running off into the morning twilight.

"Where is he going?" Mari asked, too surprised to try to stop him.

"He says farewell to the grave of his ancestor," Asha replied. "Last night we also saw the room where the departed Mechanic Dav of Midan once lived."

"You did see the room?" Alain asked. "It is the place I thought you should see. What did you think?"

"I think, Mage Alain, that Dav is an even finer man than I once believed, and that his family is a fine one as well, perhaps even fine enough to accept a Mage."

"Accept a Mage?" Mari asked.

"I have decided to accept Dav's promise to me," Asha said. "And to give him my promise."

"Why didn't anybody tell me about this?" Mari said, throwing herself at Asha and hugging her tightly. "I'm so happy for you."

Asha, stiff from the unexpected human touch, recovered quickly. "We owe it to you, Mari. Thank...you. Dav returns."

"We should go," Student Leo urged.

"Right." Mari shouldered her backpack and hefted her rifle.

Ndele and Leo led the way to the main gate, where the guards looked innocent and opened the gate without question.

"How many of you students are in on this?" Mari asked as the group trudged across the open area outside the walls.

"Twenty-four walking with us, Lady," Leo said. "Sixteen helping to carry and eight guards. Plus a few dozen more at the gate and elsewhere, helping to cover up our absence from those who might ask the wrong questions."

"I hope you don't get in too much trouble."

"We are in trouble all the time now as it is," Ndele said. "Since you came and showed us how to use the Mechanic tools, we have wanted to use them on other things. And you told us of the world outside Marandur as it is today, rather than how it was when the city was sealed. We want to talk about that and address it in classes, but few of the professors will permit it."

"You got them thinking, Mari," Dav said.

"That's one of my bad habits," Mari said. "Ndele, Leo, everyone, I promise you I will not stop trying to get the Emperor to lift the ban on this city enough for you to get out if you want."

"Would it be possible to come with you?" a student asked.

"I'm sorry," Mari said. "Our ship will barely be able to hold us and these texts, and the risks getting back are going to be pretty huge, and once it was known that any of you had come out of Marandur despite the ban, the Empire would not cease sending assassins until you were dead. I've been an assassin-magnet myself long enough to know that's not anything to wish on anyone else."

They were almost into the ruins, the sun having risen enough to light up the field, when shouts could be heard faintly from the university walls behind them. Alain looked at the students, but all acted is if they had heard nothing. They did, though, refrain from looking back, and moved into the ruins with extra speed until the university was lost to sight.

The journey back to the river was no less difficult, but not as frightening with so many men and women around them. Querulous whistles began sounding on all sides, but they remained far enough off to make it clear that the barbarians had no wish to tangle with a group of nearly thirty.

Some of the students—those who had sometimes gone into the ruins to salvage materials—led at a better pace than Alain and the others had managed on the way in. They had learned how to move fairly quickly and surely over the debris, and how to avoid the most dangerous areas.

Someone or something had tripped the deadfall since Alain and the others had passed this way. The front of the ruined building had collapsed into the rubble-choked street, partially filling the pit trap. No one was interested in seeing if there were any victims buried beneath the wreckage.

It was only late morning when they reached the bank of the Ospren, most of the students gazing in amazement at the river. "We live so close to it, but we hardly ever risk coming this far," Student Leo said.

"If I have my way, someday you'll get to see the Sea of Bakre," Mari said, waving toward the tangle of wood that marked the *Terror*.

The students pointed, calling out to each other in delight, as Captain Banda came out on deck, a coil of light rope in one hand with the Mankey fist on the end. Banda spun the weight rapidly in a circle and cast it toward the landing, where a dozen eager hands grabbed it before it could slide back into the water.

In a short time, the light rope had been used to pull across a heavier rope which Dav and some of the students tied securely to a stone bollard that had not seen use for over a century. Next the boat was pulled across, fastened by some Mechanic link that Alain puzzled over, loosely holding it to the heavier rope so that the boat could not be lost to the current. With the students pitching in enthusiastically, all Alain and Asha had to do was stand sentry, watching the ruins inland and to either side along the river as Mari and Dav supervised shuttling loads of sacks and backpacks to the *Terror*.

Students Ndele and Leo, back from helping on the latest boat run, stopped near Alain, their eyes lit with awe. He realized that the *Terror* was probably the first new thing these students had ever seen, but instead of being afraid of it they were embracing the moment.

"I cannot believe such things as that craft exist, sir," Leo said. "Even if I had any doubts about what the Lady does, they would be gone now. Is it true that Mages can see the future, sir?"

"Sometimes," Alain said. "Though even when we have such visions, understanding them can be difficult or impossible."

"Do you know if she will succeed?"

Alain did not let any trace of his worry for Mari's future show as he answered. "She has a chance. But many work against her."

"Why, sir?" Ndele asked. "Why would anyone try to stop such wonders from happening? And she said that there is much trouble coming if she fails? Why would anyone want that?"

"They do not believe the troubles will come," Alain said. "Or they do not wish to believe the troubles will come. Or they fear to do anything and think that not acting will protect them from what comes. Or they think only of what will bring them gain in the days just ahead, without regard to what might happen in the months and years beyond that."

"Like the rebels?" Leo gestured to the ruins. "We look on this every day of our lives, and we wonder why. What was the point? What was the purpose of so much death and destruction? The rebels must have thought there was a reason, a reason so strong they were willing to die for it, but it brought them nothing."

"I do not pretend to understand the way all men and women think," Alain said. "I was taught to think differently, but perhaps even if I had not been so taught, I would never have understood a willingness to see a city of people die for what I wanted for myself."

"Mages are wise," Leo said.

"Not all Mages," Asha replied, putting a trace of humor into her voice that surprised Alain. "Some Mages are wiser than others."

"Like the Mages who walk with the Master Mechanic?" Ndele asked with a grin. "There go the last of the bags. Leo, we have to get back."

"Yes," Leo agreed. "We shouldn't have trouble making it before dark if we start now." He shrugged. "And we can spend the trip back thinking up apologies for, uh, misinterpreting the wishes of the professors."

"You are not the first to be led off the path of obedience by Lady Mari," Alain said. "You will not be the last."

"Thank you!" Mari called from the boat as Dav untied the rope from around the bollard so it could be hauled in. "Everyone! Thank you!"

Alain and Asha got in last, Alain nerving himself to step into what still seemed too frail a craft to dare the river amid the ruins of Marandur. He took a moment to watch the students moving off into the ruins, their ancient robes making them look like ghosts of Marandur's past become visible in the light of day. And yet in their minds they held more of the future than did many of their professors. Certainly they had done far more to help bring a hopeful future to this world.

Mari and Dav rowed as strongly as they could, but the current pushed the boat downstream a bit before it reached the *Terror*. Alain and Asha pulled on the rope tied to the *Terror* to get the boat all the way back to the ship. After unloading, Mari helped Dav strap the boat below the waterline of the *Terror* again, hiding it from view.

Alain and Asha helped bring down the last sacks, then could do nothing else but move them as directed by Captain Banda, stacking bags here and there, making the already tight spaces below deck feel even more constricted.

"Why do we move these and then move them again?" Asha asked.

"We have to trim the ship," Banda explained. "Like balancing the load on something you carry so it doesn't weigh too heavily on one side. Some of it is trial and error."

"And, unfortunately," Dav added, "every error means another trial of moving junk around."

After that, the Mechanics did obscure things with their pumps and other devices as Alain and Asha kept watch on the outside. The *Terror*, riding low under the extra weight, rose up again as the pumps hummed, then dropped a little as Captain Banda adjusted the ballast tanks so that the driftwood camouflage once again rode just on the surface like a natural tangle of wood.

They all sat down for a few moments to rest, the Mechanics looking weary.

"We can travel during the day on the way downriver as long as we match our speed to anything being pushed by the current," Banda said. "But I want to wait until dark to leave Marandur so we can get past the guard posts along the river without risking that anyone might want to physically check for passengers riding the driftwood downstream. We know they'll let us slide past by night, so let's stick to that."

"They might be able to see something of the *Terror* through the driftwood from their watch towers," Mari agreed. "Like sunlight reflecting off something. We should do what worked last time."

"I guess everything went well," Banda commented, causing Alain to realize that no one had yet had a chance to tell him of their visit to the university.

"It ended well," Mari said. "The professors didn't want to help us at all, but fortunately they forgot to tell the students that."

"Didn't want to help? Did you tell the university professors about the ship from another star and how about important these texts are?"

"No," Mari replied, her voice taking on sadness. "I didn't trust them. If they weren't confined to Marandur I'd worry about them alerting the Empire. I'm glad we're leaving tonight." She yawned. "I guess I didn't get that much sleep last night."

"I'll take first watch on the boiler so you can crash and sleep until tonight," Dav said.

"Dav, you're a lifesaver. Oh, I forgot to offer my congratulations," Mari said.

"For what?"

"Didn't Asha—?"

Dav looked at her. "Asha?"

"Should I have told Dav earlier?" Asha asked Mari.

"Probably," she said with a laugh. "But I don't think he'll be too upset when you tell him now."

Captain Banda had taken the *Terror* as far downriver as he dared before nightfall, waiting for darkness before approaching the Imperial watch towers guarding the river. Alain felt uneasy as he saw the towers finally come into view. "There are more lights."

"Yes," Banda agreed. "A lot more lights, and they're down by the river banks as if the Imperials are expecting someone to make a break tonight. I'm going to take this very slowly, making sure we look like that wood on top is drifting along with the current and nothing more."

"Boats," Alain said.

"Blast. I see. Looks like three of them putting out into the river with lanterns on them. I can see the Imperials doing that when it gets foggy, to keep anyone from slipping past. But even if it might get heavy tonight it's not nearly foggy enough for them to be putting out already. Make sure Mari and Asha are alert. This is looking bad."

Alain slid down the ladder and warned Mari and Asha, then climbed back up to his seat. Mari appeared at the foot of the ladder, looking up. "How are the boats spacing themselves?"

"Pretty evenly across the river," Banda said. "One in the center and two toward the river banks. If I continue to play at drifting, we'll probably swing close by the one in the center."

"Alain, are there any Mages in the boats?"

"I sense none," Alain said. "There is a Mage well off to the left. He or she may be approaching, but has far to come."

"If we get close to that center boat, can you or Asha make their lantern go out? That's a small spell, right?"

Alain considered the question, then nodded. "Yes. I could make something go away to cause the lantern to stop giving light. It would reveal little to the Mage coming this way."

"Why don't we try that if we have to? If it looks like the Imperials might see something through our camouflage? Captain Banda, what do you think about opening the top hatch so we can hear anything the Imperials say while we drift past them?"

Banda looked down at her, frowning. "Do you think they'll say something of interest?"

"Maybe. I've been around soldiers enough to know they pass the time by talking about women, men, sports, various forms of alcohol, and sometimes even about what they're supposed to be doing. If this activity isn't normal, I think there's a decent chance the Imperials might be gabbing about it."

"I think you might be right," Banda said.

"Alain? Does the idea of opening that hatch cause any forewarning for you?"

"No," Alain said, "but you know how little that means. I do agree it is important to hear, if the legionaries talk about why they are guarding the river this way tonight."

"Everyone has to stay very quiet," Banda cautioned. "We don't want the Imperials hearing anything from inside the *Terror*. And make sure that curtain blocks all light from the inside." He stood to lift the hatch, swinging it carefully all the way open so that it lay back concealed among the branches.

Alain sat, trying to be as quiet as possible, as the *Terror* drifted with the current toward the Imperial guard boats, which were holding their positions in the river. "They must be anchored," Banda said in the merest whisper to Alain. "They're well forward of the watch towers with the bright lights. That makes sense if they want to spot something in time for the watch towers to attack it as it goes past. But it means we'll deal with the boats and then the towers, not both at once."

The only light was that filtering in from outside, but Alain could hear faint noises from the shore and on the boats as orders were called and acknowledged.

As Banda had guessed, the *Terror's* path took her closer and closer to the middle boat. A lantern was mounted on a staff on the bow, held by a hook on the top. The sound of an authoritative voice came faintly through the hatch. "Is there anybody on that rat's nest?"

The reply was just barely loud enough to hear. "I can't see anyone."

"Check it out when it gets closer."

"I thought we were looking for a ship? Some sort of Mechanic ship?"

"That's right."

"What's it look like?"

"We don't know. The dead one who called out to our sentries from the city walls got taken out by the barbarians before he could say much. But it's a ship or boat of some kind, made of metal and big enough to carry four people plus cargo."

Dead one. That was what the legionaries called anyone inside the city, because by Imperial decree all of them were officially dead. The voices were growing very clear in the otherwise silent evening. Alain gazed through the small windows giving the best view of the guard boat, his spell ready, as the *Terror* drew so close that Captain Banda began trying to gently, unobtrusively steer away.

"Remember," the boat commander said, his voice loud enough to be heard without trouble. "Normal orders for anyone leaving the city don't apply. Don't kill whoever's on that ship if we see it. If it's who the dead one said, whoever captures her will win the Emperor's favor."

"Her? It's…her?" one of the legionaries asked with a slight quaver.

"Just do what you're told! And don't let that pile of junk hit us!" the boat commander ordered. "Can you see anything on it?"

A legionary was standing up and leaning a bit toward the *Terror* as the light from the boat's lantern illuminated the driftwood hiding the steering room. His expression grew puzzled. "What is—?"

Alain had kept his eyes fixed on the hook holding the lantern. His Mage training told him it was an illusion of a hook, holding the illusion of a lantern. There was not much power available on the river here, but there was enough to allow him to temporarily lay a very small illusion over the one that Alain saw. The hook was not whole. The part at the top was not there.

In that instant Alain felt his strength drain a bit, and the top of the hook vanished.

The lantern dropped straight into the water.

The legionary leaning to look at the *Terror*'s disguise swung his gaze and attention to the fallen lantern, which was bobbing on the water and rapidly sinking.

The light went out.

A babble of voices erupted, yelling out curses and commands, as the *Terror* drifted on past the boat. Looking back, Alain saw the legionaries, dimly illuminated by the other lights in the area, trying to get another lantern lit and hung up.

By the time they succeeded, the *Terror* was well past the boats.

One of the watch towers briefly played its mirror-focused light on the *Terror*, then went back to concentrating on where the boats were maintaining a picket line.

Banda slowly increased speed, drawing away from the line of Imperial defenses. He took the time to close the hatch again, then called down to Mari. "How much of that did you hear?"

"Enough," Mari said, looking up toward Banda and Alain. "I guess we underestimated how much some of the professors wanted to stop me. They decided to warn the sentries around the city."

"The professor Don could have ordered someone else to carry the warning," Alain said. "Some student who would be willing to take such a risk."

"You're probably right," Mari said. "I can't see any of those masters making it to the wall through the ruins. It's a good thing the barbarians got whoever it was before they could say too much. I wouldn't normally wish that sort of fate on anyone, but I have to make an exception in this case."

"Those river defenses were still being improvised tonight," Banda said. "If the Imperials had had more time they would have put up something a lot tougher to get through. Fortunately, they seem to have a misleading description of this ship."

"Yes," Mari agreed. "Whoever it was heard something from the students who helped us carry the texts to the river, but may not have heard about the camouflage or how low this ship rides, or maybe just didn't have time to tell the legionaries about it. Even if they took off at a run from the university as soon as they got that information it would have taken them until at least sunset to reach the wall and call to the legionaries."

"They want you alive," Banda said.

"Lucky me."

"Why did that one soldier sound scared when he mentioned you? Like…*her*."

Mari did not say anything, so Alain answered. "Mara."

"Oh! That's right. Like the ones around Landfall. I'm sure if there was any truth to that Mara stuff, Mage Asha wouldn't have left you alone around Dav."

Mari glared up at Banda. "Not funny."

Banda was looking ahead, chewing on his mustache. "They'll send word down the river as fast as they can. Do you think they'll ask the Mechanics Guild to help pass the word? If so, we might as well give up now."

"The Imperials won't tell the Guild," Mari said. "They suspect what I came to Marandur for, and the Emperor wants that for himself. He knows if the Mechanics Guild hears about it they'll grab it. Maybe the

Imperials will let the Mages know enough to pass messages by their own means, but given the stakes I bet the Imperials will keep it all to themselves and depend on fast couriers."

"I hope that you're right. But keeping ahead of fast couriers riding relay horses is going to be hard for us. And as soon as the Imperials at each location along the river get their orders, they'll start throwing up blockades, the sort of thing even a pile of driftwood won't be able to get through."

Mari sighed. "Can we stay ahead of the Imperial preparations?"

"I don't know." Banda increased speed again. "We'll need to run like blazes. And if they've already sent word to the chain, we'll have problems right off. We'll get there in about half an hour. Tell Dav that we'll be running all out until we reach Landfall and get out to sea. No stops or slowing down during the day."

"That means several days straight of sailing. Who's going to steer?" Mari demanded.

"Me. If we hit some quiet stretches, you or Dav can handle it for a little while." Banda glanced back. "Is this something you or Asha could do, Alain?"

"I do not think so," Alain said. "I see what you do. But I cannot see how to do it."

"That's all right. Your contributions are valuable enough. That one legionary had spotted something under our camouflage. If you hadn't made that lantern drop, he would have alerted the others and one of them would have climbed on to search us." Banda rubbed his eyes. "Mari, I'll have to slow down a lot when we near the chain, because if it has been raised and we run into it at high speed, the bow could be stove in. We'd sink in no time at all."

"What can we do if the chain is raised?" Mari asked.

"Send someone ashore to try to get it lowered again."

Alain nodded. "I will go."

"Not alone," Mari said. "That chain is Mechanic equipment. You'll need me to tell you how to break it."

"Shouldn't we send Asha and Dav?" Banda asked reluctantly.

"No," Mari said. "They haven't done this kind of thing. Alain and I have."

Alain did not think much time had passed when Banda began slowing the ship. Mari went out the aft hatch and climbed forward, staring ahead into the darkness. "It's getting really foggy out here. I can't see much ahead of us."

Banda had slowed the *Terror* to a crawl when Alain felt a jar and the ship stopped moving.

"We hit the chain!" Banda called to Mari. "We can't get past it."

"Come on, Alain!" Mari had already loosened the boat again. Alain helped her pull it up to the surface, drain the water and set the boat upright.

Asha came out on deck as well. "What can I do?"

"Guard the ship," Alain said. "Captain Banda says there may be more boats patrolling along the chain."

"We will deal with them if any appear," Asha said.

Mari helped Alain into the boat, then pushed off and began rowing. "Come on, Alain! You've seen rowing. I need help with this."

Alain did his best. He knew he wasn't doing too well at it, but he put enough force behind his clumsy strokes to help drive the boat to shore.

"The current carried us past the chain," Mari panted as they dragged the boat onto the river bank. "Banda said the fortified winch house is on the other bank. We need to go back up this river bank and find the place where the chain is fastened. It shouldn't be nearly as heavily guarded as the winch house. Is the mist getting thicker?"

"Yes," Alain said. Between the night and the mist he could barely see beyond a couple of arm lengths. "I must be able to see what I place a spell on."

"I know. We'll get you close enough to see it. Let's go."

Mari hurried. Alain hastened to keep up, worried at her pace in the fog. "Mari, if there are guards at the chain—"He stopped speaking as Mari stumbled to a halt. Directly in front of her a legionary carrying a lantern had appeared out of the mist. Alain reached for his long knife as Mari and the legionary stared at each other.

chapter thirteen

before Alain could do anything, Mari straightened and beckoned to the legionary, who was just out of her reach. "Come, young one. I hunger," she said eagerly. The mist curled around her, giving Mari a mysterious and haunting appearance.

"Wh– what?" the legionary gasped, his hand frozen in the act of drawing his sword. His eyes on Mari widened in fear.

"I need you," Mari said. "Do you have friends with you? Other young men? I need them."

The legionary stumbled backwards, Mari following and Alain walking cautiously in her wake.

"Hans, what the blazes are you—" – Three more legionaries appeared out of the mist behind the first and halted as they saw their friend and Mari.

"She's...she's..." Hans tried to speak but could only gesture wildly.

"Where is the Emperor?" Mari purred. "You will take me to him, so I can rule alongside him just as I did with Maran when the world was young. But first," she continued, putting hunger and desire into her voice, "you are young, and I must feed."

Mari stepped forward, reaching, and all four legionaries bolted into the mist, almost immediately crashing into a fifth, who did not pause to ask questions but ran with his companions.

"Alain," Mari said, breathing deeply, "you are never to tell anyone anything about this. Do you understand?"

"I understand."

Mari took three more steps, stopping before a massive chain that Alain could see stretching into the river. A torch burned nearby, its light absorbed by the mist but reaching far enough to illuminate part of the chain as well as the packs the panicky legionaries had left behind. "The end is anchored somewhere up there," Mari said, gesturing inland. "We have to break the chain here so it will drop and let the *Terror* through. Can you do that? We have to act very fast before those legionaries get their courage back or reinforcements show up."

Alain nodded, studying the links closely. The metal was as thick as his wrist, formed into loops that were interlocked. "I will remove part of a piece so that the next one slides out. The chain just lies there and is very heavy. Will it slide?"

"Yeah. It should slide. Do it, Alain!" Mari was staring into the mist, her pistol weapon now in her hand.

Alain felt more power available to him here on the land, enough to get the job done without tiring him very much. He concentrated, creating the illusion that the lower half of one of the links was not there, gathering the focus and the power he needed.

Mari gasped, leveling her weapon out toward the water, but Alain redoubled his efforts and completed the spell. The bottom half of the link was gone.

He had expected the chain to slide slowly away, but instead it whipped toward the river faster than any snake could strike. Alain felt the rush of wind from the massive links that passed just in front of him, then saw the blur of motion as the loose end of the chain snapped up through the mist, sliced completely through a boat that was approaching the shore, and then vanished into the water. The legionaries in the boat, startled by the sight of Mari, had no chance to react as the chain tore apart their boat and hurled those unfortunate enough to be in its path far out into the river.

Mari grabbed Alain's hand and rushed back down river toward

their own boat. "Alain, I should have realized how much tension that chain was under because of the weight dragging on it! When you released one end it snapped back with enough force to rip through armor plate! I nearly killed you!"

"It missed me," Alain said as they reached their boat.

"Not the point! I should have warned you not to be too close! Stupid! I let myself get distracted and didn't think things through and it nearly killed you!" They wrestled the boat back into the water as alarmed shouts rose up and down the river bank. Somewhere on the other side of the river one of the brass Imperial trumpets began calling every legionary within earshot to action.

They rowed out into the river, Mari working with savage anger at herself and Alain with clumsy force. "Captain Banda!" Mari began calling.

"Here!"

The big pile of driftwood floated into sight. Banda steered the *Terror* close and Mari helped Alain onto the wood, then as she climbed onto the ship tipped the boat into the water so that it began filling and sinking. "No time to recover the boat!" she called to Banda. "Get us out of here!"

As Alain and Mari made their way over the tangled mass of wood toward the aft hatch, the *Terror* surged forward faster and faster. Asha raised herself from the forward hatch enough to hand Mari one of the Mechanic rifles. "Captain Banda says we must watch for boats," she said.

"Alain and I will stay up here," Mari said. She took up a position near the aft hatch, wedging herself among the branches and pointing the rifle back the way they had come. Alain took up a similar position, looking out into the mist. "I hope Captain Banda knows this part of the river well enough to go this fast in such bad visibility," Mari said, staring outward.

Alain concentrated on watching for trouble, but even though he heard shouts on the river banks and from boats on the water, the noises gradually faded behind them.

"How can you ever forgive me?" Mari said just loudly enough to be heard over the rush of water along the sides of the ship.

"It was a mistake. It is not the first mistake one of us has made," Alain said.

"Alain, if you had been a little bit closer that chain would have taken your head clean off." Mari's voice choked on the last words.

"It was a big mistake," Alain said, trying to think of the right thing to say, torn between his own belated reactions to the brush with death and his desire to comfort Mari. "I have made big mistakes as well."

"Not like that. Alain, we run enough risks as it is." Mari closed her eyes for a moment, shaking her head, before opening them again to search for threats. "To almost get you killed because I wasn't thinking…"

"I love you," Alain said. That usually worked to comfort her.

Not this time. "You love me? The woman who almost got you decapitated?"

"Yes." He decided on simple honesty. "If I were going to be decapi⊠ have my head taken off, I would want it to be with you."

She spared a moment to give him a baffled and appalled look. "What?"

That obviously had not sounded right, either. "Mari, if I had done such a thing, endangering you, would you forgive me?"

She paused to think. "Eventually."

"And so I forgive you. I know it did not happen by choice and I know you will strive never to repeat such a mistake. That is enough. And you love me. That is enough."

Mari shook her head again, smiling and blinking away tears. "My father is such an idiot. I don't deserve you. I do promise to forgive you as well if something like this happens in reverse, but I really hope it doesn't."

Not long afterwards, Asha raised herself up again through the forward hatch. "Captain Banda says you should come inside and close the hatch."

"Thank you, Asha." Mari let Alain go first, then followed him down, sealing the hatch. She paused to hug him tightly before looking up the ladder leading to the steering room. "What's the plan, Captain?"

"We charge ahead as fast as I dare in the fog," Banda replied. "And we keep going. Mari, Alain, get some sleep," he ordered. "We'll call you when it's time to take over from Asha and Dav, or if we run into any more problems."

"Go ahead to the bunks, Alain," Mari said. "I'm going to check on Dav and fill him in on things. He must be going crazy having to sit tending the boiler while everything is happening outside."

"Mari?" Alain said before she left. "You are all right?"

She gazed back at him. "A short time ago I nearly killed you, and you're worried about how I feel?"

"Yes."

"I'm fine, Alain. As long as you're with me. Try to get some sleep. I'll be right there."

He went forward to the cramped living area, now lined with sacks of the most precious documents in the world, and lay down on his bunk. In a world that was an illusion, he had no illusions about being able to sleep. The blurred image of the chain whipping past his face kept running through his mind. But he did not feel fear, or anger. Instead there was a sense of wonderment, and a question about whether fate had spared him so that he could continue to help Mari.

She showed up fairly soon and climbed into the bunk above his. "Too bad we can't share a bed. I could use your arms around me. Alain, we think the Imperials suspected I got banned technology texts from Marandur the last time we were there. Now they know I've gone back there and left again. The Imperials will be sure I've got more banned texts, and they will move mountains to stop us before we get to Landfall and out to sea. They want those texts, and they want me."

"They will not get you," Alain said.

"You will remember never to talk to anyone about what happened on the river bank, right? Not the chain. You can let everyone know what an idiot I was about that. The other stuff."

"I was surprised how convincing you were," Alain said, looking up at the bottom of her bunk. "You manipulated the illusion very well."

"Yeah, that's me. A natural when it comes to convincing people I'm a vain, blood-sucking, undead monster. Stars above, if Alli ever heard about it…just let's never mention it again, Alain."

"As you wish."

Alain was surprised to be awoken by Asha. He had not realized that his fatigue had been so great that he could fall asleep despite the desperate nature of their situation. Mari waited a moment at the bottom of the ladder as Alain took his seat once more behind Captain Banda. "How are you doing?"

"Could be better, could be worse," Banda replied, not taking his eyes off the view ahead. "The fog has dissipated, so we've got a clear view ahead. Mari…"

"What?"

"We're probably an hour away from dawn. Pretty soon after that we'll be running through Palandur in daylight at high speed, something I never meant to do but which is our only chance of getting through, if that is still possible." Banda paused. "I can slow down now, bring the ship close to one of the banks, and you and Alain could get ashore. The attention of the Imperials is fixed on the river. Once you got far enough from the river, you'd have a good chance of making your way to the coast without being caught and stealing a boat to take you out to where the *Pride* will be waiting."

Alain, looking down at Mari, saw her feelings change from curiosity to upset as Banda spoke, but she kept her temper from showing in her face or her voice. "Captain, I really thought that by now you knew me better than that."

"Mari, Palandur is going to be hard to get through. Landfall…I don't how we can manage that. If the mission is going to fail, you need to do what is necessary to save yourself. For the greater good."

Mari shook her head. "The mission isn't going to fail. And I am not going to abandon you, and Asha, and Dav. If I do, you wouldn't stand a chance."

"But if it is necessary—" Banda began once more.

"I don't do what's necessary. I do what's right."

Alain had seen something in Banda as he spoke. "You were tasked to tell Mari this."

Banda didn't look back at Alain, but he nodded. "Certain individuals ordered me to do my best to save Mari if it looked like we wouldn't be able to save the texts. Mage Alain, you understand why I'm urging this course of action, don't you?"

"Alain should have a vote," Mari agreed. "Alain, as an impartial and disinterested party, what is your opinion of what I should do?"

"I am not impartial in any matter concerning you," Alain objected, wondering why Mari would have said that.

"That was a joke," she said.

"Ah. I understand." Alain did not have to think about his answer. "I do not know what Mari should do. I know what she *will* do. Mari does not leave anyone behind. She will not leave you to save herself."

"It would also save you," Banda pointed out. "Surely that matters a great deal to Mari."

"*That* is a low blow," Mari said, anger finally entering her voice.

"I know how much it matters to her," Alain said. "And I know she will not sacrifice others for a selfish reason."

Banda sighed heavily. "I did my best. Mari, I don't mind admitting that I am glad you're so stubborn and so insistent on doing the right thing. Tell Dav and Asha we'll wake them before we get to Palandur. We'll need everyone awake and ready when we charge through, because the capital is guarded by the best the Imperials have—not like the legionaries we encountered around Marandur and at the chain. Those were less trained and less capable because the Empire assumed they'd never face much in the way of threats. If you pretending to be Mara would have worked with any legionaries, it would have been them."

"Too bad we didn't get a chance," Mari said, her eyes on Alain.

He nodded back, watching as Mari went back to take over from Dav at the boiler.

Alain settled in to watch the sides of the river roll past in the darkness.

As light grew, he could make out more and more details. A single barge tied up alongside the river bank. A small town whose buildings and landing on the river the *Terror* passed quickly.

Captain Banda, watching the landmarks alongside the river, sent Alain down long enough to wake Dav and Asha. Alain found Asha awake, watching over the sleeping Dav, told both they were nearing Palandur, then hurried back to his watch post.

Dav paused at the bottom of the ladder. "Who do you want on the boiler when we go through Palandur?" he asked Banda. "Me or Mari?"

"You're both equally good," Banda said. "The question is, who's the better shot if we have to fight our way through?"

Dave grimaced. "Mari. She's also a whole lot better at coming up with plans if we face a fight. I'll take over the boiler and send her up here."

"Thanks, Dav. Giving us maximum power is just as critical a job as the other."

Mari and Asha soon stood together at the bottom of the ladder, Mechanic jacket next to Mage robes. Alain could not recall when that sight had become familiar rather than shocking. Familiar among Mari's followers, anyway. To the rest of the world, such a pairing would still seem inconceivable.

"Our plan," Banda said, "is to keep going as fast as possible until we're past the city and any Imperial attempts to stop us there."

"Where do you think they'll try to stop us?" Mari asked.

"At the bridges and when we pass the Imperial military dockyard. As soon as they heard the news out of Marandur they would've started trying to string barges and ships between the bridge piers and tie them in place. If they've managed to get any such barriers in place, we'll be stopped."

"No, we won't," Mari said.

"You have Mages," Alain reminded Banda.

"That we do." Banda's voice regained a trace of hope.

They were already racing past the scattered buildings outside Palandur. The walls of the city were visible ahead.

"Hang on, everyone," Banda said. "I'm going to keep moving fast no matter what as long as we can."

Men and women appeared on the decks of barges and boats laid up for the night, attending to required chores at the start of their day. More and more of them caught sight of the apparent large drift of wood racing past much faster than the current could account for, pausing to stare and point.

A string of four boats appeared in front of the *Terror*, one of the boats still moving into place to help form a waterborne skirmish line of sorts. Alain could see legionaries with crossbows and swords on the boats, looking up the river expectantly.

None of them paid attention to the driftwood at first. They were clearly looking for something else. But Alain saw first one, then another, legionary point and call out. No one looked alarmed yet, just puzzled.

As Banda steered the camouflaged *Terror* quickly between two of the boats, Alain saw an officer staring at the ship with an expression of dawning realization.

"That is the boat we're looking for!" the officer yelled loudly enough for Alain to hear.

Several crossbow bolts chased the *Terror* down the river, but the two that hit only lodged in the driftwood camouflage.

The first bridge had activity on the nearest river banks, but no boats had put out yet. The *Terror* raced between two of the piers without hindrance. Looking back, Alain saw Imperials on the bridge pointing at the *Terror* and yelling words impossible to hear at this distance even if the hatches had been open.

He had never thought to wonder how fast words could travel without the aid of Mage spells or Mechanic far-talkers. Could descriptions of the *Terror* get ahead of the ship quickly enough for the next row of defenders to be ready?

An answer loomed not far ahead. He could see another bridge, this one the closest to the Imperial dockyard. A war galley was underway, gliding out into the river, her crew at their battle stations. In the light of the rising sun the galley was a magnificent sight, long and lean, her low deck rising to fighting platforms on the bow and stern, two masts soaring skyward, and the banks of oars on each side moving like the graceful wings of a bird skimming the surface of the water. Near it were two boats that Alain recognized as dockyard patrols, pressed into service now on the river itself.

He heard the clunk of a hatch opening and looked back to see Mari climbing out onto the aft deck, staying low to be as concealed as possible by the driftwood, one of the new rifles in her hands. Alain had pushed open the hatch above him and stuck his head out before he realized he was moving. "Mari, there is little power here for Mages. It will be hard to fight our way though."

She wedged herself into the wood before replying, her voice carrying against the wind of their movement. "You're actually telling me to get back inside, aren't you? Sorry, my Mage. All we need to do is discourage that galley long enough to get past it."

"What of the boats?"

"I was hoping that you and Asha would handle them."

Alain scrambled out of his hatch, knowing that he would be at least partly visible to any watching Imperials. Asha came out of the aft hatch, her knife in her hand. They knelt side by side just behind the steering room while Mari took aim from behind them.

The war galley's oars flashed in the growing sunlight as they swept up and back, the bow of the warcraft turning in a graceful arc to head toward the path of the *Terror*. Either the Imperials had managed to pass word down this far already, or the commander of the galley had realized what the mass of driftwood really was.

Mari began firing, not the slow repetition of the old rifles, but the rapid shots, one right after another, of one of Mechanic Alli's new guns. Alain saw the officers and sailors on the quarterdeck of the war galley ducking for cover from the fusillade.

The galley veered off course as those on the helm sought protection from the hail of bullets. The legionaries along the deck also crouched low, pointing and shouting to each other. They could see that only one person was firing, quickly and accurately, and they obviously were not happy to be facing such a weapon.

But being legionaries, they would face that danger if so ordered.

Mari paused to reload. The galley was swinging back onto course, legionaries forming a wall of shields to protect the helm from another barrage. She glared at the Imperial warship, then with a grimace of inner pain shifted her aim.

As Mari fired rapidly again, Alain saw splinters flying from the hull of the galley near the places where the oars entered the ship. The places where the rowers would be sitting.

The smooth rhythm of the oars on the side facing the *Terror* faltered as several rowers lost their stroke and banged into the oars nearest them, causing those oars to slam into others. The rowers on the near side of the galley fell into confusion, the thrust from the rowers on the other side causing the galley to spin. The crew of the forward ballista vainly tried to keep their aim as the galley's bow swung past the *Terror* and on around.

As the *Terror* tore away from the floundering galley, one of the patrol boats bore down on it. If Captain Banda veered to avoid it, he would get too close to the second patrol boat, so the *Terror* kept on.

The patrol boat's bow grated against the driftwood, two legionaries in the bow leaping onto the *Terror* as others moved up to also jump.

They met Alain and Asha, waiting with knives in hand. Even the bravest legionary would quail at facing a Mage. These two, unable to retreat, tried to block the Mages' knives, but the legionaries were tangled in the driftwood, unable to move to defend themselves.

Alain killed one, Asha the other, with the swift, efficient blows they had been taught as acolytes. As they braced for the next pair, Mari went back to firing.

The next two legionaries were hit and fell back into the boat. Alain leaned out and pushed it away, fending off a sword blow. A crossbow bolt thudded into the wood near him and another sighed over his head, but then the boat was behind them and losing ground fast as the *Terror* kept moving with a sustained speed that neither sail nor oars could match.

Alain looked upward as the *Terror* passed between two piers of the bridge. Imperial citizens were crowding the walkway, watching the unfamiliar spectacle of a river battle on their doorsteps and drawn by what must have sounded to them like the firing of many Mechanic weapons.

The *Terror* passed the third bridge before the Imperials could put together any defenses there. Ballistas on the walls of Palandur hurled shots at the *Terror* as it raced down river, but failed to hit their unfamiliar and fast-moving target.

The way was not exactly clear, though. The alarm was for the moment behind them, but now they began to encounter shipping traffic putting into the channel, barges and boats moving slowly and steadily up the river or downstream at better speeds. Captain Banda steered the *Terror* through the obstacles, keeping to the center of the channel so that the ship could slip between the ships going down river on one side and those heading up on the other.

Startled skippers moved their craft away from the path of the strangely animated pile of driftwood, not wanting to risk a collision with either the branches and trunks or with whatever was causing them to move along so swiftly. But barges and similar boats responded slowly even when alarmed. Captain Banda had to slow the *Terror*.

"They are catching up," Alain said, pointing just ahead. Legionaries were dismounting from lathered horses and yelling orders to barges on the water.

"I don't know how to get these barges out of our way!" Banda seethed. "They're spending too long trying to figure out what we are before they clear the channel!"

"Our illusion is the wrong one," Alain said. "We must show them something that frightens them at first sight." He pushed open the hatch again. "Asha, hold my legs when I stand."

Alain clambered out onto the top of the steering room and stood up, Asha coming up the ladder to take his place behind Banda. No one could see her hands gripping his ankles to keep him from losing his balance.

Alain stood with legs slightly spread, folded his arms, let his cowl fall back, and gazed straight ahead.

Those watching saw a Mage standing erect on a frail raft of driftwood, the wood moving with unnatural speed down the river as if at the Mage's command. An uncanny sight—a terrifying sight to those who knew Mages as dangerous and powerful, whose paths were not to be crossed or obstructed.

Shouts sounded along the river, including at least one scream.

Boats began to move more quickly out of the way, frantically racing for the river banks to leave a clear path, warning cries racing from boat to boat down the river.

The legionaries who had been working to force boats and barges out into the river stood transfixed, staring at Alain as he moved past without any apparent effort.

"A Mechanic boat," Banda said with a laugh. "The Imperials are looking for a Mechanic boat, and here is a Mage riding on a pile of driftwood. Well done, Alain."

"The Imperials at the dockyard spoke of not taking action against Mages," Alain said loudly enough so that Banda could hear. "If those orders are widespread, they will need approval to attack us. That will take time, even if the Empire invokes the aid of Mages who send messages or uses the Mechanic far-talkers."

"How long can you stand there?" Banda asked.

"As long as I must," Alain said. As much as he had been around Mechanics, he was still surprised by questions like that. Mage acolytes were trained to endure whatever physical trials they faced, so he and Asha would of course bear any strain that must be borne until either the need passed, or they collapsed.

Alain put himself into a mental state in which he was barely aware of the passage of time and the growing strain on his body. He felt the hands holding his ankles change at times and knew that Mari had given Asha a rest break. At one point he saw a group of three Mages walking along the road next to the river. The Mages looked toward Alain as he passed them. They would be able to tell that he was not employing a spell to move, but having been taught that Mechanic toys were elaborate frauds, the Mages would not consider a Mechanic ship to be an explanation.

He wondered if any of the three could create heat or cast lightning. Or if any of them might spot part of the *Terror* and make it temporarily go away, thereby causing water to flood the boat.

But the Mages did nothing, simply watching until Alain could no longer see them. They would doubtless ask the first elders they encountered for an explanation of what they had seen, and would doubtless be told that they had not seen it, that the world illusion had confused them.

The river ahead of them stayed clear, boats and barges clinging to the river banks as their crews stared anxiously.

He could probably sit down. He would still be visible, and it would be much easier to maintain such a posture for the rest of the day.

Alain sat down, crossing his legs in a meditation stance.

Lost in a daze of mental disassociation and physical tiredness, he hardly noticed the sun setting in the west. "They can't see you anymore," Mari said from inside the steering room. "Get back inside."

It took considerable effort to unlock his stiff muscles, but Alain managed it. Mari was sitting in Banda's place, steering the ship with intense concentration. "Captain Banda is getting a few hours' sleep," she said. "Hopefully I won't run this thing aground. Have I told you today that you're a genius?"

"Not that I remember," Alain said.

She stole a glance his way. "Oh, you're exhausted. Yes, you're brilliant. Wake Asha to stand guard up here and you get some rest."

The night apparently passed uneventfully, though Alain was not sure if he would have awoken even if another battle had erupted nearby. Asha woke him at dawn. He ate quickly to give himself strength, then resumed his place seated on the top of the steering room.

Captain Banda was back at the wheel. "None of the boats out there are getting underway. They're leaving the river clear for us."

"That is a good thing," Alain said.

"Yes and no. It means that word of our coming must be spreading much faster than we're moving. If the Imperials have managed to hear the news as quickly as these boat crews, we'll face more trouble today."

No danger materialized until the afternoon, though, as the *Terror* came in view of another bridge across the river. "It's the Mechanic railroad bridge," Banda said. "Get everyone awake, fast."

Alain roused the others, then rejoined Banda and took up his seated position. Mechanic Dav and Asha had come out the aft ladder onto the deck and were waiting behind the steering room as the bridge drew closer. "They've got legionaries on the bridge!" Dav called. "There's smoke there, too, and it's not from a locomotive."

"Why would the legionaries have fires?" Banda wondered.

Alain saw the first crossbow bolts flying their way, striking the water short of the *Terror* and sending up sporadic bursts of smoke as they landed in the river.

"They're firing flaming bolts!" Dav yelled. "That's what the fires are for! Alain, get inside! They must have orders to shoot at us even if a Mage is with us!" Alain dropped inside the steering room as Dav knelt, aiming his rifle over the top of the steering room, and began firing back at the legionaries.

Some of the legionaries fell, but the others kept firing. Alain heard bolts slamming into the driftwood and saw flames springing to life.

Dav shifted his aim to the crew of a mobile ballista. The heavy bolt went wide, but the crew worked to reload.

As the *Terror* raced past under the bridge, lit torches were thrown down by the Imperials. Most missed, but three caught.

Alain pulled himself out of the steering room, uncaring of the crossbow bolts still being flung after them. Asha was already using her long knife to hack away at the driftwood, freeing sections that were aflame or smoldering and casting them into the river. Alain joined in, nearly losing his footing more than once as he struggled to break loose the flaming camouflage. The pieces had been strongly joined together, so the Mages were forced to hurl large sections of intertwined branches into the river. Mechanic Dav put down his rifle as the threat receded and began helping as well.

By the time the fires were out, little remained of the protective driftwood. Alain, Asha, and Dav, tired out, dropped back into the *Terror*.

"Well done," Captain Banda said. "Get some rest, Dav, and you Mages work out a schedule to sleep and keep watch up here. I don't think we'll run into anything else today or tonight."

"Why not?" Dav asked, nursing a burned finger.

"There aren't any barriers like bridges between here and Landfall, and the Imperials have already learned that we can break through improvised defenses." Banda shook his head, his voice grim. "The Imperials won't waste time or resources trying to stop us before Landfall. Not when they can concentrate on stopping us at the mouth of the river. Get what rest you can and tell Mari to do the same. At the rate we're going we'll reach Landfall just before dawn, and we're very likely going to face the fight of our lives."

chapter fourteen

"There's a slight curve in the river up ahead," Banda said. "When we round it, we'll see the river mouth." Outside the *Terror*, the world slumbered in the pre-dawn hush when the sky was darkest and every living thing slept deeply. But inside the ship, the three Mechanics and two Mages were as awake and alert as they could be after the strains of the past few days. Alain, recalling how Mage Guild elders spoke disdainfully about "weak" Mechanics, thought that many Mages would have had trouble keeping up with Mechanics Mari, Dav, and Banda since leaving Marandur. Watching Captain Banda stay awake by sheer willpower after three days with very little sleep, Alain believed that no Mage could have done better.

"Nothing," Mari said, looking around the outside from the aft hatch. "Landfall is quiet and dark. No defenses on the bridges we passed. No barriers."

"They're waiting at the mouth," Banda said. "And they will be waiting in strength."

The *Terror* rounded the curve in the river, coming into full view of the river mouth.

"Oh, blast," Banda said in a weary whisper.

A solid wall of ships stretched across the river mouth, several of them Imperial war galleys and the rest large merchant ships. The dark of night was banished here. Torches and lanterns flared all along the barrier showing every detail of the legionaries crowding the decks. Light glinted off of crossbows, swords, shields, and the great bolts loaded onto ballistas on the decks of the galleys. Alain could see more ballistas being moved into position on the river banks, ready to fire at anything approaching the barricade, and even more ships being moved into place to form a second wall behind the first.

It was obvious that the Imperials were working to further strengthen the barrier, but it was already a formidable obstacle.

"We can't smash through that," Banda said.

"We cannot go between the front of one ship and the end of the next?" Alain asked.

"That's what I'd try to do if we could. The Imperials know that. See how they're tying up the second row of ships so that they're overlapping the bows and sterns of the ships in the first row? They haven't nearly finished, and that could have given us a chance, but the first row of ships is already lashed together. See? The fact that we can see the lines from this far off means they used rope far too thick for us to have any hope of snapping those lines even if we hit them at full speed. Oh, we'll do damage to the ships we hit, but we'll be stopped— and once we're stuck, the legionaries will swarm down on us from the decks of those ships, and it will be all over."

Alain gazed ahead, studying the barrier. At least the Imperial lights made it possible to see details. "There are two lines? I see two lines."

"Um…yes. Two lines fastening each ship to the next. As I said, they look thin from here, but each will be as big around as our arms."

"Only two. And I see no Mages on the decks of the ships. There is a chance," Alain said, "if we go between two of the ships where another is not yet in place behind them. But it will require both Asha and myself casting spells at the same time."

"You can't go topside! The legionaries packed on those ships would put a dozen crossbow bolts in you as soon as we got close enough!"

"Then Asha will have to fit up here beside me."

Mari called up. "I just told Dav what we're facing. If Alain says we have a chance, then we have a chance. Do as he says. I'm going to go back to the aft ladder, ready to go out and shoot if we have to, or stop anyone who tries to come in."

Alain moved as far to one side as he could, facing forward, as Asha wormed her way up beside him. The space available, slightly cramped for one person, was so tight that Asha had to press herself hard against him in order to fit and be able to look forward as well.

Despite their desperate situation, despite the robes shrouding both of them, Alain found himself becoming distracted.

Asha must have noticed. Her face was right next to his, but she could turn enough to eye him. Alain was familiar with the eye-rolls that Mari sometimes directed at him to accompany the one-word comment "Men," but now Asha accomplished the remarkable feat of giving him a feminine eye-roll without moving her eyes or changing her expression. He was trying to figure out how she had done that when Asha said three words in the tone of a Mage addressing an acolyte. "Mage Alain. Focus."

"Yes," Alain said, directing all of his attention forward. "Here is what we must do. There are two heavy lines connecting each ship to the next. You see the place directly ahead where two ships are joined in such a way to block us. There is little power here, but I think enough that I can cause the illusion of one line to have a gap. Can you do the same to the other?"

Asha paused. "There is little power." She looked ahead as well. "There are no Mages with the Imperials who might also draw on the power available and leave too little for us. This will exhaust us both. But I can cast the spell on one line as well."

"Captain Banda, Mari," Alain called out loudly enough for Mari to hear, "Mage Asha and I will cause the lines ahead of us to part just before we reach them. You will have a chance to ram us through between the two ships. But both Asha and myself will be exhausted by the effort and unable to do anything else."

"Got it," Mari called. "We'll be ready to do any fighting. Dav! We're going through! Be prepared to leave the boiler unattended for a few minutes if you need to help fight off any boarders. Give us a warning just before we hit, Captain!"

"Five minutes!" Banda yelled back. "If that! Give me all the power you can, Dav! We're going to need all the speed and momentum we can manage!"

The *Terror* trembled like an eager steed as Banda advanced the throttle and steered toward the wall of ships. "The place is right ahead," Banda said. "Where I'm aiming between the bow of that war galley and the stern of that merchant ship flying the flag of Marida."

"Yes," Alain said. "How well do you see the farther line, Asha?"

"I see it well. I will take the farther line." Her soft voice, dispassionate and matter-of-fact, her breath on his face, were no longer distracting to Alain, but instead part of the illusion that he could disregard.

"I will take the closer line," Alain said. "How will we act at the same time?"

"Say *now* just before you cast your spell," Asha said, "and I will immediately cast mine."

The wall of ships grew closer with dismaying speed, but they dared not slow down. They could see the masts of other ships being frantically moved by the Imperials to block the small gaps beyond the two ships like that the *Terror* was aiming for. Alain could see legionaries shouting, but heard nothing with the hatches closed and the boiler creature roaring inside the *Terror*.

The ballistas mounted on the galleys and along the river banks began firing, bolts flying toward the *Terror*. Alain heard thunks as some of the heavy bolts fell short and struck the *Terror* underwater, most of their force fortunately absorbed by the water. Two other bolts tore through the remnants of the driftwood camouflage, sending splinters and branches flying. Another hit the metal hull at a low angle, bouncing off with a clang that reverberated through the ship.

Alain tried to ignore all of that. Perhaps only a Mage could have done so, trained to be able to focus on a spell no matter what distractions were staged or physical blows inflicted. He was no longer aware of Asha pressed up against him, no longer noticed the ballistas firing on the *Terror*, did not really see the wave of crossbow bolts fired as the ship came within range of hand-held weapons or hear them strike like a thunderous rain on the metal, some sticking or penetrating the skin of the ship, one cracking the small window right beside Alain's head. All of those things were only illusions. His attention remained centered on the illusion of a heavy line fastening a war galley to another ship, the slight curve of the line dipping down between them, the torches on the ships lighting up the top of the line. Illusion, all illusion. And he could change that illusion for a very brief time, overlaying the illusion of a gap on that line. Just a small gap, barely enough to see, but enough to momentarily leave the line in two pieces rather than one.

They were very close, the sides of the ships looming ahead.

"Now," Alain breathed.

There was so little power to draw on, and Asha was drawing on it as well. Alain's strength drained.

But it was enough. Bare moments before the *Terror* struck, the two lines suddenly fell slack between the Imperial ships, both cut clean in the center.

"Hang on!" Banda shouted.

The *Terror* hit the gap between the ships like a bull striking two sides of a heavy gate. Alain and Asha, still upright only because they were pinned in place, were jolted forward by the impact, barely aware of the sound of the crash filling the ship as tortured metal and hardwood protested the collision. If the lines had still been in place, the *Terror* would have been jerked to a halt as her hull, mostly underwater, slammed into the unyielding bow and stern of the ships ahead. But with the lines severed, the *Terror* was slowed but not stopped. Grating against the bow of the war galley and the rudder of the Maridan merchant ship, the *Terror* forced her way through the great barrier.

Alain, trying to maintain consciousness, heard thumps and felt the *Terror* jolt as they passed between the two ships. Through the small windows, he saw legionaries who had jumped from the ships onto their own craft.

The legionaries were trying to get footholds when the bow of another ship moving to block the gap thudded against the side of the *Terror*. Some of the legionaries were hurled off by the impact, but more jumped down from above as Banda maneuvered the *Terror* past the ship and headed into the harbor.

Alain saw a legionary scrambling for a hold and sliding off into the water as the *Terror* began gaining speed again.

Another got a purchase on the outside of the steering room, drawing a sword.

A third knelt, crossbow in hand, raising it to aim through the cracked window just beside Alain's head.

The crash of Mechanic weapons sounded behind Alain. He saw the legionary with the crossbow jerk the weapon to point aft, but get jolted by the impacts of bullets before falling off the ship.

The thunder of gunshots kept on. Alain, his normally suppressed emotions further restrained by the haze of exhaustion, wondered how many legionaries had reached the deck of the *Terror*.

The legionary who had a handhold on the steering room was crouching, blocking Banda's view forward as the legionary hid behind the structure. He swung the hilt of his sword against the nearest window, trying to break it so his sword could reach those inside.

Alain saw Mari appear outside the window closest to him, implacable and fierce, her pistol out and firing.

The last legionary gave a despairing cry and fell, sliding off the hull into the water.

"What's wrong with my power?" Captain Banda shouted. "We're losing steam pressure!"

Unable to supply an answer, Alain managed to twist his head enough to watch as Mari scrambled back to the aft hatch. He could not see Mechanic Dav, but finally spotting him lying near the hatch, holding on to the ship as if that was all he could manage. Crossbow bolts were still falling in a deadly rain around the *Terror*, some striking the ship, as Mari grabbed Mechanic Dav and pulled him with her down the ladder.

"Asha!" Mari shouted from inside the ship. "I need you here to help Dav! He took a bolt in his hip! Get down here! I have to get to the boiler!"

Asha's limp body stirred. "Dav," she muttered, forcing herself away from Alain and down the ladder, moving clumsily and nearly falling. Alain saw her stumbling aft, one of the medical bags in her hand.

Mari needed him. Alain bent his entire will to recover, trying to clear mind and body of overwhelming fatigue just as Asha had. Captain Banda was steering the *Terror* between the ships and boats in the harbor beyond the barricade, his hands locked on the wheel. Alain looked back and saw that the barrier was a mass of confusion. The place where the *Terror* had punched through was marked by a widening gap as the barrier ships drifted apart in response to the impact. Soldiers and sailors worked to free them to chase after the *Terror*.

Off to his right, Alain saw a darker cloud against the night sky, lit beneath by sparks. He had seen that before. Where? Julesport. "There is a Mechanic ship," he said to Banda. "On the right."

Banda stole a glance in that direction. "The *Queen*. Mari! We need to call the *Pride*! The Guild is getting the *Queen* underway! They must have figured out what's going on! If they can't catch us, they'll sink us to keep the Empire from getting those texts!"

"I have to run the boiler!" Mari shouted. "The shock of the collision rattled the boiler so badly it almost put out the fires!"

"I can handle the boiler," Dav insisted, his voice thin and high with pain.

"Dav!" Asha protested.

"Ash…help me there."

Alain breathed deeply, clearing his mind and looking around one more time. "There is a galley on the left. It is coming this way."

"He's behind our beam," Banda said. "As long as the fires don't go out in our boiler he won't have a chance of catching us." Banda spun the wheel and the *Terror* heeled wildly to one side as it tore past a harbor patrol craft. "Please don't go out," he muttered as if talking to the fires.

"I will help Mari," Alain said. He heard water falling as he staggered partway down the ladder and saw leaks in the hull where crossbow bolts had penetrated or glancing blows by ballista bolts had bent and cracked the metal. There were other gaps, which must have opened when the *Terror* hit the Imperial ships. Whenever outside water washed across those spots an erratic rain fell inside the ship. That probably ought to worry him, Alain thought, seeing drops of water glance off the bag protecting one set of texts. But he was emotionally numb, too tired, too focused on helping Mari, to spare concern on something he could do nothing about.

Mari came running forward. "Are you all right?" she yelled at Alain as she fumbled with a control one-handed. A rough, rhythmic thumping sound began. "I started the bilge pump!" she called to Banda. "We're taking on water! Alain, help me get the aft hatch open. I need to transmit from there."

Alain fell more than descended the forward ladder and stumbled after Mari, wondering why droplets of a deep red showed on the deck plates. When he reached the aft ladder, Mari was leaning against it, breathing hard, her face drawn. Horrified out of his torpor, Alain saw blood dripping from her left hand and a big puddle of blood at her feet. "Mari!"

She gave him a strained look. "Most of this is Dav's, but I'm having trouble with my left arm. Help me get the hatch open."

Alain lunged past her, his fatigue momentarily vanquished. He climbed up enough to push the hatch open, then reached down and helped Mari up. She lay on the open deck, momentarily out of breath, while the *Terror* heeled again as Banda raced toward the harbor entrance.

He clamped one hand on the edge of the hatch and put the other arm around Mari to hold her. She managed a grateful smile for him before fumbling out her far-talker with a grimace of pain.

Inside the ship, the roar of the boiler had masked most other noises except for the sound of Mechanic devices like the pump. Out here on deck, Alain could hear the blare of Imperial trumpets, the clanging of alarm bells, and a low roar which was the sound of thousands of men and women on numerous ships and boats trying to catch the *Terror* before she could get away.

"Help me stand up," Mari gasped. "I need better range."

She was doing what she must despite her fears. He could do no less. Alain got to his knees, still holding on to the hatch, and helped Mari stand, his other hand now locked on her belt as she stood next to him. Mari used her good hand to hold the far-talker. Her left arm hung useless, droplets of blood still falling to mingle with the harbor water puddling on the deck.

He heard the crash of Mechanic weapons in the distance followed by the snap of bullets flying past. Looking toward the sound, Alain saw a familiar shape silhouetted against the lights of Landfall. "It is the ship that once captured us," he warned Mari. Bright flares of light sparkled along its deck. He had learned what that meant. "There are Mechanics on it shooting at us."

"Let's hope they don't use the deck gun."

Alain heard a loud crash and the shriek of a shell, followed by a fountain of water rising not far from the *Terror*.

"Never mind." Mari caught her breath, then began speaking slowly and clearly into the far-talker, her voice an odd oasis of calm in the chaos of the harbor. "*Pride*, this is the *Terror*. *Pride*, this is the *Terror*."

The ship shuddered under Alain. He heard Dav cursing at the boiler. They surged ahead again as sparks and a gout of smoke billowed from the short stack behind him.

A high-pitched ping sounded as a Mechanic bullet bounced off the ship next to Alain's foot. He heard another huge boom, another shriek of a shell, then watched the shell burst in the wake of the *Terror*. The ship changed course abruptly and he held onto Mari as she staggered on the deck.

Something tugged at the sleeve of Alain's robe. He looked at it, seeing a ragged hole where a Mechanic bullet had just punched through, passing between him and Mari. That probably would have frightened him if he had been able to spare the energy or the attention to think about such things.

Mari kept speaking into her far-talker, as calmly as if she were a Mage, totally focused on her task. "*Pride*, this is the *Terror*. *Pride*, this is the *Terror*."

They had gotten far enough away from the Mechanic ship that no more bullets were coming close, but the deck gun banged again and another fountain of water rose, near enough to Alain for him to feel mist wash across him.

"*Pride*, this is the *Terror*. *Pride*, this is the *Terror*."

"*Terror*, this is the *Pride*!"

He felt Mari tremble as the reply came in, but her voice remained steady. "*Pride*, we're approaching the harbor entrance," Mari called. "The Guild ship *Queen of the Seas* is getting underway to chase us. We've suffered damage. Over."

"Understand you are approaching the harbor entrance. We're on our way. Over."

"Mission successful!" Mari said. "Do you understand? We have what we came for. We need help as soon as possible. Over."

"Understood. Coming at best speed. Out."

Mari sagged to her knees next to Alain, breathing hard. "What am I forgetting?" she asked in a raspy voice, putting away the far-talker as another shell from the *Queen* tore into the water behind them. The *Terror* heeled again, water washing across the deck. "The stack. We have to raise the stack before we get out into open water. Help me, Alain."

He had to let go of the hatch, helping Mari farther aft to where the stub of the stack poked up. Very hot air was erupting from the stack. "Here," Mari said, shaking her head as if dizzy. She pointed with her right hand. "We need to unfasten that. Alain, please. It takes two hands. I can't. Please figure out how to do that!"

He looked at the Mechanic equipment helplessly before an idea came to him. "One of my hands and one of yours," Alain said.

"Yes!" Mari laid down on the deck, reaching, placing Alain's hand on something she told him to press, while she shoved something else with her own hand. "That's got it. Let's get it raised. Blast!" She slid to one side as the *Terror* swerved again, Alain catching her before she slid off into the harbor. "Like this. Up. Yes. See, it just pivots on the hinge. No problem. Up. All the way."

Alain helped push the higher stack up, seeing one end of it fall onto the shorter one. He felt the higher stack almost immediately grow warm, then hot, from the air coming from the boiler creature.

He held Mari from sliding again as she used her good hand to flip closed some objects that fixed the tall stack in place. "Got it. Let's get inside."

The distance back to the hatch was fairly short, but it seemed incredibly far away. At least the line of sight had been blocked by other vessels and the Mechanic ship's deck gun was no longer firing at them. Once again Alain blocked out distractions, focusing on their path and keeping one hand on Mari. Reaching the hatch, he helped her down the ladder, then crawled in and pulled the hatch shut.

Mari dropped to the deck, landing in the puddle of blood Dav had left. She fell to her knees. "Alain...help...me up. No, check...Dav."

"Your arm—" Alain began, seeing her through a haze of exhaustion.

She waved him off. "Check Dav."

Alain staggered back to where the heat of the boiler made sweat spring onto his skin. Mechanic Dav half lay, half sat on the seat near the boiler, eyes on the controls, his face a mask of pain and determination. Asha knelt beside him, bracing him in place and holding a blood-soaked bandage tightly over his hip. Only another Mage could have seen the fear with which she watched him. "We're all right," Dav said, his voice quavering with agony and barely audible above the roar of the boiler. "How's Mari?"

"All right," Alain said. Asha, catching the anxiety behind Alain's words, spared him a concerned look before centering her attention back on Dav.

"Dav is all right," Alain said as he reached Mari again. It was a lie, but it was Dav's lie, and it was what Mari needed to hear.

She was sitting against one side of the ship, looking dazed, her left arm hanging limply. Alain forgot his own tiredness again for a few moments, grabbing the other medical bag and pulling off her jacket, ignoring Mari's gasp of pain.

It looked as though a crossbow bolt had struck her upper arm a glancing blow. There was a bloody slash in the flesh, surrounded by a deeply bruised patch of skin as large as Alain's fist. Barely keeping his emotions tamped down, Alain wrapped a bandage around her arm to stop the bleeding and then looked at her helplessly, his stock of medical knowledge exhausted.

Mari blinked her eyes as if trying to focus. "Get me up...with Captain Banda."

"Mari—"

"I can sit. I can call...the *Pride*. Get me up there."

It was not easy for him, after the spell and his other exertions, but Alain managed it, never able afterwards to recall precisely how he had hoisted Mari up the ladder and into the seat behind Banda as the *Terror* neared the exit of the harbor.

Mari pulled out her far-talker again. She looked at Alain. "You'll have to...guard...the rear hatch. Be careful."

Alain nodded. "You, as well."

"I love you," she whispered, knowing they had no time for any more words.

"I love you," Alain said, knowing that nothing else needed to be said between them. He slid down the ladder, not at all certain how he was still moving. Exhaustion weighed his every step and, water trickling down from dozens of holes in the ship's hull made the footing treacherous, but he made it to the after ladder, ensured that he still had his knife, then climbed upward until he could shove the hatch open again and stick his head out.

The motion of the *Terror* changed as the ship left the harbor. Ballistas on the breakwater fortifications hurled more bolts toward the struggling ship. Swells coming in from the sea made the *Terror* roll like a drunken sailor trying to walk as Captain Banda swerved erratically to throw off the aim of the ballistas. Several times Alain had to quickly slam the hatch as swells rolled over the deck, then open it again to resume his watch.

Looking back toward Landfall, Alain was startled to realize that the sky was beginning to lighten in the east. He saw the distinctive shape of the Mechanic ship beginning to move past the masts of the sailing ships, the smoke from its stack rising until it was lost in the fading remnants of the night sky.

Behind the Mechanic ship, three Imperial war galleys forged toward the harbor mouth, also chasing the *Terror*.

Alain sensed something wrong about the motion of the *Terror*. Its movement felt sluggish. He looked down the hatch, seeing that the trickles of water where the hull had been pierced turned into erratic streams as the ocean swells rolled over the damaged areas. Did that mean trouble? Only the Mechanics would know. He could do nothing but guard this hatch.

The *Terror* forged ahead, drawing away from the harbor as the Mechanic ship and the Imperial galleys made their way through the clutter of shipping, losing ground in their pursuit.

The roar of the boiler creature faltered.

Caught again.

Faltered.

Asha called loudly from near the boiler, spacing out her words as she repeated what Dav told her. "The boiler...is going out...the fuel...is almost gone...the tank...must have been...broken open... by the...collision."

The *Terror* was slowing. Alain could feel the ship still moving ahead but failing to maintain speed. The thing Mari had called a bilge pump was also slowing as the power from the boiler fell.

He looked back again at their pursuers, wondering if they would be caught before the ship sank beneath them.

"There is...nothing...left," Asha called, the direness of her words offset by the emotionless way in which she said them. "The boiler... is about...to go out." Never had a death sentence been pronounced so dispassionately.

Alain gripped the knife he held, thinking of what Mechanic weapons could do when their pursuers caught up. Even if any power had existed out here to help cast spells, he was too physically exhausted to manage any. It would not be a long fight.

He knew that Mechanic Dav would not survive the sinking of the *Terror*. And that Asha would not leave Dav's side.

Alain wondered if there was any way left to save Mari.

The sun had not yet risen, but the sky to the east was much brighter now, silhouetting the shapes of the Mechanic ship and the Imperial galleys sharply and clearly against it. The *Terror* was well away from the harbor, but the other ships had left the traffic there and were catching up as the *Terror* wallowed helplessly, barely moving as the boiler's roar faded into nothing.

He heard a boom, and looked for the puff of smoke from the front of the Mechanic ship that marked the firing of its deck gun.

There was no smoke.

Alain heard a rushing sound overhead.

Something struck the water near the Mechanic ship, exploding with enough force to throw up a column of water twice as tall as that from the *Queen*'s deck gun.

Startled, Alain spun to look ahead. The west was still dark, but he could make out against the pre-dawn sky that the *Pride* had approached, concealed by the last vestiges of the night. As he watched, the big gun that Mechanic Alli had installed boomed again. A black speck flew overhead, landing closer to the Mechanic ship than the first shot had.

The *Queen* came straight on, not altering course, as another shell threw up a fountain of water so near that it must have splashed on the Mechanic ship. Was it arrogance that kept the *Queen* from dodging? Or blind obedience to the same tactics that had always worked in the past? Or was it due to an inability to believe that someone other than their Guild could produce a deadlier weapon?

The *Queen*'s deck gun fired, but the shot fell short of the *Pride*.

The fourth shot from the *Pride* slammed into the *Queen*. The

Mechanic ship reeled from the blow, smoke billowing from one side.

The two ships each fired another round, neither scoring a hit. But the *Pride*'s sixth shell landed directly on the *Queen*'s foredeck, where the deck gun was located. A titanic cloud of smoke and debris blossomed as the *Queen* staggered off to the side, speed falling fast as her shattered bow dipped toward the water.

Alain was still staring at the sinking Mechanic ship and the figures of men and women leaping into the water when he heard the *Pride* fire once more. This time the shell fell just ahead of the three Imperial galleys heading for the *Terror*.

The Imperial warships kept coming, their oars flashing as they rose and fell.

The *Pride* fired again.

The shot hit the leading galley in the center. The explosion blew the galley in half. The splintered remains of the wooden ship's bow and stern spun away, pointing skyward as they sank.

That was enough for the other two galleys. They twisted about under the push of their oars, racing back to the harbor where more Imperial ships were getting underway.

Alain was still looking toward the harbor, feeling stunned, when the *Pride* coasted alongside, all of her boats already dropping into the water.

Mari managed to raise herself halfway out of the forward hatch, waving her good arm at the approaching boats. "We're sinking! The boiler has stopped! You have to get the texts off!"

Alain dropped through the aft hatch, nearly falling when he reached the deck, and went back to where Asha still knelt beside Dav, holding her knife ready for use. She gave Alain a steady look. "Dav is unconscious. How close are those who pursue us?"

"The *Pride* has driven off our enemies. Boats come. Our friends. They will take Dav to the healer on the *Pride*." Asha's eyes lit at the news, as despite her Mage training she inhaled a shaky breath that revealed her relief. "Stay with Dav, Asha. Stay with him as he stayed with you in Emdin."

Feet clumped on the deck, and sailors started coming down in a rush. Alain made his way to the forward ladder, looking up to where Captain Banda was slumped over the wheel, Mari lying back in her seat behind him. "Is Captain Banda hurt?"

Banda raised his head. "Too worn out to think, Sir Mage. Am I imagining things? Is the *Pride* really here, or is this the last illusion of a drowning sailor?"

"It is an illusion," Alain said. "All is an illusion. But you will not drown this day."

Streams of water were still pattering down from the breaks in the hull. Alain could hear water sloshing under the deck plates as sailors hauled Dav from the ship, Asha following. "Mari, we should get out."

She shook her head. "Not until the texts are off."

"We can wait on deck. There is no reason to wait inside."

Mari finally nodded, the motion wobbly. "All right."

She stood up and started to climb up and out. Alain, all of a sudden reminded of how worn out he was, struggled up the ladder and helped her onto the top of the *Terror*. Captain Banda followed, moving like a very old man.

Sailors from the *Pride* had formed a chain and were quickly passing sacks and backpacks full of texts up the ladders and into the *Pride*'s waiting boats. Alain saw the *Pride*'s smallest boat, carrying Dav, Asha, and several sacks of texts, already heading back to the *Pride*.

"Lady!" The sailors holding one longboat close to the *Terror* gestured to Mari. "That ship is going down! Come on!"

Mari shook her head, leaning against Alain as he steadied himself on the top of the steering room. "Not until it's all off."

Alain looked down through the hatch, seeing water now washing across the deck plates. The *Terror* was noticeable lower in the water, especially in the front. "We do not have long."

"Not until it's all off," Mari repeated.

"Sir!" a sailor at the aft hatch called to Banda. "That's everything!"

Mari tried to move toward the hatch. "I need to check. Need to be sure."

Banda stopped her. "Master Mechanic, I'll check. I know where everything was stowed." With a grimace, he gestured the sailor aside, swung into the hatch and dropped down.

Alain watched and listened anxiously as Banda searched the interior of the small vessel. The section of deck where Mari and Alain stood was now completely awash, the sea water swirling around their ankles but the cold barely registering on Alain's overstressed senses. The aft hatch was about to go underwater when Banda reappeared and pulled himself up with surprising speed and headed for a boat. "It's all out, Mari. We've got it all."

Alain shoved Mari into the arms of the waiting sailors, feeling the deck of the *Terror* falling away beneath his feet. He sank waist deep into the water, his arms catching at the side of the boat, before the sailors hauled him in as well and sat him next to Mari.

He held onto her as the sailors rowed the short distance back to the *Pride*. Alain looked back as he was helped up the ladder, seeing that there was nothing left of the *Terror* but a few pieces of wood bobbing on the surface and steam bubbling up from below as the boiler creature gave up the last of its heat.

Mari had to be pulled up in a sling, then refused to leave the rail, watching as the boats were recovered and the sacks of texts transferred to the *Pride*.

"The Imperials are coming out again," said someone next to Alain. He turned to see Mechanic Deni standing there, immensely comforting in her strength and confidence. "A lot of them. Enough to take us even with Alli's big gun. But we'll be done and steaming away before they get close enough to worry about," she added. "Master Mechanic Mari, you should see the healer."

"Not until it's all aboard," Mari insisted. She was leaning heavily on the rail, left arm hanging uselessly. Alain held her right arm to keep her standing.

Captain Banda staggered up to Mechanic Deni. "I am in no shape to resume command of the *Pride*. Continue as acting captain until I get about two days of uninterrupted sleep."

Deni grinned. "You getting old, Captain?"

"Feeling as old as if I had sailed under Jules," Banda said. He looked at Mari, a slow smile coming to his face. "Then again, in a way I did sail under Jules. Master Mechanic, thank you."

Mari turned a puzzled look on him. "For what? None of you gave up. That's what got us through."

"We didn't give up because you wouldn't give up, and we didn't want to let you down." Banda saluted Mari, then let a sailor help him toward his stateroom.

"That's the last," Mechanic Deni said as sailors carefully brought a final sack onto deck. "I'll personally see it securely stowed below. You can see the healer now, Master Mechanic."

Mari swayed against Alain. "Dav. Where is Dav? How is he?"

"He's with the healer. As you should be."

"I will take her," Alain said, not certain that he would be able to support Mari that far. But sailors came to help them both along, moving slowly across the deck as the *Pride* turned under the push of her new steam propulsion. The deck canted and shadows from the rising sun shifted rapidly as the ship swung about before steadying back into a westerly course. The last things Alain saw before going below-decks were the frustrated Imperial warships once more losing ground in their chase, and the stern of the *Queen of the Seas* sliding beneath the surface to join the *Terror* in a watery resting place.

The healer and his assistants rushed Mari to a bunk, stretching her out despite her weak efforts to resist. "Dav. How is Dav?" Mari demanded.

"Right over there," the healer said. "I think he'll be all right. The hip may never be the same. Lost a lot of blood, but he's young, and the Lady Mage provided him some of her own."

Alain had sunk down on a stool next to Mari's bunk, his sluggish thoughts realizing that of course Mari would not think of herself until she knew that everyone else was all right. He looked across the room to see Asha lying next to Dav.

"Mechanic Dav talked the Lady Mage into getting a physical on the voyage out," the healer continued as he carefully unwrapped the crude bandage that Alain had wrapped around Mari's arm. "That's how I knew her blood was compatible with his without having to test it. Good foresight on his part, eh?"

"It was not...foresight," Alain mumbled. "That is a Mage art."

"Sorry, Sir Mage?"

"Nothing." Alain looked at Mari, whose eyes were glazed from weariness and the effects of her injury and loss of blood. She seemed unaware that the healer was working on her arm.

"We really did it?" Mari whispered to him.

"We really did it."

"We all made it," she added as if seeking reassurance.

"Everyone made it," Alain said.

"Where will you be?"

"Right here," Alain said.

"Good. That means I'm safe." She closed her eyes.

He did not realize until much later, when he finally woke again, that he must have passed out as well, still sitting next to her.

Mari woke up, aware first of the gentle motion of the *Pride* as she headed west with following seas and second, that every single piece of her body hurt. She had been looking upward for some time at the play of reflected light and shadow on the overhead planks when the healer noticed that Mari had awakened.

"How do you feel?" he whispered to avoid waking anyone else.

"Like I'd been shot out of a cannon," Mari whispered back.

"You'll be all right. That's just your body complaining about the way you abused it." The healer pointed to her bandaged upper left arm. "Except for there. You were very lucky. If that crossbow bolt had been just a little closer to you it would have broken the bone and made a lot bigger gash in your arm. As it is, it will hurt longer than the rest of you, and you won't be able to comfortably use the arm for a little while, but you'll be fine. Make sure you see a healer once a week until the injury has healed enough for the stitches to be removed."

"Dav?"

The healer scratched his chin as he thought. "He'll live. We got past the immediate danger, and the new antibiotics that you, Master Mechanic, helped us learn to make using techniques from the banned technology should keep him from getting an infection. But his hip bone was cracked. I don't think it can heal straight. He'll be able to walk, but he'll likely limp all his life."

Mari felt tears start. "It's my fault."

"Everyone is telling me the only reason he's alive is because you got him inside the ship after he'd been hit, despite having been hit your-self. I guess it's your fault he lived long enough for me to save him." The healer gestured toward his feet. "This one wouldn't move."

Mari was barely able to lean out enough to see Alain, wrapped in a blanket, sleeping on the deck next to her bunk. "No. He won't move. How is Mage Asha?"

"A little weak from giving blood, that's all. And Captain Banda is fine. Just as worn out as you are, but without the arm wound."

The healer gave her a drink that knocked out Mari again. When she awoke once more, Alain was sitting beside her. "Hello, my Mage."

"Hello, my Mechanic."

"What's happening?"

Alain indicated the deck above. "We continue toward the west. There is a spot along the coast where Mage Alera and Mage Saburo will be waiting with their Rocs to take us back to Tiae."

"Back to Tiae on Rocs?" Suddenly the *Pride*'s narrow bunk felt like the most desirable, comfortable place she could imagine for the next few weeks. "When? Do we get any chance to recover first?"

"You have been asleep for a day and a half. Captain Banda says we should be where the Mages wait in another half-day."

Mari inhaled deeply, then regretted it as her body protested the exertion. "I know I'd agreed during planning that the *Pride* would take the texts home while you and I flew back, but I don't want to leave them, Alain. What if something happens to the *Pride* before she reaches Tiae?"

"You are needed back in Tiae. To lead those who follow the daughter, to give guidance to those who follow your orders, and to prepare for whatever must be done next."

"I know, but—"

"Mari," Alain said, "have you not had enough adventure for a while?"

She made a face at him, grateful that her facial muscles didn't hurt too badly. "I'd say a few days on a Roc flying back to Tiae qualifies as an adventure. Most people would think so, anyway. Can I fly with my arm like this?"

"The healer says you should be fine."

"That figures." Mari nerved herself, then rolled to a sitting position, wincing. "Ow. I was hoping I wouldn't be able to move so I'd have an excuse for staying in a bed another day or so."

Alain shook his head. "That would mean doing something the easy way, and you always do things the hard way."

She gave him an annoyed look. "I never should have told you that about me."

"I believe I would have figured it out on my own."

"Yeah. Probably."

Half a day later, with the *Pride* putting in toward shore where the huge shapes of two Rocs could be easily seen through far-seers, Mari paused beside Dav's bunk in the healer's room, where Asha once again sat by his side. "How are you feeling, Mechanic?"

"Ready to work," Dav replied, his voice and smile both weak.

"You put up a great fight against those legionaries. I'm sorry you got hurt so badly."

"It could have been a whole lot worse," Dav said. "How did you wrestle me down that hatch with only one arm?"

"I don't know. A lot of things are kind of hazy, you know?"

"Yeah. For me, too." Dav looked at Asha. "We figured it was over. So don't apologize, Mari. You got us out of there. I've been thinking that my ancestor can rest in peace now that the job he began is finally completed."

Mari smiled at Dav. "I'll bet he's happy that his namesake played such a vital role in getting that job done."

"I can't wait to tell my parents. Hurry up and get your job done, Mari. Get the Great Guilds overthrown. What's the hold-up?" Dav gave her another frail smile as he tried to sound like a Senior Mechanic berating an Apprentice.

"I was going to take my time," Mari said, "but since it's important to you, I guess I'll speed things up a bit. I'll see you back in Tiae. You take care of yourself, Dav."

"I don't think Asha will let me do anything stupid," Dav said.

"Anything else stupid," Asha said in her Mage voice.

"We never should have taught you Mages humor," Mari said. "Thank you for all you've done as well, Asha. It all may be just an illusion, but you've played a big part in changing it for the better."

"I have already gained a reward," Asha said, giving Dav a sidelong glance that made him smile again.

The forbidding cliffs that edged the southern Sea of Bakre featured a few narrow inlets that were too small for any town or village to take root but were large enough for a pair of Rocs to land and take off again. Mari felt every movement in her aching muscles as the *Pride's* boat rowed her and Alain to the gravel beach.

Alain and Mechanic Deni helped Mari out of the boat, but she still had to grit her teeth when some pressure shot a stab of pain through her left arm. "Hold on." Mari got out two of the pills that the healer had given her and swallowed them down with a slug from her canteen.

"Why didn't you take those earlier?" Deni asked.

"The healer said they'd help the pain but also make me woozy. I didn't want you guys to have to strap my limp body to the Roc." But Mari still needed extra help getting up on Swift, Mage Alera assisting in strapping her to the harness.

"Swift wants to know if you are hurt," Alera said.

"He does?" Mari, lying on the huge bird's back, reached out her good arm to stroke some of the nearby feathers. "Yeah. Nothing serious. Tell Swift thanks for caring."

A few minutes later the two Rocs vaulted into the air. Mari had a dizzy view of the *Pride* shrinking in size as the Roc climbed, then buried her face in the feathers before her. It was probably just the healer's pills, but maybe Swift took extra care with his injured rider. Whatever the reason, Mari was able to handle the long flight that day, sleeping for most of it.

Three days later, they reached Tiaesun.

Mari caught a quick glimpse of a large encampment of her soldiers outside the city. Why were they there instead of inside Tiaesun where she had left them? The pair of Rocs skimmed over the battered walls, rising slightly to sail over the taller surviving buildings, then banked to fly around the edge of the great plaza. As her Roc circled, Mari saw the banner of Tiae flying above the building where Princess Sien had established her court. But Mari's banner of the new day was gone. In its place flew a banner of gold that Mari had never seen before.

chapter fifteen

he Rocs circled the plaza twice as people in the open area below scurried to shelter like chicks seeking safety from hawks.

Mari winced as the Roc landed, the bump jarring her left arm and setting off another jolt of pain. Despite Mage Alera's help, unstrapping herself was a clumsy process with the full use of only one hand. Alain was already waiting to help her down from Swift by the time Mari was ready.

Having seen the sort of garbage that had littered the plaza before Tiaesun had been liberated, Mari resisted the urge to kneel and kiss the stones of the pavement. But she smiled while she waved goodbye to the Rocs and their Mages as they rose back into the sky with a thunder of wings and a gale of wind. The smile faded quickly as she looked at the strange new banner flying next to that of Tiae. "Have you ever seen that banner before?"

Alain shook his head. "Many of your soldiers are outside the city."

"I saw. Let's talk to Sien and find out what's going on. Sien would not betray us, so there has to be some other explanation."

Alain walked beside her as they strode toward the building, Mari frowning as she realized something else. "What happened to the work teams cleaning out and clearing off the streets and this plaza? All I see are people standing around."

She went up the stairs, entered the heavy door scarred by years of neglect and vandalism, and found herself in a familiar anteroom. The scene inside was different, though. A string of forlorn-looking visitors sat along one wall as if they had been waiting a long time and expected to wait longer, and a richly dressed man sat behind a desk beside the closed door that led into Sien's audience room. Mari felt a growing sense of unease as she and Alain walked toward that door.

The grandly dressed man slid smoothly to block their path. "You desire an audience with Prince Tien?"

Mari stared at him. "Prince? What prince? We're here to see Princess Sien."

The man shook his head with obviously mock regret. "There is no…princess. Tiae is ruled by Prince Tien, who a week ago returned to his land to assume his rightful position and authority."

Mari was still staring in disbelief at the man when he smiled. "You may request an audience with the prince." He gestured toward the line of despondent visitors. "He is very busy, though. If you wish to see him quickly, a contribution to the maintenance of the court might be wise."

"Hold on," Mari said, wondering if she had heard right. "Did you just demand a bribe as the price for letting us see this Prince Tien?"

"It is a fee for expenses," the man repeated. "Those who cannot assist in the upkeep of the court cannot complain if that means their petitions take more time to process." He smiled again.

His smile abruptly faded as he looked at Mari. She wondered what her expression looked like at the moment. If it matched her mood, there was little wonder the man looked worried.

Before he or she could say anything, Alain intervened, using his Mage voice. "We will enter now."

The man looked at Alain, swallowed nervously, and tried another smile. "Perhaps I could—"

"Now," Alain said, the single word falling like the crack of doom. Alain raised one hand toward the man, who stumbled back a step, fear springing to life in his eyes.

"I am c– certain that the prince will see you. Now."

He hastily opened the door and stood aside as Mari stalked inside, Alain beside her.

The back third of the house's former ballroom had been roped off and was now occupied by a bevy of men and women whose clothing indicated they came from a wide variety of places. One richly dressed woman was wearing the latest style from the northern parts of the Confederation. Near her were some men and women in nice suits that reflected fashions of the Western Alliance, and several others wore grand outfits that could only have come from Syndar. Tables and chairs, many mismatched but all looking comfortable and in good repair, were spaced around the area for the use of the group.

In front of that group, what was probably the grandest chair left in Tiaesun had been mounted on a low platform draped in green and gold fabric. Seated in that chair was a man in his late twenties who looked as though he had been cast as the prince in a play. He wasn't so much handsome as he was perfectly turned out: hair styled just so, clothing shouting wealth and power. His body reflected plenty of exercise to keep his shoulders broad; his waist was narrow and his arms brawny. He loosely held the hilt of a naked cavalry saber in one hand, the point resting on the platform in a dramatic display that would have earned angry rebukes from any swordmaster who saw a new recruit mistreating a weapon in that manner.

Prince Tien vividly brought to Mari's mind memories of a certain kind of guy she had encountered at times, the sort who had come on to her as if she should be grateful for their attention and eager to hang on their arm where everyone could see. There was some family resemblance to Princess Sien, but it was hard to make out how much beneath the carefully sculpted appearance and expression.

The wall at the back of the room where Mari and Alain had entered was lined with soldiers of Tiae, but the area around the prince was guarded by soldiers wearing the uniform of one of the Syndari city-states.

"Your name!" the door warden whispered at Mari. "So I can announce you properly!"

Mari had thought she disdained the trappings of power, so she was surprised how much the doorman's failure to recognize her stung. Her unhappiness with herself made her voice even sharper as she replied. "Master Mechanic Mari of Caer Lyn."

"And you are?" the man prodded Alain.

Alain turned his most Magelike face on the doorman, causing that worthy to step back again, shaking visibly. "Mage Alain of Ihris."

The man gulped, stood forth, and began to speak loudly. "Master—"

"Never mind!" Prince Tien called, flipping a dismissive hand at the man. "I could hear. So, the Mechanic has finally deigned to respond to my summons?"

Mari, not wanting to sound too angry, silently counted to five before answering. "*Master* Mechanic. *Lady* Master Mechanic. What summons?"

"You were ordered to appear before me," Tien said, frowning majestically at her.

"I've been away. Where is Princess Sien?"

Tien's annoyance grew. "There is no 'princess.' There was a commoner who claimed to be part of the royal family. I did not bother to learn the name," he added nonchalantly, punctuating his words with another exaggerated gesture.

Mari, fearing that harm had befallen Sien, almost exploded at the prince. Fortunately, one of the well-dressed men behind the prince pointed an accusing finger at her before she could speak.

"We know that your soldiers have given shelter to the pretender. She must be turned over to the crown at once!"

"Yes!" Tien agreed, nodding vigorously. "At once!"

"Why," Alain asked, "does a Prince of Tiae have traces of Syndar in his accent?"

Tien paused, looking affronted but apparently lost for a reply.

Another advisor spoke for him. "Many of the prince's tutors and protectors were from Syndar."

"How strange," Alain said tonelessly, "since all of Princess Sien's teachers and protectors have been from Tiae."

"Do not say that name again!" Tien said loudly, pointing an imperious finger at Alain.

Alain gazed back at Tien the way most people would gaze at a dead insect.

"Are you seriously trying to intimidate a Mage?" Mari asked the prince. "Maybe we should talk privately."

"About what?" Tien asked, peevish now, one hand twisting the hilt of the saber as he gazed at Mari.

"I have an agreement with Tiae—"

"There is no agreement," Tien interrupted with another indifferent wave. "You, and your followers, are not welcome in Tiae. Tell her," he ordered another of the foreigners behind him.

That woman, with a soft smile and very hard eyes, spoke to Mari as if she were a recalcitrant student. "You are to leave Tiae. All of your followers are to leave as well. This must be done immediately. You are to take nothing but the clothes on your backs, and leave to Tiae that which you have illegally and improperly taken from Tiae's land and Tiae's people. This particularly applies to everything at the illegal encampment at Pacta Servanda."

Mari had listened with growing disbelief. "Leave immediately and leave everything behind? All of our workshops and tools? All of our weapons?"

"That is correct."

"No, that is ridiculous." Mari looked to the soldiers of Tiae lining the back of the room, finally spotting Colonel Hasna among their number. She knew it would hurt their pride for her to say the truth: that the army of Tiae was too small and too weak to have liberated any of Tiae on its own, and that it existed only because of Mari's own efforts. She couldn't let this prince, if he was a prince, goad her into harming her relationship with Tiae.

"My followers and I have fought alongside Tiae," Mari said, spacing her words and speaking clearly. "We have been proud to do so. We have passed on to Tiae weapons and armor so that Tiae's army could once again fight for their country. We have worked together to turn back the Storm—"

"Storm?" Prince Tien looked around demandingly. "What storm?"

Mari counted to five again before answering. "I'm talking about the Storm that will destroy all of Dematr if not stopped, a storm of anarchy and violence spawned by the long slavery of the common people to the dominion of the Great Guilds. Tiae has been playing a very important role in the overthrow of the Great Guilds."

"Tiae has no interest in war, except in the pursuit of what is Tiae's," Prince Tien said. "And Tiae will fight for what it owns by right."

"The Great Guilds are already fighting you," Mari said.

"The Mechanics Guild has done Tiae no harm," one of the advisors insisted.

"How can you say that?" Mari demanded. Her arm was hurting again, and the various aches caused by the long flight from the coast of Bakre were driving the last vestiges of patience from her.

"It is the truth! The Guild will help Tiae more than you ever have!"

"You work for the Guild?" Alain asked.

The advisor held out his hands in protest. "I am not a Mechanic—"

"That is obvious," Alain said. "But I read the larger lie in you. How much does the Mechanics Guild pay you?"

"I– I'm not—"

"That much?" Alain asked, the lack of feeling in his words giving them more force.

"I will not have my advisors insulted," Prince Tien said severely, raising the saber to point it at Alain. "You will do as commanded," he told Mari.

"I'm never been all that good at doing as I was commanded," Mari said, crossing her arms and gazing back at Tien. "I have been trying to do good for Tiae. I don't know what your game is, or your advis—" She paused, seeing someone she recognized in the well-dressed group. "You! You were a city official in Edinton! Why is a Confederation politician here?"

"I don't know what you're talking about," the man Mari pointed to said. "I have never met you."

"Another one who lies," Alain said. "A ruler who surrounds himself with those who not only lie but are foolish enough to try to mislead a Mage. Do none of you know what Mages can do?"

"Is that a threat?" Prince Tien cried, rising from his seat to sweep his saber in a grand curve above his head. "You dare to threaten me and my advisors? Soldiers of Tiae! Take these two! They will be held—" He cast an aggravated glare at two advisors who were whispering frantically to him. "All right!" he hissed in a low voice to them, before speaking loudly to the room again. "Leave the Mage alone, but take the woman until she agrees to abide by my commands!"

Shocked, Mari heard the soldiers behind her begin to move. She paused, not wanting to draw her weapon on soldiers of Tiae.

Alain did not hesitate. "If anyone touches her, it will go ill for you." He was looking directly at Prince Tien with the dead Mage expression that terrified commons. At the same time he raised one hand to his waist, the forefinger and index finger pointed toward Tien.

Whatever else Tien was, he was enough of a common to be frightened by that look and that gesture.

But at least one of his advisers was not. "Do not attempt to bluff us, former Mage!" a woman shouted. "Though you show us the face and voice of a Mage, you have done that which is forbidden and lost all real power!"

Mari had rarely known Alain to become furious, but she felt that now in him even though Alain kept the dead expression of a Mage.

A chair not far from the woman erupted into flame.

She stared at it, eyes wide, as everyone else edged away from her.

"Nothing is real," Alain said, his voice filling the room. "However, my power is enough to turn this illusion into an inferno. Do you doubt me?"

The woman shook her head, trembling. "No."

"The elders of the Mage Guild do not know how weak their wisdom is, or how strong I am. Do not test me again." That was clearly aimed at everyone in the room.

Mari turned, finding herself nearly face to face with Colonel Hasna, who had advanced along with her soldiers at the command of Prince Tien but now stood unmoving, waiting for further orders.

"It is unseemly to brawl here," Tien said, unexpectedly pragmatic. "Let them go. I will deal with them later."

"Why are you here instead of with Princess Sien?" Mari asked Hasna in a low voice. "Why are you following his orders?"

Hasna's eyes flashed with resentment. "You would not understand honor. I am bound by my oath to follow the orders of Tiae."

"I understand that I left Tiae under the rule of a strong, intelligent leader and return to find it led by a pretty jackass with a pack of liars telling him what to do. You've traded a princess for a puppet."

"Do not mock my loyalty," Hasna ground out between clenched teeth. "I love Tiae more than you can imagine."

"Then I hope with all my heart that none of my followers ever love me as you love Tiae," Mari said. "Get out of my way."

Hasna's face tightened with anger, but she roughly gestured to her soldiers to stand back and allow Mari and Alain to pass.

"It was dangerous to provoke her so," Alain murmured as Mari stalked back into the anteroom.

"I know! And I did it anyway! Because sometimes I just can't help telling people what I think!" Mari stormed out of the building, but came to a stop as she saw a large group of her soldiers headed toward her at a fast pace. "Ah! As rescues go, it's a little late, but maybe they'll help keep me from saying anything else I shouldn't."

"It would take many more soldiers than that to prevent you from speaking your mind," Alain said.

He must have learned to understand her very well. A brief, involuntary laugh slipped through her anger as General Flyn strode up at the head of the soldiers.

"Lady, I have brought an honor guard to escort you to your headquarters in Tiaesun."

"Thank you, General," Mari said. As they began walking back across the plaza, the soldiers formed ranks ahead, behind, and to each side, enclosing her and Alain in a box bristling with weapons. "Where is Princess Sien?"

"Officially, I have no idea," Flyn said. "Unofficially, she has sought protection in a place where the soldiers of a close friend can be counted upon where the soldiers of Tiae could not. Speaking of safety, I assume that you're all right?"

"Close enough," Mari said.

"You were wounded by an Imperial crossbow," Alain said.

"Yes, I was." Not wanting to make too big a deal of it, Mari lightly tapped her upper left arm. "Just a glancing blow. Sort of a farewell gift. I'll be all right."

Flyn nodded. "And the items you sought?"

"Safely aboard the *Pride*, on their way back to Tiae. So are Mechanic Dav, Mage Asha, and Captain Banda. It was...sort of close, but we made it." Mari looked around at the soldiers surrounding her, their faces grim and rifles at ready. "And now I'm back in another fire. How many troops do we still have in the city?"

"This is half of what remains. I left the others at your headquarters to ensure the safety of...everyone there. The rest of your soldiers who were helping to garrison Tiaesun have moved to camps outside the city."

"We saw. How is the army of Tiae able to garrison all of Tiaesun already?" Alain asked. "They did not have the numbers needed when Mari and I left."

"And they don't have the numbers now," Flyn said. "By order of that prince, Tiae's army has effectively ceded a third of the city, including the entire port, to the Syndari mercenaries the prince brought with him. Ask me how happy the people of Tiaesun are about that."

"What about fixing up the city?" Mari asked. "What happened there?"

"According to my sources," Flyn said, "an exclusive cleaning contract has been granted to one of the prince's advisers. The workers who were doing the job were all let go and told they could reapply at a later date for the same jobs under the management of that adviser's foreign company."

"Unbelievable. Who is that idiot calling himself Prince Tien?"

"Apparently," Flyn said heavily, "he is Prince Tien."

There were so many sentries posted around Mari's Tiaesun headquarters that it looked more like a fort inside hostile territory than an encampment in a friendly city. The local citizens, whom Mari had seen mingling with her soldiers after the city's liberation, were now standoffish, their attitudes those of people who had always expected the worst and were now about to see it come to pass again.

That deflated her anger. Instead, she felt hurt that these people who had suffered so much were once more turning into pawns in someone else's game.

The headquarters had once been a large inn catering to travelers. It had enough room for the soldiers and an attached stable for the horses. Mari followed General Flyn across the courtyard and into the main building, then to what had once been a small meeting room.

Inside, Princess Sien sat in a battered chair. Her dejected expression changed to a smile as she saw Mari and Alain. Mari rushed to her friend, hugging her with one arm and feeling the other's tension. "What the blazes happened?"

Sien shook her head. "He– What's the matter with you?"

"It's just my arm. A crossbow bolt. No big," Mari said dismissively. "It didn't go in. It just took a piece out of me."

"Alain," Sien said, turning an angry look on him, "you said you would protect her."

Alain nodded. "I did. But the ship was under attack, and sinking."

"Did you get—," Sien began, then waved an angry hand to cut herself off. "That's not important. Not compared to you two being safe. What did you ask? The prince. He looks like my older brother Tien. He has some proofs of his status, including the mundane crown of Tiae, meant to be worn on a daily basis. How that survived, I don't know. When he sailed into port along with those proofs, and his advisers and his Syndari mercenaries, the army of Tiae accepted him as the true ruler."

"We saw. How did Tien survive?" Alain remained standing as Mari and Sien sat down close to each other.

"As near as I can determine, while I was being traded among various opportunists and criminals until I escaped and found supporters, he was spirited away to an isolated villa in the mountains north of Daarendi," Sien said bitterly.

"He spent all those years hiding in a villa, while you stayed here in Tiae?" Mari was unable to hide her incredulity. "While you were threatened and fought and struggled to help your people, he stayed hidden in comfort? And your army turned Tiae over to him when he showed up?"

"He is older," Sien said.

"So what?"

Flyn answered to spare Sien. "The laws of Tiae are fairly simple in that regard. The eldest living man or woman in the direct royal line is king or queen."

"He's an idiot!" Mari said, frustrated.

"The law doesn't care."

"Then the law is idiotic! Sien, you can't just accept this. I saw enough of Tien to know that he's just being used by those advisers—"

"No," Sien broke in. "He is playing at that. I have been watching, mostly from afar once Tien realized that my existence was a threat to his rule. Tien plays at being merely a grand shell of a prince, but under that he has been ruthless and decisive when necessary. The advisers, some of them, are fools who think to use Tien to enrich themselves. They will discover too late that Tien has used them to enrich himself."

"How can such people be fooled when you are not?" Alain asked.

"Because they consider themselves to be very, very clever," Sien said. "Too clever to be taken advantage of or misled. If you want to take a victim, Sir Mage, choose one who thinks he is too smart to be taken. And Tien has no mercy for those who underestimate him. Did you see him smile? What did you see in that?"

"Nothing," Alain said. "There was no feeling behind it."

"Really?" Mari asked, shocked.

"Nothing," Alain repeated. "His eyes…they reminded me of the eyes of Mage elders who have divorced themselves from believing that any shadow matters."

"Yes," Sien agreed, her voice growing sad. "My brother. And he looked at me and evaluated my worth to him and my potential cost to his plans, and that was all he saw. He did not realize that I had been trained in very harsh schools to see what was in the heart of those I dealt with, and so I could see what little was in his."

"I'm…so sorry," Mari said, imagining how she would have felt if her mother had acted like that upon their reunion. "You said only some of the advisers are like that?" she asked, wanting to change the subject. "I recognized a politician from Edinton who had struck me as a weasel, but not a greedy weasel."

"Not all of the advisers are motivated by hopes of profiting from what they squeeze out of Tiae," Flyn said, "or hoping to gain power here. Others, including whoever really employs that man from Edinton, have taken note that with your help Tiae has struggled back to its knees, and they want to make sure that the country never gets back on its feet again. There are powerful people elsewhere in Dematr who see Tiae only as a potential rival and threat."

"What?" Mari asked. "They want Tiae to stay broken?"

"Before the kingdom broke," Alain said, "Tiae and the Confederation were often in conflict, though rarely fully at war."

"Why?"

Flyn shrugged. "Fighting over land, water, resources…the usual things."

Mari pointed north to where the Confederation lay. "I just flew over a lot of the Confederation, and there is a lot of empty space still in its territory. The areas east of Debran are sparsely populated. And Tiae has lots of room to expand to the south and east. What land and water and resources were they fighting over?"

"Things along the border between them," Flyn said. "Are you looking for any rationality in that, Lady? You won't find it. Two countries that could have gathered strength to contest with the Great Guilds instead spent it fighting over river fords and islets and watering holes that had little real value. Meanwhile, trade disputes with the Western Alliance and Syndar occasionally led to Tiae's use of privateers, which enriched the owners of the privateers but caused hardship everywhere else."

"Being far too young, I had no role in that," Sien said. "From the perspective of too many years of fighting battles that had to be fought, I cannot understand picking fights over such minor things. But apparently there are those in the Confederation, in Syndar, and in the Western Alliance, who think that a reborn Tiae would return to that combative role against them."

"I'm sure the Empire and the Great Guilds are trying to pull strings as well," Flyn added.

"The Great Guilds surely pulled such strings in the past to keep Tiae in conflict with its neighbors, and they seek to do so again. One of the advisers we saw is paid by the Mechanics Guild," Alain said.

"But if the commons from other countries succeed in messing up Tiae's chance at recovery," Mari said, "it would just set them up to be toppled when the Storm sweeps over their lands. I have sent messages and warned the leaders of those places. Why is it so hard to get people to listen?"

"You were told of the storm by Mages," Alain pointed out.

"Yes, but the signs are there for anyone to see! The riots and the civil disturbances and everything else. The common people are ready to blow up, and their own leaders will be the first targets of their fury!"

"Many see that," Flyn said. "We wouldn't be getting the volunteers and aid we have been if powerful people in the Confederation and the Alliance weren't looking the other way and lending covert support. But others, for reasons political or personal, are pursuing different objectives that they see as important to them."

"If the Storm does triumph, it will be because of people like that! Princess Sien, what can we do?" Mari asked.

She looked unhappy. "The last thing I want is to trigger a renewed civil war between my supporters and those of Tien. That will shatter any chance of the kingdom's rebirth and serve the desires of our enemies. But it may not be a choice I can make. Tien's actions are alienating more and more people and soldiers. They will turn to me, and I will have to decide whether to reject their loyalty and let Tien and his advisers destroy Tiae slowly, or whether to fight and quicken the final death of Tiae myself."

"How did Tiae end up a monarchy, anyway?" Mari asked. "Maybe if we look at that we'll find a solution. Tiae was the last of the countries to be established, right?"

Alain, as usual, provided the historical background. "Tiae came to be as the result of people moving south from the cities around the Sea of Bakre. Some sought new land, while others wanted new beginnings. The Confederation was going through a difficult time, with different cities feuding over issues of control and authority. The Western Alliance had expanded as far as it could to the west and north. Those wanting to leave the Free Cities had nowhere closer to go. The histories I have read say the Mechanics Guild could not halt those changes to Dematr and appeared to be experiencing some kind of dysfunction of its own, though that is not explained."

"One of the purges must have taken place about then," Mari said. "When the Senior Mechanics killed or imprisoned a lot of Mechanics to stop any revolt against their authority."

"Mage Hiro once saw documents of the Mage Guild," Alain continued, "which said that the elders allowed the founding of Tiae as a counterweight to the Confederation, which the elders did not want to expand to the south and continue to grow in size and strength."

"How does all of that produce a monarchy in Tiae?" Mari asked again.

"The histories do not say. They only report that the monarchy was established."

"I do not myself know the reasons," Sien said. "I was told many times that the founder of the royal family was a man of great strength and skill, someone others were willing to grant power to. But there is this also. My advisers have told me that before the kingdom broke, every attempt to expand the powers of the parliament was met with objections that it would grant too much influence to those who made a living from politics. Keeping power in the royal family would prevent that. I wonder if some of those who came from places like the Confederation were tired of the failures of their political leaders and sought a simpler and stronger system."

"Princess, your people would not be the first to have little regard for politicians," Flyn said. "But if that attitude led Tiae's citizens to grant most political power to the royal ruler, it left the fate of the country subject to the roll of the die. If chance granted a good king or queen, the land would prosper, but if chance gave them a poor choice for the role, the land would suffer."

"Simple solutions," Mari said. "Simple answers to complicated problems. Isn't that what happened? Choosing leaders, good leaders, is hard. So don't. Set up a system where the leader happens automatically."

"All agree the first king was worthy," Sien repeated, looking unhappy again.

"I have no doubt. That probably made it easy to decide on monarchy as a solution. But that leaves the problem of succession."

Flyn nodded. "People want to believe that the child is the heir to all things from the parents, even though it often happens that the child is very different. For better or for worse."

Sien bit her lip, her gaze on the table. "There's little happiness in what I remember of my parents. They often seemed sad. They did their best to rule Tiae, they did their best to fulfill the duties laid upon my father by his birth, but I do not think it was a role they would have chosen. And all accounts agree that they were not well suited for it."

"Your people still want a strong leader," Flyn pointed out. "Perhaps now more than ever. They want someone to defend Tiae, and more importantly to defend them. You have proven yourself well suited to that role, Princess."

"I agree," Mari said. "Which, unfortunately, is going to lead to exactly the problem that Princess Sien fears. Soldiers and people will leave Tien for her, and if Tien is as cold and calculating as you say, Princess, he won't let that continue."

A knock sounded on the door. General Flyn went to check, listened to a whispered message, and turned back to Mari. "You have a visitor. Colonel Hasna. She's unarmed, and says she has a message from Prince Tien for you."

Mari frowned. "Hasna and I didn't exactly part on good terms a short time ago. Tien must have seen and heard that. Why did he choose her as a messenger?"

"To drive home to her that she is under his authority," Sien said. "And to offer you the sacrifice of her dignity by forcing her to serve as your messenger with the reply. It puts Hasna in her place, and lets you lord it over her."

"She's just another pawn? If I wasn't still mad at her, I'd feel sorry for Hasna. Should she see you here?" Mari asked Sien.

"I wish her to see me," Sien replied, her voice hardening.

Mari nodded to Flyn. "I'll accept the message."

Hasna was escorted into the room, fixing her eyes on Mari to avoid looking at Sien. "I was ordered to give this to you...Lady Master Mechanic. And...await your reply." She offered an envelope.

Mari took it, impressed by the quality of the paper. It must have been brought from some expensive stationery store in Syndar. Inside was a single page, the writing on it in a fine, firm hand. Tien had obviously worked hard on his penmanship, but then that was part of the whole image thing. "He says it's unfortunate that our first meeting did not go better. Nice wording. It sounds like an apology but it's not, and it leaves open the question of whose fault that was. He says I am obviously...oh, blah, blah, flattery. And not to be taken lightly. All right. I'll admit I wasn't at my most diplomatic. He wants..." She reread the words. "He wants to meet, just him and me. To discuss matters of mutual benefit. You don't have to shake your head, Alain. I'm not doing it."

"You should," Sien said, surprising Mari. "But with proper safeguards. Tiae is on the road to destruction. Perhaps you can change that."

Mari, tired and physically battered, didn't feel like sticking her neck out. But Sien had a point. Mari looked at Hasna. "You can tell Prince Tien that I will meet privately with him, but only if accompanied by Mage Alain."

"Have Colonel Hasna give her word you will not be harmed or detained," Sien said.

Mari looked at Hasna, who spoke slowly. "I give my word of honor that you will not be harmed or detained."

"Thank you," Mari said. "May I ask you something?" Mari added as Hasna started to turn away. "It's a question I've been wanting to ask someone. Why do I have to fight people like you? You're not a bad person. You're trying to do what you believe is right. But you're *wrong*. You're taking this kingdom back down the same road that caused it to be broken before. Why can't you see that?"

"Perhaps I see things more clearly than you think," Hasna replied, her voice cold.

"More clearly than Princess Sien? Do you honestly believe that Prince Tien is better able to lead this country than Princess Sien?"

"That is not my decision to make. Tiae broke because too many people questioned who should lead. You would not understand."

Mari felt the pain behind the harsh words, so she held her temper in check. "But what led them to question their leaders? Princess Sien told me what set in motion the collapse of the kingdom. Rulers who weren't up to the job but held it because of an accident of birth. Would you choose officers that way? The Empire doesn't decide who will be emperor based on birth. I spent enough time in Palandur to learn that Imperial succession is built on survival of the fittest. The Imperial heir gains that status by being the smartest, meanest, cleverest, most ruthless adult in the Imperial household. Sometimes they're not even related to the prior Emperor until they marry into the family."

Hasna did not reply for a moment, then spoke in a lower but still forceful voice. "Tiae needs order. You cannot understand how it felt to have your world crumble."

"Not in the way you endured it, no," Mari agreed. "But the wrong leaders seed disorder. There may be new confrontations. I am going to do my best to defuse them from this point on. I give my word to you on that. But there may come a time when you'll have to decide in your heart what is really best for Tiae. I hope we're on the same side when that happens."

"Do not presume that you know what is best for Tiae," Hasna said, pivoting to march out of the room.

The meeting occurred late that night in a small side room of the royal residence. An escort of Mari's soldiers waited outside, as did a force of Tiae soldiers under Major Hasna. The two groups, formerly allies who had mingled without concern, now stood uneasily apart from each other.

Prince Tien, seated at a desk, waved Mari to a chair before it. Alain stood to one side of her.

"Let me speak first," Mari said. "So that we all understand the stakes involved. I've seen your advisors. I've dealt with many like them. You are smart enough to know that they serve the interests of others, the interests of their own leaders or of their own greed, but the master they truly serve is grim and awful, a Storm that will bring us all to ruin regardless of the wealth and power some gather before then."

"Dire words," Tien observed. In private, he didn't display the same grandiose gestures and bombastic speech. "What arrangement can we come to, then?" He smiled at her. "Everyone kept telling me about the idealistic daughter who did nothing for herself. I had not realized how cleverly you have managed others' impressions of you."

Mari, not happy to be told that her candor had been interpreted as stage management, made a vague reply. "I do my best."

Tien flashed another smile. "The act with the Mage is truly brilliant."

"You think so?" Mari asked, wondering exactly what Tien meant.

"Of course. Pretending that he's in a relationship with you not only makes you look mysterious and powerful, but also causes commons and other Mages to believe his powers are gone." Tien spread his hands. "It's always good to have some surprises up your sleeve, isn't it?"

"I've always thought so."

"Your left arm is injured," Tien observed. "Another assassination attempt?"

That sounded partly like sympathy, partly like a warning. Mari shook her head. "It was in a battle. At Landfall. A little over a week ago. I had business in the Empire, and the Imperials tried to stop me."

Tien eyed her. "Interesting. We do what we must, I suppose."

"We make choices, Prince Tien," Mari said. "I've seen and heard what's been happening here since you arrived. You may think you have things under control, but the Syndaris can't be trusted and the people of Tiae can only be pushed so far. The first time a ship laden with loot extracted from what little the people have left tries to leave this port or any other, the people are going to riot."

Tien made a dismissive gesture. "I have an army."

"That army is going to be very reluctant to fight their own people."

"Then my hireling soldiers from Syndar will deal with it." Tien leaned forward toward her, his eyes intent. "Unless trouble is stirred up. I have what you want: access to the people and the resources of Tiae. You have the pretender. I could be persuaded to make a deal for what you want, if you give me what I want."

Mari shook her head. "Princess Sien is not part of any deal. I won't betray her."

"How noble." Sien cocked his head as he studied Mari. "But you want to stop this Storm. What does the fate of one person matter? How many people did you kill at Landfall because they were in the way of what you wanted?"

Tien had probably meant the words as a statement of pragmatism, but they hurt deep inside her. "I don't know how many I killed in Landfall," Mari said in a low voice, trying to keep all feeling from her voice.

Apparently interpreting that as callousness, Tien nodded. "So, we understand each other. You cannot hold onto Pacta Servanda without Tiae's agreement, despite the power of your army. We could besiege you in that town, and privateers could blockade your harbor."

"The Syndaris are using you."

"They think they are," Tien said. "There is my deal, Master Mechanic. You turn over to me the pretender, and I will reach an agreement with you to allow continued use of Pacta Servanda, though I will want more access to your weaponry if Tiae is to be an ally."

"Let me think about it," Mari said. "You'll have my answer before sundown tomorrow. What will your advisors think of such a deal?"

Tien grinned conspiratorially. "Any who disagree too sharply will find that their lives become much more difficult. And perhaps much more short. That's true of all my enemies. I don't let people do things that work against me. You understand, don't you? Do you require one of my advisors be handed over to you as part of the deal? I won't ask any questions about what you do to, say, the one who is on the take for the Mechanics Guild."

"That won't be necessary," Mari said, trying to keep the revulsion from her voice.

She walked rapidly from the building, the soldiers in her escort hastening to keep up. Alain walked close beside her, speaking in a low voice. "Every word he spoke regarding agreements between you were lies. Tien would not keep any agreement, but instead demand more concessions at every opportunity."

"For once," Mari said, "I didn't need a Mage to tell me that. But he was telling the truth when he threatened us. He thinks I'm like him, Alain. How can he think that?"

"Like so many of your enemies, he is seeing what he expects to see. You fool others not by managing your words and actions, but by being exactly who you are. That is the one thing they cannot understand."

At the encampment, General Flyn and Sien waited. "How did it go?" Flyn asked in the tones of someone who thought he already knew the answer.

"Ugly," Mari told him. "He thinks I'm mulling over a deal to betray

Princess Sien. Princess, we need to get you out of Tiaesun. There's no telling what Tien will try as long as you're in the city. Once we get you out among the rest of my soldiers here, Tien won't be able to touch you. We'll march back to Pacta Servanda and try to figure out what to do next."

Sien looked away, angry. "And once more I am a thing to possess."

Mari felt a sick sensation in her stomach. "No. That's not what I want. I'm sorry that came out like an order. You decide, Princess."

She gave Mari a flat look, then nodded. "I agree with you, Mari. Thank you for letting me make that decision."

"You're still the ruler of Tiae as far as I'm concerned," Mari said. "And you'll always be my friend. General, let's try to sneak out before dawn. Hopefully, Tien won't expect us to act so quickly."

Chapter Sixteen

Mari's soldiers had marched into Tiaesun as liberators, greeted by the cheers of the people. Now, in the hour before dawn, with just enough light to move without lanterns, they began marching out of the city like a column sneaking through enemy territory.

A dozen cavalry rode in the lead, followed by Mari, Alain, Sien, Flyn, and some of Flyn's staff. Behind them came the foot soldiers. Mari could sense their unhappiness, but also that it was directed outwards at the people of Tiae who seemed to have betrayed them.

"What are our chances of getting out of the city without confrontation?" Mari murmured to General Flyn.

"I'd say they were extremely poor, Lady. But we will do what can to avoid it."

The general's words were all too quickly proven true. The column had ridden only a few blocks before it reached a large courtyard close to the royal residence. As Mari rode into the courtyard, she saw the other three streets leading out were all blocked by soldiers of Tiae drawn up in combat formation. Despite the very early hour, the sides of the courtyard not guarded by soldiers were occupied by crowds of people who were watching with a strange mix of dread and apathy. Year after year of anarchy and war had left them expecting the worst and unable to rouse themselves to fight against the seemingly inevitable.

"Keep riding," Flyn said to Mari in a low voice. "Let's see if they give way when we approach."

Princess Sien shook her head. "They would not be here if they intended to give way."

"I don't sense any stomach in them for fighting us," Flyn objected.

"These are my people, General. Push them the wrong way and they *will* fight."

Mari led her column of soldiers as far as the center of the courtyard, the people of Tiae watching silently and the soldiers standing firm. She came to a stop, though, as a stallion came prancing into the courtyard, his rider sitting tall in the saddle, light cavalry armor gleaming.

Prince Tien drew his saber and flourished it in the air. "I command you halt!"

"Hold," Mari called, her soldiers coming to a stop. "What do you want?" she said to Tien. She could see his foreign backers standing behind the prince and the ranks of Tiae soldiery.

"I require you to surrender the pretender, as you agreed, that she may be judged and dealt with," Tien said.

"I made no agreements with you. Princess Sien is under my protection," Mari said.

"She still hides behind the swords of foreign fighters?" Tien said mockingly. "If she is truly a princess, why does she not trust in Tiae?"

Sien brought her mount to the forefront, her expression hard. "I hide behind no one. I stayed with Tiae through the dark years, I stayed with my people, while others hid in comfort among the foreign hills of Syndar."

"Watch your tongue when speaking to the ruler of Tiae!" Prince Tien commanded, theatrically pointing his sword at Sien from across the distance separating them. "You wanted to give the kingdom to that outsider, the woman who rides beside you. I will not permit that! Nor will I allow you to leave this city and raise rebellion in the countryside. But I am merciful. I will allow you your life, if you first renounce your claim to be of the royal family, second swear your loyalty and obedience to me as the rightful ruler of Tiae, and third vow never to seek or serve as ruler of Tiae under any conditions."

"You ask me to renounce my mother and father?" Sien cried, her words filling the courtyard. "Never! Tien, drop this pretence that I am not your sister. We lived together in the royal nursery." She pointed toward a hill topped by a ruined palace. "You know this is true!"

"I know that one of my sisters, the six-year-old girl named Sien, disappeared in the chaos of Tiaesun's fall and most certainly died, perhaps at the hands of the same forces that now elevate you in her place! It pains me that you would use her memory in such a selfish fashion. If you love Tiae," Prince Tien announced, "you will not place your low-born ambitions above what is best for the kingdom."

Mari saw Sien's face tighten with anger. The princess almost spurred her horse forward, but halted herself. "You accuse me of the very crimes you commit against Tiae? You and the foreigners who surround you? It is your desire for wealth and power, and your lack of compassion, which makes you weak! Too weak to rule this kingdom!"

That barb went home. Tien glowered at Sien, curbing his restless stallion with a vicious jerk on the reins. "You dare to speak so to me? Perhaps I have been too merciful. Perhaps you were best given quarters in the prison next to other traitors to Tiae!"

"I would rather rot in a cell next to such brave men and women than spend even a moment in the finest apartments near a coward such as you!"

"This isn't going well," General Flyn commented as if discussing a change in the weather.

"Soldiers of Tiae!" Prince Tien called. "Prepare for battle!"

Mari did not need a Mage's skill at reading emotions to see the uncertainty and reluctance with which the soldiers lowered their pikes toward Mari's troops and spanned their crossbows. Even soldiers filled with absolute loyalty to their ruler might have quailed at fighting the battle that loomed. While Mari's force was outnumbered, the soldiers of Tiae had only two rifles among them. Mari's soldiers were almost all armed with Alli's modern rifles. A battle between the two forces would be a one-sided bloodbath.

"Lady," General Flyn muttered to Mari urgently, "we could easily win this fight, but the long-term cost of such a victory would be impossible to calculate. Tiae would not forgive us such a slaughter."

"Make no move to prepare for combat," Mari replied. "Keep our soldiers in marching order and keep their rifles in carrying position on their shoulders. I don't want a single nervous finger on a trigger causing a battle that no one except Tien and some of his foreign backers seem to want."

Princess Sien rose in her stirrups and spoke in a loud voice. "What is this? Threats against allies? Threats against those who have done so much for Tiae? These soldiers have fought alongside Tiae and shed their blood for our country! You have not!" she added, pointing at Tien. "You order others to fight your battles because you lack the strength and the courage to be a ruler!"

Tien had been looking around as well, gauging the mood of his own forces. He was shrewd enough to notice their lack of enthusiasm and the way Sien's words had hit home among the watching citizens. From Tien's jerky, angry movements, it appeared her words had also struck home with him. "It is against the laws of Tiae to speak so to a monarch!"

"There are older laws!" Sien declared. "Laws that do not permit even a monarch to hide from the truth!"

Tien responded to the princess's latest accusation with a defiant look that didn't quite mask an air of calculation as he gazed at Sien. "Strength? Courage? You say I lack those, woman? Yet I am strong enough and brave enough to risk my life for my kingdom. Here and now, before the eyes of all." He spread his arms wide and pivoted at the waist to look around the courtyard. "See me! A prince willing to place his life in the measure to prove he is right and he is strong! To fight his own battles! To prove he is the leader that Tiae needs!"

"What is he talking about?" Mari asked Sien.

"That which I know must happen," Sien said. "Though even now I cannot believe he would agree to such a thing."

"There is an even older tradition than the laws of Tiae!" Prince Tien cried. "An older law. A tradition to prove strength! To prove fitness! To prove the truth and justice of the arguments made!"

"And so it will end as it must," Sien whispered so that only Mari could hear.

"Trial by combat!" Prince Tien concluded. He pointed at Sien. "We will battle, you and I, and the winner will be proven the rightful ruler of Tiae."

A murmur ran through the watching crowd. Mari saw the soldiers of Tiae staring at the prince. "Your majesty—" Colonel Hasna began.

Tien silenced her with a gesture, still pointing at Sien. "Give your answer, woman who claims to be a servant of Tiae! I name you servant of another cause, one that seeks to destroy all that remains of Tiae! Do you fear to prove the worth of your words, the worth of yourself, in combat?"

"He knows he can't win a fight against us, and he can tell his soldiers aren't eager for such a fight," Flyn commented in a low voice. "He's trying to put this contest on grounds that he feels certain will grant him victory."

Princess Sien sat tall in her saddle. "It is you who serve malign forces," she said loudly to Tien. "By what means will the victor be determined? Who will decide which of us will be ruler?"

Tien looked back at her, thinking through her words. "Victory will be decided by the only means that produces a result whose proof cannot be debated or questioned. The winner will be the one who survives the combat."

"To the death?" Mari gasped, her words barely carrying over the eruption of noise from the crowd. "He is actually proposing to fight you to the death?"

"As he knows he must. He cannot trust others to judge as he wishes." Sien looked around, her gaze traveling slowly over the soldiers of Tiae and others in the courtyard. "And still they fear to act in my favor." She called back to her brother. "What other rules? By what terms would the combat be held, and who will enforce those rules against us?"

"No other rules!" Tien shouted in reply. "No rules to hide behind! We fight until only one of us remains. To prove that the winner is the stronger and therefore the rightful ruler of Tiae. Are you unwilling to measure yourself against the old laws?"

"Sien, this guy is taking sibling rivalry to a crazy extreme," Mari said. "He can't be serious."

"He is." The princess gazed steadily at Mari. "He will hold to this. He is confident he will win, and he would rather see Tiae fall into bloody anarchy again than see anyone prevail over him. This is what must be." She raised her voice again. "What weapons?"

Prince Tien smiled. "Saber and dagger, on foot, in the classic manner of duels."

"You wear armor," Sien said.

"I will remove it. We will fight on equal terms!" Tien announced with a grand flourish.

"Sien, there has to be another way," Mari said.

The princess shook her head. "No. There is not." Sien gazed toward one of the ruined palaces looking down on the city. "Forgive me, my mother and father, for what I must do." She inhaled deeply, then called across to Tien. "I accept your terms."

The sound coming from the crowd this time carried a clear note of dismay, and the pikes held by the soldiers of Tiae wobbled in unsteady hands as Princess Sien dismounted and walked with slow dignity toward the center of the courtyard left open between the opposing sides.

"Alain," Mari begged, "can't we do anything? Sien is being forced to fight her own brother!"

"Did you not hear what she has said to him?" Alain asked. "Sien pushed Tien to this, maneuvering him by her words so that he himself set the terms she desired for this fight."

"She wants to fight Tien?" Mari said in disbelief.

"She wants it no more than you wanted to return to Marandur. And she does it for the same reason you did return there. Because it is needed for the sake of others."

Prince Tien slid lightly from the saddle, raised his arms as an aide unbuckled his cuirass, then swung his arms to loosen his muscles, walking around with a pleased smile.

Mari saw Princess Sien stretching and flexing her arms and legs in a much more subtle fashion, keeping her eyes on Prince Tien the whole time.

Another aide ran up to Sien and knelt to offer her two weapons. Sien took up the saber in her left hand and the dagger in her right, making a few practice passes to assess their balance and appearing slightly awkward in holding and handling the weapons. "What of injuries?" she called to Prince Tien. "Should our duel include a means to halt the combat?"

Prince Tien took a saber and dagger as well, deliberately paused to sweep them through the air in elaborate, graceful arcs, then turned to Sien. "The duel is to the death. You agreed to that."

"There will be no halts?" Sien said, sounding surprised and perhaps a little fearful.

"She's good," General Flyn murmured to Mari. "Watch what he does now." Tien shook his head firmly. "A halt might leave the kingdom threatened. A true royal would not fear injury in the pursuit of truth. The fight will continue to the conclusion. No one will intervene or interfere."

"Anything else would be a sign of weakness, would it not?" the princess asked, looking directly at the prince.

"Yes," Prince Tien agreed, his voice getting tense and what seemed oddly to Mari to be almost a little eager. "No one will stop this fight before one of us is dead. That is my order."

Alain shook his head and leaned close to Mari, his voice a murmur. "Tien means this. I had wondered if he only sought to injure Sien or frighten her enough to cause her to beg for mercy, but he intends to kill her."

"Even though she's his sister?" Mari whispered back, horrified.

"That means nothing to him. She is a piece on the game board whose presence creates problems for him. It is as I said of Tien. Though he freely displays emotions, each display is calculated. Like a Mage trained by the elders, he does not consider other people to be real, and he does not care what happens to them."

Mari stared at Princess Sien. "What will Sien do?" she asked both Alain and Flyn.

"That's clear enough," Flyn said. "Princess Sien knew that a fight between your forces and those of Tiae would create ill-will that would never be overcome. Instead, she maneuvered Tien into challenging her one on one and pretended to be unused to sword fighting so that he would order no one to interfere. She knew that Prince Tien meant her death by one means or another, and intends killing him instead, to save the kingdom."

"No wonder she looks like that," Mari whispered, suppressing a shudder.

Sien walked slowly closer to Prince Tien. "You look happy, brother," she said, her voice flat.

"I always enjoy a good fight," Tien replied, whipping his saber through a few more swift and showy passes. "You will provide a good fight, won't you?"

"I only fight when I have to," Sien said, "and then I do it because I must, not because I enjoy it." She raised her sword's hilt to her face in the old ceremonial salute.

"You've missed out on a lot of fun," the prince answered. He came to attention, used his sword to present a jaunty salute in return, then settled into fighting posture. "Too bad you've run out of opportunities to have a good time."

Prince Tien advanced, the confident smile still on his face, his right hand holding the saber forward and his left hand grasping the dagger in front of his body. Mari had seen a few formal duels while she was in Palandur, between fencers advertised as the finest in the Empire. As far as she could tell, Tien's form was flawless.

Sien held both weapons just before her at waist height, the points slightly elevated. Unlike Tien's erect posture, standing sideways with his legs in line toward his opponent, Sien stood in a slight crouch, fully facing him, one leg slightly back and the other slightly advanced. Mari heard sniggers and derisive comments from some of Tien's foreign supporters about the princess's lack of form and polish. But to Mari's eyes the stance of the prince looked stylized, something conforming to rigid formal requirements, whereas Princess Sien's posture much more closely resembled how Mari had seen Imperial legionaries and other soldiers engage on the battlefield.

"Only one rule?" Sien said again as Tien drew close, her voice ringing through the courtyard. "To the death, the survivor to be ruler of Tiae?"

"That's right," Tien agreed, his smile broadening and taking on a cruel, excited aspect as he made a few feints toward her with his saber. "That is the only rule."

Princess Sien began a long lunge toward Tien, who skipped backwards, smiling.

But Tien's smile changed to surprise and then annoyance as Sien's attack turned into a feint. She halted her lunge when it was barely begun, instead also falling back fast.

With the distance between them too far to allow a quick attack and Tien mentally off balance, Sien flipped her saber to her dagger hand so that the dagger's blade slid between the saber's guard and hilt to hold it, pulled her shirt half off, flipped both weapons to the other hand, finished tearing her shirt from her body, then rapidly spun the shirt around her lower right arm. By the time that Tien began to advance, clearly puzzled by her moves, Sien gripped the dagger in the hand of the protected arm, her saber ready in the other hand.

"Do you think to distract me with a display of flesh?" Tien asked mockingly, once again feinting attacks as Sien circled just outside the reach of his saber. "I assure you, I've seen better."

"I didn't learn how to fight in fancy fencing salons," Sien said. "I learned on the streets and in the deep woods, where a misstep meant more than a lost point." She advanced, her weapons held out slightly to each side.

"Maybe you should have learned to fight the correct way," Tien said, abruptly leaping into an attack. His moves were practiced and sure, the point of the saber coming toward Sien in a thrust she could easily parry. But as she did so, Tien swept his dagger toward her chest, trying to take advantage of Sien's focus on the sword attack.

It could have been a lethal blow. If the princess had not been waiting for it.

Sien deflected the prince's saber with her own, but instead of parrying the dagger strike with her own dagger, Sien caught her opponent's blade in the folds of the shirt protecting her arm, entangling the weapon so she could yank it from Tien's grasp.

Thrown off by a move contrary to the rules of the fencing salon, Tien was just beginning to gasp, "You can't—" when Sien finished knocking aside his saber and swung her own sword's guard into his jaw.

Prince Tien staggered backwards, a trickle of blood flowing from his lower lip, his expression showing disbelief and bewilderment. He parried frantically as Sien struck at him again, this time with the edge of her sword. "Regulations do not permit such moves!" he yelled.

"One rule!" Sien shouted back. "That was your word! Do you think this is a *game*? Do you think I must fight to suit your manners when the fate of Tiae is at stake? While you played at fighting in Syndar, the people of Tiae have suffered and fought and learned that war is not sport!" Her dagger came in fast and low, nearly cutting into Tien's arm while he was busy beating off another saber attack.

"Witch!" Tien spat the word at her. "A king needs no lessons from a slut of the streets." His saber wove a complex pattern of attack, forcing Sien to drop back. "I will make your death a slow one, and then have your body tossed on the garbage heaps."

"A true king would not speak so to anyone," Sien said, her voice controlled but furious. She used her dagger to parry another attack as her sword point dipped to the street and flicked a loose stone toward the prince's face.

Tien, startled, brought his saber up to protect his head, leaving his body exposed.

The princess had already begun a lunge with her dagger, slicing into Tien's side before he could evade or bring his saber back down to parry the blow. She danced backwards out of range as the prince aimed a frenzied slash at her.

"I call foul!" Tien screamed, blood spreading across the side of his shirt where Sien's dagger had slit the fabric and the skin beneath it. "Stop her! I command it!"

Mari looked at Colonel Hasna, who gazed back at Tien, her face a mask. "You forbade anyone to intervene," Hasna said. "I follow your command."

Tien stole frantic glimpses to the side, where his foreign backers were now hemmed in by grim-faced soldiers of Tiae, and all around, seeking some support from the crowd or an exit from the courtyard. But every way was blocked by the silent, dour people of Tiae or by Mari's soldiers. "Sister! This was only a test of you! There is a place for you beside me on the throne!"

"I am sister to you now?" Sien demanded, pressing her attacks so that Tien had to constantly retreat around the open area. "You chose this. You have already been tested. And found wanting." She aimed a thrust at his throat that Tien narrowly parried in time.

The prince rallied, beating and striking with his saber in a desperate flurry of blows that Sien parried or dodged. Exhausted by the failed efforts and weakened by the flow of blood from his side, Tien dropped back a step, his sword arm shaking. "I should have killed you the moment we met. I knew you would betray me!"

"You were my brother!" Sien cried, renewing her attacks. "I will never forgive you for forcing me to do this. But the people of Tiae, *my* people, have suffered enough. I cannot let you destroy what they have begun to rebuild!" As Tien managed to deflect another blow from Sien's dagger, her saber sliced across his upper arm.

"I am Tiae!" Prince Tien shrieked. Rage and fear fought for dominance in his expression as Tien raised his saber and charged at Princess Sien, swinging a wild blow at her head.

Sien ducked under the attack while she also moved forward, using her own saber to deflect Tien's sword as their bodies came together, the shock of the collision halting both in their tracks.

Princess Sien took several steps back, lowering her sword.

Tien staggered forward slightly, then looked down at the handle of Sien's dagger where it stood out from his chest, the blade buried in his heart. He raised his gaze back to her, suddenly perplexed. "But... no one can..."

Prince Tien of Tiae fell like a puppet whose strings had been cut.

Princess Sien, breathing heavily, hurled her saber from her and glared around the courtyard. "*I am Tiae!*" she cried fiercely, her words echoing. "Does anyone deny me?"

Colonel Hasna dropped to one knee, those around her doing the same, until every citizen of Tiae was kneeling to their princess.

"Present arms!" General Flyn ordered. Mari's soldiers brought their rifles up before them in salute.

Mari dismounted and walked out into the cleared area. Sien spun to look at her, the princess's eyes still lit with the fire of battle, her posture that of someone ready to fight again. "Princess," Mari said in her most formal voice, "may I assist the ruler of Tiae?"

Sien's eyes cleared and she inhaled deeply. "I would be grateful. I am forever grateful for the support and friendship of the daughter of Jules."

Mari helped Sien unwrap the torn shirt from about her arm and put it back on.

Princess Sien looked down at the body of her older brother, blood pooling beneath it, then slowly raised her gaze to Tien's foreign backers, her expression as hard as stone. She brought up one arm to point at them as if aiming a weapon, each word she spoke falling with the finality of a hammer coming down. "Arrest. Those. Persons."

Most of the foreigners were too stunned to resist. They held their open hands out in surrender, but one, bolder or simply stupider than the rest, yelled an objection. "You have no right to—"

"Silence!" Sien looked angry enough to order his execution on the spot, but after several long moments she unclenched her jaw enough to speak in a more normal voice. "The blood of my brother stains the streets of Tiaesun. I blame all of you for this! Your greed, your lies, your mindless pursuit of power no matter the cost to others! Tiae has had enough of such vultures! I have not yet decided on your fates. Do not tempt me further to crush you just as I would any parasitic vermin. Get them from my sight!" she ordered the soldiers of Tiae, who rushed to obey.

Covering her face with one hand, Sien breathed slowly several times, then lowered her hand and looked to one side. "Colonel Hasna."

Hasna marched steadily up to Sien. "My fate lies in the hands of Tiae."

"And yet the fate of Tiae lies in the hands of her defenders," Sien said. "Did you defend Tiae well?"

"I would die for Tiae," Hasna answered immediately.

"That is not what I asked. How can Tiae trust in you again?"

Hasna struggled for words. "I followed the law. I followed the orders of the one designated as our ruler by the law of Tiae."

Sien nodded. "The fault is in that law. The fault was in granting power to someone chosen by no one. I vow that law will be changed. But Tiae must be made whole. And those who failed Tiae must be punished."

Hasna stood rigidly at attention. "I accept the price for my failure, but beg that you take my death as the full price and spare those who in good faith followed my orders."

Sien shook her head at the colonel. "Death? No. I will not let you off so easy. Death is a simple thing. I will demand more of you."

Mari waited, wanting to speak to Sien, to ask for mercy, but knowing that would be wrong when Sien was in front of her subjects.

"Colonel Hasna, I sentence you to serve Tiae." Sien paused for a moment, watching the shock that Hasna could not conceal. "I am not doing you any favors. See me. I have slain my brother this day. For Tiae. I sentence you to suffer the same fate as mine: to live and to fight and to serve, all your life, no matter the personal cost."

Hasna's steely resolve broke. She dropped to one knee again, her body shaking. "Forgive me, Princess. I vow to serve Tiae just as you demand while life remains in me."

Sien nodded. "Then here is your first command. Gather a suitable honor guard and see that the body of Prince Tien is given due honor and proper treatment for one of his rank. His body will be interred with those of my parents."

Colonel Hasna got to her feet, saluting. "It shall be done, Princess."

"Where is the crown?"

"In the prince's apartments, Princess."

"Send someone for it. Bring it here."

Hasna hurried away, but Sien stood without moving.

"Are you all right?" Mari asked. Sien turned her eyes on Mari, causing Mari to flinch at what she saw in them. "I'm sorry. What can I do?"

"Stand beside me," Sien said. "You and Sir Mage Alain." The princess shuddered slightly. "I have had to do many things. This was the worst."

"He really would have killed you."

"I know. I could see it in him. And my death would have brought him pleasure. I do not remember what he was like before the kingdom broke. Did the life he led shape him so, or would he have grown into such a monster even if no ills had befallen this kingdom?" Sien watched, silent again, as soldiers arrived to lay out Prince Tien's body, place it on a pallet, and carry it toward the palace.

Colonel Hasna came back, carrying a rather plain wooden box. She knelt to offer it to Sien.

The princess looked at it, then around at the crowd watching. "I nearly failed you," she said in a voice loud enough to carry. A murmur of dismay and disagreement rose from the people but halted as Sien raised a hand for silence. "These events have made clear to me what Lady Mari has advised in the past. The Great Guilds have claimed superiority over us all because of the blood they claimed made them better. They were always wrong. No one should rule by right of blood alone. Tiae must change. The kingdom will be reborn in full, and then the people of Tiae will decide a means to choose not just their representatives but their rulers, to ensure that whoever stands as Tiae is truly one deserving of that role. I here and now vow that I will lead only if the people of Tiae wish me to be their ruler. And if the time should come when I have children, I vow that none of them will be entitled to the throne simply because I am their mother. They must earn that right, and prove their worth, and if they are lacking then will yield to someone deserving of the crown. Henceforth the line of the royal family will be joined not by blood, but by their worth to fill that role. This is my promise to you. What say you? Will you have me as queen?"

The roar of approval from the crowd nearly deafened Mari.

Sien gestured toward the crowd. "The little one there. The child in red and gray. Come here."

A man and a woman led out a small girl, all three of them staring around anxiously.

Sien reached into the box held by the still-kneeling Colonel Hasna and brought out a headband of gold with a large emerald set on the front. She looked at it, then at Mari. "The mundane crown of Tiae is a simple, straightforward thing, is it not? Yet despite how light it seems, I expect it will weigh heavily on me."

Turning to the little girl, Sien offered the crown. "It is for the people of Tiae to crown their ruler. You will represent them, for you are among those who will inherit this kingdom when it has been reborn."

The princess knelt before the little girl, who with shaking hands and nervous eyes set the crown on Sien's head.

Sien stood up, adjusting the crown so the emerald gleamed on the center of her brow.

Colonel Hasna stood as well. "All hail Her Majesty Sien, Queen of Tiae by right of blood and right of worth, the choice of her people and the savior of her kingdom!"

The crowd roared again. Sien gripped Mari's arm, and Mari felt the tremors in the new queen. "Stay with me," Sien murmured just loudly enough for Mari to hear. "It has been a hard day."

"Alain and I will stay with you," Mari said.

"Thank you. Colonel Hasna! One more task for this morning. Find the commander of the Syndari troops in this city and inform him that he has until sunset to have them all aboard their ships and out of our harbor. Post guards to ensure that none of the Syndaris take anything with them that they did not bring."

By the time the rains ended and the land grew firm enough for campaigning again, Mari's arm had healed. Only a scar remained to remind her of the injury. To her surprise, visions of Marandur came far less frequently in her nightmares. Perhaps Alain had been right that returning there had helped her deal with some of the inner scars of her first visit to the forbidden city.

The *Pride* had safely reached Pacta. Word came to Mari that Dav was still unable to walk without assistance, but was recovering well with constant attention from Mage Asha. The texts had been off-loaded and safely placed within an old bank vault. A few weeks after the *Pride* arrived, so did a ship from Altis carrying a dozen men and women who identified themselves only as librarians and had with them a letter from Mari authorizing them to copy the texts. Only Mage Alera, Mage Alain, and Mari knew where Alera had delivered that letter along with news of the texts' recovery.

Other ships had carried copies of one of the technical texts to every country on Dematr as concrete proof that the technology the Mechanics Guild had long monopolized would be shared with everyone. As Professor S'san pointed out, the text also served to demonstrate that even though the technology had been shared, making use of it would still require trained Mechanics, thus reinforcing Mari's messages that no retaliation or reprisals should be taken against members of the Great Guilds. Mari had carefully chosen a text which dealt with medical devices, to ensure what was in it couldn't be used against her.

A few more would-be assassins tried the defenses of Tiaesun and failed to reach Mari. Otherwise, the Great Guilds were suspiciously quiet. Mari feared that it was because they were husbanding their strength, but the spies sent to learn more of what the Great Guilds were doing either disappeared without a trace or could find out nothing. New Mechanics and Mages continued to arrive to join Mari, but not in the numbers they once had. Those who were willing and able to leave their Guilds had done so. The remainder were either loyal to the Guilds or unwilling to risk breaking away from them.

Rumors had worked their way west and south from the Empire, offering a distorted version of the recovery of the texts. The people of the Empire were trading stories that Mara the Undying had come out of Marandur again, had threatened the Emperor personally and strode across the waters to cast Imperial warships into ruin before flying into the west. The Emperor had vowed to destroy the Dark One.

Alain and other Mages had been working with some children who showed aptitude in Mage skills, trying to find new, non-abusive ways of sparking the ability to cast spells. There had been no success yet, but some promising signs.

Prince Tien's body lay in the old royal mausoleum. Queen Sien had told Mari that most of her subjects appeared eager to forget his existence, but she intended to remind them strongly once Tiae's government had been rebuilt enough to be able to undergo some significant changes.

More rifles came to Tiaesun, along with more volunteers for Mari's army.

And, as the skies cleared, Mari faced another decision.

General Flyn sat down, facing Mari. "Lady, it's been a hard year and more for you. While others rested, you always had another task ahead, often one requiring personal risk and danger and tremendous physical exertion. Yet the greatest demand on you is yet to come, when the Great Guilds cease trying lesser measures and hurl their utmost forces at you. It would be well if you were rested in body and in mind when that challenge came."

Mari sat back, blinking eyes tired from going over documents. "What exactly are you suggesting?"

"That we do as we have discussed in the past: send the army on campaign without you." Flyn held up a hand to forestall Mari's objections. "You yourself have said numerous times that it is dangerous for the cause of overthrowing the Great Guilds for it to be dependent on one person. If we can show your army that they can work together and fight well without the daughter being there, they will be better prepared to cope if the worst happens."

"The general speaks wisdom," Alain said.

"I know he does." Mari squeezed her eyes shut, then opened them again. "The plan is still for the army to march south to Siadarri and then east to retake Awanat and Trefik before coming west back to Pacta, right? We shouldn't face anything worse than petty warlords."

"If handled well, the campaign should go as easily as such things can," Flyn agreed. "Ambushes would be the greatest danger, but with your Mages scouting ahead on Rocs they can spot such traps before we walk into them. After we return to Pacta, we can quickly refit. We've been concerned about being able to free all of the Confederation from the domination of the Great Guilds in one campaign. But if the army sees it can be led by someone other than you, we can enter the Confederation using two columns. You can lead the more powerful one up the coast through most of the major population centers, while I lead the other up the center of the Confederation. With the willing assistance of the Confederation's own forces, we should be able to free the entire country in one campaign."

"This is a very good plan," Alain said.

"I think so, too. But…please let me tell you what I'm thinking," Mari said. "I'm thinking that I don't like fighting. I don't like worrying about myself and my friends dying, and I don't like having to shoot at other people. And I am tired. I really want to do as you say. And that worries me. Am I inclined to agree because it is the easiest course for me rather than the best thing for our army and our cause?"

"Lady," Flyn said, "may I be blunt?"

"Always."

"I think you also fear to leave the task to another. That you want to be on the field because those who were there might not handle things as well as you."

Mari paused, looking down at her desk. "Yeah," she finally said. "It's sort of hard to let go. Which is ridiculous. You're much better at commanding armies than I am. You've got good subordinates. There are good Mechanics to send in place of me or Alli. And if Mage Dav goes he can help with any problems with our Mages. Why do I feel like this?"

"Because you're human," Flyn said. "The cause, the army, everything, is your baby. Your responsibility. And because you are Master Mechanic Mari, you do not want to pass off any of that responsibility to others. But you must. Not only to rest yourself, but to prove to yourself that you are the person you have always claimed to be, the one who does not think she is all that special, who does not want power but only that her actions benefit others."

Mari snorted in self-mockery. "You're right. I'm starting to like being the daughter in some ways, to think maybe I am… That's scary. All right. Let's do it. The army will finish reclaiming most of Tiae without me. I will stay here in the luxury of Tiaesun and take long baths and sleep in a bed every night and not tell anyone what to do."

"Including me?" Alain asked.

"I'll try," Mari said. She laughed. "Oh, it feels so good to have made that decision. I didn't want to, even though I knew it was right."

"There will still be danger," Flyn said. "Assassins will still seek you here. But I believe this is the right decision, even if it is hard for you."

❦

It was harder still the day Mari had to watch her army march past, the soldiers waving at her as she sat astride a horse for the sake of ceremony and waved back. Calu, riding along with some other Mechanics, gave her a jaunty salute. "Don't get hurt!" Mari yelled at him. "Alli would never forgive me!"

The cavalry and the foot soldiers and the wagons kept going past for a long time. Mari kept waving, hoping that none of these brave volunteers would be hurt, but knowing that some would be. The thought almost made her ride into the column to join them, but she managed to stay where she was. Having Alain alongside her may have been all that gave her the strength to do that.

Afterwards, despite the soldiers of Tiae whose numbers and abilities were now enough to control and defend the capital, the city of Tiaesun felt oddly empty to Mari. Regardless of the nearly constant stream of documents arriving by ship and riders from the north, all demanding her decision and response, Mari felt detached from important matters. And she worried. The limited range on even the newer far-talkers meant she couldn't stay in touch with her army. They had kept one Mage who could create Rocs available in Tiaesun in case of emergencies, but when word came that a soldier's spouse was very ill Mari authorized the Roc to fly the soldier home.

She found herself staring at the ceiling one night, unable to sleep.

"You are not resting," Alain said.

Mari sighed and held him, resting her face near his shoulder. "It's too hard. I keep thinking of things that could go wrong. I keep thinking I should see my mother to let her know I'm all right, and talk to my father and maybe finally resolve that. I keep thinking I should see the texts again myself. We should head back to Pacta."

"If it will allow you to relax, perhaps we should."

"You're all right with that?" Mari asked, feeling combined relief and happiness. "I know Sien will be unhappy, but—"

The messenger who pounded on their door was out of breath from running. "Lady, Sir Mage, there is a courier from the Confederation." The messenger paused to catch his breath. "I was told to bring you as quickly as possible."

"That doesn't sound good," Mari said to Alain. She threw on her clothes in a rush, but she refused to run as they followed the messenger. Seeing her running would set in motion a flurry of rumors, most of them bad. She had to walk. Quickly, but still in a walk. Anyone watching would think the message was something urgent, but nothing she couldn't handle.

Mari reminded herself to tell Alain later that she also had learned to create illusions.

Queen Sien was waiting in a small room. With her was a man in the uniform of the Confederation army, his face drawn with fatigue, clothes dusty and sweat-stained. When he laid eyes on Mari he knelt before she could stop him. "Lady, in its darkest hour the Confederation begs the help of the daughter of Jules."

"What's happened?" Mari asked. "Get up and tell me." She helped the man to his feet.

The courier paused, recalling the exact words of his message. "This is an official request from the Bakre Confederation to Lady Master Mechanic Mari, the daughter of Jules. The Confederation and all of Dematr are in great peril. We have discovered that the Empire has reached an alliance with the Great Guilds, in which all will combine their strengths to defeat the daughter. In pursuit of this goal, the Empire has prepared the greatest military expedition in the history of the world, with full backing from the Mechanics Guild and the Mage Guild."

"That is dark news," Queen Sien said.

"There is darker," the courier replied. "The expedition is supposed to sail very soon from the Empire. It will face contrary winds but could arrive at Dorcastle within a couple of weeks. Our spies report that the Empire and the Great Guilds mean to demand the surrender of Dorcastle, and if the city does not yield they will overrun it."

Alain turned a somber look on Mari. "Even Dorcastle could not stand against such power."

"No, Sir Mage," the courier said, "it could not. And if Dorcastle falls, the legions will continue south to seize Danalee before striking at the daughter's growing army in Tiae. Half of the Confederation would be gone, and the rest exist only at the sufferance of the Empire." The courier blinked, concentrating his thoughts. "I am also to inform the daughter that the Empire has formally annexed the Sharr Isles, and now has complete control over those islands."

Mari shook her head in amazement. "The Great Guilds are giving the Empire everything it ever wanted. They must know how hard it will be even for them to control the Empire if it grows that powerful."

"The Great Guilds must be desperate," Alain said.

"There is more," the courier said. "Syndar has gathered forces in secret and intends soon striking at Pacta Servanda and other places along the coast of Tiae. Syndari warships are already positioning to attack shipping and may already be picking off ships traveling between the Confederation and Tiae. That is why I was sent overland with the warning."

"It is well that General Flyn left sufficient forces at Pacta to defend it," Sien said.

"The Confederation has just learned all of these things?" Alain asked. "At the last possible moment when we can act?"

"I do not know the whys and hows of it, Sir Mage," the courier said. "But leaders I believe in told me that the information was true to their best of their knowledge."

"I believe the why is clear enough," Queen Sien said. "Who would benefit from Lady Mari hearing that Dorcastle was so threatened? That news would have caused you to strip forces from Pacta and send them north."

"Leaving Pacta a much easier target for the Syndaris," Mari said. "So the Syndaris grab Pacta and everything there, while the Empire and the Great Guilds take heavier losses attacking Dorcastle. It's all good for Syndar. That's why they leaked the news of the Imperial expedition. But then who leaked to the Confederation the news about the Syndari attack plans? Oh." The answer had come to her as she asked the question. "It was the Senior Mechanics. The Mechanics Guild would have wanted the Syndaris to hit us in Tiae to keep our forces pinned down while Dorcastle and Danalee fell. But the Senior

Mechanics don't want the Syndaris to get their hands on the technology and weapons at Pacta, even though they probably promised the Syndaris just that in order to get them to attack us. They covertly let us know about the Syndari plans so we'd reinforce Pacta, and then we and the Syndaris would take losses fighting each other while the Great Guilds and the Empire rolled through the Confederation."

"It is useful when enemies work at cross-purposes," Queen Sien said. "The selfishness that led our enemies to ally against us has also caused them to betray each other. Unfortunately, both were wise enough to provide the information about the other with just enough time left for us to react, but not enough time to plan and prepare."

"We know what is coming," Alain said. "What do we do with this information?"

"Lady Mari," the courier said, his voice strained, "the Bakre Confederation begs your presence. Without you, Dorcastle will fall, and half the Confederation will be conquered in short order. Please come to Dorcastle."

Mari felt a strange sense of inevitability fall over her. It was finally happening. The great battle at Dorcastle that Alain had seen soon after they had met. Everything she had done to try to avoid that battle had failed. "Certainly we will come. If Pacta is threatened, I can't draw away any of the forces defending it, but the rest of my army will come. It is marching to the east and south of Tiae, so it will take some time to get word to them, and for them to countermarch back here, a week at least, but as soon as they get here…" Her voice trailed off at the despair on the courier's face.

"Daughter," the courier said, "the expedition could arrive at Dorcastle at any time. We think there is only a week or two at best before the hammer of the Great Guilds and the Empire falls upon Dorcastle. If the daughter is not in the city, the Confederation cannot sacrifice Dorcastle and a large portion of its army in a hopeless fight. We will evacuate the city and yield it to the Empire. But if the daughter is there, the Confederation will fight."

Mari spread her hands helplessly. "My army can't get there any faster, and I can't pull forces out of Pacta since the Syndaris are planning to attack there."

"We need *you*, Lady. We need *you* in Dorcastle. Without you, there is no hope. With you, we will believe victory is possible."

She finally understood. They needed the daughter.

Her. Not her army. Her. Against the Great Guilds and the Imperial legions.

Sien was staring at her as if she were seeing Mari for the last time.

Alain touched her arm lightly. "You will not be alone."

"I have to go, don't I?" Mari asked him.

"I believe so. My vision showed us that long ago. Dorcastle is where the Storm will either break on this world and begin the final clashes that will tear it apart, or where you and I together will help break the Storm as it dashes against the walls of Dorcastle."

"I can't believe this," Mari said, a hundred emotions swirling inside her at once. "All that work to build up and equip an army, and it's not going to be there when we need it."

"It will be," Alain said. "Part of your forces will keep Pacta safe. We just have to help Dorcastle hold out until the rest of your army can arrive there."

"Oh, well, that's not so hard, is it?" She couldn't believe that she had been able to make even that feeble a joke. Mari closed her eyes, mustering her inner strength to help her say the words she had to say despite her desperate wish not to. The fears she had denied fought to control her, but in her mind she saw the people of Dorcastle when she had been there last, and the people of the Sharr Isles, and the librarians in Altis, and Sien and her people, and even the students trapped in Marandur. All depending on the daughter to save them.

Because no one else could.

Mari opened her eyes, reached out to grip Alain's hand, looked at the courier, and spoke in a voice that didn't sound like her own. "I will go to Dorcastle. We'll leave at dawn."

18794546R00202

Printed in Great Britain
by Amazon